PRAISE FOR SARAH PINBOROUGH AND *THE HIDDEN*!

Quite unique... Ms. Pinborough does an amazing job. ...A great read."

—The Horror Channel

"Original and gripping."

—Horror Web

MESSAGE FROM NOWHERE

After staring in mounting annoyance at that tiny white flashing line, he got up and shimmied along the wall to the plug socket where he flicked off the switch. He waited for the sound of the machine switching itself off, but the hum continued. Swearing, he yanked the plug out completely. That should do it.

Standing up, he noticed that the hum was still there, and his anger faded into confusion as he saw the white line still flashing rebelliously against the black. Just what was going on here? He checked that he pulled out the right plug, and followed the disconnected cable with his eyes until it vanished into the back of the IBM. How could it still be on?

He wondered if there was a faulty connection and somehow the computer had switched to battery. But if so, then where the hell was the Windows screen? It didn't make sense.

Suddenly, the hum mounted into a high-pitched squeal, and just before Rob expected to see smoke rising from the back, the screen burst into action, the words appearing from nowhere as if someone were typing on his keyboard faster than he could see:

MAKE HER COME HOME MAKE HER COME HOME MAKE HER COME HOME HOME HOME HOME HOME HOME HOME HOME HOME HOME HOME HOME HOME HOME HOME HOME HOME....

Other books by Sarah Pinborough:

THE HIDDEN

THE
RECKONING

SARAH PINBOROUGH

LEISURE BOOKS NEW YORK CITY

For Mum, Dad and Laura with much love.

A LEISURE BOOK®

October 2005

Published by

Dorchester Publishing Co., Inc.
200 Madison Avenue
New York, NY 10016

ISBN 0-8439-5550-3

The name "Leisure Books" and the stylized "L" with design are trademarks of Dorchester Publishing Co., Inc.

Printed in the United States of America.

Visit us on the web at www.dorchesterpub.com.

THE
RECKONING

Your house is your larger body.
It grows in the sun and sleeps in the stillness of the night
and it is not dreamless.

—*The Prophet* by Kahlil Gibran, 1883-1931

PART ONE

PROLOGUE

Syracousse—Twenty-five years ago

Cooled by a breath of September, the summer sun floods through the large clear windows from the garden outside and drenches Camilla's face, replacing the natural color that has drained away with a golden yellow sheen, giving her an unhealthy jaundiced look. She can't feel its warmth on her skin. She can feel nothing but the cold that is creeping up her numbed legs. The old swing outside, her swing from a childhood long gone by, creaks backward and forward as Gina rides it, screeching out the passing seconds on rusted hinges as she stands there and stares in disbelief. Oh God no, Oh God no, what has she done?

The blood moves toward her across the tiled floor, slow and unrepenting, darker and thicker than she expects; but then this liquid that seems like crimson mercury sucking at her shoes is not from a frivolous scratch or graze, pink and light, to be laughed away. No, this is life's blood, Philip's life blood, and it is leaving him furiously, escaping in floods, no longer needed.

Her shaking hand releases the carrot that will no longer be eaten for dinner tonight, the carrot she'd been so angrily chopping, teeth gritted, wishing he would just SHUT UP, while her husband shouted. Shouted with all that blood pumping healthily, visible through the throbbing veins on the side of his head. Shouted the words that seemed to echo around her head, the words that he never seemed to tire of.

Kneeling by his body, his blissfully quiet body; she reaches for the knife that has slid several times into his large torso before settling in its final resting place at the center of his chest. Oh God, it won't come out, it won't come out. Will this red that is creeping up her cotton dress ever come out? Leaving the weapon embedded there, she rocks backwards and forwards on her heels for a few seconds, her hand pressing against her mouth, unaware of the stain her fingers leave there. Has she done this? Had she wanted to do this? It has all happened so quickly and she is sure, she is sure . . . She lets out a small hysterical giggle. One minute in my hand. The next minute it was gone. And for my next trick ladies and gentlemen . . .

Her knees are starting to hurt, and she slowly pulls herself to her feet. There is nothing to be done. Nothing more can be done. The sound of her heels clicking on the wooden hallway stabs at her brain, too real, too loud, and it is a relief when she reaches the phone.

Her voice is even and calm as she speaks, and when it is over she goes to the large stairway and sits on the second step watching the front door. Her hands absently caress the wooden banister, seeking comfort in the familiar carvings, knowing each shape and indent from a lifetime spent here. Her house. Her home. Letting out a long sigh, she hopes the policeman will arrive before Gina comes in from the garden.

CHAPTER ONE

Soho, London—The present

"Congratulations, mate." The man with the sweaty face slapped him hard, maybe a little *too* hard on the back as he passed the bar. "Great party!"

Rob gave him a perfunctory grin, his cocaine-tightened jaw muscles aching. The stranger disappeared into the mass of dancing bodies, praising along with Fat Boy Slim. Who the hell were all these people anyway? He scanned the crowd for Janine but couldn't make her out anywhere. She was probably in the toilet topping up her party spirit, and with the way he was feeling maybe he should join her. He drained his glass of champagne and shrugged off the idea. Shit, there was enough of Columbia's favorite export rushing around his system to make an elephant high, and if it wasn't working by now why keep trying?

He sighed as the pounding bass line invaded his skull. What was the matter with him? He should be feeling on top of the world. New book, great reviews. Hadn't that been the story of his life ever since he'd penned *The Pyra-*

mid Man more than ten years ago? Life had been easy for Robert Black, literary genius extraordinaire. Well, maybe not quite a literary genius, but his books sold, sold a lot, and that's what counted in the big, bad world. So why the hell did his soul seem to ache so much these days?

For a moment he wished Michael were still here, but his agent had left hours ago along with all the journos and reviewers, sensing rightly that as usual the party was heading off in a new and psychedelic direction. And Michael hadn't even bothered trying to lecture him this time. Maybe he was finally giving up on getting his star writer back on the straight and narrow, who knew? And who the fuck cared, he still got his ten percent, didn't he? Rob was still producing the goods, ever-increasing cocaine habit or not, which was something of a mystery to himself as well as the rest of the world.

Turning around and leaning his torso on the black marble bar, he tried to get the attention of the girl who was opening yet another bottle of champagne to fill the empty glasses of all those people who'd turn up to the opening of a can of baked beans if it meant a free drink. She finally caught his eye and brought the bottle over, frowning when he told her in no uncertain terms to leave it with him. Hah. At least he was the mug paying for it. For a fleeting moment he wondered just how much this party was going to cost him, and then he caught sight of his reflection in the wall of mirrored glass that lined the back of the bar.

The sweaty, pale face he barely recognized stared back at him with empty eyes. He could see his jaw muscles working in his thin face, the face of someone who was in danger of looking much older than his thirty-seven years, the hollowed-out cheekbones creating lines where there shouldn't yet be any. But the face he could live with. It was the eyes that worried him. They were unhappy eyes that skulked beneath the dark hair, hopeless, blue in all sense of the word. They weren't his. They belonged to a stranger. *This is no way to live a life,* they screamed silently at him from their prison in the glass. *This is no way to live our life. Nothing works anymore.*

As he stared at himself, the atmosphere of the club suddenly seemed oppressive. For a moment Rob felt a rush of nausea. He turned away from his reflection and back toward the throng of people having a good time. He ran a hand through his short hair and felt the chill of damp skin as his fingers brushed his forehead. It was time to get out of here. It was definitely time to get out of here. But where the hell was Janine? Cursing under his breath, although he may as well have been shouting for all his words could be heard over the music, he started to push his way through the groups of dancing people, eyes scanning in the flashing lights for her shock of peroxide hair. The heat on the dance floor was unbearable, and he could feel his shirt sticking to his skin. Finally he spotted her, her red dress flashing in the lights as she moved her slim form energetically in the middle of the room. Yeah, that was just like Janine. Had to be center of everything. He wondered whether she actually knew him any better than any of the other strangers who surrounded him. Probably not, he decided as he reached for her shoulder. But then, that was what you got when you started screwing a model with a coke habit, ten years younger than you. It was hardly going to be a relationship based on mutual respect and understanding.

"Robby, honey!" She squealed and threw her hot arms around his neck. Her mascara had run down her cheeks and her long hair was sticking to her face. "Where have you been?" Rob noticed the two men she'd been dancing with throwing him a dirty look, then moving on. He ignored them.

"It's time to go," he shouted, hoping she would read his lips, as he took her arm and pulled her through the overfilled club. When they reached the slightly quieter bar area, he felt a petulant tug on his arm and turned to face her. She looked sulky.

"You're kidding, right? The party's just getting going." He stared back at her, not in the mood for an argument.

"You can stay if you want, but I'm going. I'm not in the mood for this tonight. I've had enough." *And the party was supposed to be about me, remember?* he wanted to add. *About me and my book.* "And anyway, it's three in the fucking morning. We've been here since six."

Janine was chewing her bottom lip with indecision, but he knew she'd come with him. After all, most of her modeling career these days was based on the fact that they were an item. Photos of them together in the tabloids were invariably accompanied by articles wondering which one of them would burn out first. She was becoming too unreliable to employ, even by modeling standards. Hating himself for being so harsh, he kissed her on the forehead. None of this was her fault. Being a shit was something he seemed to be getting pretty good at these days. No, it wasn't Janine's fault and if nothing else, they were at least convenient for each other. "Now come on home and make an old man happy." This time when he tugged at her arm, he didn't feel any resistance.

Not that many hours later his own desperate voice woke him, the force of the dream making him call out as he sat bolt upright in bed, panting, eyes suddenly wide open as consciousness flooded back. The ghost of the word still hung invisible in the air in front of him. *TEACHER.* Leaning back against the headboard, he took a deep breath as his eyes adjusted to the morning sunshine and his heart slowly calmed down to its normal steady beat. Jesus, why would he be dreaming about Teacher after all this time? That shit happened more than twenty years ago, probably as long ago as he'd last thought about it. What the hell made his brain bring it up now? He didn't really need anyone to answer that one for him. All the goddamn fucking drugs and booze, that's what it was. What a fucking mess.

He swung his legs over the side of the untidy, empty bed

8

and got up, pulled apart the curtains and tugged open the sash windows, needing to feel the morning sun on his face, wanting to rid himself of the lingering unsettled feeling, the residual sadness of the dream. The warm breeze caressed him, lifting his hair, the mingling smell of fresh coffee and sweet pastries floating up from the smart Soho cafés below. He stood there for a few moments with his eyes closed enjoying the sensation, until he heard the toilet flushing. Janine. He'd forgotten she was there.

Sighing, the private moment over, he pulled his head back inside and took his white dressing gown from the back of the door and put it on. His head and body ached from the excesses of the night before. Shit, if he were honest he ached from the night before, and the night before that and the night before that. Hot coffee and a long shower. That was what he needed. The clock by the bed read 9:30 AM. He probably could have done with another couple of hours' sleep, but there would be no point in trying now. He'd never been one of those people. The minute his eyes opened, that was it. No going back, a new day had begun whether he was ready for it or not.

Padding out of the bedroom, he yawned as he made his way down the hardwood hallway and into the large open-plan living room and kitchen. The sun was bursting through the skylights and reflecting off the pure white of the walls and furniture, filling the enormous area with brightness. God, he loved this flat. In the eyes of some it probably would have been seen as overclinical, but for Rob it was perfect, the lack of clutter and color soothing his mind, enabling him to work. This room was where he wrote, ate and sometimes slept. It was his sanctuary from the darkness inside him.

This morning its tranquillity was somewhat ruined by the sight of Janine kneeling by the square, glass-topped coffee table, dressed only in a t-shirt, her hair hanging lank and unbrushed as she concentrated on chopping herself out a large line of coke. Feeling his disgust at her, at both of them, rising from his stomach, he watched her for a minute. God, she wasn't looking so good these days. She was getting old before her time, not a good thing in her profession. Guilt gnawed at his stomach. What the hell was he letting her do to herself? The guilt made him angry.

"Shit, Janine, at this time in the morning?" Ignoring him, she started to roll up a twenty-pound note, and lower her head over the table. Not wanting to watch, *not wanting to be tempted*, Rob went to the kitchen and turned the coffee machine on, hoping the familiar rumbling would drown out the sound of her snort. There was nothing sexy about watching beautiful women take drugs. He opened a cupboard and pulled out a large white mug. Maybe it was the hangover making him so ratty. He should be used to Janine's ways by now. Christ, he was hardly that far behind her himself and not really in any position to throw stones. She wasn't such a bad kid, just a fuckup like the rest of them.

"Did you have that bad dream again? The one about your teacher?" She giggled behind him, and he turned around to see her wiping the dregs of powder from her nose and licking her fingers. "What did that guy do to you at school anyway?"

He ignored her and went to the fridge to get the milk. Janine was not a person he would ever want to talk to about Teacher. In fact, he hadn't talked about it since that summer, since there had been the four of them: him, Jason, Carole-Anne and Gina. Anyway, big deal though it seemed at the time, it probably had been just their overactive imaginations. He was about to pour the coffee when something Janine had said made him stop in his tracks and look at her quizzically. "What do you mean, 'again'? Have I had that dream before?"

Still kneeling by the table, she nodded. "Sure. You've woken up shouting that word at least three or four times in the last fortnight." She raised an eyebrow. "Probably more, but that's the amount of times you've woken me up." She held up the twenty-pound note. "Want one?"

He looked at her, at the note and at the paper wrap on the table, and that was when it struck him. It was time to go home. It was time to get out of all this while he still could. Maybe that's what the dreams were about. *It's time to go home.*

An hour later, he was just getting out of the shower. Janine was gone. He'd sat down, drunk his coffee and gently explained to her that he was going home to the country to clean up. It was nothing personal, but he just couldn't do this anymore. He needed to be straight. He needed to concentrate on his work. All the usual platitudes you come out with when you want someone out of your life. Quickly. There had been a few tears but nothing major, and part of him had been slightly disappointed with how well she'd taken it. But then, the parting gift of his stash of grade-A party chemicals probably had gone some way in softening the blow. The glittering London scene was nothing if not shallow, so what had he really expected? Still, the whole experience left him feeling hollow, emptier than normal, if that was possible.

He'd made the right decision. He knew that by the sudden keening ache he felt to be back home. Somewhere that he had roots. Somewhere he could rediscover himself, the person he should be. Someone *happy.* Shit, maybe he'd even write a book, *the* book, the one all writers want. His magnum opus.

He pulled on his jeans and a white t-shirt, and rubbed the towel vigorously over his head to dry his hair before going back barefoot into his blissfully empty lounge. He sat on the sofa and opened his address book, then punched in a number. It rang for a second before a voice answered. "Property-Lettings, can I help you?"

"Can I speak to Richard Mills, please?" There was a moment of Robbie Williams singing as his call was transferred.

"Richard Mills speaking."

Rob had pulled a cigarette from the packet Janine had

left behind and lit it. You could only give your vices up one at a time. "Hi, it's Robert Black here. I just wondered if you'd let my parents house out yet?" The old tenants had moved out a week ago, and although there had been a few repairs to do, Rob knew that the agency was good and invariably had people ready to go straight in. They'd been looking after the house since his mother died, and that was coming up for five years now.

"I've got a viewing on it this afternoon, but the decorators are still in there. I should have it let for you in a couple of days."

Smiling, he inhaled. It must be destiny. "Hold that thought. I'm going to come and live in it myself for a few months. Sorry to give you such short notice, but I only decided this morning."

The voice at the other end remained friendly. "No problem. I can have the keys ready for you to pick up in a couple of days. That'll give me time to make sure all the work's been done properly. Are you going to write a new book while you're up here?"

"Something like that. I just need some peace and quiet to get my ideas in order. I'll see you in a couple of days, then."

As soon as he'd hung up, Rob started making the next call. He didn't need his address book for this one. Michael had been his agent for so long that even if they never spoke again Rob probably would be able to recite the number on his death bed without any difficulty at all. His grin stretched as he heard Michael's laconic drawl at the other end. His agent was just going to love this.

CHAPTER TWO

Streatford wasn't a town that had much going on for teenagers during the weekend. Not unless you counted the youth center on London Road, but no one over the age of ten who didn't want to get beaten up at school would even think about going there. Not even the nerds, or the posh kids who lived in the village rather than the estate on the outskirts. Their parents normally drove them and their friends up to Fat Sam's at the city center or the big multiplex cinema for their Saturday nights. But Sharnice wouldn't go there even if her mum offered to take her. Not that that was very likely.

The evening was chillier than she'd expected, and although the walk down from Gallows Hill had warmed her up, as she waited for the boys in one of the alleyways behind the small high street, she shivered, pulling her denim jacket tighter around her thin mini-dress. What was taking them so long? It had only just turned six, so the liquor store wouldn't be too busy, and they hadn't done this for ages so the cashier should be off his guard. There shouldn't be a problem. Darren and Lee had been experts

13

at nicking since they'd been about eight, around the time the three of them had started hanging out together. The liquor store jobs always took two people, and she couldn't do it because her mum went in there too often.

It worked like this. One boy would go in and start to browse the shelves. A couple of minutes later, the other one would follow. They would act as if they didn't know each other. The first boy would take a bottle of something expensive, like champagne, from the shelf and make a run for it. There was only ever one staff member working at that time of the evening, and he would invariably give chase. Then the second boy would take a bottle of something they really wanted, like Thunderbird, and saunter happily away. The first boy would abandon the champagne farther down the road to save being chased further, and go and meet the others where agreed. Job done. It never failed. On the couple of occasions that the shop assistant had been too fat and lazy to give chase, it just meant they'd had a huge bottle of champagne to drink. But nice as it was, the Thunderbird was more in line with their fifteen-year-old palates. It got you drunk quicker.

Moving from foot to foot in an effort to shake off the cold, Sharnice smiled as she saw Lee strolling toward her. He unzipped his large Puffer jacket and tugged out the bottle with the red label. "Worked like a fucking dream. Those wankers will never learn." He pulled a packet of Marlboros from his pocket, took two out and lit them before handing her one. They smoked in silence until they heard the pounding of Darren's sneakers on concrete as he emerged from the increasing gloom. He stopped, and leaned against the wall, panting as he laughed. "Christ, that bastard could run! I thought he was going to fuck the champagne and come after me." His acne-ridden face was sweating as he paused and grinned at the others. "He was severely pissed off. Next time, you can do the running."

Lee laughed and slapped him on the shoulder. "Only if you think you can't handle it, you fat bastard."

Sharnice watched them play wrestle each other for a few moments, their carefully gelled hair glinting along with the gold earrings they each wore in their right lobe. She ground the finished cigarette out beneath the sole of her sneaker. "So where shall we go then?"

The boys separated and Darren snorted and then spat the phlegm away onto the pavement. "I dunno. The cemetery?" He looked at the others for approval, but they didn't seem too enthusiastic.

Lee shoved his hands into the pockets of his baggy jeans. "Bored of that. We always go there. Why don't we go down to the river?"

Darren and Sharnice shrugged and without the appearance of a better idea, it seemed the plan for the evening was fixed. They made their way through the village toward the lane that led down to the fields and the water, the crunching of gravel beneath their feet the only sound to invade the comfortable silence that came with years of unexamined friendship. Before long, the track meandered past the last of the houses and down to the small overgrown path along the riverbank. The evening air was dimmer here away from the streetlights and as Sharnice followed the boys across the old wooden bridge covering the slow-flowing Ouse with its wild, living borders, it seemed as if the edges of their bodies had blurred with the grayness of the fields in front of them. She moved faster to keep up with them as they strode across the grass to the old playground where they had played as children. Darren sat on a swing that came barely up to his knees and lit a cigarette, before hawking and spitting; a habit rather than a necessity.

"Give us a drink before I die of old age, mate."

Lee laughed, and pulled the bottle out of his coat, opening it with a flourish before taking a long swig and passing it to Darren. He nodded in Sharnice's direction. "Ladies first."

She smiled, and the sweetness of it transformed her plain

15

face into something almost pretty. Darren and Lee were like the brothers she never had, like the family she never had. Especially Darren, whose home life was like a reflection of her unhappy own. Things perfectly understood without ever having been spoken. Lee was slightly different. His parents were together for a start, they both worked and they never got drunk and hit their kids. Sure, they may live on the estate and they might not have much money, but it was wasn't the same. It definitely wasn't the same.

She took the Thunderbird and a satisfying swallow, feeling the liquid warming her insides. Still she was cold, the wind stronger here on the edge of the countryside. Flicking her mousy hair out of her face, she screwed up her nose. "We're not going to stay here all night, are we? I hate this fucking place." Her tone was dull, belying her unease. When she was seven, she'd almost frightened herself to death here. She had come down to play alone after school, her mother unable to control her daughter's unruly behavior or her own. While Sharnice was throwing rocks into the water with a child's enjoyment found purely in the splashes, the old man had called out to her with that papery voice, making her jump and turn to see him shuffling toward her on the bank smiling a terrible, old wrinkly grin, those old withered hands reaching for her.

Oh, how she had run. She had run and run until her breath burned in her chest, her ankles twisting under her, threatening to give way as her feet pounded all the way home. She had run from his oldness and his terrible smile and all his yellow and brown teeth. She had dreamed of those teeth for months, getting closer and closer to her as if that awful mouth could swallow her whole. And although real life soon put that small episode into perspective—the old bastard probably was only going to ask where her mum was or something—it had left her with a nervous dislike for these wide-open spaces surrounded by bushes and trees. Dark areas where anything could be watching and waiting. Old things with yellow teeth.

Lee scuffed at the ground with his sneakers. "God, this town is shit. There's nothing to fucking do here. We might as well be fucking dead." He took another mouthful from the bottle.

Sharnice wrapped her arms around herself. "Well, if you two are just going to hang around here, then I'm going home. It's too fucking cold to sit around in a pissing field."

Darren scowled at her. "Sometimes, Sharny, you sound like all those other dumb bitches at school. What do ya want to go home for? Your mum's only going to have some drunk bloke there." He ignored the sharp look that came at him through the murky twilight. "Well, isn't she? At least we've got booze and fags. So what if it's a bit cold? Get over it."

"I told you. I hate this shithole." Leaning on the climbing frame so she didn't have to look directly at him, she sniffed loudly, her nose beginning to run. "Anyway, I don't have to do what you tell me," she said to the invisible ground. "I don't have to do what any wanker tells me. So go fuck yourself." Pushing herself away from the metal, she got ready to head home.

"I know where we can go. Somewhere we haven't been before."

Sharnice stopped and looked at Lee. Darren was looking, too. "Oh yeah? Where's that, then?" His curious tone was tainted with annoyance that Lee had come up with an idea before him. "It'd better be good."

Lee stuffed the bottle back inside his jacket and zipped it up. "It is. Come on, then." Grinning, he started walking down to the towpath. Sharnice and Darren looked at each other, their disagreement forgotten while they decided whether to follow their undeclared leader. Lee had stopped at the bridge. "Well, come on!"

The other two started walking like they'd known they would. "Aren't you going to tell us where we're going?" The dampness of the grass was soaking through Sharnice's shoes and she was glad to get back onto a dry surface, pleased to see the pale yellow of the path reflecting the last of the dying light.

Lee poked her in the ribs. "I'll tell you when we get there." Looking at his friends' doubtful faces, he held his hands up in supplication. "You'll like it, I promise! You'll both like it, honest. I just wish we'd thought of it before. Now get your arses moving!" Laughing, the three of them started out on the towpath.

They had only been walking for about five minutes or so when the path came to a T-junction and disappeared into a gravel track just wide enough for one car to drive down. Darren and Sharnice instinctively turned left to head up toward the main road, but Lee called them back. "We're going this way."

Sharnice giggled. "But there's nothing down there. Just that old house on Toombes Meadow. And that's all boarded up."

Lee was smiling. "So? You reckon I can't get in if I want to?"

Darren was looking doubtful. He'd heard that place was alarmed. They used to have dogs patrolling it, although he had to admit, that was a long time ago. To tell the truth, like most of the town, he'd kind of forgotten that the house was there. "I dunno, Lee. Maybe it's not such a good idea."

Sharnice said nothing, but Lee's enthusiasm was infectious. In the end, he took the decision out of their hands. "Don't be a pair of pillocks all your life." He started to jog away from them, calling over his shoulder, "I'll race you. Last one to the gates has to go to school for the whole day tomorrow. Now come on!"

Sharnice was laughing as she broke into a sprint. "Just don't drop that fucking bottle!"

18

Darren watched her tearing down the lane, kicking dust up in her wake, before grinding out his cigarette. "Stupid bastards," he muttered to the empty air, before starting to run himself. "Oy! Wait for me!" It wasn't long before he caught up.

After easily climbing over the old chin-high wrought-iron gates, ignoring the tatty "Keep Out" sign hanging limp from the railings, the three of them stood panting on the neglected drive gazing at the house. It wasn't yet dark, although the moon was beginning to show her face, and the building was like a rebellious shadow reaching up toward the sky instead of clinging despairingly to the ground.

"Fuck me, it's huge, innit?" Lee said.

Darren shrugged and coughed, the run in the cold air hurting his lungs. "Nah. It's not that big. Just looks it 'cos it's all by itself."

Sharnice was glancing nervously at the hulking shapes of the sprawling plants and trees that surrounded them. "Got a big garden, though. Does the wall go all the way around?"

"Yeah, I think so. I guess they must have wanted their privacy, building a house out here. Let's see if we can get in."

They walked three abreast, sniffing in the chill, until they were close enough to see the huge sheets of stained wood that covered the windows. Lee took the two stone steps leading up to the chipped front door in one bound. "Well, there's no padlock or nothing," he called to Sharnice and Darren, who were off to his left trying to find a weakness in the nails hammered down tight years ago. He gave the heavy wood a shove, then stood there for a moment. "Hah! Fuck me! It's fucking open! I don't fucking believe it!" He laughed, before disappearing inside.

Standing behind Darren, looking at the curving staircase in front of the open doorway, Sharnice licked her lips apprehensively. "Don't you think it's a bit weird?" Her voice wasn't much more than a whisper.

The boys were moving away from her, eager to explore

19

their new territory. "What are you on about?" Lee was behind the stairs and opening a door that may once have led into the kitchen, but was now just another ripped out room.

Sharnice didn't move. "Well, don't you think it's a bit weird that the door was open? I mean, all those windows boarded up, but the door is fucking open? Maybe there's squatters here or something." *Or maybe just something old and horrible with yellow rotting teeth.* She shivered the thought away.

Darren had come down the stairs and met Lee at the bottom, the two of them opening the door to their left. Lee smiled at Sharnice and shook his head. "No squatters here. There's no water or electricity or nothing. It was cut off years ago." His arm vanished inside the room and he flicked the switch. Nothing happened. "See?"

She stuck her tongue out at him, then followed them into the room. They sat down in the middle of the dusty floorboards, the boys cross-legged, Sharnice with her legs tucked sideways under her. Lighting cigarettes for all of them, Lee passed around the bottle of Thunderbird.

"It's warm in here. Feels like someone's had a fire going or something, don't you reckon?" Darren was staring up at the high white ceiling. "This house must have some kind of insulation to keep it warm when it's empty."

Sharnice took several gulps from the bottle. She didn't like this house. She didn't like it one little bit, and she didn't know why. "It wasn't warm when we came in. It was freezing. It's only just got warm."

The two boys looked at her for a second, and then at each other and laughed. "Sappy cow. Are you going all psychic on us?" Darren said.

She didn't get a chance to answer as the bulb above them flickered for a few seconds and then came on, bathing them in yellow light. "I thought you said this house didn't have no electric?" she breathed.

Lee shrugged, looking slightly confused. "Well, that's

what my dad said. He must have got it wrong." He grinned. "Lucky for us, eh?"

Darren stretched out backwards, resting his elbows behind him. "How would your dad know anything about this house anyway?"

"He does the cleaning at that law place on the high street, you prat. They look after this place."

Darren snorted into his drink. "I wouldn't exactly call this 'looking after the place.' It's a fucking abandoned ruin! Why don't they let it out or sell it?"

Lee took the bottle. "You don't know much about this place, do ya? Didn't your mum tell you the story when you were a kid? Mine's still got the old newspaper pages. It was the biggest thing to ever happen in this shitty town."

Sharnice frowned at him. "Our mums never told us stories when we were kids. And the closest mine gets to a newspaper is when she buys her fags at the shop."

Darren laughed. "You're right there, Sharny. I know exactly where you're coming from. So come on then, posh boy, what's the story?"

"If you want to hear it, then you can cut out the 'posh boy' shit, all right?"

Sharnice edged in closer. "He didn't mean it. Come on, tell us what happened." It was definitely warmer in here now, and she took off her jacket. Maybe it was just the booze heating her up from the inside. That's what she liked about Thunderbird. It gave her a comfortable muggy buzz in her head. She had that now, here with her old friends.

Lee sniffed. "All right then. Some of this I know from what my mum told me, and some of it's what my dad said from what he's heard when he's cleaning." He paused to make sure he had his audience's full attention. "This house belonged to some woman who was married with a kid. Her dad used to own that mill, you know, the one that burnt down a few years ago, the one at the other end of the towpath?"

21

Sharnice and Darren nodded. They knew the one. It had been closed for years before the fire destroyed it.

"So anyway, he was pretty rich and he bought Toombes Meadow and built his house here. When the woman grew up, she got married, and when her parents got too old to manage by themselves she put them in some posh old folks home and her family moved back in."

Sharnice raised an eyebrow. "Charming. She could have at least looked after them." Not that she'd do it for her mum, but then her mum was different. Her mum was a cow. She took another drink from the bottle. Yeah, drunk was good.

"Yeah, well maybe her husband didn't want two droolers around the place, who knows?" He inhaled hard on his cigarette. "And it wasn't like they couldn't afford to pack them off. The husband was pretty wealthy. Worked in London in stocks and stuff."

"Lucky old him," Darren said.

Lee laughed. "Not so lucky as it turned out. One day, the wife stabbed him fifteen times in the chest while cutting up the vegetables for dinner. Their kid was playing outside. My mum says she was still screaming when the police turned up. Standing in the kitchen over her dad's dead body, screaming her guts out."

Sharnice shivered even though she was warm. "How come the police came?"

"The wife rang them. Calm as anything. Told them there'd been 'a terrible accident.'" He snorted. "She had a way with fucking words, you got to give her that. She's just knifed her husband to death and she wants to call it 'a terrible accident.' I mean, fuck me!"

Darren was smiling. "So what happened then?"

Lee stubbed his butt out on the floor beside him. "Well, the mother ended up in some loony bin somewhere, and the little girl went to live with some relatives. The house is hers now. From what my dad said, when she was little, the people she was living with wanted to sell it for her, but she wouldn't let them. I think she's grown up to be a bit of a loony tune like her mother,'cos even though she doesn't want anything to do with this place, she won't sell it or let it out. She just wants it to rot until it falls down or the council knocks it down. She doesn't want anyone to live in it again. Ever." He paused. "Now that's what I call fucking weird."

The light above them flickered as Sharnice shook her head. She wished she hadn't encouraged Lee to tell them the story. She hadn't liked the place to begin with and now it was starting to make her feel claustrophobic. "I don't think it's weird. I mean, who'd want to live here anyway? It's a horrible creepy old place. If it belonged to me, I think I'd demolish it. Break it down so there was just dust left. Not even one fucking brick."

She got up and started to pace the room, enjoying the light-headedness while the boys drained the last of the bottle. The bulb above them started to hiss, but Sharnice's voice drowned it out as she spun around, an excited smile dancing on her face. "Or burn it down, like someone did to that old mill! Yeah, that's what we should do, burn it down."

Darren laughed, "Yeah right, Sharnice." He shook his head at Lee.

"I'm serious. It'd liven this town up a bit for a few days. The best bonfire they've seen in fucking years. And shit, the owner'd probably thank us. Why not? No one'd know it was us. Why should they? They never found the kids who did the mill, did they?" Her eyes were sparkling.

Lee lit a cigarette as he thought. "We'd need a lot of petrol. I bet this place is really damp."

Darren stared from one friend to the other as he did up his jacket, unconsciously aware of the chill seeping back into the room. "You're not fucking serious, are you?" Neither of the others spoke. "Shit, I knew it was a bad idea coming here."

Lee laughed. "What's the matter with you? Not going

chicken on us, are you? It's not as if anyone fucking lives here, is it? It's just an empty old unwanted house."

Sharnice sniggered, unable to understand the intensity of her feelings. "Yeah, we'd just be putting it out of its misery. And at least it'd be something *to do.*"

Darren felt a small smile growing. "You two are fucking crazy, but if you want to do it, then I'm in. When?"

The idea had made them all excited, and if it were up to Sharnice they'd do it now. Tonight. Just burn it down and get rid of it. *Finish it.*

Lee passed his half-smoked cigarette to Darren. "We'll have to leave it a couple of weeks. Until it starts getting dark earlier. I know no one really comes down here, but we don't want to get seen by some pissing old dog walker as we head this way with a load of petrol. Yeah, a week or two should do it. Then it should be perfect."

"So we'll do it then?" Sharnice was jumping up and down, her small breasts jiggling with the movement.

"Yeah, we'll do it."

Smoking her own Marlboro Light, Sharnice gazed around in silence for a few minutes, imagining the walls dying with the fire, consumed by flames. Yeah, it was going to be a good feeling watching that. Standing outside in the cold, seeing the house destroyed. She'd definitely get drunk that night.

Lost in her own reverie, she didn't notice that the boys had stood up until the door slammed shut, making her jump. "Jesus, what the fuck was that?"

Staring at her, Lee shrugged. "Must be a draft." His voice was odd, quieter than normal. Suddenly, she thought of yellow teeth. An old mouth filled with yellow teeth. She wanted to get out of here. Now. And whatever warmth they thought they might have felt was gone now. "Pass me my jacket, Darren. I'm fucking freezing. Let's go. I'm bored of this place."

Neither of the boys moved, and the cold air hung heavily between them. For a moment she felt as if she couldn't breathe. A sly look passed from one boy to the other.

"Come on, stop fucking around." Walking toward them, she tried to get to where her jacket lay abandoned on the ground.

Darren grabbed her firmly by the arm. "Not yet."

Trying to pull herself free, she looked over to Lee, not wanting to let her panic show. "Sort him out, will you?" What the fuck were they playing at?

Lee giggled as he tossed the empty bottle from one hand to the other. "We're not going anywhere. Not just yet." He moved in closer as Darren yanked her to the ground. She was struggling for real now as his stale breath covered her face. "We've had an idea for something we can do right now, you see? And I think you're going to like it. I really do."

She tried to scream as Lee tugged at her clothes, before the hard punch on the side of her head left her blinded and gasping for breath. Oh God, why were they doing this to her? Why were they doing this? Oh God . . .

The light bulb, so far above her, went out, leaving them in darkness.

CHAPTER THREE

It had only been two hours since he'd locked up his flat in London, but it felt like a lifetime away as Rob stood at the doorstep of his parents' house on Dulverton Road with his laptop bag hanging over his shoulder and his one suitcase beside him on the step. Even though he'd planned all this a few days ago, it still felt surreal to him. Back in Streatford after all this time. He stared at the door for a few moments, unsure whether he could bring himself to go in. To commit himself to his "new life."

Shaking his head—after all it was a Sunday morning and the cab had left, so there wasn't really anywhere else to go—he lifted the small flowerpot to his right and retrieved the Yale key that Richard Mills had left for him earlier this morning.

Pull yourself together, Black, he thought as he slid it into the lock. *It's not exactly like you're going to be walking into a house full of memories, is it? It's been decorated and refurnished at least a couple of times since you last saw it, so get a grip.*

Still, as he stepped across the threshold, the smell of

fresh paint lingering in the peach hallway, it felt like coming back home. The color may have been different—*I mean, peach?*—but the structure of the house remained the same. And peach wasn't that far off his mother's love of pinks and purples and terrible combinations of the two. The thought of her awful taste in decor made him smile, although there was a tinge of sadness there. He should have made more of an effort to visit. Especially in her later years, once he'd finished boarding school and university. He'd been a late child, so she'd been in her sixties by then. He was all she had, and he knew how proud of him she'd been from all her letters. Why had he always been too damn busy to come?

He slammed the door shut firmly behind him. *Cut the self-analytical crap. The past is dead and buried. It's been dead since you put her in the ground next to Dad, Dad who'd been waiting patiently for her for such a long time. It's done. Over. Let it go. Check it in at the door.*

Leaving his emotions for another day, he made his way through the large Edwardian terrace, refamiliarizing himself with it. Even though compared with his Soho flat it seemed over-furnished, in actual fact, it wasn't too bad. All the colors were pale and, thank God for small mercies, there were no floral curtains. The large rooms with high ceilings gave similar feelings of space, and looking at the old fireplace in the lounge, he pushed aside the dark thought that threatened to rise, and instead remembered the joys of sitting in front of a real fire. Yeah, this is where he'd do his reading, and probably any rewrites, should he get that far. He probably should pick up a bag of coal this afternoon from the garage. It was definitely getting colder outside, now that summer was ending. He'd have to go out for groceries anyway. Making his domestic plans, he felt his spirits start to lift. A fresh start, that's what he was giving himself.

At the other end of the long hall was the kitchen, not that different from how he remembered it. As a child, it had been his favorite room in the house, its largeness broken by the breakfast bar, with a pine table that could seat eight on one side of it. He loved the bank of windows down one wall that let in so much light; even now that winter was coming. This would be where he would write. At this table, never far from the coffee machine. He could see it now, padding down here first thing in the morning, getting his ideas down while they were still fresh, the smell of warm coffee for company. That was another thing he would have to buy. He'd rented the house out with all the basic kitchen crockery and utensils, but a coffee machine wasn't among them. He felt the urge to fetch his laptop and set it up now all ready for the morning, but he figured that could wait. He had to sort out the practical things today.

He went to the cupboard under the stairs and took note of the meter readings to give to the gas and electric people on Monday morning, and then he dragged his suitcase up the steep flight of stairs. How the hell did she manage these? he wondered, thinking of his fragile seventy-something-year-old mother. He had a vague memory of tumbling down them himself when he was three or four. He'd cracked his skull on the edge of the radiator at the bottom. Somewhere, under his hair, was the scar to prove it.

At the top of the stairs, he put the suitcase down on its wheels with a relieved sigh, and started to pull it down the corridor to the room at the bottom next to the bathroom. Opening the door and looking in at the queen size bed and small wardrobe, he stopped and grinned to himself. Old habits died hard.

This was his childhood bedroom. Tucked away at the back of the house, far enough away from his folks so that they didn't have to sing along with every terrible record he'd played. Mum used to joke that she could put him in a house at the other end of the street and she'd still be able to hear his music. He'd lived in this room for twelve full years, and then all the school holidays from boarding school until he turned eighteen. Standing there, he could feel the ghost of the teenager inside him stirring, and he was tempted to stay where he was and unpack his suitcase. It was a strong temptation. To go back to a time full of hopes and dreams. He paused. But time had moved on and you could never go back, however much you might like to, if even for only a day or two. And it was easy to forget that they hadn't all been good times in here, tucked up in that bed. *It isn't even that bed. That bed would have been chucked out years ago.* He picked up his suitcase and turned around. This was about fresh beginnings.

He made his way back to the top of the stairs and turned right, pushing open the door to what had been his parents' bedroom, their twin beds pushed together, her side with a thin duvet, his with a thick one. Well, the twin beds were gone, replaced by a king-size, and although there were still built in wardrobes along the far wall, they were different too. What took his breath away was the complete whiteness of the room, from the carpet to the ceiling. It definitely hadn't been like this when he'd been a child. If he remembered correctly, there'd been a hideous lot of tans and beiges, but one of his recent tenants must have partly shared his love of clinical emptiness. Everything was white, the bedside table, the phone on the bedside table, the chest of drawers, and the net that hung around the top of the four thin wooden posts that rose from the modern bed. Shit, it was perfect. No clutter, no bookcases, no TV. Just pure relaxing white. Yeah, he could sleep in here. No problem with that. This was fucking fate.

Having left his suitcase in the hall, not wanting its navy blue to disturb the pureness of the room, he picked up his keys and headed out into the street hoping to find somewhere open to buy his basic necessities for the night. This wasn't central London, and he wasn't sure when stores opened on Sunday in the village. The big supermarkets out of town would probably be open, but without the advantage of a car, he wasn't willing to trek that far. There was a lot to get used to, being back out of the big city, and as he strolled along the quiet road he found he was looking forward to it.

It was nice to take a walk in peace, a walk for its own sake instead of being caught up in the bustle of everyone just trying to get somewhere.

He turned away from The Plough, a large pub on the corner that had been there as long as he could remember (although he had a vague memory of his mother telling him that it used to be a schoolhouse back at the end of the last century, *maybe there was a story to be found there*), and headed up the narrow high street.

He was pleasantly surprised to see how little had changed. Sure, most of the businesses had changed hands, but there was still a small newsagent's on the left, and two family butchers a little farther up on the right, separated by a couple of craft and gift shops. It still felt like a small village center, despite the increasing amount of housing estates being built closer and closer to its borders. It was a tiny pocket in time, and Rob felt so many hints at memory, many just sensory glimpses of a past long ago abandoned.

He almost laughed out loud when he saw the familiar green paintwork outside a double-fronted shop, its window displaying all kinds of hardware and household goods, from garden furniture to curtain rails, the big black lettering on the awning proclaiming that you were passing O'Neale's. So old man O'Neale hadn't been forced out by these changing times, well there was a lucky surprise. He was glad about that.

O'Neale's had *always* been there, the kind of shop where you could get exactly what it was you needed, and the old man always knew exactly where to locate the tiniest item among the thousands of tiny drawers behind the counter. An old-fashioned shop. Old man O'Neale would never have a computerized stock system. He'd never need one. Everything was locked neatly in that brain of his.

Shit, with all the time that had gone by, the old man was probably dead by now. One of the twins must run it. It was strange to think of those two little boys, a year or so below him in school, now grown men taking over the family business, bringing it to a new generation. Strange, but heart-warming. There was a solidity to life in Streatford that would never exist in the fast river of London. People *knew* each other here. They knew the stories of whole family trees. *I always knew she'd be a problem, didn't you? After all, surely you heard about her great-aunt Beatrice? Well, you know what trouble she got herself into, and I can see this one turning out just the same. It runs in the family.*

Yeah, this really was the kind of town where old ladies gossiped in the street or over their fences. Blood was thick here. There was no anonymity. Maybe that was why he'd stayed away for all this time, he thought as he pushed open the door to the tiny Spar supermarket, nestled next to the old church of St. Mary and St. Giles. Maybe somewhere deep inside he didn't want to face the ghosts.

The middle-aged woman behind the counter gave him a cheerful grin, *pleased* to have his custom, no indifferent and exhausted foreign language student with broken English serving here, and he found himself smiling back. A genuine smile. Yeah, it was good to be home.

CHAPTER FOUR

When the front door slammed shut, Carole-Anne let out a small breath and shut her eyes, waiting for the sting in her cheek to fade. Her skin tingled as the pain was replaced by numbness, and her shoulders sagged as she leaned her heavy body forward on her forearms, the sturdy kitchen table used to taking the weight. Some women got a kiss good-bye from their husbands in the morning, or so the fairy tales always told you, but not her. Not Carole-Anne Locke. However, there was the small bonus that this time when he'd told her she'd deserved it, there was some truth in the statement. There were no tears today, though. She was all out of tears after all these years.

At least the boys hadn't been there for Daddy's daily outburst. *How can someone be so ugly and so stupid all at the same time? Swallow that fucking food and answer me that, Carole-Anne.* No, Luke and Mark had already left for school. Not that she really cared anymore. Sometime, a long time ago, they had been her babies, but now they were their father's boys. Strangers grown inside her, and although deep down somewhere she knew she must love them, if she were honest she didn't like them very much. She tiredly wondered whether her increasing fatness was a reflection of the growing weight inside her as she pulled the local paper over from Jimmy's side of the table next to his cooling coffee.

She stared at the front page, needing to think. The headline, in bold black print read, LOCAL TEENS CONFESS IN RAPE CASE. But she ignored the article, having learned all there was to know about that three days ago in the butcher's. Her eyes were drawn to a smaller column down on the right-hand side. This was what was unsettling her. FAMOUS WRITER COMES BACK TO HIS ROOTS. It went on to say that best-selling novelist Robert Black had returned to his hometown of Streatford after an absence of almost twenty years. The paper hoped to interview him in the near future, and ask if he intended to write his next book here, and would the town feature in it in any way? All the usual local news crap.

So Rob was back in town. Three of the four of them were here. Her, Rob and Jason. Only Gina was missing. Not that Carole-Anne saw Jason much anymore, just the occasional awkward 'hello' if they had to pass each other in the street. After that summer, even though they stayed—had no choice but to stay, stuck here in this dead-end town—their friendship had drifted, oozed quietly away. She'd pretended that it was a natural thing, just part of becoming a teenager, but she'd known deep inside that wasn't it. After that summer, she hadn't really *wanted* to see him, to see any of them. And she guessed it was the same for him.

By the time she'd met Jimmy two years later—and oh, what a glorious thing that turned out to be—she and Jason were virtual strangers. New friends, new lives, as if none of it had ever happened. Unlike Gina and Rob, she and Jason may not have left Streatford in body, but somewhere in their spirit they did. And slowly she'd forgotten. Put that summer away in a box of hazy childhood memories, barely ever revisited. Real life had taken over. The serious business of growing up and being grown up. Until today. Today, the rusty hinges of that mental treasure chest were creaking open.

First, that awful rape up at the house. *They say she'll never be able to have children. What did those boys do to her? I hear there was a bottle involved. Girls these days never seem to learn . . . .* And then one week later Rob was back. Could it just be a coincidence? But why the hell would Rob, the big success, want to come back here?

Not that Rob had done much better than the rest of them. Not really. She'd read the stories in the papers, sometimes with a touch too much curiosity for Jimmy's liking. He'd never forgotten that she'd once had such a crush on Robby; although how anyone who didn't give a shit about her himself could get jealous over some schoolgirl thing from so long ago, she'd never understand. But hey, that was her Jimmy, lucky girl that she was. Yeah, she'd read all the stories, and if even only half of them were true then despite all his money, Rob Black was in a pretty sorry state. The drugs, the booze, the girls, all those girls, pretty and blond, sharing an empty few months before the next one took her place. She watched his life in pictures as it all took its toll. When Jimmy had last ripped a tabloid from her hands and seen what she'd been looking at, he'd snorted in disgust. "How can someone have all that and still look so fucking miserable?" But then, Jimmy didn't get Rob. Jimmy would never get Rob because, after all, Jimmy didn't *know.*

But she knew. She knew, even if he himself didn't, that Rob didn't want to be happy. He didn't think he deserved to be happy. And she knew that because she was there that summer, and maybe she knew because she'd never gone away. She didn't have so many places to hide. Even Jason eventually had gotten away from time to time, if you can call the odd stretch in Parkhouse, getting away. Sometimes she wondered whether he made sure he got caught

34

just so he could go somewhere he could breathe. It was a crazy idea if he had, because now he'd trapped himself in Streatford. Who would employ an ex-con these days except someone who knew you, or your mother, or your auntie? And you had to give that to this town. It definitely knew you.

That summer had tainted them all, and now she had a feeling in her blood that it was happening all over again. Again, but different. Maybe they had gotten it wrong back then. Maybe they hadn't understood at all. Something was starting; she could feel it fizzing in her. She'd felt it when she poured the boiling water from the kettle over Jimmy's arm only half an hour ago, and she could feel it in her last night when she took the kitchen scissors to the boys' clean clothes in the washing basket waiting for ironing, and then hurriedly hid them away when she realized what she'd done.

She sighed and pushed the paper away, no answers to be found there. Because maybe there was nothing but her. Maybe she was just going a little bit crazy. How had her life come to this? A husband who beat her, two kids she didn't like, not even a little bit, her looks disappearing long ago into her saggy waistline. Where was the point of it all?

She remembered a time, back at the beginning of that fateful summer, when she'd believed that life would hold better things for her. The future looked exciting, so full of possibilities. She'd wanted a family, yes, but not one like this. Not like this at all. She'd wanted a happy family, a man who would work hard, a man who wanted to get off the estate as much as she did. She'd wanted a life where the sun shone and she'd been damn sure she was going to get it. When had that carefree girl died? A long time ago, that's when. She'd died before Carole-Anne Bradley had even set eyes on Jimmy Locke. Maybe she too hadn't felt she deserved to be happy. Maybe that's why she'd chosen Jimmy.

Pushing the chair away from the table, she hauled herself to her feet and picked up the cheap plastic handbag that she'd once thought might be a passable imitation of soft leather. Whatever was or wasn't going on with that house named Syracousse, she had things to do. The last installment of the electric had to be paid; they'd had another one of those nasty letters threatening to cut them off, and so that was going to be the last of her cleaning money gone. Not that the two hours she did each night between nine and eleven brought in very much, as Jimmy was so fond of pointing out. She pushed her bitterness aside as she pulled up her jacket and opened the front door. Maybe the walk down to town would help clear her muggy, disturbed thoughts.

The gravel track hadn't changed in twenty years; the only difference she could see was that it had gotten smaller. But she knew that wasn't possible. A road was a dead thing; it didn't gain and lose weight, withering to nothing like those who trod along its way. No, the track hadn't shrunk; it was that she had grown. The last time she'd come down here, Carole-Anne Bradley had been just about to turn thirteen. A slim, shining girl with her whole life ahead of her. Now that girl was dead, and this enormous husk was all that was left behind. As she walked, the wind stung her eyes, creating a camouflage for the tears that were threatening there.

Why she had turned away from the high street and headed for the river she didn't really know; it was as if she had done it on automatic pilot, the course change completely out of her control. Maybe a search for answers had driven her, a need to understand what had happened to them all that time ago, a need to unlock the secrets in her head, a child's secrets too complex to understand. To see whether what she suspected was right. And the only place she could do that was at Syracousse, the house that was the root of it all.

Her breath was rapid as she saw the walls and gates

coming up ahead of her, her pace brisk, unsure of whether her fear would make her turn back if she slowed her feet down to her normal speed. Why was her heart pounding? "It's just a house," she whispered to the wind. "It's just a house."

She passed the main gates without glancing at the solitary building and followed the curve of the bricks, leaving the gravel that headed up the drive. She picked her way through the overgrown grass and stinging nettles. They had never used the front entrance, and that wasn't where she wanted to do her thinking now. She had to go back, back in her memory, back to where it had all started. Her heart had slowed down now that she had finally arrived, and she could almost hear the ghosts of carefree childhood laughter. The laughter of three ordinary children coming to play with their extraordinary, beautiful friend.

The old oak tree stood where it always had, and would stand for decades to come. Just a little to its left, she fought through the long weeds and brambles until she found the tiny gate, the wood almost black where the damp had seeped into it time and time again over the abandoned years. Peering through the mess of the gardens, she could just make out the top of the old swing they had played on, although it was now listing dangerously to one side, and somewhere beyond her vision was the large pond, probably now dried up or covered with algae, something at least living in this rotting home.

We are both shells, she thought, as she gazed at the walls that rose not so very far from her. *We are both empty shells in which people used to live. What happened to us?* She rested her hand on the gate and felt a surge of warmth go through her. The wood was feeding the heat to her, and her body started to tingle with the strength of it.

She wasn't surprised when it swung silently open on hinges that should have roared with pain, and beckoned her in. The glow had reached her head now, dulling her senses like a good joint used to back when she first met

37

Jimmy. But better, better than that, because for the first time in a very long time, she felt a little of the old Carole-Anne stirring, waking up in her light-headedness. Her feet itched to move forward, to walk through those gardens she'd tried so hard to forget. *Why, why had she wanted to forget something so beautiful, so peaceful? How silly that she hadn't come back before. Why hadn't she come back before?* She wanted to find a way in, and sit in the kitchen and dream for a while. Everything was fading from her, Jimmy, the kids, Rob and Jason. Nothing was important except to be here. Where she had been *happy.*

Far below, her feet started to move slowly forward as she gazed through half-shut lids at the past. Everything would be better now. Everything. She had come back home. The scented air filled her lungs as her mind drifted, confused by sensation.

The kestrel dived with an ear-splitting screech toward its small prey, its wings beating past her cheeks as if she weren't there, so intent was it on its kill. Gasping with shock, Carole-Anne stumbled backwards, her senses reeling as the chill flooded through her limbs, numbing her fingers as if it had never really left. Once again on the other side of the gate, the safe side, her head felt as if it had just been submerged in icy water, her thoughts clear again. Her thoughts her own.

What was I doing? What did I think I was doing? Her heart was pounding again, and her head began to ache, to throb in time with her internal beat. She looked at the gate, which still stood open and inviting, with wide eyes as the awful realization dawned inside her.

Oh Jesus, we got it wrong. We got it so wrong all that time ago. She resisted the impulse to laugh, to laugh or cry, undecided as to which urge was stronger. *We were children, and we didn't understand. But oh God, I think I understand now.*

She had to talk to Jason and Rob. She had to find them and explain. They'd listen to her. They wouldn't think she was crazy. They were the only ones who could stop it. She'd put an end to this if she had to drive the bulldozer herself.

She reached for the gate and defiantly grabbed it, pulling it shut.

"Shit!" she yelped as a splinter embedded itself in her finger, pushing out her blood. She pulled her hand away and sucked it, then peered at it, trying to squeeze out the wood, but it was lodged deep. God, it hurt. Why did the little cuts always hurt the worst? Shaking her wrist to try to alleviate the sting, she glared at the house before turning away. She'd get the fragment out with tweezers when she got home. Pay the electric, get rid of the splinter, then ring Jason and Rob. That's what she had to do today. It was time to end it. To finish what had started around them, what had never really let them go. Deep in her pocket, the tip of her finger turned purple as the silent secret expanded through her capillaries, merging into the warmth.

CHAPTER FIVE

"You ought to put something on that hand. It looks like you might have a bit of blood poisoning there." Connor O'Neale's concerned face appeared beside Carole-Anne as she stared at the row of colorful bottles in front of her. For a moment she looked down absently at the mottled red that was spreading up from her wrist and then grunted without concern.

"I have weeds. Weeds that I just can't kill." Her voice was a monotone and she didn't look at the man who had once had a soft spot for her when he was two years behind her in school. Well, a soft spot probably wouldn't be the right way to put it. A *hard spot* would be technically more correct. Carole-Anne Bradley had been his masturbatory fantasy for six glorious months of his third year. That was the longest he'd stayed faithful to one girl in all his short, solitary sexual life, and he'd been vaguely sad when his mind and hand had moved on to Jenna Compton of the short skirts and too tight shirts.

Carole-Anne sniffed and wiped her nose with the back

of her injured hand. She didn't see the man grimace with distaste before he spoke.

"What kind of weeds?"

"Weeds that won't stop growing. I've got to get rid of them. They're over-running the place, destroying everything." She seemed to be talking more to herself than him, but Connor was a professional and continued in his cheerful, soft lilt.

"We can't have that, can we? You probably need something like this." He pulled a blue spray bottle from the shelf that had a big 'Pet Friendly' label attached to the front. "It needs about three applications, but it works rather well and is a good value for the money, especially if your garden isn't too . . ."

"Don't have pets." She picked up a smaller plastic container and turned it around carefully in her large hands. Her eyes lingered on the on the danger warnings declaring the contents toxic and corrosive. "What about this?" For the first time she turned to look at Connor with his ruddy face and green overalls, the small logo over the chest pocket reminding her where she was shopping.

Connor looked concerned. "Well, that's not one I normally recommend. It has to be diluted quite a lot and you have to be careful handling it. I'd normally only sell it to farmers or agricultural experts."

Carole-Anne's eyes showed signs of life for the first time in the increasingly dazed hour since she'd left Syracousse. "Why is that?"

"It contains Paraquat. It's quite a newly developed chemical, and although it does the job well, it's very poisonous and there's no antidote. Just a small amount can make all your major organs fail. Not one to have around kids."

She chewed her bottom lip before silently mouthing the name on the label. Clean-Sweep. Yes, that would suit her very well. Clean-Sweep. She smiled gently. "My boys aren't babies anymore. I'll take it."

Before Connor had a chance to protest, she pushed him out of the way and went to the long old-fashioned payment counter behind which there was a backdrop of a thousand tiny drawers, the contents of which Connor and his brother knew by heart like their father before them. Connor watched the fat woman walk away for only a moment before moving to help an elderly gentleman in search of garden shears. His days of following Carole-Anne around were well and truly over.

"Good morning, Your Honor."

The old man hadn't been a judge in twenty years, but Connor never forgot to address him that way, in the shop or in passing, and the old man appreciated it, especially now that most of his contemporaries were either dead or had moved into that awful sheltered housing next to the cricket ground, full of remains of people who no longer seemed to count. Connor always made him feel as if he still counted. But then Connor had lived in Streatford all his life.

"Good morning, young man. Good to see you. Now could you tell me which of these shears has the sharpest and strongest blades?"

By the time Jimmy got home, the boys had been upstairs deafening her with music and television for more than an hour, but today she didn't mind. She wasn't in much of a mood for conversation. After leaving O'Neale's she'd gone to the butcher's and then trudged home with her shopping before sitting at the kitchen table, staring at the bags in front of her for two hours, maybe three, her head empty, void of rational thought. Finally, she'd gotten up and started to make the dinner. Her hand was in a bandage, not that it hurt; in fact, it felt fine, but she didn't want Jimmy questioning her about what had happened to it. You could still see the purply blue halfway up her forearm, but with her sleeves pulled down that would stay invisible.

Jimmy stood in the doorway as she stirred the contents

of the pan, the spicy aroma filling the room with warmth. He watched her warily. Carole-Anne's cooking normally ran to pizza and oven chips. Anything that just could be thrown in the oven and that went with chips, that was her forte.

"What are you doing?"

She looked up and smiled at him, ignoring the pasty paunch that hung out of the top of his trousers, ignoring the oil and petrol that covered his hands and t-shirt from a day tinkering around under cars. He'd been covered in dirt so long she thought it had probably seeped through to his soul by now, although maybe that was a place where filth had always lived. Maybe the dirt was leaking from the inside out.

"I wanted to make it up to you after my accident with the kettle this morning. I'm cooking your and the boys' favorite. Chicken vindaloo."

She saw the look of uncertainty on his worn-out face beneath the patches of thinning hair that he refused to accept could no longer handle the slightly long style he'd had since school.

"Don't worry. I've followed the recipe very carefully. It'll be delicious." She walked over to him and kissed him on the cheek as he took his seat at the table. She opened a drawer, pulled out some knives and forks, and then handed him a can of beer from the fridge. He took a long swig as she arranged the cutlery around him.

"But you don't like Indian."

Laughing lightly, she shrugged. "That doesn't mean I can't make it for you, does it? I've put a lasagne in the oven for me."

He grunted. "Well, I hope it's good. I'm fucking starving. Is it ready yet?"

Carole-Anne called down the boys.

She didn't have to worry about them not eating it. If the Locke men were anything, it was greedy. Mark had started developing little love handles when he was ten, and now at nearly fourteen, they were full-grown rolls of fat. Luke, only one year behind, was thinner but not by much. By the time she sat down and started nibbling at her lasagne, the three of them were guzzling the curry. She felt a wave of disgust behind her numbness. Her ears filled with the sound of smacking lips and slurped food. Animals. That's what they were. Fat, slobbering animals, no use to anyone.

Luke grinned at her from behind his fork as he chewed, his blue eyes sparkling. "This is great, Mum."

Mark nodded in agreement. "Wicked."

She smiled as she watched them eat.

Ten minutes later the boys didn't think their dinner was quite so wonderful anymore as the blisters started bursting on their lips and in their mouths. When Jimmy stood up, clutching at his chest, trying to wheeze out a scream, staring at her with those angry, terrified eyes, Carole-Anne decided to go lock herself in the bathroom. She didn't know how long this would take, and it was better to be safe than sorry. After all, who knew better than she just how angry Jimmy Locke could get?

She pushed past Mark, who'd slid to the floor and was trying to clutch at her leg, and went out to the hallway. She pushed down the handle on the front door, and after turning the key in the lock, pulled it out and held it tight. Luke had dragged himself into the hallway behind her, whimpering for her attention just like he had when he'd been a baby, before he could even crawl properly. His eyes were pleading at her to help him, to make the pain go away, and for a moment, beneath her haze of nothingness, she thought she felt something. Love even or maybe just pity, but whichever it was, in a second it was gone. He wasn't her baby anymore; she didn't know who *this thing* was, and she just wanted him gone the same as the others.

Turning her back on him, she went into the downstairs bathroom and bolted the door quickly behind her and sat down heavily on the lid. Soon it would be over; she just had to wait. A little patience was all that was required. She jumped a little as two walls away the kitchen table toppled over onto its side, the plates smashing beneath it. That would be Jimmy. So there still was life in the old dog yet. Never mind, there was nowhere for him to go, however much he wanted to have his little tantrum. The door was locked and she had a vague memory of cutting the telephone wire this afternoon.

Luke was scratching weakly at the door in front of her, and she kicked out at him from the other side. Why couldn't they just damn shitting well leave her in peace? That was all she wanted. Some peace and quiet. Some time to herself. Why couldn't they give her that? Why did they have to be so fucking selfish?

After a few frantic minutes, the scratching stopped. *Hallelujah, praise the Lord.* Shutting her eyes, she leaned to one side and rested her head on the wall. Maybe she should stay in here a little while longer, just to be sure. It had been such a long day, and she was so tired. Yes, maybe she should just sit here where it was nice and quiet; sit here with her eyes shut and rest. That would be nice.

In less than a minute, she was asleep, snoring softy.

It was pitch dark when she awoke with a start, her face still sweating from the nightmare. The first thing she noticed was the pain that seared through her arm. What the hell was it? And where was she? Trying to shake away the fuzz in her head, she reached up for the light switch. The brightness made her head rage, but ignoring it, she stared at her hand. There was a vague memory of bandaging it, but she had thought that was part of her dream. Just what the hell had been going on with her today?

Suddenly she was terrified of opening the door. Why had she fallen asleep in the downstairs bathroom? She racked her brain for something that made sense. The last thing she remembered clearly was standing outside *that house*, trying to suck the splinter out of her finger. *Surely*

that tiny piece of wood couldn't be causing all this pain?
The rest of the day was a series of fragmented images.
She'd been cooking, that much she did know. She'd been
cooking something unusual. What was it? A curry? Yes,
that's what it was. She'd cooked a curry. A curry with a
special ingredient.

Leaning back against the wall, she moaned slightly as a
memory engulfed her. She was in O'Neale's, and Connor,
no longer the spotty teenager who used to moon over her
in corridors, was trying to warn her about something.
Something she wanted, something that would "do the
job," whatever that meant. Weed killer. Why would she
want to buy weed killer?

She'd needed a special ingredient, that's why.

"Oh dear God," she whispered softly. "Oh my dear
God, no." Oblivious to the pain, she raised her shaking
hand and pulled back the bolt. What was going to be out
there? Was her baby lying out there? The tears were already forming in her eyes when she tentatively opened the
door, but the blurriness of her vision didn't stop her seeing her son far too clearly, lying in the hallway, one hand
still reaching for her. His eyes were wide open, full of
shock and surprise, and oh God, far too much pain.

"Oh Luke, oh my baby boy, what have I done to you,
what have I done?" Falling to her knees she took his head
and cradled it carefully, keening through her tears as she
rocked backwards and forwards, smothering his cold face
with kisses, calling for him to wake up, wishing for him to
wake up, to wake up from this terrible nightmare that
she'd infected them with. How long she sat there with the
light from the open bathroom doorway shining down on
their tragedy, she didn't know and didn't care, her grief
uncontrollable as she whispered to her youngest baby, trying to comfort him in the dark.

Eventually, when her legs felt as cold and numb as his
did, she lifted her heavy head, and gazed along the corridor to the kitchen doorway. Gently kissing Luke good-

night, she laid him back on the carpet and hauled herself to her feet. She could see Mark's arm on the floor before she'd crossed the threshold. As she forced herself forward, her feet squeaked on the cheap linoleum. She sunk into a chair, reached down and took her eldest son's hand, holding it against her cheek, trying to savor its smell, to remember its living scent. Beneath his gelled dark hair, his eyes were squeezed shut, as if he couldn't bear the pain. His mouth and tongue, like Luke's, were a mass of red sores and swollen blisters. "Oh my babies," she said. "Oh my poor, poor babies." She was no longer crying, the sheer desolation of what she felt inside too much for tears to keep up with.

From behind the tumbled pine table she could see one of Jimmy's work boots, lolling toward her. He was her husband. There had been some good times, hadn't there? A long time ago, maybe, and maybe their love had died along the way, but he had given her beautiful boys, her sons, who sometimes drove her mad, but they had been all hers, *her babies*. They didn't deserve this. None of them did.

Unable to bear the thought of Luke alone in the corridor, she got up and carefully dragged him into the kitchen, whispering lovingly, laying him beside his brother. She wanted her family around her. She wanted them all to be together. One last time.

Taking a black marker from one of the drawers, she went to the large upright fridge in the corner, pulling away the Post-it reminders from a life gone by. When it was a clear canvas of white, she lifted her hand to write. Those who needed to understand it would, as long as they got to read it. And if they didn't? Well, she was just about past caring. Hers eyes filling at the thought of the sheer ridiculous waste of it all, she wrote her simple message.

TEACHER
We got it Wrong

Her hand didn't seem to write so well anymore, but the words were legible and that was all that mattered. She'd done her bit. Oh God, had she done her bit.

She turned away from the fridge, picked her way over Jimmy to the stove and lifted the pan of congealed leftover curry. Taking a spoon from the draining board, she sat on the cool tile between Mark and Luke, resting her back against the uncomfortable cupboards. Placing the pan beside her, she pulled the boys' bodies closer until their heads were resting on her lap. She stroked their hair for a while, a small sad smile dancing across her lips, before picking up the pan; and with a cool, clear head, she started to eat.

CHAPTER SIX

Jason's shoulders had started to ache at seven-thirty that morning regular as clockwork, but he'd stayed silent as the two of them humped the boxes into the back of the van, the frosty air burning his face. He knew better than to complain. As Bob had pointed out on his first morning at Brown's when Jason had mentioned blearily that getting up at 4:30 AM to go the farmers' markets was no way for a man to start his day, he was lucky to have the fucking job at all. *He* wouldn't have employed him. The old man must be losing his marbles to want a parolee on his payroll. But then, Bob was the size of an ox and had been working for the fruit and veg shop pretty much since he was born. This was his fucking chosen career.

Jason almost laughed at that thought until the truth of the grunting giant's words hit home. He *was* lucky to have this job. And to be lucky to have a job humping sacks of potatoes and endless crates of apples and carrots, when you were in your thirties was a pretty shit position to be in. That was the fucker of it he couldn't deny. So for the past six weeks, he'd worked silently, doing what he was told, and keeping his endless aches and pains to himself. He didn't want Bob to tell old Mr. Brown that he wasn't up to the job, even if his thin, lanky frame was telling him otherwise.

At least today it was Bob's turn to do the van run. Brown's did a good trade in supplying restaurants, and also delivering to houses in the small surrounding villages. The last crate stacked, Jason slammed the van doors shut and slapped the side, letting Bob know it was all his from here. He watched as it pulled away down the tight alley at the back of the small warehouse behind the shop, and waited until Bob had turned the corner before pulling a cigarette out of his overalls pocket and lighting it, leaning gratefully against the wall. A precious hour to himself before the shop staff arrived.

The smell of diesel hung in the cold, still air. Yeah, Brown had done well out of the deliveries, and Jason had a good idea that that was why the old bugger had given him the job when no one else was exactly eager to employ him. The deliveries had, after all, been Jason's idea, back when he was fourteen and the acquisition of a Raleigh Chopper with a Sturmey Archer three-speed gear selector was his ultimate aim. He *had* to have one. He had to have one so badly it hurt. His first sight of one of those bikes had made him feel alive for the first time since all that shit at Gina's place. Yeah, the Raleigh Chopper. The king of bikes. His stomach would churn with envy whenever one sped by. And that was how he ended up with the summer job at Brown's.

The old man had been taking a chance then, given that Jason's dad was hardly a pillar of society—like father like son—but Jason hadn't let him down. He'd worked all hours, sweeping and cleaning, moving sacks that seemed twice his weight—that still seemed twice his weight—carrying old ladies' baskets for them, until finally, he had enough money, with the little bit his mum had thrown in. But during those few months of what felt like back-breaking labor, carrying the cut-out picture of his prize in the back pocket of his jeans to keep him going, it was he who had mentioned to the not yet old Mr. Brown that the business could be expanded by delivering, and that no shopkeeper could feel secure because 'the age of the supermarket' was approaching. Brown had laughed him away, but the idea must have stuck because within a few months, he'd tentatively bought his first van.

And the rest, as they say, is history. Mr. Brown expanded his business, and Jason got his chopper with the three-speed gear selector that nearly castrated him on several occasions.

He stubbed his cigarette out and went back into the small warehouse to make himself a coffee. He still had plenty of work to do, get the shop stocked up and the outside display ready, but caffeine was what he needed first. Nicotine and caffeine. A man's two best friends.

By ten-thirty Bob wasn't yet back, and the shop was open with its usual steady stream of regular customers. Different day, different regulars. The people of Streatford were creatures of habit, invariably shopping on the same day of each week. Jason was pottering about in the warehouse without much to do, although he was sure that when Bob got back, he'd find something. Bob *always* found some unnecessary job for Jason to do. Any chance to exert his limited authority.

The phone on the wall rang, and he picked it up. It was Jan at the register. "Can you bring me out another box of Cox's Pippins? We're having a bit of a run on them this morning."

"No problem." Picking up a small box along the left wall, he walked down the small corridor and into the warmth of the shop, heading over to the depleted straw tray of apples, and started refilling it, keeping the fruit in its purple tissue-paper wrapping. The contrast of color always made the apples look crisp and fresh, even if they had been out back for longer than they should. This was one of his ideas that had really gotten Bob's back up, especially as the old man had gone along with it. He was going to have to learn to keep his big mouth shut, or else Bob's general dislike would turn to hate, and he was getting too old for making new enemies.

The box empty, he turned around to head back to the warehouse, and almost knocked over the man standing behind him. "I'm sorry, I didn't see you there. Are you okay?"

The man smiled back at him, and Jason's heart sunk. It was Rob. Fucking Robert Black standing there in a casually expensive cashmere sweater, head to toe oozing success, staring at him in his too big Brown's overalls. Jesus. Just what he fucking needed. For a second, he thought he might be able to slip away, and then Rob's head tilted quizzically. "Jason?"

Well, well. The bigshot recognized him after all these years. Should he feel flattered? Trying to swallow his bitterness and embarrassment, he smiled. "Yeah, it's me. I heard you were back in town. How are you?"

Rob shrugged. "Okay. What about you?"

Jason's eyes slipped away a little, focusing on old Judge Matthews checking the tomatoes just outside the shop, before they came back to Rob. "Same as ever. No wiser, just older."

Rob laughed. "Yeah, that just about sums me up, too."

Maybe, except you're a shitload richer with it, Jason thought. But then, he could hardly blame Rob for the mess he'd made of his own life, no matter how much he wanted to. There was a moment's awkward silence before Jason's curiosity got the better of him. "What made you come back here, Rob? The rest of us dream of getting away. You could go anywhere in the world if you've had enough of the big city. Why the fuck come back to a shithole like Streatford?"

This time it was Rob who looked away slightly. "I don't really know. I guess it's home, that's all."

The old man had come in from outside and was reaching for some bananas on a hook above where they were talking.

"Let me get them for you, Judge Matthews. How many would you like? It's three normally, isn't it?" The old man nodded, as Jason put them into a paper bag.

Putting them into his green plastic basket, he looked up and smiled. "Thank you, young man." He looked at Rob for a second and then his smile froze as he glanced backward and forward between the two men, who were smiling back at him. He didn't move.

"Are you okay?" Jason asked, gently touching the fragile man's arm. The judge pulled away, muttering under his breath, and started to move to the register, glancing nervously over his shoulder, barely waiting for his change before scurrying out of the shop.

The strangeness of it broke the tension between the two men for a second, as they looked at each other with raised eyebrows. "He must finally be going ga-ga."

"Did you call him Judge Matthews? Is that really him? God, I didn't recognize him. He's looking so old." Rob was still staring at the space the judge had vacated.

"Yeah, well time didn't stop here just because you left, Robster." The bitterness in Jason's voice, combined with his involuntary use of the old childhood nickname, must have hit a nerve, because Rob looked as if he'd just been slapped.

"You're right. I just didn't expect to see him like that. I guess I just always thought he'd go on and on exactly as he was. He was one of those kind of men. Like an invincible army brigadier or something. Stupid, huh?"

Jason smiled, wondering where this conversation was going, and not wanting to rekindle any long-dead friendships. Some things were better left alone. "Look, I'd better get back into the warehouse. I've got tons of stuff to do."

"Sure, of course." Rob was rummaging in his back pocket and pulled out a small notebook and tiny pen. He grinned sheepishly. "Tools of the trade. I take them with me everywhere in case any lightning bolts of inspiration strike. That's the theory anyway." He scribbled a number down and tore out the sheet. "I'm at my mum's old house. That's the number. Maybe we could go for a beer or something one day?"

Rob still had the notebook open, and Jason found himself reciting his cell number. *Oh Lord, Robster wants to exorcise his demons.* He folded up the piece of paper and slipped it in his overalls. "Yeah, maybe."

Nodding farewell, he went back to his sanctuary of the warehouse and lit a cigarette before pulling out the scrap of paper and staring at it as he smoked. There was no way he was ever going to call that number, and he had a feeling it was the same for Rob. The time to talk was far too long ago, and now they were too grown up to know where to start. The past was done. It was best left alone. His face in a frown, he balled up the paper and tossed it into the bin.

CHAPTER SEVEN

When he'd been in London, Rob considered it a good day's work if he'd gotten a couple of thousand words down by about two. Then he'd normally call it a day and start planning his evening's entertainment. Although he was giving up the partying, he'd expected his writing output to have stayed at about the same level now that he was in Streatford. So he was somewhat surprised to see that it was four o'clock when the ringing phone dragged him out of the world in his laptop and that he'd done just over four thousand words. He had a sneaking suspicion that they were damn good words, too.

His legs felt stiff when he got up, a testament to the hours he'd spent sitting at the kitchen table, and his neck was in agony, but he felt good about himself despite it all. He was working. Working on something good.

"Hello?"

"Rob? It's Michael. How are you getting on?"

He smiled to hear the familiar voice. "Great. Better than great. I'm working on something new and although it's early days, I think you're going to like it. I've been writing since eight this morning, and I've only just stopped. I think this might be my best work since *The Pyramid Man,* I really do."

"Good, I'm glad to hear it." Michael didn't need to mention that the sales figures for his latest book hadn't been as high as expected. Rob was painfully aware of that fact. Still, it was hardly losing money, even if it had just missed the top ten spot in the bestseller lists. Maybe the paperback would pull it back.

"So how's country life? Bumped into any old flames back there? I hear Janine is missing you." Rob didn't miss the hint of sarcasm in his agent's voice, and he smiled wryly. He'd seen the papers. Janine had moved on pretty instantaneously to some up-and-coming pop star.

"No, no old flames, thank you very much. I think I've earned a break from women. Seriously though, I'm just keeping pretty much to myself." He didn't mention bumping into Jason yesterday. After all, Jason didn't really qualify as an old flame. And anyway, weird though it was, he hadn't expected to bump into him at all, as if he belonged to a Streatford stuck in another time and shouldn't be in the here and now. On top of that, it had looked as if Jason hadn't wanted to be bumped into. Not by him at any rate.

"You should come down and visit for a few days. It'd be great to see you. Just give me a couple of weeks to sort the place out properly."

"Yeah, I'd like that. Anyway, I'd better go. Deals to do and all that jazz."

"Okay, just as long as they're deals for me. I'll call you in a few days."

After saying good-bye and hanging up, Rob started to make himself a ham sandwich. Yes, it would be nice to see Michael, but not just yet. That's why he'd come out with the small white lie about getting the house ready. The house was fine. He was just enjoying having it to himself for a little while. He wasn't ready to share his peace and quiet yet. Not even with Michael, who was probably the best friend he'd had since . . . well, since Jason. And after their awkward meeting yesterday, it was hard to believe that they'd once been best buddies, their friendship bravely crossing the gulf of the '70s class divide. Maybe that's why it was doomed not to last. Maybe that's why Jason had done that shit in class about Rob's dad; maybe he'd been glad that Rob's world wasn't so perfect after all.

As an adult he could see it clearly, but at the time he hadn't forgiven Jason, even if he'd said he did. The cracks in their friendship were pretty huge by the end of that summer, even before all the weird crap that happened with Gina. Yeah, their friendship was fatally damaged when it was only the good stuff going on. They just hadn't realized it yet. But that was all just part of growing up. You make friends. You break friends.

He turned the radio on for company while he ate his sandwich, and instantly wished he hadn't. It was the local station and the news had been dominated by the story of the woman from Gallows Hill who'd murdered her family and then herself a couple of days ago. The reporter was saying that it might have been brought on by guilt over an extra-marital affair.

Turning it off, he went into the lounge to light the fire. It seemed like there was nowhere in the world safe from these awful tragedies anymore, and he didn't really want to hear about them if he didn't have to. He'd set the fire first thing that morning and was glad of it now, only having to light the scrunched up newspaper at the base to start it blazing. The work he'd done today was catching up with him. His head was drained and tired. He thought about sitting in the armchair and having a snooze for half an hour or so to revitalize him. Then the thump of a paper hit the carpet in the hall, and he went to see what it was.

Of course, he thought as he picked up the thick tabloid-sized newspaper. *The Citizen's Companion.* How could he have forgotten? Delivered every Thursday afternoon. Always had been and always would be, he suspected. Still, it was a lot thicker now than he remembered it. No doubt full of motor or property supplements, the scourge of the modern newspaper world. He took it back into to the warming lounge and sat in his armchair, laughing a little, because he suddenly felt like an old man. All he needed to complete the picture were some tatty slippers and a pipe. If only Janine could see him now.

The main part of the front page was taken up with a photo of a woman with a fat, sad face and greasy hair. He didn't recognize her, and even when he'd read and reread the name written in bold underneath, he still didn't recognize her. Despite the fire, a chill had settled on him, a chill that started deep inside him and worked its way out, and it took a few seconds before he could bring himself to accept the words that his eyes were reading. He looked at the picture again. Could that really be Carole-Anne? Could it? Not their Carole-Anne. Surely not. The picture swam a little before him. But there was something in those eyes that was familiar, and maybe the shape of the mouth. He looked at the name again. Carole-Anne Locke. So she'd really gone and married that arsehole Jimmy. Why the hell had she done that?

He took a cigarette from the packet on the mantelpiece, lit it with shaky hands and inhaled deeply before starting to read the article. "Jesus, Carrie," he muttered to himself. "What the hell have you done?"

He read the words without really accepting what they were telling him. It couldn't be true. It couldn't. She would never have done anything like this. She didn't even swat flies, for Christ's sake.

Apparently, she killed her husband and two sons by poisoning their dinner with a highly toxic weed killer, before poisoning herself. She left a cryptic note that led police to believe that she may have been having an affair with one of the teachers at her boys' school. However, all staff vehemently denied the allegation, and there was now suspicion that Mrs. Locke was suffering from some kind of delusional fantasy that got out of control. Sources reveal that the message, which was believed to have been written on the family fridge, read, "TEACHER. WE GOT IT WRONG."

As he stared at those words, Rob felt as if his sandwich was about to come up. He read it over and over again, feeling twelve once more, feeling helpless in the presence of the words. Carole-Anne had left the message for them, she had to have. No one else knew about Teacher. No one. But Jesus, what had driven her to this? How could something from so long ago have made her do this?

The butt of his cigarette burned his fingers for a second or two before he realized and threw it into the fire, shaking away the pain. What the hell was going on here? He'd dreamed of Teacher. That was what made him think of coming home, and now this. Could it just be a coincidence? God, he needed to talk to someone. But who?

Before the answer had consciously come to him, he'd gone to the kitchen and picked up his notebook. There was only one person who would get this, and he needed to talk to him whether he liked it or not. He dialed the number, and it rang twice before someone answered.

"Hallo?"

"Jason? It's Rob. Have you seen the paper?"

Jason sighed wearily at the other end. "What? About Carrie?" His voice was slightly slurred, and Rob got the distinct feeling that wherever Jason was, he was drinking.

"Yes, about Carole-Anne. Did you see the message she left? She was talking about Teacher."

"I'm not really interested, Robster. It's all a long time ago. I haven't really seen her since, well, since school. Since you and Gina left. She may as well be a stranger now. Just like she is to you. I didn't notice you going to any great lengths to keep in touch over the years."

Rob let the slurred knock go unnoticed. "Yeah, well I guess I just thought you two would end up together."

Jason laughed, although there was no humor in it.

"Well, I'm fucking glad we didn't! Didn't you see that photo? She's looked like that for years. It was all downhill for her as soon as she started shagging that wanker Jimmy Locke. So, no. We were never going to get together." He paused for a second before he added softly, "Anyway, we were both in love with Gina, weren't we? Carrie never really got a look in."

Rob wondered whether it was as hard for Jason to mention Gina's name as it was for him to hear it. He let out a sigh of his own. "Look, you know when you asked me yesterday why I'd come back to town? Well, there was more to it than just coming home." He waited for a second, but Jason said nothing. "I'd been dreaming of Teacher. Bad dreams. I didn't think anything of it, but now with this. . ." His voice trailed off. "Maybe we should get together and talk about it."

Jason's laugh was a bark. "Why? So you can write another book about the shit that happens to people around you? Like you did with *The Pyramid Man*? I don't think so, mate." So he'd read that book, even if he hadn't gotten the point of it. Maybe he had. Maybe he just had his own guilt on that score. There was a tired exhale on the other end of the line. "Look, I'll see you at the funeral. When they issue a date that is. And that's if I go. I'm not sure I will yet, but if I do, then we can talk there. Will that do you?"

Rob muttered a yes.

"Good. 'Cos that's all you're going to get." The phone clicked off. Still cradling the receiver to his cheek, Rob chewed the inside of his mouth. Why the hell did Jason sound so scared? And if he thought he could fool Rob with all that crap about not giving a shit, then he was wrong. Rob knew him too well, even after all these years. He'd been in love with Carrie in his schoolboy way long before Gina came along. And Gina, well it was never quite real love, was it? She was too ethereal, too strange, too beautiful to *really* love. And too goddamn weird.

It seemed like the floodgates of his memory were about to open, and he locked them shut. Not today. He didn't want to remember all of that today. Yes, Jason would be at the funeral. He wouldn't be able to stop himself from saying good-bye. Couldn't if he wanted to.

He went back into the sitting room, and threw the newspaper onto the fire. Watching it burn, he thought for a moment, that he was going to cry.

CHAPTER EIGHT

The new shears he'd bought a few days ago from the young O'Neale boy sliced easily through the overgrowing greenery at the bottom of his rambling garden. It was the joints in Judge Matthews's hands that were struggling, the pain causing him to occasionally grunt quietly to himself as he worked, a constant reminder that the best of his days were over, and now he was left playing the waiting game with God. Not that he believed much in all that heaven and hell preaching; although sometimes, as the nights silently ticked sleeplessly by, he wished he did. There seemed to be little comfort in old age.

A satisfyingly large piece of blackberry bush fell by his feet, and admiring his handiwork, he decided that within another forty minutes or so he'd be able to see the river from his conservatory as he liked to, all through the approaching winter. He rolled his creaking shoulders, feeling the twinges there. It didn't seem so long ago that he'd have had this job done in twenty minutes, and something in that thought made his heart ache, but only for a moment. He wasn't a man who liked to dwell too much on things that he couldn't do anything about. It was hard to stay down with fresh air in his lungs and the sweet mingling smells of the countryside dancing in his nostrils. On the other side of the water, a herd of cows was grazing in the fields, their quiet sounds keeping him company, and there was something about it that made old age seem the most natural thing in the world, which, he guessed on reflection, it was. The last of the summer midges darted about his head, and he blew them away.

There were plenty of people who would think him a fool for being out here working at his age, for not hiring someone, but he didn't care. As long as he could do for himself, he'd be damned if he'd let anyone look after him. And anyway, that young doctor down at the surgery had told him the best thing for his rheumatism was to try to keep himself active. Some gentle walking. Keep himself as flexible as possible. He snorted out loud as he snipped away at the brambles. Not that that young tyke could know anything about the soul-destroying pain of rheumatoid arthritis. But then, Ernest Matthews consoled himself, should the young GP reach his ripe old age, then more than likely he'll have first-hand experience.

He smiled, peering over the section of trimmed bushes at the river beyond. The young always looked at the old as if they were from a different species. Aliens; tolerated, but not really understood. They never seemed to realize that the walking stick and reading glasses were really only a blink of an eye away. Still smiling, he shook his head. Still, that was the way it always had been, and always would be. It was how it *should* be. If you couldn't believe in eternity when you were young, then what was the point of it all? What would be the point of your hopes, your dreams? They would all grow up in time, and sooner than they expected. Just look at those two boys he saw in Brown's this morning . . . He pushed that thought away, working vigorously with his shears.

Seeing those two had unsettled him, brought him out

into the garden to work away his unease, although why they should have bothered him he didn't know. It wasn't as if he hadn't seen Jason Milburn plenty since the Grace case, mainly in the dock just like his father before him. It must have been seeing him with the writer that had brought back the old memories. Seeing the two of them all grown up, men now, no more carefree days racing around town on bikes for them. It was like seeing them, but not them. The children he'd known briefly all those years ago, the ones he had talked to, in his own way tried to reassure, were long gone. Strangers with only shadows left behind. In the case of poor Carole-Anne Bradley, she was gone forever.

His work was almost done, and something in his newly clear view distracted him from his immediate thoughts and took them down a new road. Looking to his left, he heard himself take a sharp breath. Surely that couldn't be right. He'd have noticed it before. Why hadn't he noticed it before? He'd lived here thirty years and more; he knew every inch of the view across the river. So why was he only seeing it now? Putting the unwanted shears down on the lawn, he stretched his back and stared, puzzled.

The top of the house on Toombes Meadow was clearly visible, even the chimney stack, unused for so many winters now. He blinked a few times, to clear his mind as well as his vision, but every time he opened them, it was still there, clear as day. "Well, I'll be," he whispered, not sure what to make of it. Maybe it had always been there and he just hadn't noticed it. That had to be the case; there was no other alternative. Maybe it was seeing those boys today that made him spot it. After all, it wasn't exactly right in front of him or anything. It was possible he could have missed it for all these years, if he wasn't looking for it. Or maybe he was just a useless old man with rheumy eyes and couldn't trust his sight anymore. He wasn't convincing himself very well.

He was sure he never used to be able to see the house

from here. He'd have remembered a thing like that, forgetful though he may be these days. As he stood there, his brain worked overtime to find a logical reason for this new information, and when it came up with one, he grabbed it and clung on.

Someone must have cut a few trees down over there. Or maybe they had come down in those gales a few weeks ago. Yes, that must have been it. That was why he could see the house now. Feeling a rush of relief, liking his explanation, he let the world settle back to normal around him. His mind was still his own; he wasn't joining the drooling brigade just yet.

Calmer now, he squinted at the house for a few moments longer, cursing whoever had cleared the view. He'd never understood why old man Cowley had wanted to build on that land in the first place. He'd even asked him, to which Cowley, canny businessman that he was, had laughed and given him that big, open smile of his, and told him, "Because it's cheap, Ernie, because it's cheap." He was a good man, Cowley, and God knew he himself had never been prone to superstition, it wasn't a good quality in a judge, but that meadow had been unused common land for so many centuries, there was almost something sacred about it. Still, Cowley was right. He'd gotten himself a big, private house for his family for half the money he'd have paid anywhere else. Not that Cowley couldn't afford it, but he always was a man who liked a bargain. At least he'd never let his wealth give him airs and graces, like that son-in-law of his, who'd turned out to be not quite so well off as he liked people to believe. People were strange; his life on the bench had taught him that, if nothing else. There was no accounting for folk, as the old saying went.

Feeling his melancholy settling back in, he bent down slowly to pick up his shears and put them in the shed, not wanting to dwell on events so long past. He'd liked Camilla. She'd been a lovely girl, and it had hurt his heart when she came up in court before him, but there was no doubt about it: She'd killed Philip Grace—no matter what she said—and he'd had to judge her for it.

Locking the shed, he sighed. Still, that place out by Ashburtle probably hadn't treated her too badly over the years. They'd be giving her the care she needed, and mainstream prison hadn't been the place for a fragile woman like her. By the time the trial was over, and he'd made it as swift as possible, all Camilla would do was giggle into her hands and rock backward and forward. Backward and forward for hours and hours. Lost in her own world. She was probably still lost there now. It had been the little girl that he'd most felt sorry for. Her guilty eyes, as if the whole sorry tragic episode were her fault, trying to take the blame herself. Kids were strange creatures. As strange as the adults they would one day become, that much was for sure.

Eager to leave his thoughts in the garden, he leaned on the open patio door handle to pull off his muddy shoes before going back into the house. His gloved hand stopped as he grabbed the leather of his heel. What was going on out here tonight? Leaning down closer to the pale paving stones to get a better look, he scanned along the wall to see where the little devils were coming from. His eyes came to rest at the fence that separated his house from Daisy's. There was a tiny stream of black ants marching from her side of the brown wood to his, running all the way to his patio door, where they seemed to be just milling about, as if waiting for further instruction. He shook his head, not sure whether to trust his vision for the second time this evening. Ants this late in the summer?

Keeping his shoes on, he went inside and locked the sliding door firmly behind him, peering at the growing multitude through the glass. Ants. Well, it must just be the evening for unusual things, and it wasn't as if the summer were quite over yet. Maybe this was their last supper before the hard frosts came.

He pulled his shoes off on the mat, and replaced them with his loafers, ignoring the scream in his back as he straightened up. Maybe he'd overdone the recommended gentle exercise slightly, but at least the pain let him know that he was still very much with the living. Checking the carpet, he saw with relief that none of his six-legged friends had made it in with him, but he liked to open the door in the mornings and let some air in, so something was going to have to be done about his new garden inhabitants. He wouldn't normally bother, but there just seemed to be so damn many of them.

The only thing for it was to pop next door and see where they were coming from. Daisy would want to know if she's gotten a bit of an infestation anyway. A damn fine woman, Daisy Roper. She'd run the haberdashery in Market Square for years back when she'd been *a real person,* just like he'd been; and just like he, she was damned if she was joining the retirement home brigade, mid-eighties or not. That haberdashery had been a feature of the town for two decades, back in the days when haberdashery shops were a lady's must, before a new generation came and took over, quietly pushing the old ways out, usurping from the inside.

Unfortunately, the only thing that knocking at Daisy's door revealed was that she wasn't at home, and back in his own kitchen Ernest Matthews boiled a full kettle of water, starting to feel irritated at this interruption to his evening. He just wanted to sit in front of his fire, (gas these days, although still coal effect; the body wasn't up to the rigors of maintaining a real fire anymore), and do the crossword while listening to the radio 4 play on the wireless.

Trying to shake off his internal grumbles, he tugged the lead away from the steaming kettle and headed toward the patio. He'd treat himself to a nice whisky when he'd finished. That would ease his aches and pains, physical and otherwise. Unlocking the door, he slid it open, and noticed with amazement that the mass of black insects was making its way onto the wooden lintel of the door-frame. They were persistent little buggers, he had to give them that. Tipping his wrist, he started to pour, and wondered momentarily, how much pain they'd feel.

CHAPTER NINE

Kelly was glad she didn't have her high heels on today as she almost jogged out of the school gates before anyone could grab her. A free period at the end of the day was a rarity and with her year ten English group away on a trip, she intended to make the most of the extra hour. Once a safe hundred yards away, she slowed her trot down to a brisk walk, pushing her blond hair away from her face so she could see where she was going, her breath quick in her chest.

Time to start going back to those aerobics classes before your body completely goes to pot on you, she chastised herself. Slim didn't always mean fit, and the busyness of home and work that made her forget to eat was the same one that left her too tired to exercise. It was a lose-lose situation. *Next week, I'll sign up again,* she thought with a wry internal smile. *And pigs might fly. Do white lies count when you only tell them to yourself?*

Her brown eyes, unusual for a natural blonde, were sparkling as she strode down the long road that separated Dulverton from Streatford. It was about four miles between the two villages and the school was somewhere about halfway, but she figured if she kept up her pace she'd make it in time to get to the nursery, where her father would be waiting. She got to pick up Tabitha so rarely these days that every opportunity was precious. It sometimes seemed it was only yesterday when she was a tiny wrinkled bundle smelling of talcum powder and baby formula; but her baby days were over and she was four and growing up fast.

Thinking of her daughter, Kelly's delicate cheekbones were highlighted with a smile. Yes, Tabby was great, but with the way her mother's love life was going—not going would be closer to the truth—there weren't going to be any baby brothers or sisters coming along to keep her company. At thirty-five, Kelly could feel her body clock ticking away, like some internal countdown to barrenness, and there was no hint of Mr. Right grinning at her from the horizon.

Passing under the bridge, what she considered her halfway mark on her daily walk to school, she checked her watch. Good, she was in plenty of time to meet Tabby and the only man in her life she'd ever been able to rely on, her father. Under his and her mother's gentle insistence, she'd tried dating most of the single men in town, none of whom really caught her eye apart from the occasional short-lived exception, and most of those relationships had been driven by the dawning realization that she was being considered by the chattering masses of Streatford to be an ideal candidate for the position of village spinster. Well, she managed to avoid that title quite dramatically when Tabitha came along. Village spinsters did not generally have children out of wedlock. That had caused a little stir amongst her parents' generation, of which there were plenty. *Did you hear about Kelly Hollingsworth? At her age you'd think she'd know better, her a policeman's daughter, too. They say the father's a married man. Her poor mother must be devastated.*

The Reckoning

It had been a long few months, but she'd kept her head held high and rode the wave until some juicier gossip had come along, which of course always happens. And yes, they'd been right. The father was a married man, and a lying shit to boot even if he had given her a beautiful daughter. At least once she'd told him in no uncertain terms that she wasn't going to have an abortion, no matter how much he pleaded with her, he'd had the decency to pack up his house and his wife and move out of town. Far out of town. Every cloud had a silver lining if you looked hard enough.

She'd reached the top of Dulverton Road and started following the long stretch of pretty Edwardian terraces down toward the high street, her spirits high. It wasn't as if she needed a man, anyway. Her life was pretty good, all things considered. She had her wonderful child, a job she loved, and she had her father, who was finally starting to get over her mother's death two years ago. They were both getting over it, comforted by Tabitha and her startling resemblance to the woman who had been the heart of their lives for so long, before having to leave them to face the world on their own. No, they were doing pretty well. Her mum would be proud of them, and looking after Tabby with her was good for Dad, keeping him busy. *And* it was great for Kelly. She didn't know what she'd do without him.

Turning down a side street before the crossroads at the bottom, she joined a gaggle of mothers heading toward the small primary school to pick up their kids. Tabby only went for the afternoons, but was loving it already. She was a clever little girl and had already decided she was going to be a "pleaseman" like Granddad when she grew up. Kelly had a sneaking suspicion that the little girl knew how to pronounce the word perfectly well, but kept up her baby word to make an old man happy. It never failed to make retired Detective Sergeant Jack Hollingsworth laugh when her heard her say it, and anything that did that was fine with his ladies, as they called themselves. Especially over the past couple of weeks, since that terrible rape at Syracousse.

Neither of them had been laughing much since then. Kelly had taught those kids, and unruly as they were she couldn't imagine what could have made them do something like that, especially not to Sharnice. Those three had been close. They had been friends. It was such a terrible, terrible business, and she only wished she could understand it.

Spotting her father's gray hair above the crowd of young mothers, she waved to get his attention. His face creased into a smile when he saw her and looking at him leaning on his walking stick, she felt a soft stabbing pain inside. *When did you get so old, Dad? When did it happen, and why didn't I notice? Was I too busy growing up myself?*

Pushing through the throng, she made her way, breathless, to his side. "Hello, Pops." She squeezed his arm and planted a kiss on his cheek, before she heard the familiar squeal.

"Mummy!" The small girl threw herself at them, and Kelly bent over to hug her, kissing the top of the dark head.

"I thought I'd come down and surprise you. I finished work early. Pleased to see me?"

Tabby squeezed the lower half of her mother's body in response as the three generations of Hollingsworths made their way out of the crush and headed home to Horsefair Green. "Look what I made! Look what I made!" Skipping slightly ahead of the two adults, she turned around and held up a piece of green sugar paper, daubed with colorful paint, depicting a large house and garden full of trees and plants. Kelly exchanged a smile with her father. Children's imaginations were really something else. If that's what Tabby thought their little terraced cottage was like, then they had it made.

She ruffled the child's wild dark curls, a legacy from her grandmother, that had escaped from her ribboned ponytail. "Is that our house, honey?"

Tabitha looked at her mother as if she were mad, a small furrow of impatience forming in her soft, smooth brow. " 'Course not!" She glanced at the painting again as if to make sure, before smiling. "It's the house I'm *gonna* live in. It's my house. I dreamed it."

With the amused love only a mother could feel, Kelly laughed. "Well, if you want a house like that, young lady, my only advice to you is don't become a teacher."

"Or a policeman," added Jack, sharing the fun. "But it's good to have someone with ambition in the family. You'll be able to keep us in our old age."

Tabby was still holding the picture out in front of her, looking at it almost wistfully while she walked. "My house."

Taking it from her, Kelly held it carefully as she took her daughter's hand to cross the road. "Tell you what. We'll put it on the wall when we get home, and then when you get bigger and you don't want to do your homework, you can look at it to remind you what you want in life. Deal?"

Tabby giggled and led the way home.

The little girl was happily ensconced in front of CBBC, surrounded by toys, when Kelly came down the narrow staircase changed into her jeans and sweater. Time for half an hour relaxing with a cup of tea before the usual evening round of dinner, baths and then when Tabby was asleep, marking. Well, at least she'd gained an extra hour today, although that would fly by quickly enough. She saw with a smile that her father had already pinned up the picture in the kitchen by the door and was pouring out the tea. "Thanks, Dad," she said, gratefully taking the mug and sitting at the tiny table. "So what did you get up to today? No wild house parties I hope."

Jack Hollingsworth didn't smile, but pulled out the chair opposite her and sat down carefully, wary of the pain that tended to flare in his right hip. "I went up to the station. Thought I might talk to someone about those boys."

About to take a sip of her drink, Kelly paused, and put the mug down, untouched. She looked intently at the old man. "Darren and Lee?" Her tiredness was forgotten now.

Her father nodded. "I've still got some clout up there. Some of those high-flyers trained under me." He rubbed his hands over his eyes and sighed.

Kelly's eyes were alert. "Did they tell you anything? Did you get to speak to them? Was it drugs that made them do it?" The anxiety in her voice was plain as she leaned forward.

She cared about all the students in her school, but these three had been in her tutor group, and she hated that she hadn't noticed that anything was wrong outside of their normal erratic behavior. She should have sensed there was a problem. That was her job. Three young lives were ruined, and maybe if she'd been paying attention, she could have done something to prevent it. Ever since the awful news had broken, she'd been eating herself up with guilt.

Her father let out a long sigh. "No, I didn't speak to them. They're on suicide watch at the moment. DS Keery says they'll be transferring them up to the young offenders unit soon, and then you can probably get a visit, if they want to see you. I don't think they're in a good way."

Kelly's heart ached. "So what happened?"

Her father shrugged, meeting her gaze with a frank stare, reminding her that although his body was letting him down, he was still a policeman through and through. "It's hard to say. When they turned themselves in, they were taken separately for interview. They both came out with the same story, which isn't much of a surprise since they'd been hiding out in the allotments overnight. Plenty of time to come up with something." He grimaced as he flexed his leg. "The thing was, they didn't. Not really, although their story is pretty strange."

He paused to sip his tea, thoughtfully, and Kelly had to restrain herself from screaming at him to hurry up. But she knew her father. His speech was always ponderous when his brain was working fast.

"Keery says that they both admitted to stealing a bottle of something from the liquor store on the high street, which has been confirmed by the manager, and then meeting up with Sharnice and going down by the river. Apparently, Sharnice didn't want to stay there and so they went up to the Grace house, Syracousse. They'd never been up there before, and they claim that the front door was open. One of the boys knew a little bit about the history of the place because his dad works cleaning the offices at Greenslade's, the solicitors that manage the property."

He paused to sip his tea. "Anyway, they went inside, switched a light on in the front room and starting drinking. Sharnice decided that maybe they should burn the house down for bonfire night. She was really adamant, and the boys went along. It was at about this time that the lights went out, and the boys can't explain what happened next."

Kelly was puzzled. "They can't explain it? Are they claiming that they're innocent?"

Jack shook his head. "No. They were both very calm. They admitted they did it, but neither of them could explain why. They said something made them do it. Made them *want* to do it. Just before the lights went out. Something they couldn't control. When it was over, they carried her out onto the front door step and then went to call an ambulance. They said they hadn't wanted to move her at all because she was so badly hurt, but at the same time they didn't want to leave her in the house."

Kelly didn't know what to make of it. Why had they been so worried about her after they'd hurt her so badly that she was still in intensive care? After what they'd done with that bottle when they'd finished raping her, stamping on her abdomen, smashing it inside her. She shivered at the thought of the girl's pain and terror. "That is strange."

Jack Hollingsworth shook his head. "That isn't the

strange part. You see, there is no electricity at Syracousse. Keery was adamant about that. It was cut off years ago. There's no way they could have turned on a light. What's even stranger is that there is no way they could have gotten into the house by the front door either. It takes three keys to open, and they're all housed at Greenslade's."

Kelly frowned slightly. "Well, maybe the last time someone went to look it over they forgot to lock up behind them."

Her father shook his head. "No. No one's been up there in ages anyway, and if that were the case, then why was the door fully locked and untampered with when the ambulance found Sharnice? It just doesn't make sense. Also, there were fresh cigarette butts on the floor in the old living room to corroborate their story"

Kelly sighed, and leaned back in her creaking chair. "They must have been taking something. Maybe they were high. Maybe Lee got his dad to steal the keys or something."

Jack raised an eyebrow. " 'You're a policeman's daughter all right. That's the theory Keery's working on, although the father is adamant he didn't have anything to do with it. But the drug thing is a definite no."

"Why? Did they test them?"

Jack looked weary as he spoke. "Well, it turned out that the reason they were both so calm was that they'd downed a load of any pills they could get their hands on before going into the station. That's why they were so eager to make their statements quickly. They both collapsed within a few minutes of each other and had to be rushed to the hospital for stomach pumps. They were tested for illegal substances then, and there was no trace."

He stood up to pour himself another cup of tea from the pot. "So I can't see why they would have any reason to lie about anything, if they were planning to kill themselves. It wouldn't fit with the stereotype."

Kelly sat thoughtfully for a few moments, not knowing

what to say. It was a terrible, terrible thing to happen, and she still felt none the wiser, but she was grateful to her father for getting the information.

"Thanks for finding out for me. I know you're retired and probably had enough of all this kind of stuff years ago. I'm really grateful that you put yourself out." She stood and rinsed her mug out in the sink, wanting to go and spend some time playing with Tabby. That always helped to raise her spirits.

Jack smiled at her. "I knew it meant a lot to you. I'll just have to have my wild party tomorrow."

He watched his little girl disappear into the lounge and then turned to gaze out the small kitchen window, looking at nothing in particular, sipping his cooling tea. He hadn't been entirely honest with Kelly. If it had been only she who had been so unsettled about the rape, then he would have probably told her to let the police get on with their jobs in peace, and she would have to wait until it came to trial to get her information, like everyone else. He was retired. He'd done his time. It was nothing to do with him anymore.

But it wasn't only she who needed to know what had gone on. The irony was that he was probably more disturbed than she was by the recent events. Ridiculous as it sounded, he'd kind of forgotten that the house was there, as if the years that had passed had erased it, made it invisible to the mind. But of course it hadn't gone anywhere, the bricks and mortar standing the test of time far better than his flesh and blood had done, and when he'd seen the name there in the newspaper, heard it whispered in the streets, it was like cold water hitting his face, the spell broken. In his head, he could hear the words as easily as if they'd been spoken yesterday by that cool, composed voice.

"You'd better come quickly. There's been a terrible accident. I don't understand how it happened. One minute in my hand. The next it was gone."

He hadn't understood what Camilla Grace née Cowley had been talking about until he'd gotten there. And then, with the sound of that little girl's awful screams coming from the kitchen, as her mother calmly opened the front door and invited him in, it had all become crystal clear.

But even that memory probably wouldn't have been enough to make him go up to the station today. If anything, it would have kept him away. It was something Kelly had said yesterday that made him get his old suit on and shake off the cobwebs in his brain. She'd been reading the weekly rag and pointed out in passing that the woman up at Gallows Hill who killed her family and herself had been one of Gina Grace's circle of friends at school. Just like that writer who'd come back to town last week.

Something was disturbing his sleep, and it was nothing he could put his finger on, ghosts of the past whispering in his head. All he knew was that Streatford didn't have crimes like this, not one on top of the other. People in this town did not go around hurting each other and themselves. At best, murder happened once in every couple of generations; everyone knew each other too well here. Murder and suicide tended to happen in communities of strangers.

He chewed his bottom lip. He may not understand it, but something was happening in Streatford. Something bad, and it started with that rape.

That rape broke the spell.

The thought made no sense to him, but it felt right. A flash of pain surged up his lower spine from his hip, making him catch his breath. He waited for it to pass before attempting to move. *Maybe something is happening here,* he thought as he trod carefully toward the door. *And maybe it isn't. Maybe it's just your old man's imagination. But one thing's for sure: you're too damn old to do anything about it, so just let it go. It's not your business. Not anymore.*

For the first time in the years of his retirement, that thought brought him some comfort as he settled into the armchair to watch the news.

CHAPTER TEN

In the four days since he'd read about Carole-Anne in the paper, Rob's work had slowed down. The book that he'd thought was so fantastic now just looked like words on a page, thin and lifeless. His characters seemed two-dimensional as they wallowed aimlessly in his stagnant plot. Staring at the screen, he decided enough was enough. Without bothering to save his new pages, he switched the laptop off and refilled his mug from the carafe of his new coffee machine sitting on the breakfast bar. No milk this time, black moods called for black coffee. He smiled to himself. Shit, he was even thinking in clichés.

Rolling his head, he felt the tense muscles stretching in his neck, and sighed. There was nothing wrong with the book. It was a good piece of work. The problem was with him. Since his conversation with Jason, he hadn't been able to concentrate, Carrie's final message playing over and over in the back of his mind. *Teacher. We got it wrong.* Jason might have been able to drink it away, but he couldn't. Not now he knew about that rape case as well.

79

That one local paper had a lot to answer for. With his hermit lifestyle these days, there was a good chance he never would have found out about that if Carrie hadn't been blazed across the front page in all her destroyed glory. Local papers had never been his idea of reading; he'd probably just have used it for starting the fire, and he wasn't a TV man. He'd learned everything he needed to know about the world from *The Sunday Times*, and local rapes, no matter how horrific, weren't going to make a mention there, even if Carrie had got herself an obituary.

He wondered briefly whether Gina had seen it, wherever she was these days. Did she sit there in a daze and think of her childhood friend, or did she blithely move on, cold and uncaring, to the financial section? Probably the latter. Gina, for all her terrible and wonderful strangeness, had always been untouchable. Well, that was how it had seemed to an infatuated twelve-year-old, anyhow.

He yawned and then downed the rest of his coffee in an effort to quash his tiredness, ignoring the heat that seared his insides. His sleep hadn't been good either, his nightmares a mish-mash of Teacher, his father and Syracousse, none of it pleasant. He seemed to be spending an awful lot of his nights running from something, trying to escape, and often woke up more exhausted than he'd been when he'd turned out the light.

Maybe it's the lack of Grade-A's in your system, he mused while lighting a cigarette. *Maybe your body's just readjusting. God knows all this clean living's got to be a shock to the synapses.* The combination of smoke and coffee was drying his mouth, but he didn't care, as he went to the hall and gazed thoughtfully up to the landing. He'd given up kidding himself a long time ago, and he knew his unsettled feelings had nothing to do with the coke and the booze, and everything to do with the past. *His past.*

"Maybe it's time to start a little self-help therapy," he muttered, climbing the stairs, his eyes fixed on the large wooden loft door in the ceiling above. Maybe it's time to face down the memories. And here's a really good place to start. *Let's start with Dad. You and Jason and Dad. Thirtieth May, 1976. You can face this one without even leaving the house, Robster. So let's give it a go, shall we? How hard can it be?*

Chewing his bottom lip, Rob studied the attic hatch. This was the one part of the house he hadn't explored since his return. Shit, he hadn't been up there since that afternoon, and he'd made sure he was at Syracousse when his mother's friends came to clear it out, his father sitting like a zombie in front of the test card on the TV. That was before the doctors came and took him away. His father had known what executive burnout was long before those boys in the city gave it a name.

Not wanting to delay, to lose his nerve, Rob opened the laundry cupboard by the small boxy room and found what he was looking for inside the lintel of the doorframe, what he'd *known* would be there, forgotten but waiting. Wrapping his hand around the old wooden pole, he felt the memories flooding back.

"Are you sure this is okay? What if your mum comes back and catches us? She'll go mad." Jason's eyes were shining with excitement as Rob pulled the long pole out of the cupboard, its length almost twice his height, unwieldy in his small hands.

"She's not going to catch us. I told you, she's walking up to Dulverton to see a friend. She'll be gone for hours. Anyway, I've just got to see what he does up there all night."

His dad had started using the attic as a study weeks ago and spent all his time at home locked away in it, and Rob's curiosity was starting to drive him crazy, like the itch under his plaster cast had when he broke his ankle the summer before. No one was allowed up there, not even Mum. Not that she'd go up there anyway. She never went up ladders, not beyond the second step anyway. She said that it wasn't dignified for ladies, what with their dresses and everything, but he was pretty sure she was just plain scared. Girls were like that. Even Carrie got funny sometimes, like when she wouldn't go up to the highest branch in a tree just 'cos it was getting a bit thin. Gina probably wouldn't do it either, but then Gina was different. She wouldn't be scared of it, though. Not with the kind of things she could do. No way.

Jason gripped the other end of the pole as they maneuverd it into position under the latch, ready to slide it back. He was an inch shorter than Rob, but his thin, pale frame was wiry, and he managed to steady the wobble. "Do you really think he's working on something top secret up there?"

Rob grinned as the hatch moved back, leaving a gaping square of blackness above them. "Gotta be. I reckon he's got a prototype of a new kind of gun or something up there. Maybe even a nuke."

Jason snorted. "Sure thing, Robster. I bet they all get to take the nukes home." He paused. "A gun'd be cool, though."

Rob was pleased that Jase was as excited as he was. He was proud of his dad, who worked in London for the Ministry of Defense. He loved the sound of the words when he said them. They sounded special; important, and he knew that Jason was pretty impressed, too. But then Jason was pretty impressed with most of Rob's life, had been since they were kids in preschool. Jason's dad worked part time in one of the new factories that were springing up around the town, and he lived on the Hill like Carrie, not here in Streatford where it was nicer. They didn't go up there much.

Maybe Jason was more impressed with Gina's life right now, but they hadn't been friends with Gina that long, only since Carrie had introduced them after deciding she needed another girl in their gang. And anyway, Gina may *have been rich and able to do weird stuff, but she didn't have the Ministry of Defense.*

They waved the pole around the edge of the square until they felt it connect with the ladder. "You'd better stand back, this ladder kind of comes down fast." There was a loud clattering of metal as the ladder crashed down, its joints crunching as they slotted into place, and Jason dived for cover into Rob's parents' bedroom doorway.

"Shit, that's loud." He laughed, as he straightened up and stared at the metal stairway that now rested on the carpet.

Rob too was looking, wondering for a second just how the hell they were going to negotiate it back up again, not knowing that in about one and a half minutes that was going to be the least of his worries. Oh well, the ladder was down, and they might as well use it. His stomach contracted, knowing his questions of the past weeks were about to be answered.

"Come on, then," he whispered over his shoulder as he gripped the cold rough steel and started to climb.

No further. Not yet, Rob told himself, firmly pushing the memories away. The rest could wait a few minutes longer. The pole was light in his hand, and he slid the cover away with ease. No need for two this time, Jason old buddy. The hook edged under the bottom step of the ladder and he eased it down slowly, letting it drop by itself for only the last few inches. His heart beating in his chest, he stared at the rungs in front of him for a few moments before glancing up into the darkness and reaching for the first step. "Come on, then," he whispered to the emptiness as he headed into the past.

He could feel Jason close behind him as he stepped over the final rung and into the attic room. They stood silently, side by side, for a moment, their breath sounding harsh in the quiet as they enjoyed the final moments of unsatiated curiosity, the anticipation like Christmas morning, know-

ing you can finally rip all that pretty paper up and get to the gloriously unknown present inside.

"It smells sort of funny in here." Rob couldn't see Jason's face in the gloom, but he knew he'd be crinkling his nose in the same way he did when he smelled cabbage as he waited hungrily in the queue for school lunch. Jase was right; it did smell strange, something strong and sweet had invaded the musty wooden scent that lived in all lofts, something sickly and new challenging the rights of the old, traditional comforting odor. And then there was the buzzing, the discordant hum coming from somewhere in front of him. In that second, Rob didn't want to turn the light on, didn't want to be here at all, and if he'd been on his own he'd probably have just turned right back around. He was starting to think there were some things best left unexplored. Things that smelled like this. Things that smelled wrong. He swatted something, maybe a cobweb, away from his face.

"Well, turn the light on then, slowcoach." Jason elbowed him. "I want to see this gun." Rob wondered momentarily why they were talking in whispers alone at the top of an empty house as his hand moved involuntarily up to the light switch above his shoulder. Flicking it down, he squeezed his eyes shut against the glare of the light. No turning back now, he thought to himself. For a long second he heard nothing, except that awful buzzing that sounded like a live electric cable hissing at them, and then Jason, whose breath had caught in his throat, finally let out a long whistle that was more like a sigh. "Holy moley. Holy, holy moley." He giggled slightly, a jagged sound from a boy whose only response to something he didn't understand, couldn't understand was to laugh instead of show fear.

Rob slowly opened his eyes and looked at the scene that presented itself to him, looked into his father's office, into his father's mind. Something secret had definitely *been going on here, something top secret, something the Ministry of Defense would surely love to know about.*

The desk that David Black had built himself was pushed against one wall, the chair neatly tucked beneath it, to make room for the pyramids that covered the ground, covered its surface. The triangular piles were everywhere, in all sizes, the walls covered with newspaper, official documents all made into the required shape. Rob's eyes moved around the room in disbelief. This couldn't be right, this couldn't be right at all. In one corner there was a pyramid of neatly folded towels and dishcloths, and it looked from here as if the base was made from his mother's guest valance she kept clean in the spare bedroom for visitors who were never invited. How could she not know it was missing? What did she think had happened to it? Maybe she didn't want to know. He could feel his whole body shaking, but still he stared, couldn't help but stare at all his father's hard work.

Down to the left by his feet was a carefully constructed pyramid of playing cards whose point came above his knees, and he thought he saw traces of glue holding it together; his father had glued it together, determined it should not collapse, it was important that it stood impervious to movement. Rob's stomach turned and he was unaware of the bubbling sound his breath was making as it escaped between his clenched teeth. His head was filled with the image of his father, huddled over the pile of cards, carefully, painstakingly gluing them all into place. Hours and hours of concentrated effort. How many hours, Dad?

Finally, unable to resist any longer, he turned to face the pièce de resistance, his father's masterpiece that took up most of the space in the center of the room. The other pyramids were inconsequential next to this, like artist's sketches made before undertaking a work of magnificence. From the corner of his eye, Rob could see Jason staring at him, staring at him as if his father's madness were catching. With a small moan, he stepped forward, gazing at the three-foot-high mountain—not mountain, it was a pyramid fit for the pharaoh of rats, not a mountain at all, built entirely from rotting food, the flies, black and angry, swarming madly around it protecting their domain. There were remains of every evening meal his mother had carefully prepared for weeks, his father smiling and telling her he'd eat it in his office, "So much work, so little time. Got a country to protect from the Commies, you know." An hour later he'd reappear with the tray telling her how delicious it had been. There were sandwiches in there, his father's packed lunches brought carefully home, and Rob noticed as his insides freewheeled that there were things there, other things, like used tea bags, half-eaten items no longer recognizable, moving with the maggots that squirmed inside, blending into the green that was overtaking them, turning them into something else, something new and not yet formed. Things that his dad could only have got from the rubbish. "What did you do, Dad?" He whispered to the monstrosity in front of him, as if its decaying form could give him an answer. "What did you do? Did you sneak out in the middle of the night to see what you could find?"

He felt Jason shaking his arm, and looked numbly into those wide, scared eyes. "I think we should get out of here, Robster. I think you should go find your mum. I don't think this is right."

It was then that Rob began to laugh, laugh louder and louder until he thought his deadened heart would burst with the sound of it, his eardrums aching with the unwelcome noise. He felt like he would laugh forever, laugh at the ridiculousness of it, at the ridiculousness of him and Jason and no, he didn't think it was right either, definitely not right at all. He stepped backwards on unstable legs, sliding down the back wall, wanting the wood to absorb him into its solid stability. Somewhere in the movement, and for the life of him he didn't notice when, it seemed that the laughter had turned to tears, tears that wouldn't stop, tears that threatened to choke him, and he felt Jason slowly sitting down next to him, uncertain of what to do, clumsy with the emotion. Eventually, Rob felt Jase's slight arm around his hunched, hot shoulders, the gentle pressure slowly calming his emotions, slowing the flood to a stream. And there they stayed, sitting like lords of the flies amidst the ruins of Rob's perfect life, until his mother got home.

Crouching against the wall in the empty room, the musty scent, lonely after all these years making way for its one-time visitor, Rob cried for the second time that week, cried for the boy he had been, for his father who died of shame, misunderstood in an unforgiving era, abandoned and alone in the company of strangers. A man whose heart attack had been a relief to his family. Had been a relief to his son. *Jesus, Dad, I'm sorry. I'm so sorry.* The thought felt useless, the sentiment too late. He wiped his eyes. He'd gone twenty years or more without shedding a single tear and now that he was home, it seemed they wouldn't stop. *Christ, you were a shit as a child, and you're sure as hell a bigger shit now. Some things just don't change, do they? You're not such a bigshot now, are you, Robster?*

He could hear Jason in his head voicing his internal thoughts, not the stranger that he'd met the other day, the *Jason-in-disguise,* but the Jason from that day, from this room, the Jason who'd been his best buddy, the best buddy a boy could ask for. The Jason who would never, ever have done that terrible thing on the hot last day of term in the classroom, if Rob hadn't driven him to it. The Jason who had tried to help Teacher when he and Carrie had just looked on in horror. The Jason who was special and funny. The Jason he'd thrown away out of shame by closing himself off, by put-downs and barbed remarks. By the kind of cruelty that only kids are capable of.

Yeah, that Jason in his head was right; the twelve-year-old Jason who never minced his words. He was a shit. A

Grade-A shit, through and through. What the hell had he been thinking, coming home? Facing his demons? What the hell good was that now? Couldn't help him or Carrie or his dad or even goddamn poor Teacher.

Suddenly he was laughing, the tears evaporating, welcomed by the musty air. And he'd thought coming up here might make him feel better? The irony was a little too much and he snorted into his hands, emotionally exhausted. *Kill the self-pity,* he told himself, his own voice this time. *A bastard you may be, but hell, you're a rich one. Life could have turned out worse for you.*

He hauled himself to his feet, and switched the light off, eager to get down to the present. He'd had enough of the past for one day, and as he slid the lid over the attic a few minutes later, he got the sneaking suspicion that the past had had enough of him, too.

CHAPTER ELEVEN

Judge Matthews had quite forgotten his arthritis as he leapt his skeletal, pajama-clad body out of the bed and stood barefoot on the cold carpet. He smiled and twitched nervously as he chewed his fingernails, staring at the exposed sheets that glowed white in the moonlight filtering in through the gap in the curtains. He knew he should turn the light on just to confirm it, but he also knew what he'd find. Ants. Ants everywhere. He absently scratched himself. *Ants in his pants.* The thought made him giggle slightly, although the feel of his sharp hipbone under the thin cotton gave a small part of his mind, a part that wasn't quite yet bug obsessed, a moment of concern. He really should try to force himself to eat something tomorrow. He'd go out and eat something. That would probably be safest. Yes, that's what he'd do.

He couldn't bear to eat anything at home, not after the day before yesterday, when he'd found they'd invaded every cereal box in his cupboards, and the milk bottle, although securely fastened with the new-fangled plastic lid, had been lined with hundreds of tiny, black drowned corpses, as it stood cold in the fridge. He had a vague memory of throwing up after that, and somehow from then until now, food hadn't been high on his list of priorities.

Staring down in the darkness, he was sure he could see them scurrying around his mattress, taunting him, daring him to take action. He licked his lips as his eyes darted quickly, trying to keep up with them. Well, take action he would. He was a judge, *had been* a judge, and no infestation was going to get the better of him, no matter where it came from. Feeling for his slippers, neatly placed beside his bed, he left the light off—no warnings would be given in this war—and felt his way, stumbling slightly into the hallway. He pulled the door shut firmly behind him and then flicked the switch, muttering to himself as the stairway illuminated. There was no trace of them here, but then how they'd gotten into his shower yesterday, he still couldn't understand. He shivered with the memory of standing beneath that stream of clear water, of tilting his head back in the spray, and then gagging as the water turned into a black stream. A black stream that wanted to get *inside* him, inside his mouth. *A black stream of madness.*

He grunted as he turned on the kitchen light and switched on the kettle that he'd taken to keeping full, and boiling every half an hour or so in case of emergencies. *Madness.* Yes, that's what Daisy would call it. He'd seen it in the unhappy expression in her eyes yesterday. She thought his mind had finally caught up with his degenerating body, and maybe it had, maybe it had. In many ways he hoped she was right, madness he could live with, but the ants—the source of the ants—he couldn't.

He'd gone next door the morning after he'd first noticed his visitors, when things were still normal, to see where they were coming from. That was when the world first started to slip off-kilter, not in any noticeable way, just the tiniest slide to the left or right. There were no ants in Daisy's garden, you see. No ants at all. They searched and searched but found nothing, Daisy regarding him thoughtfully with those sharp blue eyes, the intelligence there so often missed by those who only saw her wizened face. So if there were no ants in Daisy's garden, how were they still coming through the fence to his? Where were they coming from? Slightly embarrassed, he'd left her and gone home, confused, to stare at the inhabitants of his patio through the protection of the glass.

The kettle was starting to throw out steam, and too impatient to let it switch itself off, Ernest unplugged it and headed back to the stairs.

After the incident with the milk, something had cracked. He had still been in his slippers when he headed out, this time going around the side of Daisy's house to where her fence ran alongside the path leading down to the river, the outside fence that was guaranteed to get vandalized and daubed on at least once every summer. He'd seen his breath misting in front of him as he watched the procession coming up the path with mildly hysterical disbelief. They were coming up the path like a tiny army, trudging relentlessly forward. As they reached his feet, they made a sharp right and went under Daisy's fence. *They're tunneling,* he'd thought in numb amazement, stifling the first of the unconscious fits of giggles that were to become such a part of his life. *They're tunneling under her lawn to get to mine.* He stared at the thin procession until his toes became numb, and then slowly turned and walked against the tide, his head down, studying his silent adversaries. Where were they coming from? Where were the little bastards coming from?

It was when he'd crossed the river—*how far were they traveling?*—that he'd first felt the shiver of terrified anticipation, and then, when his freezing form finally came to a stop outside those old, forgotten iron gates, he realized that he'd known; it was crazy, but he'd known all along that the trail would lead here, to this house, to Syracousse.

He'd met Daisy on his way home, while he was still

somewhere between laughing and crying. She'd taken the scenic walk back from the shops, and she looked at him, that sadness in her eyes, in her whole face, as she took in his slippers, and his laughing and his lack of a coat, and had asked him if everything was okay. That had made him laugh even harder, envious of Daisy looking so right with her Budgen's shopping and her red, sensible coat and matching gloves, when everything was so completely not okay, his world fracturing around him. "I've been on an ant hunt," he told her as they walked, she solemn and he wiping tears away from his cheeks with crippled hands. "They're coming from Toombes Meadow. They're coming all the way from Syracousse to see me. Should I feel flattered?"

Daisy had said nothing as he entertained himself with thoughts of insanity. "I'll pop in tomorrow. Have a cup of tea." He had nodded and waved in agreement before shutting his door on her. And true to her word, she had called around, he thought as he progressed back up toward the bedroom. He hadn't let her in, of course. He had been far too busy at work in the bathroom for any socializing, but she had rung the bell several times. Daisy always had been a woman of her word. A fine woman.

Opening the bedroom door, this time he did reach for the light switch, flooding the room with the yellow glare. He wasn't surprised to see the mass of black that covered his mattress, frozen in the shock of the brightness. Tutting to himself, he approached and started to pour, the satisfaction of genocide somewhat tainted by an itch that started in his ear. He couldn't quite reach it with the little finger of his spare hand.

His bed soaked, he turned to fetch a blanket from the airing cupboard, before heading back downstairs to sleep the rest of the night on the sofa. He dug his finger deeper and scratched.

CHAPTER TWELVE

It had taken Jason all of ten minutes during his lunch break to empty his meager savings account and spend it. He'd parted with most of what was left of his wages, too, leaving himself twenty quid to get through the four days until payday. *No more living the high life for me then,* he thought as he turned onto the lane that led to the rear entrance of Brown's, The Family Greengrocer. *Thirty-seven years old and twenty pounds to my name. Maybe it's time to sign up for* Who Wants to Be a Millionaire? *But then again, maybe not. No amount of money could be worth letting that smug bastard patronize you on national television.* He picked up his overalls from the shelf where he'd dumped them on his way out, and started tugging them over his boots and jeans.

Bob was leaning his heavy frame on a stack of crates by the far wall, slurping up Chunky soup; one with bits of pasta in it. He didn't wait until he'd swallowed before speaking, eyeing Jason with curious suspicion. "What did you take your overalls off for to go and get your lunch? You've only been gone quarter of an hour at most."

Jason looked at the other man for a second, and silently wondered what it was that he'd done with his life that warranted having to work with Bob. His merciless brain fired several answers back at him, none of which he could deny. Looking down, he zipped up the green canvas material.

"I had things to do." He hoped his curt, soft tone would shut Bob up, but then his colleague had never been one to understand the nuances of language, or even take a hint for that matter. Bob snorted as if Jason had said the most ridiculous thing in the world, shaking his head slightly as he scooped another spoon load into his still full mouth.

Jason's anger was beginning to rise. This wasn't the day to start pissing him off. He really, really wasn't in the mood. And who the hell did this ignorant oaf think he was, looking down on him? How could someone be that stupid and so far up their own arse all at the same time? His smile was thin and tight, his eyes colder than they'd been in a long time, probably since the days when he'd fight anyone who was willing to throw some hard punches back.

His insides had been screwed up tight since he'd first heard about Carrie, screwed up with grief and not a little fear. It seemed that the scars on his hands and arms had been itching ever since he'd read her damned suicide message in the paper, itching just enough to keep him remembering, to keep him looking at that piece of notebook he'd pulled out of the bin, the one with Robster's phone number on it, the writing blurred by thrown-away coffee. And then there was the business he'd just taken care of. That awful bleak business. Yep, all in all, his mind had been pretty fried by the events of this month, scrambled enough for him to throw his carefully applied diplomacy of the past few weeks out of the window. He paused for a second, enjoying what he was about to do, before he spoke.

His voice was soft and lilting, as if he were talking to a slow child. "It may surprise you to learn that overalls aren't always the most appropriate things to be seen in. Unlike you, I am not an ignorant fuck, and I happen to be aware of certain social protocols. Unlike you, I don't get so excited over the prospect of spending the rest of my life lugging cabbages around that I have to go home and wank over my uniform." He raised one eyebrow at Bob, whose mouth was wide open, the half-chewed pasta on display, mangled pieces threatening to fall out of the yawning hole. Jason's smile widened. "I take it that is what those stains are? I've often wondered but never wanted to ask. It all comes back to social protocols, you see."

Bob's jaw seemed to be moving, not chewing, but a jerky up-and-down action, as if it were begging his brain to give it something to say. Something, anything. Jason noticed that the big man's grip had tightened around the mug so hard that his knuckles were white. *Any moment now it's going to implode with the pressure. He's going to crush it like a tin can and then he's going to crush me. Oh boy, you really picked a good one this time. This has got to be up there in the top ten of fights with no chance of winning.*

It seemed to Jason in those few tense moments as he held the big man's stare that the walls of the warehouse were breathing with him, panting in anticipation of the blood to come. Ready for it. Tired of its vegetarian diet. *Any moment now, any moment now he's going to come at me.* He knew the signs; he knew how long the insult would take to filter into that dull brain of Bob's. His body crackled, tensing as his mind raced, mentally running through what was in the room, what he could get to, that would help him against the Goliath he'd pissed off. He really didn't think cabbages were going to do the trick.

The buzzer rang loudly three times, and both men jumped, the tension fracturing, sucked away for a second by their sharp intakes of breath. Bob dropped the mug, his brain unable to deal with the two pressing issues—wanting to kill Jason so badly and the buzzer. *Three times means trouble.*

"Shit!" The china smashed at his feet, the glutinous contents splattering all over the lower half of the overalls that started this crap in the first place. "Fucking shit!"

Jason slowly strolled past him, his heart still pounding with adrenaline. "I'll go deal with it. You stay here and clear up your mess." Going into the shop, he let out a long sigh. Okay, so he was still going to have face up to the confrontation, but at least he had a reprieve. And from what he knew of men like Bob, once the moment was gone, they weren't that likely to use their fists. *Nope, he'll just settle for getting you fired instead. This is really turning out to be something of a day.* And it was just about to get worse.

Coming through the side doorway, he saw Mary's wide eyes beckoning him from behind the register, before flicking away to her left and then back again. The only person near her was one of the old biddies from the sheltered housing community, so at least she wasn't getting robbed. One close brush with physical violence was enough for one day. He wasn't as young and feisty as he used to be. So what the hell had spooked her enough to buzz the alarm?

Walking past the register to be able to see whatever it was Mary and the old woman were staring at, his brow furrowed as he turned around the L-shaped wall. Three customers passed him as they scurried out, abandoning their groceries, unpurchased, at the open doorway. He barely noticed them. Was that Judge Matthews? Could that really be the judge?

The man, the tramp, at the far end of the shop was eagerly devouring a peach, tossing the stone to the ground as he reached for another, pieces of the fleshy meat clinging to his chin as the juices ran down his scrawny neck. There were already four pits abandoned by his slippered feet. *He's wearing slippers. And are those pyjamas peering out from under the tan overcoat? Old man Madness has finally got him.* Jason watched in silence for a few minutes before he cautiously moved forward.

He noticed that the judge was muttering to himself as he ate, spraying a fine mist of fruit with every word, and his eyes darted feverishly around him, wide and blood-shot. *I hope I go before this gets me,* Jason thought as he brought himself within two feet of the tragic old man. *I wouldn't want anyone to see me like this. To remember me like this.* But then, he considered, it wasn't really likely anyone would remember him anyway, not like they would the judge. The judge was *part* of Streatford. He'd been there forever.

Jason's nose crinkled as he came face to face with the grunting, slurping man. Jesus, he stank. A mixture of stale sweat, bad breath, pee and God only knew what else radiated from him in a warm, nauseating glow. *How long has he been without a bath? And just how long has he been wearing those fucking pyjamas?* Although they were face to face, the judge seemed to be staring right through him, and Jason gently touched his arm.

"You'll make yourself ill if you eat too many of those, Your Honor. Why don't you come around to the back and I'll make you a nice cup of tea? Warm you up a bit. It's my lunch break, and I could use the company." His voice was so different to the one of only moments ago when speaking to Bob. There was no latent aggression here, no sarcasm, just gentle compassion. This voice belonged to a different Jason; a Jason who'd almost forgotten he'd once existed, so much so that the present Jason didn't even notice he was there.

The judge didn't move, and his eyes didn't meet the younger man's, but when he spoke he seemed to be addressing him, addressing someone. His tongue darted out and moistened the thin lips of his decaying face. "I can't eat at home you see. Nothing's safe there. They get in everything, everything! Everywhere I look. If I eat at home, they'll get in me. In *me,* imagine that." He paused and scratched at his ear. When he pulled his finger out, it was pink with blood, and he examined it momentarily, seeming pleased with the results. "I can't eat. Can't sleep. Have to stay vigilant. Have to stay alert. I won't let them win. I won't!" He turned away and reached for a new piece of fruit.

Jason firmly held his arm back, careful not to hurt him, but wanting to keep his attention. "Won't let who win? Who's bothering you?"

The old man twitched. "Ants, of course. Ants everywhere." He giggled as though it should have been obvious.

Jason knew it was going to take more than ant powder to solve the judge's problems, but he figured it would be a good way to get in the house with a social worker. "Maybe I can help. I could come around with a friend and some ant powder, and give the house a good going over to get rid of them. I could come this afternoon if you like."

The old man nodded to himself, his eyes drifting off. "Ant powder. Yes, yes, that's what I need, ant powder." His voice drifted off to a mutter, and Jason thought he was losing him again. He wished Mary would stop gawking and ring social services. Out of the corner of his eye, he could see a large black shadow near the register, and he knew Bob had emerged to watch the show. He brought his focus back. He could ring social services later himself.

"Do you know where they're coming from, these ants? Maybe if we can find their nest, we can get rid of them completely. It shouldn't be hard. Nothing to worry about."

Judge Matthews started to shake as he laughed, a hard, cold, mad sound. Snot escaped his nose, and he didn't wipe it away. This time his eyes met Jason's as he lowered his voice to a whisper and drew in closer. Jason tried to ignore the stench, to not let his repulsion show on his face. "Oh yes, I know where they're coming from. Oh yes, I know. I told Daisy, but she didn't believe me, oh no, I could see it on her face. She thought I was mad." His words were clipped, hurried. "I used to be a judge, you know. I can tell a lot about people from their faces. I can see who you are in your face." He stopped and drew a sharp breath, as the shock of recognition widened his eyes. "You!"

Jason frowned, confused. "You know me, Judge Matthews. Jason. Jason Milburn. I've known you since I was a kid." Always in trouble, he almost added.

The judge nodded, hatred glowing in his twisted face. "Yesss," he hissed. "I know you, you and your friends. You and that writer and the two little sluts. I remember, you see. I remember everything. So many secrets, haven't you? So much guilt. So much dirty guilt eating at you. So much *blame.*"

Jason could hear his heart in his ears, trying to pound away the sounds of the man's accusing words. *It's just mad ramblings, just the insane talk of an old man. He'd say the same to anyone. He knows everyone. It doesn't mean a thing.* He felt his stomach lurch as the man gripped his arm tight and pulled him in closer. *Secrets. Guilt. Blame.*

"So why are they coming for me? Why are those little black monsters coming all the way from there, just for me? Can you tell me? You and your friends?"

Jason felt liquid on his face as the judge spat the words out at him and this time he cringed with the sensation. He no longer wanted to help. He was getting more than he bargained for. Now all he wanted was to get the fuck away from this ranting madman, and he wanted it more than anything in the whole world. "Where are they coming from?" he whispered, trying to pull his arm away, not liking the feel of that cool, leathery skin against his.

A slow, sly smile crept across Ernest Matthew's face. "Do you really want an answer, young man? Do you need one? Can't you feel it? I bet fat Carole-Anne could. Yes, I believe that under all that blubber her deadened soul could feel it." He paused and Jason felt those fevered eyes crawling all over his face. "Syracousse. They're coming from Syracousse."

Jason felt his skin go numb as the words echoed in his

head. *Syracousse. They're coming from Syracousse.* No, that couldn't be. That just couldn't be. His head was swimming and he badly needed to sit down. Sit down before he fell down.

He realized after a moment that the pressure on his arm had gone. The judge had let go. He stared at the old man, his whole body shaking. "What do you mean they're coming from there? Tell me what you mean, you crazy bastard!" His voice was loud and harsh, too loud, but he didn't care what Mary and Bob made of it, not caring about anything, resisting the urge to grab the man in front of him and rattle what was left of his pathetic life right out of him. "What do you mean?"

The judge's eyes had glazed over, and he was muttering to himself again as he wandered away, Jason forgotten as if he weren't even there. "Ant powder. That's what I need. Ant powder." He shuffled, lost once again in his strange world, out of the shop and across the road to O'Neale's without even glancing for oncoming traffic. Jason stared at the retreating figure, wishing that he'd just stayed out back and let Bob beat the living shit out of him. A cool sweat had formed on his face and he felt as if his insides were trembling. *Secrets. Guilt. Blame. Syracousse.*

"What did he say to you? You're as white as a sheet."

Jason hadn't noticed Mary approaching him, and he jumped. "What?"

Mary's plump face searched his. "I said you're as white as a sheet. Are you okay?"

Jason nodded, and tried to control his breathing, steadying himself. *Just the rantings of a sad old man. That's all it was. He doesn't know anything. He can't know anything. He wasn't there.*

"Yeah, sorry. I guess it just shook me up seeing the old boy like that. Never expected it of him."

Mary nodded. "He'd gone downhill quick, too. He was in last week, and he seemed fine. But then you never can tell, can you?"

"No," Jason whispered, still staring out at the street, staring but not seeing, his mind being dragged to a past he'd long ago fought to forget. "No you never can, can you?"

Mary touched his arm. "Tell you what, you go and have a cup of tea. It's still your lunch break anyway. I'll send Bob down to the health center. See if he can get someone to go give Mr. Matthews a visit." Her voice was gentle, and for a moment Jason thought the kindness in it would make him cry. He squeezed his eyes shut and kissed her on the forehead.

"Thanks. You're an angel."

The stout woman blushed slightly. "Get on with you, you'll have people talking! You know what this town's like. Doesn't take much to get a rumor started." She ushered him maternally past Bob and back toward the side door. Bob started to follow, but she stopped him with a glare. "Not you. I need you to go down to the doctor's."

Jason didn't wait for the end of the conversation, but headed gratefully into the gloomy solitude of the corridor and the cool of the warehouse. With shaking hands, he pulled his cigarettes from his jacket pocket, and went outside, where, despite his nausea, he lit one and inhaled hard.

The nicotine felt good as it flooded his system, and he slid down the rough bricks until he was crouching, his knees tight against his chest, his back supported by the wall behind him. *Just a crazy old man,* he told himself. *Just a crazy old man who didn't know what he was saying.* It sounded good in his head, but hard as he tried, he didn't believe himself. He didn't believe himself one little bit as he rested his tired head against the cement and shut his eyes and remembered. Remembered the beginning. When three became four.

"You'll really like her. And her house is just too cool, so get a move on! I don't want to be late." Carole-Anne had her hands on her small hips as she turned to glare at the two of them, her forehead wrinkling under her bangs as she squinted in the late-April sun.

"We're coming, we're coming. Keep your hair on." Rob looked at Jason and the two exchanged a conspiratorial look. Sometimes Carrie could be such a girl, and today was one of those occasions. Jason looked down at his tatty sneakers, the cloth more gray than white and stretched where his toes were getting too big for them, and watched them scuffling along next to Rob's bigger, cleaner, newer shoes.

Carrie had insisted they dress up in their best jeans and t-shirts to officially meet her new friend, but unlike Rob, he only had jeans. Old, worn-out and in need of replacing. He'd seen the embarrassed look on Robster's face when they'd picked him up in his smart new Wranglers and stain-free shirt. It was a look that kicked its owner. A look that said, *I should have thought.* If Rob could have gone upstairs and changed back into his scruffy clothes without making it obvious, then he would have.

Jason sighed, blowing his hair out of his face. Life was shit when you were poor. It didn't help that this Gina girl seemed pretty loaded, either. A big house by the river all on its own and a dad who worked in London like Rob's did. Yeah, he could just imagine what she was going to make of him. But then, she wanted to be friends with Carrie, and Carrie lived on the estate just like he did. Still, he wasn't looking forward to the pitying sideways looks, however well-intentioned, that was for sure.

He kicked a stone from the gravel track as they turned away from the towpath. *"I don't see why we have to meet this girl. I bet she's really wet and going to want to play with dolls or something."*

Rob laughed, and Jason looked up to the taller, broader boy whose smile was always wide and open, and felt a twinge of envy. Everything always seemed so easy for Rob. Great family, great house, great shitting life for that matter. How come he got to be the tallest, too? Sometimes as much as he loved Rob, it was hard not to hate him. But those moments always passed in a blink of an eye, and *then they were just best buddies again. Jase and the Robster. Sounded like a good name for a film. A film about a pair of outlawed cowboys, always on the run.*

"I wasn't being funny. Why do we need to hang around with a girl?"

Rob shrugged. "Carrie's a girl."

"Yeah, but Carrie's different. She's cool. Most of the time I don't even notice she's a girl." That wasn't exactly true. Over the past year or so, he'd begun to think about Carrie being a girl more and more. It was difficult not to, not now that she was beginning to look like one. Sometimes, he'd be looking at her and she'd catch his eye and smile and he'd feel himself tingling all over. He ignored it, though. He didn't want them to grow up. He didn't want them to change. He wanted them to be best friends forever. And now there was this Gina from Carrie's library club, and it felt like change to him. He glowered at his canvas shoes. "I don't see why Carrie needs this new friend anyway. She's got us. We don't need anyone else."

Rob elbowed him in the ribs, grinning. "Now you sound like a whining girl. You know what Carrie's like. She's probably going through one of those weird spells she has when she wants to be all feminine. You know, just like the nail polish."

Jason started to smile. Yeah, the nail polish. How could he forget? For a whole month she'd insisted on wearing that awful pink stuff; a cheap bottle off the market, just 'cos she'd seen some woman wearing something like it in a film. The problem was, she wasn't any good at putting it on and it was always all over her fingers. And she never let it dry properly so whatever she'd managed to get on her nails was always smudged into clumps.

A cool breeze brushed by them, temporarily invading the early summer warmth, and he stuffed his hands into the baggy pockets of his jeans. "You reckon?"

Rob nodded as they caught up to Carrie, who was waiting by the front gates. "Yup. By this time next week this

Gina girl will be forgotten. So let's just grin and bear it, okay?"

Jason nodded and then took a deep breath as he took in the house. "Wow," he breathed. "That's beautiful." The house looked like something out of a book or magazine, its outside painted pale yellow with perfect white window frames, and plants and flowers with a thousand colors lining the short driveway up to the front door.

Carrie slid her arm through his, and her eyes were shining. "Wait 'til you see the inside and the back garden. Come on, let's go 'round to the side gate. Gina said she'd be in the garden."

The two boys followed her as she led the way, and Jason noticed that Rob's face had grown quiet. Maybe he didn't like the fact that Carrie's new friend was better off than he was. He shook the thought away. Nah. Robster was better than that. Carrie brought them to a halt by a large tree, behind which was a small metal gate built into the wall. She swung it open and led the way. Jason felt butterflies starting up in his stomach. He hated meeting new people, and now that he was here, now that he'd seen the house, he felt like he was about to meet the shitting queen.

His feet led him behind the others, past the large pond that was more like a small lake, fish busy making their homes in it, their darting fins covering the water with ripples, and around to the garden.

A rug was laid out on the lawn and a girl in a pale blue summer dress lay on it, belly down, reading a book, her long chestnut hair held back by a yellow ribbon, the same color as the house.

"Gina!" Carrie's shout was loud, and the girl looked up, shocked for a second, and then she smiled. Watching as she stood up and brushed herself down, Jason felt his insides go all funny, the way they did sometimes with Carrie. How come he'd never noticed this girl at school?

Finally, they came to a stop in front of her. Carrie was almost bouncing with pleasure. "Gina, this is Rob and Ja-

son, the boys I was telling you about. Guys, this is Gina."

"Pleased to meet you." The girl held her hand out and Rob blushed and muttered something as he shook it. Jason wondered if his insides were going weird as well. Probably, by the looks of it. When it was his turn, he took her tiny hand, enjoyed feeling her soft skin, and smiled. Shaking hands was one of those things he'd normally laugh at; it was one of those things posh grown-ups like Rob's parents did, but with Gina it didn't seem weird at all. Her face was even prettier close up, her eyes a glorious blue, and her tiny nose made Carrie's look like a clumsy afterthought.

"Your house is great." How come he found the words so clumsy? What was the matter with his mouth? Gina didn't seem to notice, and she smiled, showing two rows of perfect tiny white teeth.

"Thanks. My grandfather built it." Jason was trying to think of something to say next when they were interrupted by a woman's voice.

"Gina!" Standing at the back door was a slim blond woman dressed in cream, with high-heeled shoes on. She was the most glamorous woman Jason thought he'd ever seen outside of a film. His mum wore stilettos sometimes, awful cheap white things, but she never looked like this. *"I've made some lemonade! Why don't you and your friends come in and get some? You can take it outside with you. There's biscuits, too."*

The woman disappeared inside, and as the four children stepped through the back door, Jason could smell the lingering scent of vanilla. He stared at the jug on the side. *"Your mum makes lemonade?"* He couldn't keep the surprise out of his voice. *"Not even Rob's mum does that."* Rob sent him a scowl, and Jason shrugged in apology.

Gina was opening a cupboard and pulling out some tall tumblers, her bare feet balancing on tiptoes. She was shorter than Jason, and he liked that. Carrie was just about as tall as he was these days. Gina smiled over her shoulder. *"She likes cooking. My parents do a lot of entertaining."*

Rob stepped out in front of Jason. "Do you want me to get those down? I can probably reach the easiest." Jason resisted the urge to dig his friend in the ribs. He didn't need any reminding that he was never going to be the first choice for a basketball team.

Gina shook her head. *"I can manage. I don't know why they're on the top shelf; they're normally kept on the bottom. Mum must have been tidying out the cupboards again."* As she spoke, one of the glasses slipped through her fingers, smashing into a thousand tiny shards on the floor. The shock sent her off balance and she stepped backward.

The next moment seemed to play in slow motion in Jason's head. The glass tumbling to the floor, exploding, covering the ground around Gina with its splintered form; and then her foot, the smooth bare sole of her small foot stepping backward as she wobbled, and he thought, She's going to land right on all that glass; she's going to cut her foot to ribbons. *And he wondered whether there was time to reach forward and grab her, but everything was going too shitting fast, and then he felt his heart stop beating for a second as IT HAPPENED.*

The glass shot away from under her foot. Every last tiny piece. It moved away from under her approaching skin; just like that experiment they did at school with two magnets, it moved as if it were repelled by something. But it wasn't just the glass she was about to cut herself on. In that split second all the glass on the floor swept itself into a neat pile by the cooker away from them all. Just like that. One minute it was everywhere, and then it was sucked away.

Gina's foot came down on the harmless tiles. No one looked at her. They were all staring at the floor. There was a moment's silence before Carrie spoke. *"Did anyone else see that, or am I going crazy?"*

"I think we're all going crazy." That was Rob, his voice barely audible.

There was the sound of ice cubes tinkling in a glass, and Jason looked up to see Gina pouring out the lemonade. "I seem to do that kind of thing quite a lot. Don't worry about it." She smiled at them, something close to pride in her face.

A long time after that day, when things had started going bad, Jason wondered whether maybe she'd broken that glass on purpose. To show off to her new friends. To make sure they'd come back. But on that April afternoon, it was just the coolest thing he'd ever seen anyone do.

"You did that?"

She nodded and handed him a glass. "I'm not sure how. Just sometimes it happens. It's like I can get myself out of trouble."

Rob was laughing. "That is just so far out!"

Carrie had found a dustpan and brush and was sweeping up the glass. "I told you she wasn't like other girls. So are we all going to be friends or what?"

And that was how the summer started. How three became four.

Jason opened his eyes and stared at the wall opposite him. His legs were starting to cramp with the cold, but he ignored them. He could still hear that smashing glass in his head. His soul ached with emptiness. How different would it have all been if Carrie had never joined that ridiculous library club? Where would they all be now? Would Carrie still be here, instead of cold and sad down at that hospital morgue? Would she have married Jimmy Locke? Or would Jason have got his wish, all he'd ever really wanted? Would they all have been best buddies forever?

The cold was making his nose run. *Guilt. Secrets. Syracousse.* Well, if the old man had been rambling, then he'd got very lucky with his guesses. His legs twinging beneath him, he dragged himself upright. Yeah, he'd talk to Rob after the funeral. He wanted to talk. Needed to talk, and the sad thing was that the rich bastard was the only person he had left whom he *could* talk to. His heart heavy, feeling like he desperately needed a drink, he went back inside.

CHAPTER THIRTEEN

Standing on the doorstep of the terraced, Edwardian house, Kelly was beginning to feel ridiculous. Why had she agreed to do this for her dad? Rob would no doubt already know about the funeral; after all, he and Carole-Anne had been good friends, even if it was a long time ago. But then, she knew her father well enough to know that this was more about matchmaking than about passing on information. Yeah, she figured she'd read her father's mind pretty well. And maybe he'd read hers with the ease at which she agreed to this visit she was now regretting. Surely he'd never noticed the crush she had on Rob when they were at school? She groaned inside. Of course he had. He was a policeman at the end of the day, and perhaps, after all the stuff with his dad and then Gina, her concern for the boy who hadn't even known she'd existed was a little obvious.

Still, she thought, drawing herself up. School was a long time ago for all of them and there had been a whole lot of bigger crushes from the time Rob disappeared off to boarding school and the day her love life died with the internal admission that all men were bastards or not worth the effort. Smoothing out her jeans, she rang the doorbell. Here goes, then. She tried to ignore the fluttering feeling in her stomach. God, this was going to be so embarrassing; standing on a virtual stranger's doorstep, looking like the village gossip. She saw a shadow approaching through the glass panel and resisted the urge to run away. Five minutes and it would all be over. Job done. She took a deep breath as the door opened.

The first thing she noticed was that he was still gorgeous in the flesh. A little thin, a little tired-looking, but gorgeous all the same. The second thing she noticed was that he looked confused.

"Can I help you?" The voice seemed disinterested, and she wondered whether she'd woken him. The more she looked, the more tired he seemed, dark circles eating at those eyes that were still as blue as the ocean.

Oh, get a grip, girl, she chastised herself. *The sight of a new man in town and you've come over all Mills and Boon.* She smiled and felt a blush of embarrassment flushing her skin.

"Um, you probably don't remember me, but I'm Kelly Hollingsworth. I was in your class at school? My dad was a policeman?" She knew the words were coming out too quickly, but she just wanted to get the job done and get out of here. "He asked me if I'd pop by, I don't want to disturb you or anything . . ."

Rob interrupted her, his face stretching into a grin of recognition. "Kelly Hollingsworth! Yeah, I remember you! You were the really clever kid who should have been in the nursery or something but instead had been moved up about a million classes!"

Kelly shrugged, not sure what to make of his memory. "Well, only two to be precise. The reason I've called 'round is . . ."

Rob had pulled the door wide. "Come in, come in. God, you've changed a bit, haven't you?" Kelly presumed he was referring to her train-track braces and puppy fat.

"Yes, well that's what happens when you grow up. Everything changes."

Rob led her down the hallway, and he cast a searching glance back at her. "You think so? These days I'm not so sure. You'll have to excuse the kitchen; it's a bit of a mess. I've been writing." He laughed slightly as if at a private joke. "Well, thinking about writing."

Now she was inside, Kelly was starting to feel awkward. Why hadn't she just said what she had to say and gone? She felt trapped and didn't like it.

Holding the coffeepot in one hand, Rob turned to face her, leaning against the sink, and she felt his eyes thoughtfully appraising her. "Kelly Hollingsworth. God, time just disappears, doesn't it? How did we get to be so old?"

She smiled, and nodded at the offer of a coffee. "Well, I hate to remind you, but you've got two years on me. I'm still only thirty-five years young."

He raised an eyebrow as he emptied the jug of water into the top and turned the machine on. "Thank you so much for reminding me. So what brought you around here?"

Her eyes slid to the floor for a moment, having until then been doing some appraising of her own, wondering what his body looked like under that black long-sleeve t-shirt. God, she must be getting desperate. Or maybe it was just that seeing him had allowed her a small trip down memory lane to a time when she'd been all hormones with a head full of unrealistic dreams. But whatever it was, all thoughts of sex were dispelled when he asked the question.

She ran her hand through her hair, something she always did when trying to broach an unpleasant subject, and then brought her eyes back to his. "It's about Carole-Anne." He looked as if he'd just been doused in cold water, the skin on his face almost goose-pimpling with the shock.

"I know this whole thing must have been awful for you, but my father thought you'd like to know that the police are releasing her body on Monday morning. The funeral's been arranged for Tuesday afternoon."

"Right. Right." His voice was soft as he turned away and started filling the mugs with steaming coffee. "Thanks for telling me. I thought it might be announced in the paper or something." He moved to the fridge for the milk and kept his eyes averted. He must be more upset than she'd first thought.

"No. I don't think anyone wants too much publicity. You know. Press and things like that." God, this was hard. She shuffled slightly from foot to foot, trying to ease away the tension in her body and the room.

"Of course. I wasn't thinking." He looked up at her, and she wondered what was going on behind those eyes. "Do you take sugar?"

She shook her head. "Look, I can just go if you want. I know this is awkward. You probably want to be on your own."

There was a moment's pause before he spoke. "No. I'd like you to stay. I could use the conversation." He was chewing his bottom lip, just like he used to when they'd had tests at school. It made her smile. So he still chewed his lip when he was thinking, just like she still flicked her hair when she had to do something unappealing. She wondered whether he even knew he did it. Probably not. Maybe they didn't change that much when they grew up after all.

She took the mug. "Well, if you're sure."

He clinked his mug against hers. "Yes, I'm sure, Kelly Hollingsworth. Cheers." He let out a long sigh, and then looked at her sideways. "Is it still Hollingsworth? Or has some lucky man dragged you down the aisle?"

She laughed aloud. "No, it's still Hollingsworth. Although I do have a daughter. Tabitha. She's four. Four and fantastic." The coffee burned as she swallowed, and she wondered why she'd brought Tabby up so quickly. Was she trying to put him off? As if he were even interested.

He wasn't fazed though, just curious. "So what happened with her dad? Divorce?"

The frankness of his question made her answer more honestly than she normally would. "Well, since you ask, he'd already dragged another girl down the aisle long before I met him. Stupid, huh?"

This time it was his turn to look embarrassed. "Sorry, I shouldn't have asked. It's the writer in me. Makes me too damned nosy for my own good."

Kelly shook her head. "It's okay. It doesn't matter." And for the first time in a long time, she realized she meant it. "What about you?"

He threw his head back and laughed, whatever weight he seemed to be carrying momentarily forgotten. When he looked at her, his eyes were full of soft humor. "Don't you read the gossip columns?"

She shook her head.

"Well, you've got a long way to go if you want to start competing with me in the 'stupid relationship' stakes. I'm the king of the meaningless fling."

She smiled, despite the alarm that rang in her head with those two words. At least he was honest, and that made a change. "That bad, huh?"

He shrugged, his face a little more serious. "Yeah, I think I am, or was. Too much success can do that to a person. Too much success, too much cocaine and not enough people prepared to put you in your place can turn you into an arsehole in no time at all, you can trust me on that one. And the London scene isn't exactly the place to go looking for a meaningful relationship."

"Especially if you're not looking for one." Her smile was wry and Rob lit a cigarette.

"Ooh, that hurt. I'd forgotten about that brain of yours. What are you doing with it these days anyway? Running Microsoft or something?"

That was the strange thing about intelligence. People always expected you to do something grand with it. All the careers advisers at her university had thought so anyway. It was as if what *she* wanted or cared about didn't matter. Her brain was everything.

"I'm a teacher. Back at Roecliffe." She shrugged apologetically and hated herself for it.

He was looking at her with that assessing gaze again, and she found that she quite liked it.

After a couple of moments, he nodded slowly. "I bet you're a great teacher." Her face clouded over as she thought of Darren and Lee and poor damaged Sharnice. "Well. Maybe not as great as I thought. Those kids involved in the rape case were in my class. I should have noticed something was up with them, but I didn't. I keep thinking I could have stopped that if I'd just paid more attention." She sighed. "So a teacher I may be, but I wouldn't go as far as to say a great one. Not by a long shot." Somehow it felt easier talking to him about this than it had to her father.

Rob was chewing his lip again, and his expression darkened momentarily. "You know, there are some things that are just beyond our control, however much we wish otherwise. You couldn't have helped those kids. I don't think anyone could."

For a few seconds he seemed to drift off into his own thoughts, before he brought his attention back to her, the darkness around him lifting again. Just what was bothering him? She wished she knew him well enough to ask. Maybe she would, but not today. Not now.

Putting her cup down on the breakfast bar, she straightened up, pushing herself away from the tall built-in cupboard she'd been leaning on. It was time to get back to her weekend. Tabby had gone swimming with one of the girls from nursery, but she'd be home soon and probably starving. "I'd better get going, I've got some shopping to do. Thanks for the coffee. It was nice seeing you."

He nodded. "Likewise. And thanks for the news on the funeral. I really appreciate it."

He led her to the front door, but paused as he reached for the knob. His voice was hesitant. "Look, this is probably a crap idea, but I was wondering if maybe you'd like to go out for a drink or something?" He seemed to be struggling for the right words. "I'd like to see you again."

Trying to stop her heart from thumping, she met his eyes warily. "I'd like that. But just as friends. I'm not in the market for a meaningless fling. Okay?" The words sounded harder than she'd meant them to, and it was his turn to look flushed and embarrassed. She thought she could see hurt in there, too. Maybe she had been a little harsh. Pulling the door open herself, she reached up and pecked him on the cheek. "You can pick me up at seven tomorrow if you like. Number seven, Horsefair Green. It's been nice seeing you again, Robert Black." Not waiting for his response, she shut the door behind her, a smile on her face. Not bad for a girl so out of practice, she thought as she headed home. Not bad at all.

PART TWO

CHAPTER FOURTEEN

By midnight most evenings, Streatford is a desolate place; last orders been and gone, all those late-night drinkers whiling away their loneliness, having meandered their way through the chill to the comfort of their own homes, hurried out by weary publicans eager for their beds. Silence rules the darkness, smothering it into submission; the last car having made its way along the winding, narrow streets like a predatory shark patrolling the almost black of the ocean bed, disappearing into the night half an hour past.

The tarmac and the pavements relax, no weight of passengers left for them to bear, apart from perhaps solitary foxes and not-so-domestic cats seeking adventure in the world that has been abandoned for a while. By midnight in Streatford, everyone has gotten where they're going; there will be no more traveling of the human kind until the sun rises and brings a new day masked in the safety of the light.

It seems that the houses lining the centuries-trodden roads, those buildings both old and new, loved and unloved, slump forward and doze like dogs sleeping with one eye open, careful not to disturb their occupants, as they lean on each other for support, surrendering themselves to the memory of so many times gone by.

The trees whisper in sympathy, their branches aching for children long since grown up, their former presence marked only by words carved in the bark with giggles and penknives. The childish laughter aches in the sap of the oak and the apple and with each bellow of wind, they call out the names they bear on their ageless bodies, silently appealing to be remembered, but knowing that none will return. No memories will be relived.

In the stillness of the night, they take comfort from the knowledge that new children will come, new families to be loved. People come and people go, time different for them than for the bricks and the wood. But people there always will be, there always have been. And they will care for them. All of them.

By one o'clock, the town has settled into its slumber, content with its lot, a happy community, secure in its place.

Just one house, a forgotten place aching with need, dreams loudly in the night. It wants to be remembered, needs to be remembered. Its hurt makes it angry, and its dreams will be heard.

CHAPTER FIFTEEN

By three o'clock in the morning, Judge Matthews's house looked as if winter were arriving from the inside out, the white powder having settled like a dusting of snow resting comfortably as it covered the carpets and furniture, creating a strange, white landscape, foreign and unnatural. Empty tubular cartons carrying various brand names were tossed carelessly about the living room, their loads dispatched, the thick cardboard shells no longer required.

In the kitchen, the fridge door stood open, no cargo left to chill, the cupboards also bare save for the powder that covered every corner of the house like overgrowing moss.

Ernest Matthews stood by the patio door in his gray underpants, whose baggy form clung precariously to hip bones that threatened to tear through the thin layer of tired skin. Staring out through the glass, his bloodshot eyes didn't waver as he scratched furiously at the red, irritated blotches that covered his body. There were lights blazing at Syracousse. Not that it was possible of course, but there they were, and he had a feeling they were shining out just for him. Just so he'd get the message. His skin burned from where he'd rubbed the ant powder in, but that couldn't be helped, precautions had to be taken. His mouth moved constantly, unconsciously, words forming silently, unheard.

He hadn't bought the ant powder at O'Neale's. He'd tried of course, but he'd read the young man's thoughts straight from his face, the minute he'd asked. Carole-Anne Bradley, that's what had run through his mind. Carole-Anne Bradley. So instead of waiting for a reply, Ernest had just scurried out of the shop. Young O'Neale hadn't called him Your Honor either as he'd stared, uncertain of quite what to do. In fact, he hadn't called him anything at all. Ernest Matthews's life was slipping away from him—being torn away from him—in more ways than one.

In the end he'd walked to Dulverton, to less cautious shopkeepers, to fetch his necessary supplies. His slippers had been worn through when he'd got back, his soles bleeding into the pavement beneath him, as he slammed the door shut behind him, wary of Daisy's concerned observation from behind her spotless lace curtains. He had begun to hate Daisy. Hate her for the proximity of her normalness. Everything on her side of the wall was just fine. Syracousse had no business with her.

From the corner of his eye, he saw something black running down the curtain. He remained still, his mouth moving, twitching into an echo of a smile. His mind was suffering a moment of clarity. So the ants were still here, nestling in the nooks and crannies above him, safe from the deadliness below. He wasn't really surprised. Nothing surprised him anymore, and his tired, crazed body was unaware of the tear that trickled down his cheek, free to run the length of his emaciated body before its own life wore out, vanishing to nothing at the end of its tiny trail, somewhere midway down his chest.

The single black insect he had glimpsed had disappeared to the floor and was now followed by a steady stream, heading back to the carpet, no longer afraid of the poison he'd laid there. Deep inside, he felt no shock. He hadn't really expected it to kill them. After all, it was just the last effort of a desperate man. This morning, as he'd stood in his garden relieving himself, he could have sworn he saw flecks of black in his urine. Flecks of wriggling black that scurried away when they hit they grass. Scurried back to the house. Was it his house or *their* house? It was so hard to tell, but he had a sneaking suspicion that they knew the answer.

The lights were flashing on and off at the house farther down by the river, and he wondered whether anyone else could see them. Probably not. It looked like someone was having a party in there, but he knew better. The old Judge Matthews, the one from a week ago, would have been indignantly dialing the local police. Trespassing was against the law, whether the house was occupied or not. The law was his special subject; it was what he'd lived his life by, proud of it, secure because of his knowledge of it. But this Judge Matthews was different. This Judge Matthews knew that should the police arrive at Syracousse, they would find it locked up and silent, mocking him with its darkness. And he didn't know quite what to make of that. He thought maybe he was being judged by a new law, a law he didn't understand for an unknown crime committed in a life gone by.

He chuckled as he stared, drool escaping his mouth, his false teeth long since abandoned—who knew what was nesting in the gums?—appearances no longer an issue. "The lights are on but there's nobody home," isn't that what the youngsters say these days?

He was aware of a tickling sensation as his housemates ran across his feet, reclaiming their territory. He didn't look down, couldn't bear to look down. His chuckle turned to a sob. What had he done to deserve this? What? Behind him, the ants were moving madly across the carpet and furniture, some in a mass, some as individuals, stirring up the powder, lifting it into the air with their tiny, frantic motions. Ernest Matthews didn't notice, his mind elsewhere, drifting into the past, into the courtroom, searching for answers.

"Camilla Grace, this court finds you not guilty of the murder of your husband, Philip Grace, on the grounds of diminished responsibility. However, in view of the evaluation report presented to me, you are to be committed to a secure psychiatric hospital until such time as you are deemed fit for release."

As the dust rose higher and higher, a cough started in his chest and his nose tickled, while in his mind the image of the woman, rocking backwards and forwards, eyes glazed from drugs or madness, he didn't know which, blurred and was replaced with a younger face, eyes wide with guilt, and he could almost feel the young hand on his arm, as she pleaded with him, the small voice calm and low. It was the day after, when her uncle and aunt had arrived to take her away. They had been in his office, finalizing arrangements for her, and he was standing at the oak door, its weight indicative of his importance, giving his condolences, when she clutched at him, tiny and almost forgotten in the midst of all this mess.

"It wasn't her, Your Honor, it wasn't her. It was me. I did it. I did it from the garden."

He had stroked her head and told her not to blame herself. The police knew what had happened. There was nothing she could have done. Her mother was sick. The doctors would look after her until the trial. The little girl's eyes had burned into him.

"But it was me," she whispered, and the three adults exchanged a look of sympathy. What a terrible ordeal. This kind of thing just didn't happen in a town like Streatford.

A cough exploded from inside him, and the shock of it brought him back to the insanity of the present, his eyes widening as he looked with shock at the powdery fog that surrounded him. What had they done? What were they doing? For the first time since they'd started, he noticed the manic activity of the ants, whirling up a dust storm in his living room. He squinted to try and stop his eyes stinging as the tiny grains attacked him. The cough wouldn't stop, and with each sucked in breath, his throat became more irritated.

Hunched over, his hand over his mouth, he staggered, choking, to the kitchen sink. Water, that's what he needed. Water. A glass of water and he'd be fine. He turned the tap, but nothing came out, no water, no ants, no nothing. The muscles in his stomach were straining, and his tongue ached as his coughing became more desperate. Stumbling toward the patio doors, he ignored the tears that streamed down his cheeks as the small blood vessels in his eyeballs burst with effort.

It was getting more difficult to catch his breath between the coughs, and he could feel his panic rising as he clutched at the small lever that locked the patio door. A small part of his mind tried to stay calm as his fingers trembled, his body shaking as he tried in vain to stop the convulsions of choking. *Push it down, that's all you have to do and you'll be out in the clear, fresh air. Just push it down.*

But the lever wouldn't go down. He could feel it pushing upward against him, and every time he pressed harder, the resistance got stronger. His tears were real now as his energy drained from him and he sank to the carpet. The world was starting to go black, and there was an awful pain starting in the side of his head. He banged weakly on the glass, terrified and frustrated.

At least let me understand! At least give me that! he pleaded inside, to himself, to the ants, to Syracousse as he gazed out at the unforgiving night. *I don't understand. I can't die without knowing why, tell me why, damn you to hell, tell me why!*

For a blissful moment, the coughing stopped, his chest suddenly soothed, and he closed his eyes, sobbing with relief, the tears and snot mixing in the wrinkled contours of his skeletal face. *Oh thank God, Oh thank God, Oh thank Go . . .*

The blood vessel that had served its master silent and faithful for so many years burst more dramatically than its tiny size would lead anyone to expect, flooding his brain with the blood it carried. For the split second it lasted, the pain was more than anything Judge Matthews had believed was possible. By the time his eyelids had flown open with the shock, the life had left his eyes. He was dead in an instant.

CHAPTER SIXTEEN

Tabby had been in bed half an hour by the time her mum came to kiss her goodnight. Her perfume smelled warm and sweet as she sat on the bed and leaned forward. Her voice was soft. "I know you're awake. I can see your eyelids fluttering."

Giggling, Tabby opened her eyes. Her mum looked different than normal, even in the pale glow of the nightlight. She wasn't wearing her jeans and t-shirt for one thing, nor her teacher clothes. Instead, she had on a black top and trousers Tabby hadn't seen before. She'd done something funny with her hair, too. She pondered on it for a moment before speaking. "You look really pretty, Mummy." Her mum smiled back, and Tabby realized she looked more than pretty, she looked beautiful.

"Thank you. Not as pretty as you, princess, but I try my best." She stroked Tabby's hair, and the little girl sighed.

"Who are you going out with?" She liked the feel of the hand running gently over her head.

"Just a friend."

"A man friend or a woman friend?"

Her mother laughed as if she'd said something funny. "A man friend. But just a friend, okay?"

The pillow rustling in her ears like crunching snow, she nodded, not really sure what she was agreeing with, but wanting to please her mum. Her mummy just didn't go out with male friends and something about it made her feel funny inside. And she wasn't sure if it was a good funny or a bad funny. It was a weird funny. Her mother leaned forward and they exchanged kisses as Tabby breathed in that comforting smell, a mixture of mother and perfume and makeup, the smell that let her know everything was well in the world, and that nothing *bad* could happen no matter how many shadows she saw in her room at night.

The bed creaked as the weight of its extra occupant lifted. "I'll look in on you when I get back. I won't be late."

"Not on a school night!" Tabby chirped from behind her duvet. Her mother laughed a little at their old joke.

"Nope. No parties for us girls on a school night!" She pulled the door so that it was almost shut, before peering her head through the gap. "I love you, princess."

"I love you too, Mummy." And then she was gone.

Tabby yawned, and snuggled down in her bed, feeling sleep calling for her. She wondered whether she'd dream of her special house again tonight, feeling a shiver of childish anticipation. She was glad she'd left her painting of it downstairs, even though at first she'd wanted to put it on the wall in her room where she could look at it on her own. Savor it. She hadn't painted it well enough, though, not by a long shot, and now when she looked at it she just felt frustrated with herself. It did look kind of like the house, but not like it was in her dreams, just a clumsy copy. She couldn't have painted it like it really was, no one could. Even the best painter in the world would fail at that. She let out a long sleepy yawn of contentment and allowed herself to drift off into the unchartered sea of sleep. It wasn't long before the dream called for her. It called, and she happily answered.

She was lying on a rug in the garden, the wool tickling her belly where her t-shirt had ridden up, her legs enjoying the warm breeze as she wiggled them to and fro behind her. Up on her elbows, she was still close enough to the grass to see a ladybug that perched at the tip of a blade, its red and black wings standing out against the deep green. She watched it, fascinated, wondering how something could be so light, or maybe it was the grass that was strong. So much to learn, so much to know. She took a long sip from the cool glass of lemonade beside her. It wasn't like the lemonade her mummy got from Budgen's. This one was all musty-colored and sharper, making her teeth feel strange with the mix of bitter and sweet. She liked it. She liked everything here.

She looked at the ladybug again, and as if it sensed her curiosity, it opened up its wings and disappeared from sight. Maybe when she was a grownup she'd understand about bugs and grass and wings. The voice that wasn't a voice, *her invisible house friend*, as she thought of it, smiled in her head. She liked the feel of it tingling in her skull. It made her feel safe and warm. "When I grow up I'm going to be a pleaseman 'cos they know all kinds of stuff. I'm going to be a pleaseman like my granddad." She thought her friend would like that, but a shiver danced over her. She shook her head, trying to rattle the feeling away. Confused, she sat up in the sunshine and tilted her head. "What's the matter?"

For a few seconds there was nothing, and she thought for a horrible moment that she'd said something terrible and her friend had gone away forever, and then the glow within her started again. The dreamy music that played inside somehow made perfect sense. Perfect word sense.

Your granddad is a bad man.

Her hand unconsciously went up to her hair, twirling a strand of her sleep-disturbed curls between her fingers. In a few moments she'd probably be sucking it. "No, not my granddad. He was a pleaseman. He's brave and kind," she said, adamantly, as if correcting a stupid mistake. She felt the voice caressing her, comforting her, and she released the hair.

He has a secret. A guilty, shameful secret. A secret from you and your mummy. He has created a house of lies. You live in a house of lies. Remember that.

Tabby shook her head, not liking this disturbed feeling that invaded her special place. Nothing should feel bad here. Nothing.

Ask him.

The little girl stood up and dusted down her clothes, brushing away the bad thoughts until later, as children so often did. "Will you push the swing for me now?"

The tune lilted behind her eyes, and she knew that everything was okay again; everything was back to normal. She held on to the chains on each side of the wooden seat, no rust there to stain her hands, and waited for the air to lift her to the sky.

Normally, when she played at school, she didn't like to swing too high, because even though Miss Parkinson said it was special soft ground, it still looked pretty hard to her. But here it was different. Here she swung so high she thought she was flying, just like that ladybug had. But then, here she knew she was safe. Nothing bad could ever happen here. Her friend had told her that. It was a promise.

"I wish I could find it here when I'm awake." Her laughter spoke for her, and the voice understood.

Soon.

CHAPTER SEVENTEEN

Rob crossed the road to the small side street leading to Horsefair green, enjoying the cool, crisp air that circulated in his lungs. He wasn't sure he should be doing this, and despite the thousands of dates he'd been on over the past few years, his stomach twitched with nerves. He tried to ignore it. It wasn't a date anyway, not really.

His tan suede jacket wasn't doing much to keep out the chill—*if it isn't a date, then why the hell didn't you put on something warmer?*—and he pushed his hands further into the pockets of his soft, brown Calvin Klein jeans. Well, whatever it was, it would be nice to spend the evening with an intelligent woman for a change, and he could sure as hell use the company. The house, which at first had seemed like a sanctuary, had become unsettling, memories threatening him from the corner of his eye and when he turned to face them, they'd gone, disappearing like shy ghosts that know they have no right to be there anymore. He sighed. Wasn't that what he'd come home for anyway? To exorcise some ghosts? Hah. Maybe he was getting more than he'd bargained for.

This afternoon he'd dozed off and dreamed of Gina. Dreamed of the time she'd kissed him—his first kiss, and boy what a place to start—and Jason had seen them and not talked to him all the way home. Another crack in the fragile walls of childhood friendship. But this time, in the dream, it was different. It was as if he was really seeing what had happened for the first time, watching from the outside, looking at the clumsy almost teenager, so smitten with this fascinating girl who was pressing her soft lips onto his and not believing he could be so lucky. Oblivious to the world outside, the world away from his lips and tongue, from *her* lips and tongue, which were sending shivers all over his body. This time he could see the way her eyes darted quickly to the kitchen window—checking to see whether Jason was there, whether Jason was watching—before she reached up for his face.

He'd woken up with a bitter taste in his mouth, for a moment no longer sure where he was in space and time. Was it real or wasn't it? And did it really matter now?

Squinting a little in the gloom, he checked the numbers on the wooden front doors that opened straight onto the uneven pavement. Still a few more to go before he got to Kelly's. It was emotional overload that was making him feel so edgy. That's all it was. Nothing weird was going on in Streatford; he'd convinced himself of that over the past couple of days. The past was done and dusted. So what about that terrible rape up at the house? And what about Carrie's message? Maybe she'd just gone crazy at the end. Shit, she'd have to have been crazy to do what she did. Sure, this stuff was unsettling, but only because of the memories it dredged up. Nothing more. And memory was a fickle friend. Maybe nothing strange had ever happened here at all. Children had vivid imaginations.

Finally, he found himself standing at the right house, soft light escaping from the closed curtains. He rang the bell, suddenly looking forward to getting the evening underway. He needed a distraction, contact with reality, and there was something about Kelly's serious, calm intelligence that attracted him. And she hadn't grown up to be bad-looking either.

She'd looked pretty good in the dim streetlights, but it wasn't until they stepped into the warm yellow glow of The Plough that he realized just how attractive she really was. Like him, she'd gone for the not-quite-date look, but the top and trousers fitted her perfectly, outlining her natural curves, and their blackness only enhanced the luminescence of her pale skin. She'd piled her hair up on her head, so loose strands were falling down the side of her face. Watching her as she took her seat at the table by the fire, carefully putting her gin and tonic down on a bar mat, he realized what was so refreshing about her. She was the first woman he'd met in a long time who was totally unaware of how stunning she actually was. He sat down opposite her and took a sip of his beer before speaking. "So who's babysitting that little girl of yours tonight?"

She smiled. "My dad. He's lived with us since my mum died two years ago. It's a perfect arrangement. Tabby's enough to keep us both busy and the extra pair of hands is a godsend." Her eyes softened. "I think looking after us stops him from missing my mother so much. It must be strange to have someone around you for so many years and suddenly they're not there anymore. I think he's a bit lost without her. I know I was for a while, and I still miss her." She raised an eyebrow at him, as if waiting for him to make a joke. "I know it must sound funny coming from someone my age, but I guess there's never enough time to say everything you want to, is there?"

Rob smiled, his heart tugging at him with memories of his own parents. He was speaking before he realized it. "I understand you perfectly. I wish now that I'd seen my mum more before she died, and I'm still not sure why I didn't. I think that after all that stuff with my dad and then going to boarding school we just drifted apart. It

133

seems stupid now." He'd told her more of the truth than
he'd ever told any other girl, but even that wasn't the
whole story. How could he explain his need to stay away
from Streatford? He couldn't even explain it to himself.

There was a moment of strangely comfortable silence
before his eyes met Kelly's thoughtful gaze as she spoke.
"It must have been tough on you when your father got ill.
Especially in those days when people didn't understand."

He almost laughed out loud at the words. *Your father
got ill.* That was an understated way of putting it if ever
there was one. For a moment his head was filled with the
sight and smell of that mountain of food, maggots and
flies.

"Yeah, it was." He pushed the image away and concentrated on the far more attractive one in front of him. "So
what about you? Do you enjoy teaching? Most people
would say it was a vocation rather than a job. Do you feel
that way about it?"

She grinned. The first real one he'd seen all evening,
and he was glad she was relaxing despite the seriousness
of their conversation so far. Somehow, he wasn't surprised
by that. He had a feeling that with Kelly, what you saw
was what you got. She wasn't the type of woman for playing games. *So just don't fuck it up, Black,* he told himself.
*If you know what's good for you, you won't piss this one
up the wall.*

She rolled the tall glass around between her hands, wiping away the condensation. "Yeah, I guess I do. The work-
load can be a pain, but every day brings something new.
You couldn't describe it as a dull job. And a school is
somewhere that you can really make a difference to people. Corny, huh?"

He held his hands up as if in surrender. "Hey, I think it
sounds great. I'd love to be able to make someone's life
better with what I do. It's a great gift you've got."

She shook her head, her face serious again. "Writers do
make people's lives better. A good book can change the

way people think about the world and themselves. At least being a writer, you don't have to face your failures close up. That's the tough bit about teaching. The holidays are great, but when stuff like this rape comes up, terrible things involving kids you know, then you wonder if you're letting down more than you're lifting up."

Rob reached across the table and took her hand. "That wasn't your fault, you know. That was just one of those awful things that happen."

Chewing the inside of her lip, Kelly nodded. "Yeah, I know that now. Apparently the kids didn't even know they were going to do it until it happened. They tried to kill themselves afterwards. God, what had they been thinking?" Her voice had lowered in the relative quiet of the bar, and she left her hand in his as she talked. "The whole thing has something weird about it."

She looked at him as if deciding whether he could be trusted or not. This time her voice was almost a whisper. "The boys told the police that the house was unlocked, but it couldn't have been. The keys were with the solicitors, and when the police went to check the scene out, all the doors were locked. How strange is that?"

Rob felt his heartbeat quickening, and wondered whether his palm was sweating into hers. *Curious things happening at Syracousse.* "Pretty strange, but I bet there's a logical explanation for it. There always is." His voice sounded calm and reassuring, as inside, his mind turned somersaults. He didn't need to be hearing this, he really didn't.

Kelly blushed slightly. "Yeah, I'm sure you're right. There's probably a good explanation for the lights, too."

Not wanting to know the answer, Rob heard himself asking, "What happened with the lights?"

"Well, this is going to sound really silly, but the kids said they'd turned one of the lights on in the house. But they couldn't have. The electricity was cut off ages ago. Freaky, huh?"

His head was starting to hurt, but he forced a smile after taking several long gulps of the beer. "Like I said, they'll find an explanation. Just remember crop circles. There's always a rational explanation for everything." Dear God, let them change the conversation now.

It seemed that Kelly felt the same way, as she almost visibly shook away her mood. "Yes. I'm sure you're right, although I'm a bit disappointed in your lack of imagination. Are you sure you wrote your books?"

He pulled his hand away and pretended to cuff her around the head with horror. "My dear, you go too far." His voice was pure Basil Rathbone, and she giggled happily.

They were on their third drink, deep in a comfortable conversation about a mutual love for fiction, when Jason came in. Finally relaxed and at ease, all thoughts of Syracousse pushed to the furthest corner of his mind, Rob didn't see him until the shadow falling across their table made them both look up. The woman standing behind Jason's slim frame had probably once been very pretty underneath all that over-bleached hair and lipstick. Jason didn't introduce her as Rob and Kelly politely nodded hello. He didn't acknowledge Kelly either, but instead leaned down on the table, blocking Rob's view of his date.

"I agree." His voice was clipped and curt, not inviting conversation. "We need to talk. I'll see you on Tuesday. We can talk after." Barely waiting for Rob's agreement, he left them and went to the bar to order a drink.

Watching him walk away, the unnamed woman behind him, Rob couldn't help wondering whether they were both seeking distractions. Both out, both with women. Maybe they were still more similar than they were willing to admit. Jason finally ordered his date a drink almost as an afterthought. She didn't seem to mind, though, as she stood there staring at him adoringly. She looked like someone who for years had admired from afar and then finally got her chance and couldn't believe it. He wondered whether Jason even noticed the way she was looking at him. Probably not. But then, Jason was another person who had never realized how good-looking he was. Jase had never really known his own goodness. Rob's heart ached for his long ago friend.

This time it was Kelly's hand that reached for his. "What happened to you guys? You two used to be so tight."

For a moment Rob was shaken, forgetting that Kelly had been there, an observer on the sidelines of his childhood. It felt strange. With everything that had gone on all that time ago, it had been easy to believe that no one else really existed. They'd been so caught up with what was happening around the four of them, the rest of the world had just been a gray, unimportant fog.

He frowned into his beer. "Just grew up I guess."

Kelly was gazing thoughtfully at the figure at the bar, shaking her head slightly. "It was weird. I wasn't the only one who noticed. You three were so close, and then Gina came along and by the start of the next school year, none of you wanted anything to do with each other."

Rob's blood rushed defensively to his face. "Yeah, well. That was a hell of a way to end a summer." His features drew in on themselves, and he tried to relax them as he shrugged. *Don't take it out on her, Black,* he counseled himself, but still the words came out barbed with sarcasm. "Then I went off to boarding school, and Gina left town never to be heard of again. I guess when your friend's mum stabs her dad to death it can change things. Life's funny like that." *Especially when you were there, especially after Teacher*, he wanted to add, but bit hard on his tongue to stop himself. Some secrets shouldn't be shared. Not after so much time.

His harsh tone seemed to run off Kelly, or perhaps she was too busy thinking to notice it. "I guess I just thought that something like that would have made your friendship stronger. Not with Gina; she wasn't like you three were, you three had been close forever. No one ever saw you when you came home on school holidays. The boys all thought you'd turned into a bit of a snob or something. I didn't, though. I'd seen how Jason and Carrie ignored each other and figured you'd all had some kind of huge row."

Rob raised an eyebrow. "I guess you could call it that." He drained his pint. "Anyway, to be honest I don't really remember, so can we change the subject now?"

Kelly smiled, and the innocence in her gentle face almost made him weep.

By the time they left at quarter to ten it was obvious that Jason was drunk, leaning precariously on the bar, laughing with the woman whose happy glow had revitalized a little of what beauty she must once have had. As Rob held the door open for Kelly, he wondered whether anyone else could hear the desperation in that over-loud sound. He pulled the door closed, embracing the cold air. He could think about Jason later. Jason was for Tuesday, not for now.

Kelly slid her arm through his, an action that surprised him, but caused a warm glow to run through his body, as they crossed the road for the short walk back to her house. It was only minutes before they were standing on her doorstep. They grinned at each other like a pair of teenagers. It was Kelly who broke the silence. "Thank you for a lovely evening. I really enjoyed it."

Rob gave a small bow. "I aim to please. Anyway, it was great having someone intelligent to talk to. Intelligent and beautiful isn't a combination I've come across much recently." He watched her face for a moment before speaking, softly this time. "So are you going to say goodnight and get into the warm, or am I allowed to kiss you first?"

Her small smile gave him his answer, and he moved forward, taking her face in his hands, kissing her gently and slowly, enjoying the feel of her warm body so close to his. He could feel himself becoming aroused, and no doubt she could too, but he resisted the urge to kiss her harder and pull her closer, instead, gently breaking away. This wasn't a situation he wanted to rush, and he had a feeling that if he pushed too hard, she'd run away and that was something he definitely didn't want. From what little he knew of her, he'd bet that Kelly Hollingsworth had had her fair share of shit from men.

Looking at her standing there on the doorstep, flushed and uncertain, he suddenly felt as if maybe spending the whole of your life with just one woman could be a pleasant possibility. The thought terrified and excited him. Not wanting to spoil the magical moment with unnecessary words or bad timing, he took a step backwards. "You get back in the warm. Will I see you on Tuesday? Are you going to the funeral?"

Kelly nodded. "I'll be there. It'll be the most original second date I've ever had."

Rob laughed and started walking away. "Well, you can't say I don't know how to show a girl a good time!" He heard her laugh just before the door shutting silenced the sound. He was still smiling as he strolled up Dulverton Road toward his own house. She'd said second date. And that couldn't be a bad thing. Maybe something good was going to emerge out of coming home, after all.

Kelly left her shoes downstairs and padded upstairs in her bare feet, not wanting to wake her father. It was only just gone ten so he probably wasn't quite asleep yet, but she didn't want to take any chances. Tabby got them up early in the mornings and after a whole weekend of her, Jack was normally pretty exhausted. She'd be tired herself if her mind wasn't racing with the memory of that kiss. It had been quite a while since her last one, but if memory served her correctly, Rob Black's effort had to be pretty high on the list of best kisses ever. *Still,* she warned her racing heart, *he's had enough practice.*

Quietly pushing open Tabby's door, she stepped into the pale, almost green glow of the small nightlight and sat down on her daughter's bed. "Goodnight, baby," she whispered, not expecting a reply.

Tabby's eyes blearily opened, still half asleep. "What's Granddad's secret?" she mumbled. "Why does he have a secret from us?" Her serious, sleep-scrunched face looked at Kelly for a moment before her eyes closed again, sinking her back to oblivion with a tiny sigh.

Kelly watched her daughter for a few seconds, making sure she'd drifted off again, before standing up. What a curious thing to have said. Maybe she'd been having a bad dream or something. Children's minds were such funny things. Carefully closing the door behind her, Kelly made her way to her own room and peeled off her clothes in the dark, before tumbling into bed.

CHAPTER EIGHTEEN

By Monday morning, the chill in the previous night's dark air had settled on the ground as a hard frost, and by eight forty-five it still wasn't showing any signs of melting away into the bright sunlight.

Standing outside Judge Matthews's house, watching the locksmith work, Jason stamped his feet a little to ward away numbness as the cold worked its way through the canvas of his sneakers. He sniffed and watched his breath vanish in front of him. Christ, it was cold. Okay, so it was nearly November, but this kind of freezing weather was normally reserved for mid-January. The tops of his ears ached, which at least distracted him from the pain of his hangover, although the drilling wasn't helping.

After setting the shop up, he'd taken five minutes to go up to the Health Center and see what Social Services was going to do about the judge. The memory of their encounter had unsettled him for the whole weekend, and he wasn't sure whether he was checking for his own peace of mind or out of concern for the crazy old guy, but whichever it was, he needed to know if the situation had been resolved.

Well, surprise, surprise, it turned out that Bob hadn't bothered going there at all. He must have just gone off to vent his steam somewhere, probably over a pint of cider. Standing in the surgery, telling the overworked doctor that he'd go and check on Mr. Matthews himself and then call the authorities, Jason had cursed his ape of a workmate for being the selfish, ignorant fuck that he was, before realizing, with a sense of relief, that at least they were even now. Old man Green wouldn't like to hear about this. He was old enough to have plenty of respect for the elderly, especially a man like the judge. He'd kick Bob's fat arse from here to Old Streatford if he got wind of this fuckup.

The door of the adjacent house swung open, and Daisy emerged with two steaming mugs of tea. Jason took one gratefully, his red hands for a moment in pain with the shock of sudden contact with heat, before the warmth started to seep through. He saw Daisy glance at his scars, but it didn't bother him. They didn't seem to bother her either as she turned her gaze to the locksmith, her gloved hands clutching her drink, her body wrapped up warm in a red, padded jacket.

"How much longer?" Jason asked, as the man rifled through his tools.

"Nearly done now." The man didn't look up, probably eager to finish up and get back to the warmth of his van. Jason couldn't blame him.

Feeling Daisy's arm brush against his, he looked down and gave her a small smile. She returned it, but Jason knew they weren't fooling each other. Neither of them was keen to find out what had happened on the other side of the lock. Daisy had come outside when she'd heard Jason banging furiously on the door next to hers, and her face had been sad then. She said that she hadn't seen Ernest— it felt weird to hear someone call the judge by his first name—for days and had been thinking about calling Social Services today. He hadn't been himself, she said, a phrase that endeared the old lady to Jason instantly. *He hadn't been himself.* Oh no, he definitely hadn't been himself. Jason had nodded and said that he'd seen Mr. Matthews last week and was worried. They had looked at each other and had a moment of complete understanding, before Daisy carried on.

He'd stopped answering the door to her, she had said, her eyes averted so Jason couldn't see the hurt there. But she hadn't been too worried because she'd heard him pottering around on the other side of the walls, all hours of the day and night. But the past day or so, she'd heard nothing, no matter how hard she tried. She was silent for a moment, before shaking herself and declaring that they both needed a nice, sweet cup of tea. Jason had just nodded, pleased that the tough old lady hadn't sought any reassurances. He didn't have any to give.

He had just taken the last swallow from his mug when the locksmith tapped the door open. "There you go. It's all yours. That'll be thirty quid please." He looked at the two of them, and Jason realized with rising embarassment that he didn't have any money.

"Thank you." Looking down at Daisy, he saw she'd pulled her purse from her pocket and taken out three crisp ten-pound notes for the man who was now stuffing them into his back pocket and gathering his tools.

Jason fought hard to swallow his shame. "Look, I'll drop that money to you this afternoon." he started, before she shook her head firmly, her face adamant. "Ernest Matthews is my friend. You've done enough by showing your concern. You're a very good young man, and I thank you for that." The sincerity and strength in her voice took Jason by surprise. It had been a long time since someone had anything that nice to say about him, and it choked him for a second. *A very good young man.*

143

He squeezed her arm. "Some people may not agree with you on that one, but thank you anyway."

They both stared at the door that now stood ajar, waiting for someone to enter, and Jason knew who that person should be. "You stay here." His own voice was firm, and when he moved away, she didn't follow. *Well, here goes,* he thought, as he gently pushed the door wide, his stomach filled with trepidation, and for a moment, as he stepped into the glare of the hallway, the lights bright above him, what he expected to see was an enormous, stinking pyramid of food, life oozing from its edges.

But of course, that day was long past, and the first thing he noticed in the judge's house, was the fine layer of dust that seemed to cover the carpet and stairs in front of him. He frowned a little with distaste. Jesus, how long would you have to leave your house for this much dirt to accumulate?

Tilting his head up the stairway, he saw that all the lights were blazing on the landing there, too. "Judge Matthews?" he called, his voice sounding strange in the quiet. Maybe he'd slipped in the shower or something. Unsure of whether to go up and look, he decided to check down here first. There was something too personal about the upstairs of strangers' houses. Even when he'd taken up burglary for that short spell—*Old Daisy wouldn't think you were such a good young man if she knew about that, would she?*—he'd always stayed downstairs. He guessed it didn't feel so much like someone else's house and possessions that way. Standing here now he wondered who he'd been trying to kid.

Taking a deep breath, he opened the door to his left and went into the long lounge. It obviously went around into an L-shape, no doubt there was a kitchen there, hidden from view, but Jason figured he wasn't going to have to look in there. He'd found what he was looking for. Oh boy, had he found it. His legs carried him forward—just where the fuck had all this dust come from—across the full length of the sitting room, until he was standing a few feet away from the patio doors. Outside, the perfectly manicured lawn waited for its owner to come outside and tend to its needs. It was going to be waiting an awfully long time, Jason thought absently, as his shocked eyes drifted downwards to the figure at his feet. He shouldn't have died like this. Not a man like he was. Jesus.

The emaciated body was curled up under the patio door, its knees pulled up to the chin, the pale, stick-thin legs emerging from a pair of baggy underpants. The face—he couldn't think of it as Judge Matthews's face— was turned upwards, its grimace frozen forever in time, the eyes completely red, like some kind of monster's eyes would be in a kid's story. *He must have burst every blood vessel in his eyeballs. Every single last one.* One thin arm was slumped over the head as if he'd been reaching for the door when it happened. Jason took the handle and slid the glass open a little. It was unlocked. So what had the old man been trying to do? Though eager to be out in that cold, fresh, untainted air, Jason reluctantly pulled the door shut again. His hands were shaking, the numbness of his initial shock slowly wearing off. Looking down at the body again, he saw that some of the grayness was caused by the dust, which looked as if it had been rubbed into the skin. Underneath it, Jason could see raw patches of irritation. Just why the hell would he have rubbed dust into himself? What would make him do that?

With widening eyes, he looked at the house around him, at the dust that covered every surface. This was too organized to be abandoned dirt. So what the hell was it?

His own words flashed into his head, and his legs started to twitch beneath him as he gazed around in disbelief.

Maybe I can help. I can come round with a friend and some ant powder and give the house a good going over.

This wasn't dust. It was ant powder, and Jesus, he'd given the old man the idea.

Syracousse. They're coming from Syracousse.

Fear and bile were rising in equal measure as Jason took a step backwards, his eyes beginning to water. *Syracousse. Guilt. Blame. Secrets.* Just what the fuck was going on here? A low, moan started deep inside him.

"Oh, Christ."

The clear, crisp voice behind him made Jason stumble backwards, banging his hip painfully into the breakfast bar. The pain rattled exquisitely through him, but he was glad of it. The relief of seeing Daisy there behind him was enough to make him almost giggle. "Jesus, you scared the shit out of me!"

She glanced up at him, and then went back to staring at her dead friend. "Sorry. I just couldn't wait out there any longer." She let out a long sigh, a sigh that told of the sadness behind that practical exterior, and Jason wished he could have her grief, any amount of grief, if only it meant a release from the terrible fear that was eating at him.

Daisy pushed her hands into her coat pocket. "I'll go and phone an ambulance. Will you wait with me?" Jason nodded.

"Then come on then. This is no place for the living." He followed her out, glad to get away from the madness. He had someone he needed to phone, too.

CHAPTER NINETEEN

By the time he'd had a quick shower, it was ten o'clock. Rob turned on his laptop and clicked the Word icon, before going to make himself a pot of coffee. The kitchen was warm, and as he waited for the black liquid to filter into the coffee pot, he stared through the window at the frosty land outside. He smiled. There was something comforting about winter weather, especially when you were on the inside looking out. He'd slept in longer than usual, but his rest had been dreamless, and judging by how refreshed he felt this morning, he must have needed it.

Something else was having a pretty major contribution to his upbeat mood, and that was the kiss he'd shared with Kelly the night before. He was feeling pretty good about that. Who was he kidding? She was the last thing he'd thought about before he'd drifted off and the first thing he'd thought about as he opened his eyes to the tranquillity of all that whiteness upstairs. Even with all that shit she said about the rape; the lights, the locked doors, all the stuff that had gotten hold of a quiet place in his mind and wasn't letting go, he still felt pretty damned great about the evening.

Pouring himself a mug of Columbia's second favorite export, he was grinning like a love-struck teenager. *Just enjoy it, Black. Enjoy it while it lasts, because no doubt it won't be long before you fuck it up. Anyway, I thought you weren't really in a position for any new relationships.* Raising an eyebrow at himself, knowing there was probably truth in the thought, he moved back to the wooden table and sat down. The book was slowly taking shape, and it was time to get down to some serious graft. Anyway, switching off from the real world and getting lost in one of his own making, was good for the soul. It was like therapy without the bill.

Putting his coffee down, he brought his attention to the screen. Weird. It was still blank, with only the small white cursor flashing in the top left-hand corner awaiting instructions. Muttering in frustration, he tried the Enter key, and then pressed the On button again. It shouldn't have crashed; the sleek model was supposed to be top of the line. Well, top of the line for six months ago anyway, which, he figured, meant by a technofreak's standards it was now a granddaddy.

Staring in mounting annoyance at that tiny white flashing line, he got up and shimmied along the wall to the outlet, where he flicked off the switch. Still leaning over he waited for the sound of the machine switching itself off, but the hum continued. Swearing, he yanked the plug out completely. That should fucking do it. He hated any delay to his work, and always feared that the pages he would have written without any distraction would be so much better than the ones he finally got down on the screen. Maybe Michael was right when he'd jokingly called him anal.

Standing up straight he noticed that the hum was still there, and his anger faded into confusion as he saw the white line still flashing rebelliously against the black. Just what the fuck was going on here? Glancing down by his feet, he checked that he pulled out the right plug, and followed the disconnected cable with his eyes until it vanished into the back of the IBM. Just what the fuck was this? How could it still be on?

Sitting back down, he wondered whether there was a faulty connection and somehow the computer had switched to battery. But if so, then where the hell was the Windows screen? It didn't make sense.

Suddenly, the hum mounted into a high-pitched squeal, and just before Rob expected to see smoke rising from the back, the screen burst into action, the words appearing from nowhere as if someone were typing on his keyboard faster than he could see.

MAKE HER COME HOME MAKE HER COME HOME MAKE HER COME HOME HOME HOME HOME HOME HOME HOME HOME HOME HOME HOME HOME HOME HOME HOME HOME HOME HOME

The word was filling up the screen, getting faster and faster, too rapid for his eyes to keep up with, and it was as if he could hear it screaming in his head as each word appeared, defying the thought that *this was not real, this was not real,* and then just before he thought it was going to consume him, the coffee pot on the breakfast bar exploded, sending the hot liquid and glass everywhere, splattering the table in front of him, sending him backwards in his chair, banging his head hard on the wall behind. And then there was silence.

Slowly sitting upright, his skull throbbing from the impact, he felt the breath trapped in his chest and forced it out. Jesus Christ. Jesus fucking Christ. Looking at the brown liquid that trickled between the keys of the laptop, he noticed with dazed recognition that the computer had finally turned itself off. He slammed the lid down with disgust, before turning to gaze at the mess that was his kitchen. Coffee had hit just about every cupboard and surface in the room, trickling down the side of the fridge and the stove. The floor glittered with tiny shards of glass. He laughed slightly, a hollow sound. Just what the fuck was going on? What the fuck was going on?

His heart pounded heavily in his chest as he stood up and went to the coffee machine, his shoes crunching on the broken glass beneath them. He'd just reached it when the phone began to ring, making him whirl round, dangerously close to slipping on the wet floor. He stared at it for a few seconds before carefully picking up the reciever. What now? What the hell now? He didn't think he could take any more surreal messages. Not now, not ever.

His voice was slow and cautious. "Hello?"

"Rob? Jason." Exhilaration flooded through his body. Jason. It was Jason. A real, live breathing person. Thank Christ. Thank Christ for that. His relief was only momentary.

"It's Judge Matthews. He's dead. I found him this morning." He paused, maybe waiting for a response, but Rob wasn't capable of giving one and Jason continued, "I saw him last week, and he said some stuff to me. Stuff about the house, about the four of us. Stuff he couldn't know." He let out a sigh, a sigh that echoed Rob's own fear. "I think we need to talk. We need to talk about Teacher, and I don't think I can wait until tomorrow."

Gazing at the wreck of his kitchen, Rob fought the urge to giggle. He bit it back before speaking. "Yeah, you're right. I think we seriously need to talk. Something just happened here that you wouldn't believe."

Jason didn't ask what and Rob figured they both had their own fears to fight today. Whatever had happened to the judge, Jason obviously wasn't ready for any more weird stuff on his plate. Rob knew how he felt. Suddenly, the idea of talking to Jason was very appealing. He didn't think it was possible for two people to go mad together, and his sanity was something he needed to feel secure in. "Do you want to come over now?"

"I can't. The ambulance has just left with the body, and

I've got some more stuff to do." This time his pause was awkward, and when he spoke, Rob knew why.

"Can you see if you can get hold of Gina somehow? I think you've got a better chance with those solicitors than I do. I'm not sure that we can get to the bottom of this shit without her."

Rob's stomach sank, but in his gut he knew Jase was right. "I can try."

Now that they were in agreement, Jason sounded more confident. Fear was obviously better shared than kept to oneself.

"Okay, you do that, and I'll come over this evening."

It was only when he'd put the phone down, that the words flashed in Rob's head again. *MAKE HER COME HOME.*

Pulling a dustpan and brush out from under the sink, suddenly exhausted as his body calmed down, he decided that if that's what it would take to get this shit to stop, then that's what he'd do. Make them come home. As he started to clear up the mess, he wondered how much his coming home actually had been his decision. Who or what had made him come home?

CHAPTER TWENTY

Shaking off the cold in the tiny hallway, Jack Hollingsworth hung up his granddaughter's tiny coat and then swallowed it up with his own, before ushering her into the kitchen for orange juice and cookies. As he got their drinks ready, he whistled happily. He loved this time he had alone with Tabby before Kelly got home. He knew that his daughter—and it didn't seem so long ago that she'd been Tabby's age—worried that it was too much of a burden on him, and no matter how much he tried to convince her otherwise, any fool could see the concern on her face that maybe he was overdoing things. He'd been sorely tempted on several occasions to tell her exactly the same thing, but it seemed that those kind of wise comments were the preserve of the young. He smiled wryly. And so the parent becomes the child. Well, there was still plenty of parent left in this old dog, and the truth of the matter was that he loved looking after Tabitha. Being around her kept him young, and anything that did that with so much charm was all right by him.

They sat at the kitchen table, and he watched as the

child in question drank her juice and nibbled on a chocolate digestive. Kelly would kill him if she ever knew how many he let Tabby have, but hey, wasn't that the kind of thing foolish old granddads were supposed to do?

He sipped his tea. "Remember that tomorrow afternoon you're going to Emma's house to play after school." Tabby insisted on calling her nursery "school." "Your mummy and I have to go somewhere, but we'll be back as soon as we can." They'd decided against telling Tabby about the funeral. There were some things that children should only be introduced to when it was relevant to them, and until it was someone she knew, neither Kelly nor himself thought it was necessary to talk to her about death. Children were curious, and Kelly wasn't happy about the possibility of her baby asking about how Carole-Anne had died. Jack could understand why. If he were honest, he hadn't wanted to go at all, but Kelly had been adamant. They'd been at school together and no matter what Carole-Anne had done, it would be awful to be buried with no one there to show respect. It had all sounded plausible enough, but Jack figured that Kelly's insistence had more to do with that other old school friend of hers, the writer.

Staring at Tabby, he realized that given their tiny family, the first funeral she attended would probably be his. It gave him a vaguely unsettled feeling for a moment, before he brushed it away. It would be the natural course of things, and he had no plans for popping his clogs just yet, no matter how much his hip ached, reminding him that the bottom of his personal hourglass was much fuller than the top.

Tabby was still nibbling absently at her cookie, and Jack wondered whether maybe she was coming down with something. She'd been very quiet since he'd picked her up. Normally, she'd be chirping away about what she'd done or whom she'd played with, but today she'd barely said a word. It was strange, not like her at all.

"Are you okay, sweetheart?"

She nodded, but as he refilled his teacup he could see her out of the corner of his eye, staring at him warily.

"Do you have a secret, Granddad?" Her voice was calm and low, and Jack's hand froze for a second before he carefully put the teapot down.

He tried to smile a little. "Everyone has secrets, Tabby. You've probably got a couple. Private thoughts you want to keep all to yourself."

Shaking her head impatiently, she kept her eyes firmly fixed on his. "Not that kind of secret. A guilty secret. A shameful secret."

Staring at Tabby, Jack felt his throat go dry. The words didn't sound like hers, they were too old for her, and he wondered angrily who'd given them to her, who'd been speaking to her. *Nobody. Nobody knows. Nobody could have told her.*

Lifting his mug to his face to hide his fear, he was unsure of what to say. "Why do you ask, sweetheart?" Under the strength of her gaze, he felt as if he were caught in a game of cat and mouse. It was ridiculous, but that's how he felt. A game of cat and mouse, and he wasn't the cat.

She put the half-eaten cookie down on her plate. "Have you? Have you got a secret from Mummy and me?"

Jack felt his stomach twist and lurch. It was nothing, just the curiosity of a child hitting a raw nerve, reopening scars, making them bleed a little. It was nothing. She couldn't know. It wasn't possible. And it was all so long ago. A lifetime ago. An old secret, a secret dead a long time. There had been a time when it had eaten him up, but not anymore. Now, there was just the ghost of shame that sometimes visited him in the long, sleepless nights of the old.

He shook his head. "No, darling. I would never keep a secret from you or your mother. Never." From behind the steam that rose from his tea, he thought for a moment that he saw a dark cloud pass in her eyes, a cloud too knowing for such a little girl. He shook off the feeling. *That's your own guilt talking, old man.* She couldn't know. Neither of them could know. And that's the way he intended it to stay.

CHAPTER TWENTY-ONE

The inside of the solicitor's office overlooking Market Square was as bland as the face of the overweight man on the other side of the modern gray desk. Rob had been waiting in reception for twenty minutes by the time the man actually called him in and his already frayed mood wasn't tempered by the knowledge that he'd been kept waiting for no good reason. No one left the office before he entered, and he severely doubted that this little place had a back entrance to stop important clients from being noticed by the proletariat. No, he knew what game the little man was playing, and he also knew that there were better and more effective ways of letting someone know that they were not impressed by money and celebrity.

He gritted his teeth and smiled as he held his hand out. "Mr. Greenslade?" The solicitor stood up, revealing that a surprisingly large expanse of stomach lurked beneath that thin, pasty face.

"Mr. Black. Pleased to meet you. Sorry to keep you waiting." He indicated a chair and sat down again before Rob did. This guy would never survive in the big city, and

Rob wondered why Gina would have left the management of her affairs in his hands. "What can I do for you today?" His attitude so far may not have been, but his smile was most certainly obsequious. He should be a maitre d' in a second-rate Italian restaurant, Rob mused, before leaning forward in his chair, eager to get on.

"I'd like you to pass a message on to Gina Grace for me."

He shook his bald head, his smile adapting itself to suit a small child, as he played with the gold signet ring on one of his interlocked fingers. "I'm afraid that Miss Grace has no desire to have any contact with her past. I'm sure you understand."

Rob resisted the urge to thump the squashy face. "Well, that may be so, but I need to discuss an urgent matter with her. Can't you just call her and give her my phone number? I think she's old enough to make the decision to speak to me or not all by herself."

Mr. Greenslade coughed quietly. "Actually, Mr. Black, Miss Grace converses with me through a London solicitor. Any contact has to be made through him." Rob's smile grew. That made sense. This guy was actually the bottom of the food chain, and the blush running through his face said that he knew he'd been found out.

Rob tried to keep his voice civil. "So call him. Tell him to call her. It's important that I speak to her. Tell her it's about Teacher. She'll understand." Taking a piece of paper and a pen from the box of Post-its by the phone, he scribbled his number down, and handed it to Greenslade. "Call him."

"I'm afraid I couldn't possibly do it now, I'm expecting a client. I'll try this afternoon, but I wouldn't expect a response. Miss Grace has always been very adamant on this subject."

His patience wearing thin, Rob stood up. "Well, maybe you could give me his number. I can try him. Save you the time."

On the other side of the desk, Greenslade also stood, drawing himself up to his full rotund five-foot-something height. Rob glowered down at him, knowing what he was about to say.

"I'm afraid I'm unable to give out that information. Like I said, I'll try to contact them this afternoon." Pulling up his cuffs, he examined his watch. "Now I'm afraid I'm really going to have to ask you to leave. Time is marching on."

Rob was already pulling open the door and looking out into the empty reception area. "Thank you very much for your time, Mr. Greenslade. Much appreciated." He already closed the door behind him by the time the solicitor told him it had been a pleasure.

Standing outside on the cobbles, under the watchful gaze of a bronze John Wesley, Rob swore aloud. Jesus, why did the world have to be full of so many pricks? Maybe he should have been more honest with the pompous arse. He could just imagine it.

"Hi, Mr. Fat Fuck Greenslade, I wonder if you can help me get in touch with Gina Grace. You see, people are dying in horrible ways and my computer's talking to me and I think wherever she is, she's doing it. Why do I think that? Oh, of course, you weren't there, were you? You weren't there when it all happened before. How silly of me."

Yeah, he could just imagine what the solicitor would have made of that little tirade. That would have gone down well. Jesus, what a mess. He wasn't even sure he wanted Gina to get in touch, although he was pretty sure Greenslade would pass on the message. That was his job, after all. Message boy and maintenance man. Rob took a long, deep breath as he started his walk home. Well, maybe that wasn't entirely true. Part of him was excited at the thought of Gina all grown up. Another part of him was apprehensive. Well, it was out of his hands now. He'd done his bit. From here on in, they'd just have to wait and see.

Jason pressed Play on the CD system and waited for the mellow, chill-out album to seep into the room before pouring himself a drink, sitting on the tatty brown and black sofa and rubbing his eyes with a weary hand. Even in daylight, the tiny flat retained a gloomy air. He put his glass on the side table and flicked the switch on the lamp, hoping it would help dispel those shadows in his mind as much as the ones in the corners of the room.

Holy fuck, what a day. Every time he shut his eyes all he could see was that old man, curled up so pathetically in his goddamn underpants, covered in ant powder. His body had been cold, too fucking cold to want to touch, like old bread dough or something. And those awful, red open eyes. At least the ambulance guys had closed them before they'd taken the judge—had that really been the judge?—away. But they weren't closed in his head. In his head he had a feeling that they'd be open forever.

Leaning back in his seat, no energy left to keep himself upright, he stared idly around at the shithole he called home. Yeah, it was clean, he was pretty fastidious about that—hey, he'd been in that attic, he'd seen what rotten food could turn into—and he'd done his best to decorate within his limited means, but however hard he tried, it was always going to be a shitty little flat in Gallows Hill.

Was this where he would have ended up, regardless of that summer? Had his dreams of better things been only that, wasted dreams? Probably. Carrie didn't exactly make good on hers either. Maybe they'd always been meant to remain scum. Maybe that's just what happened to people like them. He lit a cigarette and watched its smoke trails in the air before taking a long sip of his whiskey and water.

Well, at least he'd had those dreams once, tenuous or not. Had they died with Philip Grace? No, not then. Philip Grace had just been a grownup, a person they passed sometimes on the way out Gina's door, or as his car drove past them on the lane, they returning to their lives, he returning to his. No, his dreams were dead before Philip Grace. His dreams died when the magic went sour, two long weeks or more before the summer ended with blood on the kitchen floor. His dreams had died with Teacher.

Sighing, the pain as fresh as if it had happened yesterday, he pulled out his wallet and carefully took out the battered and faded photo. It shook in his hands as he stared. Philip Grace had taken it; he'd taken one for each of them. A picture of the four of them and Teacher, early in that summer when everything was good, before the scars that showed on his hands and hurt in his heart.

His breath caught in his chest, as he sunk into the image, and despite the ache inside that made him want to put it right away again in the back of his wallet from where he never took it out, never looked at it, hiding the too-painful memory away, he blinked back the emotion and remembered.

They'd been hanging out with Gina for maybe three weeks when Teacher arrived. During that time the three of them had decided Gina was pretty cool, even if she was a bit unreadable and aloof. She'd changed them too, or maybe it was just time that had changed them, setting their hormones racing, growing them up against their will. Carrie had turned into something of a wanna-be girl and they didn't seem to get so dirty anymore, probably because Gina never wanted to climb trees or have play fights or stuff like that, and because she didn't, neither did Carrie, and so neither did he or Rob, because they didn't exactly want her to see them as a pair of kids. Nope, if Gina didn't want to do it, whatever it was, then it just didn't happen. And nobody minded.

But then, Gina was beautiful and clever, probably cleverer even than Rob and that was saying something. More than that, she was special. After the thing with the glass, they hadn't been able to stay away.

Yeah, magic like that had lured them back, and it wasn't just the glass. As the weeks passed, other weird shit happened, and they had the feeling that whatever power Gina had, it was beginning to rub off on them. Like the time Jason had been sliding helplessly down the muddy bank to the pond, his foot tangled up with aggressive weeds, his body tumbling forward to the murky water, all balance lost, and then suddenly he was free, his feet resting on a newly dry patch of ground, the weeds dead and shriveled up, lying harmlessly by his sneakers.

And then there was the hot sunny afternoon that Rob wound Carrie up about some boy at school to the point when her fiery temper was boiling over and she was cursing loudly at him to shut up. He didn't, of course, and she went to smack him hard in the mouth, her hand too quick for him even to think about ducking away. Carrie never missed a shot like that, tomboy that she was she'd had plenty of practice, but she just couldn't connect, her arm changing direction at the last minute, sending her reeling around in a circle, her face a picture of dumbfounded confusion. She tried again and the same thing happened, by which time they were all laughing so hard, that her anger had evaporated into tears of mirth.

It seemed there'd been a lot of laughter in the early days of that long summer. Easy smiles stretched out in the warm grass, the sun on their backs. They never went to Rob's place anymore apart from maybe to pick up a record or a football or something while the girls were at the library; it just didn't have the same comforting feeling that whiling away the time at Syracousse did. In fact, they never really went anywhere else, the rest of the world had faded to a pale shimmer, and even if they'd planned to go to the Rec or to the river, it never seemed to happen. They'd find themselves heading down that dusty track to the small side gate by the tree as if they were drawn there, and maybe they were. They felt happy within the walled confines of the house and even Rob, after all the shit that had happened in the attic, seemed to find peace and the tattered remnants of his childhood at Syracousse.

One afternoon, they'd been up at the top of the house

in Gina's bedroom listening to the new Bay City Rollers album, the girls lounging on her double bed, he and Rob leaning up against the long walls of the room that was bigger than his mum's lounge up at Gallows Hill, when Mr. Grace got home. His deep voice calling Gina's name drifted up the elegant stairway. He was early. Normally he would just pass the three of them on their way out the door saying farewell with a smile and a nod, and that was only on the occasions that they didn't use the side gate in the garden. And they never usually left until about seven, just before Mrs. Grace got dinner out of the oven in perfect timing with her husband's arrival home from London, so something had to be up for him to be back before five.

Turning the record player off, Gina opened the door and ran down the stairs, leaving them to follow her, unsure of what else to do. It wouldn't be polite to stay in her room without her, and anyway, Philip Grace sounded pretty excited about something and Jason knew that the others were just as keen as he was to find out why. With a quick glance of agreement, they shut the door behind them and ran. Catching up with Gina at the bottom of the stairs, they stared at the tall, handsome figure holding a large cardboard box, which seemed to wobble in his arms; whatever was inside shifting from end to end. Gina was clapping her hands excitedly. "Is it a kitten, Daddy? Have you gotten me a kitten?" Her voice was almost a squeal, and Jason realized he'd never seen her so unreserved, so childlike.

Her father smiled, enjoying her reaction. "Well, let's all go into the kitchen and see, shall we?" Walking just behind them, Jason felt his heart pounding. What was it? What had he brought home?

Placing the box carefully on the kitchen table, Philip ignored the glare that flashed from his wife, and slowly lifted the flaps. Reaching in, he pulled out a tiny golden ball of fur, long ears flopping over the deep brown eyes, a tiny pink tongue hanging from its mouth, as the bundle of paws and tail let out a small squeak that might one day be a bark. "So what do you think? You'll have to be careful with him, he's only about six weeks old."

The light in Gina's eyes faded a little, and the disappointment was clear in her voice. "I thought it was going to be a kitten."

Camilla, leaning her elegant frame against the counter let out a long, tired sigh. "You should have talked to me about this first, Philip."

Still holding the small animal, Mr. Grace looked from his daughter to his wife, mild hurt and annoyance in his face. "But I wanted it to be a surprise. Most children would give their right arm for a puppy, isn't that right boys?" Jason couldn't take his eyes off the small animal, but he nodded slowly. A puppy. It was all he'd ever wanted, but there was no chance in hell he'd ever get one from his mother. Philip Grace had brought home a puppy. He could see Rob beaming from the corner of his eye. Yeah, Rob obviously thought it was pretty cool too, but nothing like he did. Taking a hesitant step forward, he reached out and stroked the cotton wool fur, feeling the warm breath on his hand. Philip Grace lowered the dog to the floor and Jason bent down with him, fussing the tiny creature, almost oblivious to the heated conversation above him.

Camilla's voice was sharp. "That doesn't change the fact that you should have talked to me about it. We agreed on a kitten. That *is* what she wanted after all. But you had to go and get a dog. I hope to hell it's house-trained."

"Of course it's not bloody housetrained, it's six weeks old. Anyway, it can spend most of the day in the garden while the weather's good. I don't see what your problem is."

The harsh sounds were making the little dog nervous and Jason softly soothed it. He loved the dog from that moment, watching it sitting there unsure on the kitchen floor, the floor that would soon be covered with its owner's blood, unsure and wanting only to be loved. The row raged above them in soft controlled voices leaking bitterness.

"They're so damned messy! It's going to be dragging in dirt from the garden all day and I'm going to end up spending my life mopping up after it. We agreed on a cat, Philip. I don't even like dogs, but of course you didn't take that into consideration, did you? And judging by Gina's face, I don't think she's particularly keen either. Why couldn't you just think about somebody else for a change?"

Jason could see Carrie's feet shuffling awkwardly in the tense atmosphere, and he scooped the puppy up in his arms. "Shall we take him outside, Mr. Grace?"

The man nodded, his eyes fixed angrily on his wife. Rob had swiftly opened the back door and stepped outside with Carrie, Gina close behind them. None of them were used to any kind of disharmony here and wanted to get away from it quickly, so they could pretend the argument had never happened. Jason paused in the doorway. "Don't worry, Mrs. Grace. I'll house-train him. I'll try to make sure he doesn't bring any mud into your kitchen either."

Her beautiful face gave him a wan smile. "Thank you, Jason. That's very kind. Now run along outside, I'll bring you some drinks out soon." Jason nodded, and then stepped into the warm breeze.

Joining the others on the rug, happy to be away from the awful tension inside, he put the puppy down. Carrie and Rob laughed and fussed him with Jason, the dog slowly relaxing and starting to play, nipping them with tiny sharp hot teeth. Gina petted it a little, but wouldn't let it clamber on her, not wanting to get puppy drool on her dress.

Gently pushing the excited face away from where it was trying to chew his ear, Jason smiled at Gina. "What do you want to call him?"

The pretty girl shrugged. "I don't know. You decide."

Carrie was giggling as paws scrabbled at her back to reach her hair. "I think we should call him Teacher."

Rob snorted. "What kind of a name is that for a dog? We can't call him that, it's stupid!"

"I like it. I think it's pretty cool." Jason was rubbing the small round upturned belly and his words were soft. "I think he deserves an unusual name."

Tucking her thick hair behind her ear, Gina raised an eyebrow. "Okay. We'll call him Teacher." The little puppy yapped, almost in approval, and even Gina laughed.

Over the next few weeks, Gina and her mother got used to having Teacher around, but they never really took to him as the others did, and even Rob and Carrie, who loved the little dog as if it were their own, didn't love him as much as Jason. Nobody could. Even Philip Grace, whose life barely touched those of the visiting children, grudgingly admitted that if the daft ball of fur belonged to anyone, that person was Jason. The dog loved him as much as he loved it. But then, it was Jason who spent every possible moment there playing with him, trying to house-train him so Camilla Grace wouldn't hit Teacher with a broom, and on those occasions when he had an over-excited accident, it would be Jason who quickly cleaned it up so that no one would notice.

As Teacher got bigger and clumsier, his fur losing its baby coat, growing instead in long waves of silky gold, Jason loved him more and more. He would get out of bed an hour early on school days so he could take the dog down to the river, as neither Gina nor her mother had shown any interest in taking him for a walk, and Philip Grace had to leave early to get to work. Sometimes Rob would get his lazy arse out of bed and join them, but mainly it was just him and Teach, and although he'd never tell Rob, that was the way he liked it best. Just the two of them and the smell of fresh warm summer's air, the smell that only the very beginning of a day can have, untainted by events, new to the world.

When they got back to the house, Jason would carefully

rub Teacher down with a towel, making sure he was dried off from any dips in the river, and then saying good-bye to him in the garden, he'd leave through the side gate and head off to pick up Rob on the way to school. Sometimes, he wouldn't see Gina at all during those morning visits, and although he still thought she was the most beautiful thing he'd ever seen and was completely in love with her in an awestruck kind of way, he was sad that she didn't love Teacher like he did. And the bigger he got, the more Teacher seemed to annoy her. She couldn't stand it when he jumped up at her, or shook his glorious wet, musty fur, splashing her, and Jason wondered how much of that came from Mrs. Grace.

Although the woman was never cruel to the dog, Jason knew she didn't particularly like him, and she'd even asked him once if he'd like to take Teacher home and keep him. Oh, that had hurt his heart. There was nothing in the world Jason would have liked more, but there was no way his mother would allow it. Sometimes, he would lie awake in his tiny shoebox bedroom and hug his pillow to him imagining that it was thick, warm fur he was burying his face into. The thought would help him sleep over the sound of his mother and whoever was in the room next door.

It was after a Sunday afternoon walk down by the river, when Carrie had to leave early to help her mum with something or other, that he'd dried Teacher off and then gone into the kitchen to get himself and the dog a drink, and seen Rob kissing Gina through the kitchen window. Staring at them, the tap still running, his heart had twisted in his chest. What did Rob want? Everything? You didn't have to be blind to see that Carrie had a crush on him, which didn't bother Jason *too* much anymore, but he'd told Rob what he felt about Gina, and Rob had promised, *promised,* that he didn't feel the same.

Standing there, he felt alone, truly alone for the first time in his life. Robster had broken his promise, and something in their friendship snapped inside him. It couldn't be relied on anymore. It couldn't be trusted. He still loved Rob, and the next week when they made their awful discovery in the attic, Jason's heart would break for his friend; but the seeds of destruction were sown that afternoon. Feeling a wet nose on his hand, he'd looked down at Teacher, and with eyes brimming with tears, realized that he and the dog had something in common. Neither of them were really wanted. Rubbing the head under his fingers, he took comfort in the fact that at least they had each other. At least they had that.

Looking back through the wasted years, Jason wondered whether Gina had been jealous of Teacher, jealous of the way they all fussed over him and loved him, and jealous of how he was the focus of Jason's visits now and not her. Not even the weird things she did held the allure for him that the dog did. Those he was used to, the novelty gone. Yeah, maybe she was jealous. Jealous and spiteful. He sure as hell never saw Rob and Gina kissing again after that afternoon. Well, jealous or not, it didn't justify what happened. Nothing could justify what happened.

It was a cool afternoon when the magic turned sour. They'd been out in the garden for an hour or so, the girls messing around on the swing talking girl stuff like they did sometimes while Rob and he tried to catch frogs by the huge pond, Teacher sticking his huge nose in their faces and in the jam jars, trying to figure out what they were doing, eager to be part of it. It was four weeks since the kiss and three weeks since the madness in the attic, and the atmosphere between the two boys was quiet and reflective.

It would be another four long days before Jason drove the final nail into the coffin of their friendship, his bandaged arms behind his back, standing at the front of the classroom not giving a shit about anything anymore, except trying to make someone else hurt as much as he did, as if that might somehow lessen the isolating pain that was ripping his insides apart. By then the world would have changed, but all that was in the future. At that moment, standing side by side next to the pond, there was just an awkwardness they didn't know how to deal with. Their friendship had shifted slightly, and neither of them knew how to handle it.

Silently unscrewing the lid of his jar and releasing the small frog that had been jumping at the transparent walls, Jason watched Rob's impassive face from behind his scruffy bangs. The overcast sky seemed to be reflected in the tanned boy's expression, and Jason wondered what was going on in his mind as he sifted through the mud searching for life. The more he studied his friend, the more it seemed that he was looking at a stranger, the features familiar but no longer recognizable. The ease that he had always felt in Rob's company was gone, and he didn't know how to get it back. He didn't even know whether he *wanted* to get it back.

The small frog bounded away, chirruping with joy, and Jason followed its progress with his eyes, one hand locked in Teacher's fur as the dog panted beside him. Why did life have to be so complicated? He was feeling things he didn't like, had been for weeks and he hated himself for the new darkness he'd discovered growing inside him, wishing it could just stop, stop right here and now, but it wouldn't. It couldn't. And it had all started with that kiss. That stupid kiss.

He picked up a pebble and skimmed it across the water. He shouldn't resent Rob for that, not anymore, not with everything that had happened since, but the memory of it had somehow soured the sympathy he felt for his friend. That small black area inside him that he so desperately wanted to squash was pleased that things were far from rosy in the perfect life of Robert Black. That part of him was laughing hard. Maybe now Rob would have an idea of what it was like for the rest of them. Maybe now he'd realize that for most people life was pretty shit. Maybe now he'd realize that he wasn't so fucking special after all.

Teacher licked his face, and Jason locked his arm around the dog's body. Even here at Syracousse with Teach, he couldn't shake off the heaviness of his soul. His feelings were too mixed up for that. He was angry at Rob too, angry at him for unwillingly unsettling the stability of the world. If shit like that could happen in his life, then what hope was there for the rest of them? Rob was the golden boy, everybody's favorite guy; crap like this wasn't supposed to happen in his world. His world was what everyone else was supposed to dream about. The afternoon in the attic had changed all that. Suddenly, nothing was certain anymore, and that frightened him. He shivered in the cool breeze.

Carrie was waving at them from the other side of the garden by the swing. "We're going inside! It's too cold out here."

Jason nodded back and stood up, pleased with the suggestion. The girls were right, the air was too thin to really enjoy being outside, and maybe the change of situation would help lift his mood.

"You coming in?" He touched Rob's shoulder, the other boy still crouched by the water.

Rob looked up and smiled. "Yeah, my feet are frozen to shit." He held his hand out for Jason to help pull him up the bank, and with the physical contact it seemed that for a moment the events of the past month were forgotten, the two boys grinning together as they collected their motley equipment and, followed by Teacher, headed inside.

Jason hadn't realized just how chilly it had been outside until they were all gathered in the warmth of the Graces' kitchen. Camilla had just finished peeling and chopping a pile of potatoes, and a large pan of water was boiling on the stove, the steam hovering above like mist in the mountains. She smiled cheerfully at them as Teacher beat her legs with his wagging tail.

"Look at you lot! You've got goose bumps. I can't believe you went out there without any sweaters on." She glanced through the window at the trees that swayed in the strong wind. "It seems like the summer's abandoned us for today, I'm afraid. It looks like October out there." Drying her hands on a tea towel, she headed toward the door to the hallway. "I'll go and light a fire in the lounge, so you can warm up in there. Get yourselves some drinks and I'll be back in a minute."

Carrie plugged in the kettle and opened the cupboard above it. "Well, I don't know about you lot, but I really fancy a hot chocolate."

"Yeah, me too." Rob was rubbing warmth back into his arms, his t-shirt still damp from mucking around by the pond. Jason handed Carrie four mugs from the tree next to him and she started to spoon the powder in.

Standing by the stove, Gina had opened a box of cookies and left it close to the edge of the counter, as she nibbled on a slice of shortbread. Teacher, perennially hungry, whined and slavered by her knees, gazing up at her imploringly. She ignored him. On the other side of the room, Jason cringed, hoping the dog would stop begging. It was the one thing that really made Camilla Grace angry, and Jason knew that it was his fault Teacher did it at all. The Graces never ever fed him tidbits, but Jason just couldn't help himself and always snuck his canine friend small pieces of whatever he was eating. Every time, he promised himself that he wouldn't do it anymore, but he couldn't resist those big soppy brown eyes. Yeah, if it wasn't for him, daft as he was, Teach would have learned the no-begging rule by now. Avoiding the dog's confused glances, he started adding sugar to the mugs, ready and waiting for the kettle to boil.

Gina took another biscuit, and Teacher pawed at her legs, his mouth starting to drool. "Jesus, Teacher, sod off!" Gina pushed him away and moved to the other side of the stove, mild irritation marring her beauty. Watching from the far counter, Jason saw the dog eyeing the box so temptingly close to the edge of the counter, and realized with horror what he was going to do. "Teacher, no!"

It was too late. The dog's clumsy front paws had left the ground by the time Jason got the words out, and as he scrabbled for the counter, all Jason and the others could do was watch with sickening horror as the golden pad hit the black handle of the pan, sending the boiling water up into the air, bringing it down in a waterfall directly over Gina's head. The girl flinched by instinct, but not a drop touched her as Rob—always Rob the hero—grabbed her arm and pulled her away. Instead the water squirted outwards, as if trapped in an invisible hose that someone had squeezed a finger over, spraying everything but Gina. Teacher yelped and bounded towards Jason, who hugged the dog to him, crouching on the floor. Still holding the kettle, Carrie let out a small shout as some of the scalding liquid landed on her arm. Sometime in all this, the pan clattered emptily to the floor, the noise harsh and unforgiving.

For a moment there was silence as the four children stared at each other, and then Teacher whimpered, his dog sense telling him that this was all his fault. Jason patted him gently as the water gathered in a steaming pool in the middle of the floor.

Gina's face was red with anger. "That stupid dog is always in the way. Look what it's done now!"

Camilla Grace appeared in the doorway, and took in the scene, her face confused. "What happened?"

Gina's face was as surly as her voice, and Jason felt himself falling out of love with her. "Teacher jumped up to get the biscuits and knocked the pan over. I hate that stupid dog! Why didn't Daddy just get me a kitten like I wanted?"

Camilla rushed to her daughter to check her for burns, taking no notice of Carrie who held her scalded wrist under the cold tap. "Are you okay, darling? Oh God, you could have been seriously hurt."

Jason stood up, aware of the dog crouched low and fearful behind his legs. "No one was hurt, Mrs. Grace. It was just an accident." His heart squeezed tight as he saw Carrie out of the corner of his eye turning the tap quickly off, and hiding her burn in support. She wouldn't want Teacher to get into trouble any more than he did. Suddenly Carrie's inner beauty shone for him far brighter than Gina's physical presence ever could. Somewhere in this strange summer that had gotten lost. So many things had gotten lost, and he wondered how much of it was down to Gina's strange power and the hold she seemed to have over them.

Camilla Grace's eyes were cold as she stared at Teacher. "That bloody dog's been a nuisance ever since it arrived." She pointed at the blanket in the corner of the room. "Get on your bed!" The overgrown puppy shifted forward a couple of steps, and braved a half-wag with its tail. "I said get on your bed!" Her shrill words conveyed their meaning well, and almost on his belly, Teacher skulked over to the blanket and lay down, his brown eyes gazing up at each of them mournfully.

Jason moved toward him, his heart aching, knowing this was partially his fault. If he hadn't encouraged Teach to beg then none of this would have happened, and he just wanted to stroke him and let him know everything was okay.

This time Camilla's anger was directed at him, her voice calm and quiet. "Jason, if you go and pet that dog, then it's the last time you'll step foot in this house. Do you understand me? The animal has to learn." Jason froze on the spot and nodded, unable to contemplate never returning here, to the comfort of the house, to Teacher.

"Now go into the sitting room. All of you. I've got to mop up this mess."

Subdued, Jason followed the others out, and into the lounge at the front of the house. The fire was blazing and he sat silently on the sofa next to Rob, just wanting to go home, but unable to leave until he knew that Teacher was going to be all right. Carrie took one of the deep armchairs and stared with disgust at Gina, who was sitting in the other. Her voice was low. "Why did you have to tell your mum about Teacher? That was mean. You could have just said it was an accident."

Rob slowly nodded. "Yeah, Carrie's right, you didn't have to get him in trouble. He's only a puppy. And it's not as if you were in any danger, is it? That water wouldn't have hit you if I'd poured it over your head."

Gina shrugged. "I don't know what you're getting so wound up about. It's only a dog." She sounded disgruntled, and Jason felt warmth flooding through his body, warmth and love for Carrie and Rob. Carrie, Rob and Teacher, his forever friends.

Gina got up and turned the TV on, and the four of them watched it silently, enjoying the blaze that warmed their bones from the hearth, despite the atmosphere that hung over them, the feeling unnatural in this place where they all normally felt so at ease. Jason was surprised that neither Carrie nor Rob had decided to leave yet, and realized that maybe they like him, wanted to check on their four-legged friend before heading back into their other, less consuming lives. Something in the thought calmed him. Everything was going to be okay. The poor mutt had just been given a telling off, that's all, nothing worth going ape for.

After maybe half an hour or so, Jason heard the kitchen door opening and the sound of paws scratching on the wooden floor of the hall. He doubted Teacher was out of the doghouse, but as Camilla Grace never allowed him in the kitchen when she was preparing food, then he reckoned the puppy had a temporary reprieve. It seemed he was right, because a few seconds later, the familiar panting snout came into view, poking itself around the doorway, before hesitantly edging into the room.

Jason and Carrie exchanged grins as the ungainly dog

tried to move unnoticed toward the carpet in front of the fire, his tail still hung low with shame although the tip was wagging in anticipation of forgiveness. Carrie gave him a surreptitious pat as he passed, and even Rob giggled at the sight of Teacher trying to control his happiness, while still glancing warily at Gina. Eventually, his confidence a little restored, he sat down a few feet away from the fire, pleased to be back in their company. He looked over at Jason for reassurance, but not wanting to excite Teach and make Gina, who so far had ignored his entrance by concentrating on the TV, shout at him again, he only smiled quickly and then looked away.

Teacher took a step toward Jason, wanting to curl up by his feet, and then froze and started to whine.

"What's the matter with him?" Rob had leaned forward on the sofa, and Jason had to stretch around him to see. Teacher's body looked strange, twisted slightly, as if he was wanting to go in one direction, and someone was pulling in the other. His heart started to pound. "What's the matter, boy? Come here."

The dog whined again, his eyes moving from one person to the next in confusion and rising panic. Even Gina was watching him, her face pale, as Teacher seemed to slide slightly on the carpet. Carrie's voice came in a whisper, sending a chill through Jason's body. "It looks like someone's trying to drag him by his collar." She was right. Teacher was now sitting much closer to the fire than he had been moments ago. Or was it just his imagination? How could he have been pulled by nothing?

There was a moment's pause, and then the dog stood up, his tail wagging slightly, still a little unsure, but back in control of his body. Rob looked at Gina. "What the hell was that all about?"

Before she had a chance to answer, if she could answer at all, the puppy howled, a sound too high and too loud and too afraid to come from a dog. His big brown eyes met Jason's for a brief second before something twisted the dog around and sucked it forward, plunging that beautiful golden head into the flames. The room was suddenly filled with screams, but the only ones Jason could hear were Teacher's and his own as he leapt from the sofa where Rob sat frozen, and threw himself across the room, clutching at the body of the squealing struggling dog, trying to pull him out, trying with all his might, but something stronger was holding him in there.

Screaming in frustration, ignoring the smell of burning fur and cooking meat, and ignoring the tears that were pouring down his face, Jason thrust his hands into the fire, the pain unbearable as it raced up his arms, but that didn't matter, nothing mattered, and the melting skin on his fingers made contact with the melting flesh of Teacher's head as the dog flung itself from side to side in agony, trapped in the fire. Their screams mingled as Jason tugged and tugged, the dampness on his cheeks evaporating in the searing wall of heat, and then there was only his own scream of pain and anguish abandoned by the other, as the struggling stopped and the dog went limp in his arms, the sudden weight making Jason fall backwards as the fire released its cargo.

As he knelt on the carpet, somewhere behind him he could hear Carrie's hitching breath as she whispered from behind her hands, "Oh my God, oh my God, oh my God, oh my God," to no one and everyone, but the words seemed to be traveling from another world, as was the keening, quiet wail coming from him, from deep inside him, getting louder every second as he cradled the mutilated, unrecognizable head, in his burnt hands. From the neck up Teacher had no skin, no skin at all, just something pink stretched over his bones and teeth, pulled back in agony, and those floppy, silky ears were vanished forever. Jason was rocking backwards and forwards now, as his whole being started to break, not just his heart, this was too much for just his heart, and he felt as if every organ inside was shattering, smashing themselves into nothing, leaving him hollow. Leaning over, unaware of the stench, he kissed the hot meat, held it close to him as if somehow, maybe if he wished hard enough, he could bring Teacher back, *but he's got no eyes, no big, brown soft eyes, and maybe if I'd moved quicker, and maybe if I'd never given him a treat, and maybe it's all my fault.*

The scream ripped through his thoughts, and this time he was sure it wasn't his own, he had no energy left for screaming, and then there were Camilla Grace's hands trying to pull him away, and then Rob's were there too, and then there were too many hands and he couldn't hold on against them, however much he tried, and then they separated them. They took Teacher from him. After that, it was his own howl of grief that filled his ears.

The rest of the day passed in a haze, it probably did for all of them, but Jason was beyond noticing the others. He was barely aware of himself. Camilla Grace put Teacher in a black garbage bag, he was sure of that, he could remember Rob's silent tears as he helped her, and all the while she talked about what a terrible accident it was, and how they'd bury him properly in the garden with a cross and everything, and as Jason listened numbly to the words all he could see was that black plastic bag, knowing Teacher was in it like some kind of used-up rubbish that nobody wanted, nobody had ever wanted, and he deserved better than that.

He didn't know where she put Teacher's remains, and he didn't really want to know, but after they'd "cleared up," as Camilla Grace called it, she bundled Jason and Rob into the car and took them to the hospital, her face looking old and drawn as she clutched the wheel. Carrie stayed behind with Gina, who didn't want to come, wasn't able to come, instead sitting in the armchair, her back stiff and upright, clutching at her hands as she stared at the singed area in the middle of the rug.

The doctor covered his arms and hands with lotions that felt like acid on his flesh and then bandaged him up and told him he'd have to come back and get the dressings changed in a couple of days. The words washed over him as did Camilla Grace's tears and soothing whispers. Rob sat on the chair opposite and their eyes met, both gazes now old before their time, and Jason knew that the other boy was thinking the same thing he was. Teacher nearly burned Gina in the kitchen and then this happened. Her magic had gone sour. Everything had gone sour.

The next day, he didn't go to Syracousse. None of them did. Nor the day after that. Two days later, so full of anger at the world—*maybe if Rob had got up off the sofa and helped, we could have saved Teacher*—he did the terrible thing on the last day of school, and then he didn't really see anyone for a while, except Carrie who valiantly kept trying to get the two boys to speak. But she didn't go to Syracousse either, and neither did Rob. They'd had their fill of Gina. It was two weeks before they'd go back again, sneaking in through the side gate late in the evening, not wanting to see either Camilla or Philip Grace, and only then after Carrie had insisted. It was she who had made the three of them meet up at Rob's for two long hours of discussion, trying to analyze what had really happened, each word like a knife in the aching hollow of his insides. But they'd done what she said and had gone to Syracousse, because they needed to know, maybe they needed to go back and give Gina, who had become drawn and quiet, a chance to answer for herself. That's what Carrie had said anyway, and maybe she was right. They sure as hell got more of an answer than they bargained for.

The small drop of liquid fell directly from his eye to the tatty image, and Jason carefully wiped it off before putting the photo away. Sniffing hard, he drained his glass, angry with himself. Crying at something that happened more than twenty years ago. Jesus, he didn't cry when he heard about Carrie, but he could still cry over Teacher? How fucking pathetic was that? Standing up, the walls of the tiny flat suddenly claustrophobic; he grabbed his jacket from the back of the door, and headed outside. He didn't know quite how he felt about spending time with Rob again, but at least at the moment, Robster'd be the one person who didn't think he was going mad, and even if he was, then they were going mad together. He smiled wryly as the cold wind hit his cheeks. And going mad with someone else in tow didn't seem quite as frightening as doing it on your own.

CHAPTER TWENTY-TWO

Rob had cleaned up the kitchen and the house was looking pretty normal by the time Jason arrived at six-thirty. Standing in the kitchen, like they had so many times, so many years ago, the awkwardness between them was almost visible, and under the bright lights Jason looked tired and pale.

"Are you okay, mate?" Rob grabbed the bottle of wine he'd just opened and two glasses as Jason laughed slightly.

"Yeah, but it's been one fucker of a day."

Glancing around at the cupboards that so recently had been covered with coffee, he knew what Jase meant. Boy, did he understand. "Come on. Let's go into the lounge." He didn't plan to spend any more time than he had to in this room, and he certainly didn't have any intention of turning on his laptop again. Nope, if there was any writing to be done—and he had serious doubts about that happening in the near future—then it was back to the good old paper-and-pen method.

Jason sat on the sofa and sipped his wine, his body stiff and uncomfortable as he leaned forward, resting his forearms on his legs. "Any luck with getting hold of Gina?" His blue eyes shone in the reflective glow of the fire, but their seriousness dulled them dark.

Rob shook his head. "I don't know yet. The solicitor says he'll pass the message on, but we'll see. Maybe we'll hear from her, but probably not." He sipped his own drink. "What happened with Judge Matthews?"

Jason took three or four long gulps of wine before he started his story, and Rob listened quietly without interruption, as his childhood friend spoke calmly, starting with the fight with Bob and moving to the judge's madness, and as he listened his heart chilled. *So many secrets. You and your friends. So much dirty guilt eating at you. So much blame. How could the judge have known? How? Well, if you're going to start thinking things like that, then how the hell did your computer blow up your coffee machine this morning? Haven't quite figured out an answer for that yet, have we?*

Pulling his attention back, realizing that the story was moving on without him, he focused again on Jason's words, swallowing his fear for a moment. Studying the other man's face as he spoke, seeing the self-loathing that hovered so close to its surface, he wondered whether Jason had any idea of how few people in the world, in this untrusting world, would have checked on the old man like he did? Jason had always been such a conflict of so many things, and it seemed as if nothing there had changed. He could have been anything he wanted, despite Gallows Hill, despite everything that happened to them; Gina, Teacher and Philip Grace, but there was too much anger inside him that he'd never been able to let go. Maybe it was staying in Streatford that had kept it there, locked up tight inside. Maybe Jason had thought that without his anger there would be nothing of him left. And it wasn't just Jase. Were he and Carrie so different? Carrie was dead, and he, well, the success of his books was certainly balanced by the failures in his personal life. No question about that. God, did what happened that summer really leave them all as fuckups, or should they take a little more of the blame for that themselves?

Jason poured himself another glass of wine, and topped off Rob's, his story over. "I don't know, maybe it means something, or maybe I'm just going fucking crazy. Either way, all I know is that old man put the fear of God into me with what he said. And then finding him dead like that . . . I mean, shit!"

Rob lit two cigarettes and passed one to Jason, who held it with finger and thumb, instead of the normal way between index and middle fingers, just as he had on their first nauseating encounters with nicotine down at the Rec when they were nine or ten. There was something comforting in that.

"I don't think you're crazy. I don't think you're crazy at all." Pulling deep on his cigarette, he recounted the weird things Kelly had told him about the rape at the house and then the events of his kitchen, the madness of the words that appeared impossibly on the unplugged screen, *MAKE HER COME HOME HOME HOME*, and the explosion of his coffee pot. Hearing the words aloud, his own speech more faltering than Jason's had been, it was hard to believe that it had only happened this morning; the fear seemed to have been with him far longer than that. When he'd finished, he looked up at Jason, who seemed to accept his story without questions as if he'd been expecting it, or something like it. "Do you think Gina could be doing all this stuff without realizing it?"

Jason shrugged. "Your guess is as good as mine. It's possible. I mean, she never really had control over the stuff that happened back then, did she? Whatever power she had, it was subconscious. Maybe wherever she is, she's going through some kind of trauma and this is how it's coming out." He paused. "It's hard to say. I never really felt I knew her. She was always a bit elusive, wasn't she?" A grim smile threatened to break on his face.

"Beautiful and terrible. But I guess you probably knew her better than me, so what do you think?"

Rob shook his head, not knowing if Jason had meant the comment to be barbed or not, and not really caring. "I didn't know her any better than anyone, although after Teacher came along, I guess Carrie and I spent more time with her than you did. I think Carrie knew her best, but she's not here to help us."

Jason stared into the fire. "I think Gina was jealous of Teacher."

Rob thought of the dream he'd had while dozing on the afternoon before his date with Kelly, the way he'd seen it all from the outside, Gina's eyes flicking to the kitchen window, checking to see that Jason was there before she kissed him. "I think Gina was jealous of a lot of things." His eyes lingered on the flames as the two of them sat in silence for a few moments. Despite the reason for their reunion, it felt good to see Jason again, to talk about all this stuff with someone who could understand. He pulled his eyes away from the streaks of hot blue and orange and was startled to find Jason watching him intently. The other man's eyes slipped away, looking into the red in his glass while he spoke.

"I've been thinking about Carrie's message. About Teacher. What do you think she meant by 'we got it wrong'? Do you think maybe she thought that Gina wasn't responsible?"

"I've wondered about that, too." His voice was firmer, quicker. This was no time to meander into memories. "But then I think about that last day at the house. About what Gina said and then what happened. I can't see how it couldn't be her. I mean, who else could it be? Also, this weird shit is only happening to people involved with her. The judge locked her mum away in the nuthouse, and us . . . well, we were there, we knew more than anyone what was going on at Syracousse. Shit, we loved it up there. We couldn't stay away."

Jason smiled. "It felt good up there for a while, didn't it? It was the first place that I'd really felt safe, where the world was my oyster. I was happy there." He let out a short laugh. "Sounds crazy given everything that happened."

"I think crazy is the word of the day, so I wouldn't worry too much about it if I were you." Their eyes met and it was good to see no tension there. Jason lit another cigarette.

"So if this stuff is only happening to the people who know Gina, then how do you explain the rape up at the house? Those kids wouldn't know Gina."

Rob sighed. "I can't answer that. All I know is that my gut tells me that the rape was the start of it all. It's like it flicked a switch or something, turning this madness on."

"It'd be a bit of a relief if we were just going mad, wouldn't it? We could just go and check ourselves into the funny farm and that'd be that." Jason seemed to find the thought amusing for a moment, before a dark shadow settled on his face. He glanced around the room, and Rob knew before Jason started speaking that his mind had wandered to that afternoon in the attic.

"This house brings back the memories, too. Are you sure you're okay staying here?"

Rob's insides clammed up. He wasn't ready to talk about his dad with Jason yet. "It was a long time ago. I don't really think about it much." His voice was sharp and Jason didn't look convinced.

"If you say so."

"I say so."

Suddenly the strained atmosphere between them had returned, the room filled with tension just as it had been on the afternoon that Carrie had called the powwow to talk about Teacher, and the two of them had sat just like this, not looking at each other, not even wanting to speak to each other. All that was missing was the pain of that afternoon. Time had taken care of that, but the tension had survived and seemed just as strong as ever.

Rob stood up, too drained to feel anything but tired. Maybe some things were broken forever, however much you wished you could mend them. Like a carefully repaired broken vase. It may look exactly the same afterwards, but the damage had been done, its perfection ruined. You may as well just have thrown it away.

"Look, we'll see if we hear from Gina over the next couple of days. Then we'll decide what to do, if in fact there is anything we can do without getting ourselves certified. Anyway, I'll see you at the funeral tomorrow."

Jason had stood up, and they walked into the hallway to the front door. "I'll be there."

Rob pulled the door open, the cold wind bursting in. "It's been good talking to you, Jase. It really has." He cursed himself inside for how false the words sounded, despite the fact that he meant them. Probably *because* of the fact that he meant them. Well, that was him, great on paper, pretty crap in reality.

Jason didn't look back as he stepped outside, but his voice was heavy and sad. "You too, Robster. You too."

Chapter Twenty-three

Rob's umbrella gave him some protection from the rain as he walked up to the town's graveyard on Dulverton Road, but by the time he stepped through the small black gates under the moss-covered stone arch, his legs were feeling damp beneath the trousers of his suit, and his nose was running slightly. The rain had started in the night, its constant beating at the window keeping him company through the long night as he lay awake, his small spells of sleep interrupted by dreams of Carrie as she had been and the fat, unhappy woman she became. In the end he'd gotten up at four and made himself coffee and a fire, trying to lose himself in a book until the rest of the world woke up. It didn't really work, the combination of tiredness and emotional upset, destroying his concentration.

Michael had rung at eight, and he'd mustered enough energy to lie about the progress of the book, and put the agent off the idea of coming down for a few days—"don't want to spoil the momentum"—before trying to wash away his exhaustion under the shower.

Now, as he strode through the rows of abandoned

gravestones toward the mound of dug-out earth at the back, he was glad of the rain. It made him feel alive, attacking the numbness inside him from the outside. Stepping onto the wet grass, he made his way to where the vicar was standing patiently at the head of the grave. As he got closer, the coffin came into view, next to the hole it would soon disappear into, losing the light forever. Carrie's coffin. Laughing, lively, tomboy Carrie. Gone forever. Not even a church service to say farewell, just a quick embarrassed burial, tucked away in a far corner where no one could see.

Jason was already there, standing next to the casket, his head bowed in thought. Rob nodded to the vicar, then went and stood next to his childhood friend. Close up the casket seemed thin, as if the water dripping on it from above would soon seep through, and where there should have been ornate brass fittings, there were only standard clasps, holding it shut. His heart was heavy as he stared. "God, not much of a way to go, is it? She deserved better than this."

Jason's eyes burned when they met his, his tone sarcastic. "Sorry, mate, it may not be up to your standards, but it was all I could afford."

Rob could have kicked himself for being so stupid. Of course, someone had to pay for the funeral, but it just hadn't crossed his mind, not with everything else that had been going on. He watched Jason, whose gaze had returned to Carrie's coffin, filled with anger and resentment, and felt the guilt wash over him. Jase hadn't forgotten. Jason had taken care of it, just like he had the judge, and just like he'd taken care of him on the afternoon in the attic, despite everything that happened afterwards. Jason always had been the strong one, even if he didn't give himself credit for it. Jason had always been good at looking out for everyone. Rob searched his mind for the best thing to say, but his mouth opened before he'd found the words.

186

"Do you want me to chip in? I should. She was my friend, too."

Jason spat out his laugh. "No thanks. There are some things I can afford to do by myself, even if they don't quite meet with your approval." He paused, and his voice softened. "Anyway, Carrie was never really a diamonds-and-flowers kind of girl, was she?"

"No. She wasn't."

Looking up, some of the anger had gone from Jason's face. "I take it you haven't had a call from Gina then?" Rob shook his head, and Jason sniffed. "Yeah, well, I didn't expect her to give a shit, so I'm not really surprised."

A flash of light caught Rob in the corner of his eye, and following it he spotted a small group of journalists outside the gates. "Those guys really have no respect, do they?"

Jason smiled. "What, worried about your reputation? You didn't have to come, you know."

Tired of feeling like scum, Rob's anger flared. "Tell me, just when did you turn into such an arsehole, Jason?"

The other man turned, his face only inches away from Rob's. "I don't know. Not long after you, I should imagine, Mr. Bigshot."

Rob couldn't believe they were acting like such a pair of kids. "Oh, lose the chip on your shoulder, Jase." He could see Kelly and her father walking toward them, two solemn figures in black. He didn't have the energy to argue with Jason. And he didn't want to either. *You've missed him, haven't you? Even if you don't want to admit it.*

"Look, you're right. I probably am an arsehole. In fact, I'm pretty sure I am. I didn't even think about the cost of the funeral. I don't want to fight with you. Not here. Not while we're saying good-bye to Carrie. Truce?"

Jason gave him a reluctant smile. "Deal." He looked up at Kelly, who was only a few feet away now. "Here comes your girlfriend."

Moving away slightly as Kelly linked her arm in his, Rob watched as Jack and Jason nodded at each other, and

187

he got the feeling that their paths had probably crossed several times over the years. He wondered momentarily why Jack Hollingsworth was even here. What interest could he have in Carrie? But then, he'd been a policeman in town for a lot of years, and maybe the station had asked him to come as their representative. Maybe he'd just come along with Kelly, but there must be pleasanter ways of passing the time than spending it at a murderess's funeral.

The vicar had started his short service, his voice deadened by the weather, and it seemed that all too soon the coffin was lowered into the ground. Could it really be Carrie in there? It shouldn't have ended like this, not for her. Following Kelly, he scooped up a handful of earth and dropped it into the dark hole, hating the finality of its sound hitting the wood. He felt a squeeze on his arm, and looked down at the blond head, hair getting wavy in the damp, despite huddling close to him under his umbrella.

"Are you okay?'

He nodded, taking in the sight of her flawless skin, perfect even without makeup, like a canvas as yet untouched. "Do you want to come over for dinner later?"

She smiled in agreement, and it was like a small, bright light in the darkness that seemed to surround him. God, he needed her. He needed her calmness, her stability.

Glancing over at Jason, he saw that he was still standing by the grave, staring into it thoughtfully. As if sensing Rob watching him, he looked up and signaled him over.

"Wait here for me. I won't be a minute." Leaving Kelly with the umbrella, he joined Jason, who didn't look up, his voice quiet.

"I think we should go up to the house and take a look around."

"Well, we can try, but I don't think that solicitor's going to be very willing to give us the keys."

Jason laughed and this time there was genuine humor in it. Rob had forgotten how good a sound it was. "My, my,

Robster, haven't you grown up all prim and proper? Who said anything about getting the keys?"

Rob stared at him. "You want to break in?"

"I can't think of any other way to get a private viewing. Don't look so shocked. It's not like anyone lives there or anything." He paused for a moment. "Anyway, we owe it to Carrie. What happened to her, the judge, the rape, your crazy computer—whatever Gina's doing, it's all linked to Syracousse. We might as well take a look." He looked straight into Rob's eyes, and Rob suddenly remembered how intense that blue could be when Jason was set on something. "I know Carrie would have done it for you. No hesitation."

Rob sighed and knew Jason was right. "Okay, we'll do it. When were you thinking?"

"Tonight."

Shaking his head, Rob glanced at Kelly. "Can't do it tonight. I've got plans."

Jason had followed his eyes. "She grew up to be a looker, didn't she?" He nudged Rob in the ribs. "But I'd have thought she'd be a bit bright for you. A bit old too, from what the papers tell me."

Rob knew Jason was only joking, but he couldn't help the surge of embarrassment that came with the feeling that the whole world knew his life story. The worst parts, anyway. He glanced at the journalists getting ready to snap him leaving. No, it seemed that there was rarely any time for reporting the good bits in people's lives. He looked back at Jason. "If we haven't heard from Gina by tomorrow night, we'll go then, okay?"

Leaving Jason at the graveside, he walked back to Kelly and her father, taking the woman's hand, before heading out of the cemetery and back to life, the echoes of the dead following them.

CHAPTER TWENTY-FOUR

The candles on the pine table had burned halfway to the bottom by the time Kelly put down her knife and fork and leaned back in the chair. She wasn't sure whether it was the warm glow of the flickering light, the half bottle of red wine she'd managed to drink or just the company that was making her so relaxed, but whichever it was, sitting here in Rob's house she felt totally at ease. She grinned at her host. "That was the best spaghetti I've had in ages. I don't seem to have time to cook properly these days, and Tabby's more of a fish finger and peas girl, but then I guess they all are at that age."

"Have you had enough? I've made enough to feed an army, so there's plenty more if you want some. It's the only thing I know how to cook, so I tend to get a bit ambitious with my quantities."

She sighed and patted her stomach. "I'm absolutely full up, thank you. But if the food's this good, I might eat here more often." She said it as a joke, but as Rob stood up and gathered their plates, his eyes were soft when they met hers.

"I hope you will." He smiled, and she felt a quiver in her belly. "Do you fancy an Irish coffee to finish? I'm pretty good with those, too."

Nodding, she watched him as he moved behind the breakfast bar and abandoned the plates to fill up the kettle, liking the way his body moved. She could imagine there were a few things Rob Black was pretty good at, and where her mind was at, most of them were in the bedroom. He was too damned good-looking, that was for sure. But the looks were resistible. There'd been plenty of handsome men in her life, and most of them had been disappointing, vain and dull. But Rob, well, what frightened her about Rob was that she found she liked him more and more each time she saw him, and he was so easy to talk to. He was interested in her. *You want him. You want him for keeps, and that's a dangerous way to feel. Just remember what he called himself—the king of the meaningless fling. If that doesn't tell you the way it is, then you're dumber than you thought.* She pushed the internal reprimand away, her head warm and woozy, in no mood for caution. Something about this felt right, and so what if the childhood crush she'd had was now close to becoming something so much more? Life was for living, and she was tired of being on her own.

As the kettle clicked itself off, she tilted her head. "Where's your coffee machine?"

Rob froze for a moment as he took the cream out of the fridge. "I broke the pot." Kelly wasn't sure whether it was her imagination, but his words seemed a little sharp. Was he thinking about Carrie?

"Are you okay about today? You haven't talked about it at all."

He looked up at her as he poured the topping on the coffees, and even in the dim light, she could see so much sadness in his eyes. It looked like it had been there forever. How does he hide it so well? How does he live with it? She had a feeling that there was so much more to Rob than met the eye, and she wanted to reach those parts, to understand him. He didn't speak, and she felt slightly uncomfortable.

"I'm sorry. You don't have to talk about it if you don't want to. I should learn to keep my big mouth shut. I think it's the teacher in me, always checking if everyone's okay."

He shook his head. "No. I think I do want to talk about it." He paused, seeking out the right words. "I've thought about Carrie a lot over the past couple of weeks. More than since I left town. Well, since I grew up, anyway." The vulnerability in his soft voice made her ache inside. "And it's going to sound weird, but it doesn't feel like we buried her today. Not the Carrie I remember. I guess I'm grieving for the girl I knew, and just wishing I'd taken the time to find out about the woman she became. I felt like I was at a stranger's funeral today. It was the funeral of an adult I didn't know, and maybe if I had known her, then she wouldn't have ended up like this."

It was good to hear him opening up, and Kelly smiled gently. "Do you remember what you told me about the boys in my class and what they did to Sharnice? There are some things you just can't control, no matter how much you wish you could. I think Carole-Anne was a very unhappy woman. I don't think you could have helped her solve her problems. Sometimes, terrible things just happen."

She stood and took the coffee cups from him. "Come on. Let's go sit in front of the fire."

She led the way into the lounge, put their drinks on the small table in the center of the room and sat down close to the hearth, tucking her knee-length skirt carefully under her. Still standing, Rob's face clouded over, his eyes fixed on her with concern.

She touched his leg. "Are you okay?"

He sat down on the rug, about a foot behind her. "Um,

this might sound silly, but could you move back a bit, away from the fire?"

"Sure." She wriggled backwards until she was level with him, and picked her coffee up to take a sip. Rob stared into the fire and she didn't intrude on his silence.

Finally, when he spoke, he kept his gaze on the flames and his voice was barely above a whisper. "Jason got his scars from an open fire. They go all the way up to his elbows, you know. His hands got burned the worst, but the scars go right up his arms." He paused and Kelly watched his jaw muscles clenching and unclenching in the side of his face. She resisted the urge to touch him, to try to soothe him back to calmness.

"Gina used to have a dog. A golden retriever. A big, soppy clumsy thing. Jason loved that dog. Carrie and I did too, but not like Jason. One afternoon, near the end of that summer, it stumbled into the fire." He smiled bitterly, as if at a private joke. "I sat there on the sofa and watched as it burned, too shocked to move, unable to believe an animal could scream like that, knowing I should do something, should try to help it. But it was like I froze, like my mind couldn't accept what was happening. Not Jason, though. He just leapt forward and stuck his arms into the flames, trying to pull the poor mutt out. He didn't hesitate."

Kelly gazed at the glowing reds and oranges, so beautiful and deadly. The air between her and Rob seemed heavy, almost oppressive, and she had the feeling this was something he hadn't talked about in a long time, if ever.

Her question came out in a whisper. "Was the dog okay?"

"No. No, it died." He let out an almost wistful breath. "I seem to have been thinking about that dog a lot recently."

Kelly watched him, not really sure she understood what he was saying, wondering what was the cause of the weight he seemed to carry. He seemed to have scars of his own, deep inside, not visible like Jason's, but real all the same. She gently reached out her hand and turned his face toward hers, stroking his cheek. "I think you need to take your mind off things." Leaning forward, she kissed him, softly at first, her tongue hesitantly meeting his, savoring the warmth of his mouth, and then becoming more urgent as she heard his breath quickening.

One hand came up to her face, his fingers caressing down to her neck as he moved forward, taking control, pushing her backwards until she was stretched out on the rug, him lying next to her. She moaned slightly as his mouth moved down her body, his saliva leaving a cool sensation in his wake as his fingers deftly undid the buttons of her blouse. She could hear his heavy breaths mingling with her own, and she reached down and felt for him through his trousers, enjoying the solidness there and the groan that came up to her from his mouth as he teased her nipple, letting her know that his arousal was as great as hers. His touch was getting rougher as his need increased, and pushing her skirt up around her waist, he slid one hand into her panties. Her head almost exploded as he came into contact with the wetness there. Oh God, it felt good, so good, and pushing against his fingers, eager to have him, any part of him, inside her, she felt his body shuddering as he slid farther down the rug, one hand squeezing her buttock, the other pushing the thin lace aside to make way for the heat of his mouth.

As much as her body ached to feel his tongue and lips on that part of her, that wasn't what she wanted, not this time, so she reached down and pulled him up, until his beautiful face was above hers, his eyes glazed with lust, confused to have been stopped.

"What's the matter?"

She reached down and pulled at his belt buckle, her insides contracting at being delayed. "I want you inside me. I want to come with you inside me." Tugging at his zipper, releasing him, she ran her hand down his full length, and he needed no more encouragement. Pulling her pants away, she guided him inside, arching her back and feeling the beginning of her orgasm as she rose to meet him, wanting him deep inside, not wanting him to be gentle, just wanting them both to let go and lose themselves. There would be time for gentle lovemaking later. But not now.

"Fuck me, Rob." She whispered into his ear, before biting down on the skin of his shoulder. "Fuck me till I come."

Moaning above her, Rob tangled his hands up with her hair as he surrendered, thrusting himself into her hard and fast, all control gone, until she screamed as the orgasm ripped through her, her muscles throbbing around him, not wanting to let him go, keeping him inside. A few moments later, his body stiffened as he pushed further inside her, all his muscles clenched as his body caught up with hers, releasing himself, his fluids mixing with hers before he collapsed on her, all energy spent.

They lay there in silence for a while, before their bodies stirred again. And this time, it was slow and gentle.

CHAPTER TWENTY-FIVE

The bad man's asleep. Time to go, Tabby.

Her eyes opened reluctantly, dazed and confused in the darkness, but the words, clear and musical in her head made her pull herself upright, pushing the covers away. She sat there for a second, mouth moving silently, before she managed to mumble, "I'm tired," unsure whom she was talking to, if anyone at all. Pushing her wild hair out of her face, all she wanted to do was lie back down and curl up under the duvet with her teddy bear. It was all dark now, and she didn't like it. The dream must have woken her up, and now she was sad, wanting to be back there.

This is your only chance. Don't you want to find me?

Her bleary eyes widened, and she shivered sleepiness away as the voice tickled inside her. Yes, yes, she wanted to find the house and play there in the sunshine. Oh yes, she wanted it more than anything. Wondering whether she was still asleep, still dreaming, she pulled a sweater awkwardly over her nightie, her hair rising with static, and then sat on the bed to tug on yesterday's socks, which had been abandoned on the floor. Her excitement was starting to grow. Maybe it wasn't a dream; maybe it was really happening. She was going to find the house, her house, just as the invisible friend had always said she would. As the seconds ticked by, she felt more and more awake, not like in a dream awake, but proper awake, like in the mornings. Pulling on her leggings, not able to cope with the buttons on her jeans by herself, she smiled in the darkness that didn't seem so scary anymore. She was awake, and her invisible house friend was here!

Scrabbling under the bed quickly, still not quite convinced that something didn't live there, she dragged out her slippers, and then paused, her small brow furrowing in the gloom.

"What about Mummy?" she whispered to the emptiness. There was a resonance inside her.

Mummy's not here, is she? She's found someone else to love. Someone her own age. Someone who won't tie her down. She's left you with the bad man. The bad man with secrets. I think she's forgetting you already.

Tabby paused, one slipper on, one still in her small hand. Mummy wouldn't do that. She wouldn't forget her; she couldn't. Her body ached with hurt and confusion. But her friend had been right about granddad, she'd seen it in his face, and there *was* something different about Mummy now. She'd seen her smiling all on her own for no reason, and she didn't want to play as much anymore, and when she did it was like she wasn't really there at all, but off in a place of her own. A place without her. Her bottom lip started to wobble, and then the soft tune played in her head, soothing her.

I won't ever forget you, Tabby. Come with me to the house. We'll have so much fun. We'll have an adventure. We'll never be lonely again.

The music was too lovely to resist, too beautiful to be wrong, and she picked up Mr. Pickles—she couldn't have an adventure without him—before carefully pulling open her bedroom door and creeping down the stairs, clinging on to the railings, afraid to slip and fall.

Not letting go of her bear, she took her red padded coat from the hook and pushed her arms through the sleeves, wrapping it around her instead of trying to do up the zipper. Reaching up on tip-toes for the knob, she puffed for a few seconds as her clumsy fingers slid over it, before turning the catch and pulling the front door open.

The cold, damp air swirled invisibly around her legs, and staring out into the night, she felt hesitation working its way through her. It was so dark out there; too dark for her even to see, and fear flickered in her eyes. "Is it far?" Her voice was small, and as much as she wanted to find her house, she couldn't imagine getting there. Not alone. Not in this blackness.

Not very far at all. And you won't be alone. Me and Mr. Pickles will be with you. And we won't let anything bad happen.

Hugging her bear close and feeling for the notes playing inside her, Tabby took a deep breath and stepped through the doorway, turning and pushing her fingers through the letter box to close it behind her. There was a finality to the sound of the latch clicking, separating her from her world, and she stood and stared at the door for a few moments, before her feet started to follow the music. There was no going back now.

CHAPTER TWENTY-SIX

The wind played merrily on the long stretch of London Road that led from Gallows Hill to Streatford, snapping and snarling at Jason as he strode head down, his fists balled up in the pockets of his worn leather jacket. Maybe he should have taken the back way, through the houses and coming out on Dulverton Road, but this was the better-lit route and the last thing he needed was some neighborhood watch fanatic reporting him for suspicious behavior. Even going this way, if he got stopped by a police car cruising on its rounds, he'd have a hard time explaining what he was doing heading into the village at eleven-thirty on a weekday night. But then, they probably wouldn't bother stopping anyone but the likes of him. Even though he hadn't been in trouble with the law for at least a couple of years now, memories died hard in Streatford. He knew that better than most.

His breath hung in the air before him for a few moments before dancing off into the night, and his nose ached a little, letting him know that it was turning red. The rain of earlier had faded into a bitter chill, and the idea that had been so great when it came to him an hour ago, now just seemed foolish. Just what the hell did he think he was doing anyway? He'd agreed with Rob that they'd leave it till tomorrow before they went to the house, so why had he decided to go down and take a look tonight? Suddenly, out in the cold, it didn't make much sense.

His lungs felt raw as he panted, and he quickened his pace in an attempt to warm up. As much as the cold made him question having left his flat, he knew that if he turned around and went back he'd remember well enough why he'd gone out in the first place. He was sick of sitting in that flat with nothing but booze for company, sick of thinking about the past. In fact, he was pretty much sick of thinking. It seemed that his brain had done nothing but turn over and over during the past couple of weeks. And anyway, he wasn't intending to break into Syracousse or anything, he'd do that with Robster tomorrow night—hey, hey, it might even feel like old times—no, all he wanted to do now was take a look from the outside. Watch it for a while. What he expected to see, he didn't know, but it had to be better than staying inside and going crazy. And he had a theory to check out.

Sometime this afternoon, somewhere between his second Jack Daniels and his fifth, a thought had taken seed in his mind, and it had been growing there ever since. What if someone was in the house? Maybe Gina had come back. No one had been up there since the rape, so she easily could be there without anyone knowing. That solicitor bloke wouldn't tell anyone, and if Gina *were* there, then maybe that would explain the shit that was happening. If she were this close, then maybe she could be doing it. Maybe she'd learned to control that weird power she had, maybe it had gotten stronger. So many maybes. And why the hell would Gina hole herself up in a house she'd abandoned for so many years? Even if she *had* come back to her family home, why all the secrecy? It didn't make sense, but then none of this craziness made sense.

He reached the dark hulk of The Plough and noticed the welcoming bright lights were switched off, no after-hours drinking happening tonight; Jason crossed the deserted street and headed down the narrow alley leading to Horsefair Green. Within a few minutes he'd crossed the wet grass and took the leafy far turn onto Ousebank Way; Retirement Row, as it was known to those locals under forty. The streetlights were few and dim this far away from the village center, and they cast long, distorted shadows across the pavement of the wide street.

By the time he reached the towpath across the tiny bridge, the darkness had swallowed him whole and he could barely see his feet as they moved beneath him. The walk having warmed him slightly, he unclenched his fists and pulled a pack of cigarettes out of his pocket and lit one, the burning end giving off no light, saving its brightness for itself. Not that the dark bothered Jason. It never had. The dark always hid the things you should be afraid of, and anything that did that was all right by him.

As he turned into the track leading down to the house, his stomach fluttered a little with excitement, and with the familiar crunch of gravel under his feet, for a few moments it seemed as if he was twelve again, heading down with his friends to the comfort at Syracousse. Why hadn't he been down here in all these years? Why hadn't he even come down to take a look?

Throwing his cigarette butt down and grinding it out with his next step, he sniffed hard, listening to the deafening sound of his own breath, rough in his ears. This was no time to get sentimental. He hadn't come down here because he couldn't face the memories, didn't want to face the memories. It was better to put them away and try to forget. And in the main he'd done that quite successfully, despite they way they'd itched at the back of his mind, eager for attention. Yeah, he'd locked it all up: Syracousse, Rob, Carrie, Gina and even poor Teacher. He'd put them somewhere out of easy reach. Until the rape. Until Carrie. Until Robster came back.

This was no time to get maudlin. He'd spend half an hour or so looking around, and then he'd head home. The adventure could wait till tomorrow night. Stupid though it sounded, he suddenly felt as if coming down here alone hadn't been the best idea in the world; whoever had said there was safety in numbers had a point, and the idea of having Robster with him was a comforting thought. But then, he'd always felt good around Rob; he could admit that to himself out here in the open air with no one to hear it.

Looking down in the gloom, he paused for a second, not sure whether to trust his eyes. It was pitch black under the overcast sky, but he could see his feet clearly. More than that, they seemed to be glowing, reflecting a blue-white light. Weird, too weird. Laughing slightly he looked up, puzzled as to where the light could be coming from. His breath caught in his throat as he stared, unable to take in what he was seeing. *What could do that? What the fuck could do that?*

The house was in view up ahead of him and it seemed to be shimmering, radiating light like a beacon, as if it had swallowed the moon, and its brightness was seeping out through the tiny gaps in the brickwork and window frames. What the hell was going on? There was nothing natural about it, nothing at all, and he felt a chill run through him that had nothing at all to do with the cold air surrounding him.

Standing there, his breath coming fast now, he knew it was time to go home, or better still, straight to Rob's. They needed to talk about this, oh boy did they. Things were getting seriously freaky, but he had the feeling that at the same time they were getting clearer. Veils were lifting in his mind. Carrie was right. They had gotten it wrong. His mind sparkled as if he'd been hit by a high-voltage shot of electricity. *I've been asleep for such a long time. Thinking in a daze. Did it make me that way?*

"You came down here, didn't you, Carrie?" he whispered aloud, still staring at his childhood refuge. "You came down here just to make sure. I think you suspected all along." He paused, a wave of grief flooding his system. "Clever, clever girl."

He was about to turn, to turn and get the hell out of there, when something up ahead caught his eye. The small shape was visible by its absence, a patch of moving blackness surrounded by a halo of light, and he squinted, taking a few steps forward, his curiosity overcoming his eagerness to get away. It was too big to be a fox or a stray sheep and anyway, it was moving all wrong for an animal. *It's moving like a child.* His feet started to walk faster, his synapses sending panic signals of realization to them before the thought found its way into words, flashing in his mind. *It is a child. What the hell is a child doing out here in the middle of the night?* The bobbing figure disappeared into an enormous shadow thrown down across the track like a huge black cape, and Jason broke into a sprint, all thoughts of home or Rob vanished in a second. *It's the old oak tree, that's where she is. The old oak tree by the gate. Oh shit, she's going into the house, please God don't let her go into the house . . .*

"Wait!" he shouted, as his sneakers threw gravel up behind him. "Wait! Don't go in there! It's not safe! It's not safe!"

Clutching Mr. Pickles so tightly to her chest that she was sure he would be squashed forever, Tabby kept her eyes fixed on the brightness ahead of her. The coldness had seeped up through her slippers from the ground, her socks damp and icy next to her soles, and the big toe of her left foot throbbed painfully from where she had stumbled a hundred yards or so back. She didn't look down though, afraid that if she did, the light would leave her, and that thought terrified her more than the threat of a broken ankle or a bruised toe.

She'd been so scared walking down here in the night, so scared she could barely breathe. She'd never walked *anywhere* on her own before, and even with her bear and the music inside her that's how she'd felt, all alone in the terrible blackness that was eating her body up like it had the trees and the pretty fields and the river, replacing them with something else she couldn't see, something horrible that lived in the darkness, stretching out for ever and ever, licking its lips and watching.

Despite the reassurance of her invisible friend, when she'd been halfway down the gravel track she'd almost turned and fled, back to her house if she could find it, or back to anyplace where there was light to scare away the monsters. Then all of a sudden, when the panic was about to explode inside her, there it was, right there ahead of her. The house. Her house; all lit up to show her the way, waiting for her to get there. Oh, it was so beautiful, glittering and sparkling as she got closer and closer—so much prettier than in the dreams—but although the sight of it had calmed her down a little, she still wished it were daytime, bright and sunny and friendly. But at last she was nearly there, just a few more yards to go and then she'd be safe. Safe from everything.

Hearing the man shouting behind her, Tabby let out a short yelp and whirled round, her heart bursting through her ribcage with fright. Not so far away someone was running at her, running quickly, screaming at her, a huge moving shape, lunging forward. *It's the monster. It's escaped from the dark. The monster's hungry, and he's coming for me.* Turning back, scared to take her eyes from the thing following her, but wanting to get to the house—get to the gate, that's what the tune was playing, get to the gate—she hurried onward, wishing her numbed feet could go faster, small, terrified tears forming in the corners of her eyes, blurring her limited vision.

Brushing through the thin branches that felt like old ladies' arms clutching at her, tugging at her hair, she reached for the wood of the gate and grabbed it with one tiny hand, the other holding Mr. Pickles secure. She pushed the gate forward and it swung open, as the sound of footsteps hammered the gravel so much nearer now. A silvery haze hung over the step across, separating her from the house, as if a barrier of water was reaching up from the ground, fluid and bright, not quite allowing a view through it. Tabby stared, unsure, not knowing whether to step through, but the monster was almost on her. She sobbed aloud, her fear confusing her.

Don't be afraid, Tabby. Come on in. I'm waiting for you. And the monster's nearly here.

The tree behind her rustled, and she could hear the raw breathing behind her. Squeezing her eyes shut, she jumped forward, passing through the warm, tickling air of the wall and into the glorious sunshine beyond, safe from the grasping touch she'd felt on the back of her jacket.

Can't let her go into the house, can't let her get there . . . The little girl was so close that he could make out the yellow ears of the bear she was clinging to and the long curls that hung loose from her head. She pushed open the gate and seemed to hesitate there for a moment. *That's it, baby, stay there, please stay there.* His breath ripped his lungs as he pushed himself, no energy left for yelling, through the old oak tree that seemed eager to hold him back. She was so close, so close, and he could almost feel her lifting one tiny foot, a toddler's innocent foot, as she moved toward the insane light. Lunging forward, his jump simultaneous with hers, he reached out to grab her, feeling the soft material of her jacket slipping past his treacherous fingers, and then she was gone, vanished into the garden, through the liquid air protecting it.

Alone and exhausted in the gateway, sweat freezing against him beneath his clothes, Jason let out a wail of frustration as the blue-white light sucked itself back into the house again, taking the child with it.

For a moment there was only the blinding darkness again as he stood, his soul empty, on the threshold of the gate he'd crossed so many times as a child, the wonder he had felt then replaced now with vehement hatred, as he stared at the building, the bricks and mortar as much a part of his life as his own flesh and blood. As he raged inside, at himself, at Syracousse, at all the memories, the air around him changed, charging itself up with electricity, crackling with it.

The wind howled around him, whipping him painfully. What now? What the fuck now? Not sure how much more he could take, Jason watched with disbelief as the image of the house began to distort. *It's like a trapped bubble of air under the water. The blue light's going to bubble outward. That's what it's doing. It's getting ready to attack.*

The words were clear in his head, but he stood there frozen, unable to tear himself away. There was a rumbling deep in the ground as the bubble exploded, the energy surging outward like the shockwave of a nuclear blast; powerful, angry and full of vengeance.

He managed a weak "Oh shit" before the power wave hit him, lifting him roughly from his feet, sending him tumbling through the air, and away from the house. *I should have waited. I should have waited for Robster . . .* He hit the gravel with a sickening crunch and pain exploded all over his body for a brief glorious moment of life, before the world went black from the inside. The only thing he was grateful for, in those last agonizing seconds, was that he was facing away from Syracousse. He didn't want to die with it in his eyes. But then, he thought as the darkness took over, he didn't really want to die at all.

CHAPTER TWENTY-SEVEN

It was nearly nine when Rob reached for the phone to call Michael. He'd been up about an hour, clearing away from the night before, playing the evening's events over in his head like a lovesick kid. At least thinking about making love with Kelly was a lot more pleasant than trying to make sense of the madness that was going on around him, but he had the rest of the day to ponder over that, and at the moment he was just enjoying the memory of soft skin and a passion that had surprised him. Yeah, she was special; there was no doubt about that. *And what's she going to think of you if you get caught breaking and entering tonight? How are you going to explain that?* He shrugged the thought off like an itchy sweater, irritating to the touch.

In the broad light of day, after such a fantastic night, he was in half a mind to cancel with Jason. It was a crazy idea, and he was getting too old for that kind of shit; they both were. All he wanted to do tonight was meet up with Kelly again, and he couldn't see what could be gained by traipsing around that abandoned house, freezing their arses off, when he could be curled up with a beautiful, fascinating woman.

He'd dialed his agent's number before he realized the line was empty of sound, and after a brief moment of confusion, remembered that he hadn't plugged the phone back in before going to bed last night. He smiled, laughing slightly. What would Kelly have made of that? No doubt she'd have figured it was some kind of slimy "not wanting to be disturbed while getting my action" move common amongst the male of the species, and he'd been guilty of using that one on occasions in the past. But not this time. This time, he just hadn't wanted Jason throwing a spanner in the works by calling him with more tales of the unexpected.

Sliding the connector into the socket in the hallway, the immediate ringing made him jump. Maybe Michael was getting telepathic. His heart beat quicker. Or maybe it was Gina. Hurrying back to the kitchen, he reached across the breakfast bar for the receiver.

"Hello?"

"Thank God you're there, I've been ringing all night. I even came around and knocked on the door, but I didn't get an answer. I need to know if you saw anything strange on your way home last night, anything at all. Maybe just someone looking suspicious. Tabby's gone missing, and we don't know where she is or if anyone's taken her."

It took him a couple of seconds before he realized the rambling, disjointed voice on the other end belonged to Jack Hollingsworth. He sounded exhausted and he wasn't making much sense, but alarm bells started ringing in Rob's head with the mention of the little girl he had yet to meet.

"Slow down, Jack." He kept his own voice as calm as possible. "Did you say Tabby's gone missing?"

"Yes." The old man's voice seemed anchored to the weight of that word of acceptance, as if it were dragging him down with it.

"I'll be there in five minutes." Slamming the phone into its holder, he grabbed his jacket from the kitchen door, shoved his cigarettes and keys into his pockets, and was out of the house before he'd gotten his arms through the sleeves.

The cold air conflicted with the heat inside him as he ran down Dulverton Road toward the crossroads, the muscles in his legs aching as they warmed up, but he ignored them. He had a crazy feeling inside telling him that somehow all this was his fault, that he was contaminated with something bad, and now it was taking its revenge on him for having the gall to think that he could be happy. Not stopping to check for traffic, he darted across London Road and headed into Horsefair Green, ignoring the swearing and strange looks from passers-by as he barged through them. His run eased up to a walk as the police car came into view, making Jack's message a reality. Oh Christ, Tabby really had gone missing.

Panting from his sprint, he pushed past the policeman who opened the door and found Kelly in the small kitchen, seated at a tiny pine table. Jack had been sitting with her, but he got up and moved to the hallway to quietly speak to the officer who had followed Rob in, after briefly introducing them. Rob sat in the vacant chair and took Kelly's hand and gently rubbed it, his insides aching at the sight of the tracks of spent tears down her skin, and the hollow emptiness of her eyes. She glanced almost through Rob as she spoke.

"The first thing they did was search the house. Can you believe that? As if I hadn't done that before I called them. As if I didn't know all her hiding places. She could be anywhere out there, and they want to search the house."

Rob followed her gaze to a crude, childish painting of a house pinned up on the wall. Tabby must have done it. "What happened? When did she go missing?"

"She was gone when I got home." She swallowed a small sob. "I should never have stayed out so late. Maybe she wanted to know where I was and went looking for me. I should never have gone out. Never."

A small fresh tear trickled away from her eye and Rob carefully wiped it away. "It's not your fault, Kelly. The police will find her. She won't have gone far." He hoped his voice sounded more confident than he felt. It seemed that the news was filled with stories about missing children these days, and not many of them had a happy ending. This will be different, he thought firmly as his eyes wandered over the painting. Things like that don't happen in places like Streatford. Still holding Kelly's hand, he looked at the picture quizzically. Something about it was vaguely unsettling him, and he couldn't figure out exactly what.

Kelly rested her head on her spare hand, her voice low and dead as she spoke to nobody in particular. "She took her coat. She took her red coat. Why would she have taken her coat?"

Rob got up and went to Jack, who was leaning against the doorframe. He spoke quietly, even though he doubted Kelly would be listening. She was lost in a private world of fear and grief that no one could penetrate. Not yet, anyway. But when she was ready, he'd be there. "Was there any sign of a break-in?"

The older man shook his head. "No. Wherever she's gone, it looks like she went there on her own. There's no sign of forced entry, and I'm sure no one came in the house. I would have heard them. It would have woken me up." His eyes bore into Rob's, the honesty of the pain and guilt in them, hitting the writer hard. Jack squeezed his lips tight, his gaze slipping away. "It would have woken me up."

Rob nodded, awkward in the other man's emotion, and patted him on the shoulder. He didn't think Jack Hollingsworth was a man who gave way to his emotions very often, but he seemed pretty close now. He wished there was something he could say, but he knew better than most that there were no words that could give someone peace from their internal guilt, whether they deserved to be carrying it with them or not.

His eyes were drawn to the painting again and his brain tingled. There was something familiar about it, something real in the design that the young hand had tried to re-create. Instead of trying to focus on it, bringing the image into sharpness, he let his eyes blur, seeing only the whole and none of the splotches of detail. Suddenly, he seemed unable to see anything else, nothing in the room around him was clear as the crinkled poster paint house on the wall. *Of course. It had to be. Could there ever have been a different answer?* With the knowledge came a moment of calm, followed by a surge of anger.

"Did Tabby paint that?"

Something like ice in his voice made Kelly look up. She smiled sadly. "She said it was her house. Where she was going to live one day." Her face twisted slightly and she bit down on her lip, forcing herself to breathe. "What does it matter? She's gone."

Rob stared at her. "I think I know where she is." His voice was getting louder as his excitement rose. "That house is Syracousse. Maybe she's gone there."

Kelly's eyes glowed life again as she pushed her chair away, hope oozing from her pores. Rob pulled on his jacket, ready to move. Jack Hollingsworth was still staring at the painting, his lip shaking as he muttered. "It can't be. It can't be. But she couldn't know. Nobody knows."

Kelly had barged past them and was tugging at Officer Keery's sleeve, dragging him to the door, and Rob shook Jack, bringing him around. He didn't like losing patience with the emotionally drained pensioner, but they needed to move and they needed to do it straight away. The old man looked as if he'd been slapped in the face.

"You go in the car with Kelly. I'll run down the back way, it's probably quicker." He looked thoughtfully at the other man for a moment, at the way his eyes trembled slightly at the edges. "Are you okay, Jack?"

The gray irises came back sharply into focus, their strength a reminder of the formidable man who lived inside the weakening body. "Yes, sorry. I'm fine. It's just been a long night, and I'm not as young as I used to be." This time it was he who firmly gripped Rob and pushed him toward the door. "You get running. We'll see you up there, and let's just hope to God we find her."

CHAPTER TWENTY-EIGHT

Rob turned his back on the figures clambering into the Panda car and headed over the back of the Green and onto Ousebank Way, sending a small, silent prayer to a God he didn't believe in that everything was going to be okay. That Tabby would be fine. That all this would be finished once and for all.

His legs were burning as he turned off the towpath, his feet pounding the slippery gravel with an almost steady rhythm, lungs tearing at his breath for more oxygen as he sucked desperately at the air. Jesus, it seemed like all he'd done today was run, but there was no stopping now, no matter how much he might want to. Tabby was at the house. Tabby was at Syraccouse.

The thought was a cold certainty in his mind, and he knew it was right. He knew it the same way he'd known there was no way to save Teacher back on that summer's afternoon when the dog had slid on the carpet against his will in front of the four pairs of frightened eyes, making the world tilt forever.

The Reckoning

Passing the old iron gates without glancing at them, without even thinking to pause there, Rob followed the wall as it curved away, chasing the ghosts of his childhood footprints to the wooden back gate, the secret entrance to the house of secrets; a child-sized doorway hiding and waiting beneath the protective gaze of the old oak tree, waiting for the touch of a tiny hand.

As he rounded the bend, his feet slowed to a stumble and then came to a halt, eyes squinting to make sense of what they could see. *What was that? A body?* Yes, that was it. A body too big to be a child's lying across the track from the back gate. Hands on his hips he panted heavily, a sweaty stitch starting in his side, as he became vaguely aware of the sound of the police car coming up the drive behind him, stopping on the other side of the bend at the *adult* entrance to Syracousse.

The air roared in his ears as he tried to control his breath. If the body wasn't Tabby, then who else could it be? Who else would have come to the tiny secret gate leading to the back garden? He stared at the collapsed heap dressed in black, and his pupils widened. "Oh Christ," he muttered, as his feet once more moved forward, slowly at first and then gaining speed. "Oh Christ, no."

His legs unable to move fast enough, he sprinted the twenty meters or so as if forcing himself through glue, until at last he fell to his knees next to the twisted body of his childhood friend. Oh God, this wasn't a normal way for a person to be lying. What could have made his legs stick out like that?

"Oh, Jason. Oh no, Jase." Shaking, trying to ignore the lips that were too blue to be healthy, he carefully pulled a sleeve of the leather jacket up on one outstretched arm to check for a pulse. The skin felt cold and doughy. "Come on, Jase, come on, please . . ."

For a moment his fingers felt nothing except their own blood pumping frantically through them as he cursed under his breath, cursed Jason for coming on his own—for not fucking waiting—and cursed him again for the grief that was now exploding inside.

"Damn you, Jason, you shit!" he screamed, barely aware of the policeman's shadow falling across him, and then his whole body froze as he felt a slow, desperately weak beat under his clenched fingers. He was alive, oh Jesus, he was alive.

Tugging his own light jacket off, he covered Jason's awkward torso with it as best he could. *I think he's broken his back, I really think he's broken his back, how can he have broken his back?* He looked up at Keery. "Call an ambulance. He's alive, but only just." The policeman was ahead of him, dialing already, and Rob wanted to punch the lack of hope from the man's face and scream at him that he didn't know Jason, and Jason was capable of surviving things that other people couldn't because Jason was *special,* and Jason just couldn't go and die like other people did, because there was so much left unsaid and undone and unadventured.

He was unaware of his own silent tears, until Kelly's shouts cut through his panicked thoughts. Reluctantly looking up, he saw her on the other side of the lane, holding up something small and muddy, with patches of bright blue showing through. "It's Tabby's slipper. My baby's slipper!" Without waiting for anyone to answer, she disappeared through the gate, screaming the little girl's name. Rob knew he should go with her, but he couldn't bring himself to leave his friend so close to death's door; he'd turned his back on Jason too many times in the past to let him down now. His place was here, and anyway, Keery was already darting after her, his mobile phone pressed to his ear as he shouted instructions at someone on the other end, no doubt demanding the keys to the house.

Looking around in a daze as he waited impatiently for the ambulance, time seeming to have distorted on this crazy morning, Rob thought he was alone and was startled to see Jack Hollingsworth twenty or so yards behind him. In all the madness, he'd forgotten the old man was with them, and it seemed as if Jack had forgotten the rest of them were there too, so intently was he staring at the house. *Why hasn't he gone after Kelly? Why is he just gazing at the house like that? What is he seeing?*

Focusing on Jack, he was stunned to see the anguished look on the old man's weathered face. Whatever memory he was reliving, it wasn't a pleasant one. He looked as if he were in a turmoil of emotion, and Rob wondered whether he would see tears making their way down the craggy crevices of those cheeks if he were a little closer. Something tapped at the back of his brain. What was it Jack had been muttering when Rob realized that the painting was of Syracousse? What had he said? *She couldn't know.* That was it. *She couldn't know.* What couldn't she know? Surely no one else was consumed by crazy secrets untold outside this house? Not an old guy like Jack.

The ambulance let out a small whoop as it came down the track, breaking both men's reveries. Jack's face instantly masked over, becoming calm and normal again, only the strain of the present situation tearing at his features. Rob finally got to his feet, stepping backwards to let the medics do their jobs, feeling his stomach churn as they slowly began to fit neck and back braces to the unconscious Jason, their faces serious and concentrated as they spoke loudly to the man who was in no position to answer them.

Keery came back out through the side gate with one arm around Kelly, leading her out and guiding her forward as she repeatedly glanced over her shoulder. There was no sign of Tabby, and both Rob and Jack looked questioningly at the policeman.

Keery shook his head. "We can't find her as yet in the garden, but if her slipper's here, then it's likely we'll find her asleep somewhere. One of my men will be here in a

217

minute with the keys to the house, and then we'll have a thorough search. She might have gotten in somehow." He glanced over at Jason, who was being maneuverd onto a stretcher and then looked at Rob. "Are you going with him?"

Rob nodded. "Yeah. He's a good friend of mine." Taking hold of Kelly's hand, he realized what it was that kept drawing her attention, causing her to nervously gaze over her shoulder. Pushing her hair out of her face, he kissed her on the forehead and then tilted her face up to his so that she could see the sincerity there. "Tabby wouldn't have fallen in the pond, Kelly. She'd have to climb over the little fence that surrounds it first, and that would be too high for her. Believe me, I know. I climbed over it hundreds of times when I was a kid, and it was designed to keep curious toddlers like her out. Okay?"

Letting out a little sniff, Kelly nodded; grateful, if not convinced. The ambulance men were loading Jason into the back now, and Kelly kissed Rob gently on the lips. "Will you call me later?"

Rob squeezed her tight. "Of course. And you can reach me at the hospital if you have any news or if you need me for anything. I wish I could stay, but I can't send Jase off on his own. I need to know that he's going to be okay."

Kelly smiled gently. "Don't worry. I've got plenty of people here." Her brow furrowed a bit as Rob stepped up to sit down next to the stretcher. "What do you think Jason was doing here anyway?" She didn't look suspicious, just confused.

Rob looked away. "I don't know. I really don't know."

Keery's look was hard. "Well, I'd be interested in finding that out when he comes 'round. Call me if there's any change."

Glaring at him, Rob slammed the door.

CHAPTER TWENTY-NINE

About five minutes after the ambulance had left, four policemen arrived with the keys to Syracousse, shortly followed by a van carrying more constables to help search the house and grounds. Keery had tried to keep Kelly to one side while he swiftly separated his men into parties, sending some along the lane to the river and the fields and spreading the rest evenly around the property, but she refused to remain with the young woman police constable allocated to her, insisting in no uncertain terms that she was damn well going into the house. If anyone was capable of finding Tabby, it was her. Keery had stared into her resolute, exhausted face for only a fraction of a second before admitting defeat.

"Okay, you can go in. But if anyone tells you to stop or come out, then you do as you're told. Agreed?"

"Agreed."

It took all of her restraint not to grab the keys and race ahead of the detective who seemed to be moving too slowly toward the heavy front door.

"Come on, come on," she muttered under her breath as

he worked his way around the locks. Her eyes seemed to be aching constantly, and if she looked down at the hands that held on so desperately to the dirty blue slipper, she'd have seen the cuts and scratches that were oozing and scabbing from her frantic attack on the overgrown thorny bushes that had tried to keep the precious prize from her. They were there but she couldn't feel them. She was vaguely aware of mud and blood, but there was no sensation of pain. She hadn't felt anything except an awful, hollow emptiness all day. All day and what felt like forever.

Time had passed like a hazy nightmare ever since she'd put her head around Tabby's door, still fuzzy and romantic from making love with Rob, and realized with horror that the room was empty. She had a vague memory of moving in slow motion across the landing, screaming for her father to wake up, to tell her that Tabby was sleeping somewhere else and not to be so bloody hysterical. To tell her anything except that the little girl wasn't in bed and nobody knew where she'd gone. But it didn't happen like that. It didn't happen like that at all, and now here she was, trapped in these events that didn't belong to her, as lost as her baby. *Oh Jesus, please let my baby be okay. Please let her come home. For both our sakes.*

The door was finally pushed open, and with an unconscious cry of relief she barged past the uniformed men and ran up the abandoned staircase, which seemed to eat up the large, empty hallway big enough to be considered a room in its own right. Her body surged forward on pure adrenaline and instinct.

When she came to the shabby landing that had once been cool and elegant, but which now shed its skin in patches like the dry, rotting flesh of the aged, dropping forgotten flakes of paint on the stained floorboards beneath, she stopped, her breathing heavy, eyes darting to the doors on each side, gaze stretching along the full length of the narrow walkway to the tatty, rotting window frame at the far end. *She's here; I know it. She's some-*

where here. She turned around, hesitating with this sudden, new certainty. *Oh Tabby, I can almost smell you. Where are you?* Somewhere outside of the calm island in her mind, she could hear her own straining voice screaming her daughter's name, screaming for an answer, willing it to come.

The sun was flooding warmly through the clean glass of the window behind her as Tabby giggled on the carpet with Mr. Pickles. The smell of the flowers in the garden seemed to have followed them inside, and the fresh sweetness danced along the corridor and around her, teasing her hair. She smiled happily and leaned against the golden yellow walls, the music tinkling inside her like it had constantly since she'd arrived. How long ago was that? Her young mind twisted at the puzzle, but couldn't find an answer. Sometimes she felt like she'd been here forever, and other times it seemed like only minutes. Whichever it was, the monster man who had chased her in that terrible dark seemed like a long time ago now, and that was all that mattered. She was safe here. She was safe and bright and loved.

Let's play hide and seek again, Tabby. I'll hide; you and Mr. Pickles come and find me. Let's play.

Hauling herself to her feet, she was about to cover her eyes and start counting, when something seemed to invade the tranquillity, something that she could hear above the music, unsettling her. Tilting her head, she fiddled absently with Mr. Pickle's ears, trying to tune out the lilting notes and focus on the other sound, the new and familiar one. She stood silent and still, her breath shallow as she concentrated on listening to the sound that seemed to be coming from just outside her range.

Finally she seemed to locate the right internal frequency and her deep eyes widened. Mummy. It was Mummy calling her name. Oh, she sounded upset, so upset, not like Mummy at all. Her brow furrowed, and she glanced around as if expecting her mother to appear from one of the doors on each side of her. Expecting and *wanting* her to appear. Her mummy sounded so sad, and it was all her fault. Her mummy missed her. She missed her.

The music inside started to play louder and louder, and Tabby frowned, pushing the sound away.

Come on, Tabby. Let's play. Let's play hide and seek, and she'll go away. Just ignore it and it'll go away. Let's play Tabby, let's play.

Her face furrowed in annoyance as she pushed the notes away. Why would she want to ignore Mummy? She looked at the doors, which came off from each side of the corridor that seemed to go on forever, trying to figure out where the sound was coming from. Could Mummy be in one of those rooms? How could she have gotten there? They'd played in and out of them all afternoon. Surely she'd have seen Mummy if she'd been in them. She'd explored every inch of their fairy-tale contents. Those rooms were the most beautiful and magical places she'd ever been, full of toys and sweets and princesses' beds and clothes, each unique but equally wonderful. She couldn't ever imagine being afraid of the night if she had to sleep in those rooms. Anyway, that didn't really matter, because it never seemed to get dark here. It was always daytime, and it was always sunny.

Her mother's voice cut through her thoughts, and something in it made her insides feel funny. The music was getting louder and more insistent inside her, and she screamed at it to SHUT UP. Suddenly she wanted her mummy more than anything. More than the sunshine, more even than Mr. Pickles. She didn't like hearing her screaming like that as if she were crying, when everyone knew that mummies didn't cry. Mummies made everything better.

This time when Tabby heard the echo of her name, she shouted back, shouted back with all the strength her small lungs could manage. She shouted so loudly that her throat ached with the effort. The music inside was discordant and angry, sending sharp pains across her forehead, but she ignored it. Her mummy was in the room just up a bit from her, she was sure of it. Why hadn't she answered? Grabbing the handle with both hands, she twisted it and pushed the door open. She'd been expecting to see the cool blue of the walls and the enormous toy chest open by the four-poster bed, and the shock of the change left her staring in silence for a moment at the terrible blackness across the threshold. The air that hit her was cold and stale, but it was only when she heard the wet sound of something big slithering toward her across the floor that she screamed and screamed, pulling the door towards her, desperate to shut it before whatever thing was in there reached her and sucked her in. Her eyes squeezed shut, and she held the door shut tight, tugging against the handle for a few moments until she was convinced that nothing was trying to open it from the other side.

Small tears were running down her face—her mummy had been in there, her mummy had been in there, she'd been sure of it—and she stood frozen with fear until somewhere under the awful noise inside her, she heard the faint sound of her mother's cries. Opening her eyes, she turned around, screaming in frustration.

What she saw made her yell cut off midway. Things in the house had changed, just like the music that was hurting her head. The corridor was crumbling now in the new gloom, its walls and ceiling covered with cobwebs, their silky threads thick and weighed down with dead insects. It hadn't been like this a minute ago; it hadn't been like this at all. Her body shook as she cried, confused and terrified and just wanting to go home—*please Mummy, please take me home, I'll be good I promise*—and she shrieked as a large black spider scuttled across her bare feet, pausing for a moment, its front legs waving in the air as it sensed her presence, sniffing her out.

She pushed the wisps dangling from above that threatened to trap her, out of her face, and she ran to the window that was now covered in grime, shouting and screaming for her mummy, for anyone, to see that she was in here. The garden was a dull haze, but if she looked hard enough she was sure she could see ghost-like figures moving out there. Banging on the window, jumping up and down in anxiety, she shouted again and again, her words nonsense, her small vocabulary unable to convey what she felt, just wanting someone to hear her, to look up and see her. Behind her, she was sure she could hear the spider coming back. Not just one, lots of them, and they were coming for her.

Little Miss Muffet sat on her tuffet, eating her curds and whey. Along came a spider and GOBBLED HER UP!

We can play hide and seek like this if you like, Tabby. You'd be amazed at what can live behind some of those doors. I can make it like this forever, you know. Now be a good girl and behave. I love you. You're home now.

Trying to shut the voice out, Tabby banged on the window frantically, and something fell from the ceiling into her hair. Hysterical now, she beat it out and glanced upwards. The ceiling was covered in slugs and they were dripping onto her, their small thick bodies, heavy and damp as they landed on her head, arms and shoulders. It was too much for her system to take and she slid down beneath the window frame curling into a tiny ball, her hands over her hair. *Make it stop now make it stop now I want to go home I want to go home I want to go home.* And she did. More than anything.

The music was gentler now.

You are home, Tabby. Look. You're in your beautiful house. The one you wanted so badly.

Tabby slowly opened her eyes, her nightdress sticking to her with sweat despite the chill. For a moment she seemed unable to breathe. The corridor was back to the golden yellow, no spiders now, no cobwebs, no slithering creatures coming to catch her. Pulling herself up on her knees, she peered through the clear glass of the window. The sun was shining on the perfect lawn, and the surface of the pond twinkled back up at her. She stared for a few moments, and for a second she almost believed it, but if she stared hard enough, she could almost see the blackness under there. The blackness and the bugs. "It's not real," she whispered, the loneliness eating her up from the inside. "It's not real." A small mewl seeped out of her. "I want my mummy." A pane of glass cracked in front of her, but she didn't flinch, just kept on staring out at the garden now empty of moving shadows. "I want my mummy."

Go to sleep.

The tiredness washed outward from somewhere deep inside her, her muscles aching as they relaxed. The tears were still silently flowing as she buried her face in Mr. Pickles's familiar, homely smell, and waited for her eyes to start to drift shut.

CHAPTER THIRTY

It had been two hours since Jack had finally persuaded Kelly to leave Syracousse, and the bath and brandy he'd poured her had done little to calm her. He hadn't really expected them to. Nothing would calm her apart from the return of her little girl. And despite his own veneer of calm and strength, it was only Kelly's need for him that was stopping him falling apart. It seemed as if even the house ached with the lack of Tabitha. Nothing seemed right without her. Nothing.

Kelly was staring into the flames, one hand playing with a loose strand of hair, twisting it into knots. Her voice was quiet. "She was crying. It's crazy, but I was sure I could hear her. So sure. I thought I could hear her really faintly calling for me, answering me. She sounded terrified." She paused, lost in the memory, and Jack knew that even in the midst of this terrible loss, her clever mind would be analyzing it, needing to know whether it was truth or whether her own brain was deceiving her, answering her need.

"How could I have heard her if she wasn't there? And what about her slipper? She's there, I know it." She paused. "I know it, but I just don't understand it." For the first time, she turned to gaze at Jack. "Why did they make me leave? Why?"

"They're ripping the house apart up there. If they find anything, they'll call. It's better that we're here. They need space to get on with their jobs. You know that better than most, love. Trust them." Looking down into the golden pool of brandy, Jack's stomach turned a little knowing that what he was saying was only a half-truth. Keery had asked him to take Kelly home because they needed the daylight to dredge the large pond, and that was something neither of them wanted Kelly knowing. If he were honest, it was something he could have done without knowing himself. The thought of those men looking for Tabby in all that murky water would keep him awake tonight. That thought, and so many others.

He finished his drink and poured himself another from the bottle on the floor by his chair. One more wouldn't hurt him. Kelly hadn't really touched hers, and that was probably a good thing. He'd try to get her to take one of his sleeping pills later, and too much alcohol beforehand wouldn't be too clever. But he'd resigned himself to a sleepless night, and he needed the calming warmth to help him think properly. To think without guilt and confusion and fear.

Why the hell hadn't he recognized the house in Tabby's painting? He should have; God knows, he knew it well enough. And today, going up there, seeing it standing so defiantly after everything that had happened, had brought all the memories flooding back. There were some good ones, yes, and some great ones; there was no point in try-ing to deny that. But some were painful, too painful to want to revisit. And then there were the ones that were . . . well, were downright strange. God, he was too old for this, too old to have to go traipsing around in the past again. It was done. Done and dusted, damned or oth-erwise. He let out a long sigh, but Kelly didn't notice.

What would she think of him if she knew? What would she and Tabby do if the whole mess were opened up?

Do you have a secret, Granddad? A guilty secret.

The confusion inside was making him want to scream, and he got up and went into the dark kitchen, gazing out the small window without turning the light on. The dark was the place for thinking about secrets. It was a great leveler, making distractions invisible, objects old and new, loved and unloved reduced to shadows unintrusive and unimportant. In the dark, he could forget about age and aching hips and just exist for the moment as if nothing before or after was of any consequence. When he'd been on the force, he'd done some of his best thinking late in the evening when everyone else had gone home. He'd turn the lights in his office out, put his feet up on his desk—back in the days when he could do that without thinking something was going to snap at the base of his spine—and let his brain take over. Staring out at the night sky it felt a little like that now, and the chill away from the fire seemed to make his mind sharper, more focussed.

How could Tabby have known? How could she have even known what the house looked like? Kelly and he had never taken her down there. No one ever went down there. It was a forgotten place. No one even thought about it, mentioned it. It was like a dirty secret that the town was no longer interested in. Not until that rape. What would have made Tabby go there? What would have made her paint Syracousse? It didn't make sense.

The only link between Tabby and Syracousse was himself. Whatever was going on, it had to be down to him in some way, and it wasn't only Tabby who was affected. What about Jason Milburn? Someone or something had hurt him pretty badly last night, and he didn't hold with Keery's theory that Jason had anything to do with Tabby's disappearance. Jason may have strayed off the straight and narrow in the past, but he'd never been like that, never *bad*. But just what the hell had he been doing down there?

The dark provided no answers. He turned and stared through the doorway at Kelly, and his heart felt heavy and for the first time in his life, old. Its beat was tired, an unwilling accomplice in his life. She was his baby girl. His daughter. His *youngest* daughter.

Standing there watching her, seeing her so pale and upset, he felt a sudden overwhelming urge to sit down and tell Kelly everything. To bare his soul and be damned. He'd lose her; he'd lose her for good, of that he was sure. But maybe if he told her, then Tabby would come back. Crazy as it sounded, he believed that more than he believed in anything. If he told Kelly, if he sacrificed himself on the altar of the truth, then Tabby would come back. All this would stop. It would be worth it. Losing that love to see her joy when her baby came back. And in his heart he'd know that his punishment would be deserved. Would that knowledge make the loss easier?

He felt like a man standing on the edge of a precipice, giddy eyes drawn to the tiny reflections of rocks below, wondering how large they would grow, what sharp shape they would become were he to take just one tiny forward step more, leaving land behind him and heading into the abyss. Mentally moving in a dream, he raised a foot. "Kelly, there's something I need to tell you." His words sounded as if they were coming from somewhere else, somewhere outside himself, and as his daughter slowly turned her head to face him, it almost felt like he was leaving the safety of firm ground and heading into the freefall that beckoned so invitingly.

The doorbell rang like an alarm clock going off in the middle of a deep sleep, and Kelly's head swung round away from him, breaking the moment.

"That'll be Rob." Scrambling to her feet, she was blind to the reeling step backwards Jack took, his hand reaching for the doorframe, clutching at something to steady himself mentally and physically. *What was I thinking? What was I thinking to tell her today? Today of all days?* Despite the heat from the fire, his hands felt cold and he poured himself another large brandy under the guise of fetching one for Rob.

Coming into the small lounge, the writer looked tired. There were large, dark circles clinging to his eyes, and his clothes hung lethargically from his frame, disheveled and forgotten. Kelly ushered Rob to the sofa, where she sat down close to him, her face full of concern. "How is he?"

Jack passed the young man a glass, and Rob took a long sip before answering. "Not good." His voice was hollow, another reminder to Jack of how the world had changed for them all with only the passing of one day. Each with their own burden of grief locked away inside.

He slowly eased his aching, treacherous body into the chair by the fire to hear what Rob was quietly telling them.

"They say he's lucky to be alive. I don't think I'd call it lucky. He's broken his back and fractured his skull." He took in a long, shaky breath. "He's in a coma in intensive care. If he does make it, and it seems like a big if, then he's never going to walk again."

Jack's trained eye noted the tortured way Rob's jaw twitched, and the anger hiding just below the surface of his handsome, sad face. The policeman inside, the one his body had forced into retirement, stirred. "Do they know how it happened?"

Rob's face twisted into a smile before his muscles lost their energy and his expression slackened into nothingness. "The doctors said that if they didn't know better, they'd say he'd fallen or jumped out of a third-floor window. They haven't got a clue how it happened. I'm going back up there tomorrow morning, so maybe they'll know a bit more then."

"I'll come with you." Kelly's face was determined. "Just

in case he comes around. He might know something about Tabby. Maybe he saw something."

Rob stroked her hand. "Don't expect too much. Like I said, he's in a coma."

"Anything's better than just sitting here going crazy. I've got to do something."

Jack took his moment. Kelly needed to rest, and this seemed like a good opportunity to get her to bed. "I think you'd better go upstairs and take one of my sleeping pills. I'm not letting you go anywhere tomorrow unless you get some sleep tonight. You need it. You need to be fit and well for both yourself and Tabby."

Kelly frowned. "I hate pills, and the last thing I feel like doing now is going to bed. What if someone rings?"

"If someone rings, I'll wake you up. They're not going to knock you out; they'll just help you drift off. Trust me."

Kelly looked at Rob, who stroked her hair. "Your dad's right. You need to rest if you're going to be fit for anything tomorrow. Now go and do as you're told, young lady."

Kelly didn't smile, but acquiesced, pulling herself to her feet.

Kelly leaned down and kissed Rob before going and kissing Jack. "Goodnight, Dad."

"Goodnight, sweetheart. Let's hope this whole nightmare is over tomorrow. Keery will find her. I'm sure of that."

Kelly didn't reply, but headed slowly up the stairs, leaving both men staring into space as if hypnotized by the fire. Neither spoke until they heard the dull sound of Kelly's bedroom door shutting. Jack waited a few moments before sipping his brandy and leaning back in his chair. He spoke quietly, the age in his voice like gravel.

"So what do you think Jason was doing up at the house last night?" Rob sent him a sharp, suspicious look from the sofa, and Jack shook his head quickly, a sad smile on his face.

"You're getting me wrong. I don't think he had anything to do with Tabby going missing, don't you worry about that. I had plenty of dealings with him back before I retired, but it was never anything serious. He did himself more damage than he ever did anyone else. I think he is just a very angry young man, not a bad man. He's been out of trouble for a while now." He watched Rob carefully as the writer rolled his glass in his hands, avoiding eye contact.

"I just wondered if you knew what he'd be doing up there. You boys were pretty friendly when you were kids, and you chatted for a while at the funeral. Did he say anything?"

Rob chewed his bottom lip, and Jack waited patiently for the man to find the words he was mulling over. He'd learned over the years never to push. If you pressed people too hard for an answer, they'd clam up. Let them talk in their own time. In their own words. Eventually their story would come out, whether now or in fifty years' time, it didn't really matter. You couldn't fight the truth, no matter how hard you tried. He was learning that lesson fast.

Rob sighed and ran one hand through his short hair. "When we were kids, we used to play up there. Me, Jase and Carrie." The memory of his friends seemed to stab at the skin on his face, but he carried on, his voice stilted as if uncertain of how to continue. "Only for one summer. But it seemed to last a lifetime, that summer. Carrie had made friends with Gina Grace." He laughed a little, lost in time. "I guess she was getting to that age when she wanted to have girlfriends as well as us. Anyway, things happened during those months that drew us together and then blew us apart."

Jack's eyes narrowed. "What kind of things?"

Rob shook his head. "You wouldn't believe me if I told you. Strange things. Gina things, we called them. I suppose, over the years, I convinced myself that they never happened at all. But now, after all this, I don't think I can hide from it anymore, and without Jason, I don't think I know what to do about it." He smiled bitterly up at Jack. "I sound crazy, don't I? Are you sure you want me around Kelly?"

Jack didn't smile back. *Strange things. Gina things.* Why had Rob called them Gina things? Gina didn't have anything to do with any of it. She couldn't have. Because strange things happened before Gina, he was sure of it, even if it was such a long time ago. He shook his head at Rob. "I don't think you're crazy. I don't think you're crazy at all."

The younger man was staring at him so intently, Jack was suddenly afraid of taking this conversation further, afraid of what he might say and what he might hear. He changed tack. "I know about crazy. I went up to Syracousse that day. I answered Camilla Grace's call at the station." He hated the way the words came out so clinically. So professionally. *Of course you answered. It came through on your direct line. She wasn't calling the police, she was calling Jack Hollingsworth. She was calling for help.*

"I was the one who found Philip Grace in the kitchen."

Rob had frozen, his glass half way to his lips. "That was you? You were the policeman who came?"

Jack nodded. "That was me. A long time ago."

Silence fell between them again, but this time there was an edge to it, and Rob finished his drink and stood up. "Thanks for the brandy, Jack. I'll see you in the morning." He paused in the doorway. "Maybe you should try and get some sleep yourself."

"Yes, maybe I will. I think I'll have a nightcap first, though." He raised a hand to say goodnight and Rob pulled the door to behind him.

CHAPTER THIRTY-ONE

Rob got undressed in the dark and slid into the double bed next to Kelly. The pill must have sent her off to sleep, but her body was sweating and she tossed and turned, murmuring to herself, lost in a dreaming search for her baby. Putting one arm gently over her, Rob stroked her damp hair. Where was she? Still up at Syracousse hunting through those abandoned rooms?

Although he'd come up to bed, he wasn't tired. Exhausted and aching, yes. But not tired. His mind was still racing, and always, always, flashing up behind his eyes like a screensaver on a computer, there was the image of Jason hooked up to all those machines, his face barely visible behind the ventilating equipment strapped to him. Was the past ever going to let them go?

The old man's words were still ringing in his ears. *I know about crazy. I went up to Syracousse that day.* So many doors opening into the past, and so many truths when you get there. Jack Hollingsworth had been there. Rob had been surprised for a second, and then it all made a weird kind of sense as if strands of thread were being carefully woven back together.

It was another refracted ray of someone's life slipping past the shadows of his own. Another door opened at a different angle creating a different view of the same truth. Jack Hollingsworth's truth was that he'd found Philip Grace bleeding his life away on the kitchen floor that hot afternoon, Gina probably still crying beside him. But what if he'd come five or ten minutes earlier? What would his truth have been then? His truth and theirs would have collided, and there'd have been one less secret to carry through the years.

Stroking Kelly's hair had calmed her a bit, her movements less frantic. His eyes still wide open, Rob curled in behind her, wanting the comfort of her warmth as he strolled through the past. Yes, there'd have been one less secret for all of them to carry because Jack Hollingsworth didn't find Philip Grace first. They did. The four of them.

Rob didn't know what he was doing, coming up the gravel track that afternoon. He didn't know why he'd agreed to Carrie's meeting at his house. He didn't want to hear about Gina, didn't want to see her, but he'd known the minute they'd all met up that they'd end up back here. His eyes burned into Jason's back as his ex-best friend, his now biggest betrayer, strode along ahead of him, arms and hands still lightly bandaged even though it had been two long weeks since . . . well, since Teacher. Teacher and Jason's talk at school. Rob's stomach twisted with the memory. Maybe that's why he'd agreed to Carrie's incessant demands for a powwow, not just to shut her up, but to see Jason. To see if he was sorry.

He blew his bangs out of his face, and out of the corner of his angry eye saw Carrie waiting for them up by the tree. He wasn't stupid. He knew she'd gone on ahead to leave him and Jase together. What did she think they

*were going to do, talk or something? Fat chance. He was
never ever going to forgive Jase, even if he were sorry and
there was no sign of that. Jase hadn't even looked at him
when he and Carrie had turned up at Rob's mum's house.
Yeah, Jase looked tired and had those big dark rings under his eyes, just like Mum had since the stuff with Dad,
but he sure as shit didn't look sorry. He hadn't even really
spoken, just nodding and grunting in agreement when
Carrie said they should go up and see Gina. See what she
had to say.*

*When would Carrie see that talking was worth shit?
Whatever Gina had to say it wouldn't bring Teacher back.
It wouldn't turn the clock back to the beginning of the
summer when everything was fine, and he could believe
that whatever was wrong in the world, a hot summer's
day could put it right. Jason wasn't the only one who
hadn't been sleeping. If he thought he was the only one
who had nightmares about Teach, then he was more of a
selfish shit than Rob thought. Shit. It was such a good
word. It really summed up the way the world made him
feel and the way he felt about the world. At least he knew
that he didn't have long to go here. He was off to boarding
school and for the first time in his life September couldn't
come soon enough. He stared at the strangers ahead of
him who used to be friends. Soon enough he'd be away
from them, from all this and then maybe the nightmares
of fire and burning fur would stop. Yeah, boarding school
was his lifeline, his secret. And he wasn't sharing it with
anyone. It was his. It was private.*

*He reached the shade of the heavy branches and joined
the other two. Carrie glanced from one boy to the other
with total despair and Rob slid his eyes away.*

*"Well, let's go see what she wants to say. I don't want
to be here any longer than I have to." Jason's voice was
hollow and for a moment Rob almost felt for him. Almost.*

*Carrie pushed the gate open and once again, for the
last time that summer, they crossed the threshold of*

Syracousse. Walking past the pond, Rob pointed out Gina on the old swing in the far corner, and the three of them headed toward her. As she stood up to meet them, he saw how the past two weeks had taken their toll on her, too. Her hair had lost its sheen and her slim frame was now thin, her face gaunt. The beauty was still there, but there was nothing glowing anymore. She picked at her fingers, ripping the skin from beside her chewed-down nails.

"It wasn't me. I didn't do that to Teacher. I wouldn't do something like that. You have to believe me." *Her voice was barely a whisper, and she looked close to tears.*

Awkward and uncomfortable, Rob took the swing and pushed the empty seat backwards and forwards, listening to its familiar creak. He didn't know what to think. Maybe Gina didn't do it. Or maybe she just thought she didn't do it. Jason was staring at her with hate, and something inside Rob was pleased he was looking at her like that and not at him. But then he remembered that he didn't care. He and Jase were finished. There was no going back.

Gina was crying properly now, the blotchy red beneath her eyes the only color on her cheeks. "I promise. I wouldn't do something like that. I couldn't. I don't know how it happened, but it wasn't me. It couldn't have been me. Please believe me."

Carrie took a tentative step forward and turned to face the others from Gina's side. "I believe her. No one would do something like that. Not to Teacher. Not to anyone. Look at her. She's as upset about this as we are."

The open goodness in Carrie's face would have made Rob smile in any other situation. Carrie always believed the best of everyone. Jason looked at Carrie, the hate in his face overwhelmed by tiredness, and shrugged. "I don't really care anymore. Nothing can bring Teacher back. Nothing."

Rob said nothing, his brain aching from thinking, and

just pushed the swing again and again. The back door was open and the sound of shouting and recrimination invaded their silence. Gina flinched.

"They always argue now. Ever since you all left. They think I can't hear them from my bedroom."

For a moment, the purpose of the visit was forgotten. Rob could almost see Carrie's vision of the perfect family crumbling. That's how she saw the Graces. The same way Jase used to see the Blacks. Perfect. When would she learn that nothing was perfect?

Carrie's voice was incredulous. "What are they arguing about?"

"Dad's business isn't working. Hasn't been for a while apparently, he just didn't tell us. He wants to sell the house, move somewhere smaller and use the rest of the money to pay off some of his debts."

She was speaking in barely a whisper, and Rob noticed that even Jase was fascinated. If he were honest, he was fascinated himself. The mask of the summer was crumbling further.

"Why don't they? Sell the house I mean, if it'll solve your problems." Carrie made it sound so matter of fact, but then, Rob thought, a little ashamed of himself, Carrie lived on Gallows Hill. Nobody would care if they had to move out of there.

Gina was staring at the back door. "Mum won't let him. She loves this house. She's lived here all her life. She says it's her house, not his."

Philip Grace's hard, accusing words filled the garden with their sound, and Gina's face clouded over. "He never shuts up. Never. I wish he'd just die." She almost spat the last words out, and Rob wondered just what had been going on here since the awful day that Teacher had died.

A couple of seconds later and the shouting stopped abruptly. Carrie raised an eyebrow. "Maybe they heard you."

Gina shook her head. "More likely he's just stormed out again. That's what he does. Comes in, shouts and then leaves."

The sun was beating down aggressively and a few moments later when Gina suggested a drink, none of them said no, although Jason swore he was leaving straight after.

Rob was the last one into the shade of the kitchen, and Gina was already staring at the body on the floor, the body bleeding on the floor, her breath coming in sharp, fast sounds. Out of the corner of his eye, Rob could see the orange of the pile of chopped carrots, the orange that seemed to clash so badly with the red that was covering the tiles beneath them. Jason was staring into the surprised eyes of Philip Grace, his young body visibly trembling. "Jesus shit, Gina, what did you do? What did you do?"

For a brief moment, Gina looked up at Jason in horror. "No," she whispered, "No, no." Then her voice began to rise until she was screaming the word, her hands reaching up and pulling at her long, dark hair, her long hair that had lost it's luster, pulling out clumps as she tore at it. "NO NO NO NO NO NO NO . . ."

Unable to take any more, Rob reached forward and grabbed Carrie and Jason, tugging them out of the kitchen. Without pausing to speak, the three of them ran through the garden, fighting for first place out of the gate, not stopping then but running all the way down the lane as fast as they could go. Rob's ankle twisted on the gravel, the pain shooting up his leg, but still he pushed himself forward, no amount of agony enough to make him rest this close to that awful place. His arms pumped as if trying to move through hot honey, and he wanted to run and run forever. To never have to stop. To never have to think. But once he'd reached the wall of the house that led from Ousebank Way down to the river, his blood vessels felt like they were exploding all over his body, and his legs were like jelly above his throbbing foot.

Sliding down the rough brick, Rob sat on the cool ground, drops of sweat running down his face, and shut his eyes, waiting until the pounding feet of Carrie and Jason behind him fell silent, before he opened them again.

Jason doubled over, barely able to breathe. "Holy shit. Holy, holy shit. She did it, just like she did it to Teacher." He glanced up from his crouched position, eyes full of disgust. "Why did you take us there again, Carrie? Why? How fucking dumb are you?" Pulling himself upright, the stitch that was obviously in his side making him stand funny, he spat at the ground and then started wandering slowly away up the narrow lane toward the other houses, his shoulders hunched and tired, a small patch of sweat showing through his t-shirt. Rob watched him go, no energy or compulsion to call him back.

Carrie was crying, but he ignored that too, pulling his knees up and lowering his head into his forearms. When he raised his face again, she had gone, vanished quietly as if she'd never been there.

His breath still raw in his lungs, he wondered momentarily where there was left to go. Home? What home? What did it mean, that word? At his, his mother would be hunched over the phone, whispering in a guilty voice to some doctor or nurse up at that home or hospital or wherever they'd taken his dad, whispering as if the neighbors could hear the family shame through the walls. At Gina's home, home no more, she was probably still screaming over Philip Grace's bleeding pale body, waiting for someone or something to take it back, what she did. Jason would be wandering back to his careless mother with his bandaged arms and empty eyes, and Carrie, poor crying Carrie, bereft without her friends, her hope, now full of the fear that came with knowledge. Knowledge that nothing was safe, and that nothing would ever be the same again.

No more friends, Rob thought, his sweat now cold

against his skin. No more friends like this. He didn't have it in him. If he could stay sane till boarding school, then everything would be okay. It would be a new start away from Streatford. A new start.

PART THREE

PART THREE

CHAPTER THIRTY-TWO

The walls are aching from the inside out, frustrated by the child's tears. It isn't working; it isn't working at all, not like the other little girl, the only little girl. Everything is black now, black and damp, the air rancid as the anger takes over, the inner bricks oozing slime as the constant crying whine fuels the rage.

Why can't this one love? Doesn't she understand that they can be together forever, never alone? Doesn't she understand how safe it is here, how nothing can ever harm her as long as she only behaves? Why can't she understand and be grateful, instead of this reluctance and resistance? Why can't she just be happy?

The incomprehension seethes, pulling it into itself. There is only one who would truly understand. It knows that now. It has forgotten so much during the too many years of waiting, but now it knows she cannot be replaced so easily. She was special. She is special. Together they belong.

There had been others it had loved all those seasons ago, but they had betrayed it. All of them. They wanted it destroyed. They wanted it to be alone forever. They had taken her away and now she was lost. Lost and alone. The strangers had told it that. They had made it understand.

Oh, how it had ached, hearing those words after all the patient empty days with only echoes for company, but it had taken its revenge. It had made the strangers pay. It had infused them with its anger; it had suffocated them with its pain. And it would deal with the rest until she came back. Until they made her come back.

The constant sobbing makes it wail, drowning the smaller human sounds with waves of its own discordant emotion until the child screams and falls silent. There is a victory in the peace. The girl will learn to behave. She will learn to be grateful, to understand. The fear will teach her. The fear and the darkness. It will be for the best. She will learn to do as she's told like a good little girl. She will behave while she is under this roof. It settles back, feeling the old earth secure around its foundations and relaxes. Maybe in a little while it will let in some light. Maybe. But not yet.

CHAPTER THIRTY-THREE

Rob could feel the nervous energy emanating from Kelly as they walked down the whispering corridors of the hospital in search of Jason's room. She had awoken almost as exhausted as she'd been before they went to bed, but still she'd insisted on coming. And Rob had to agree with her; what else was she to do? There was no sign of Tabby at the house and now the police were stretching their search farther, into the fields and back into the village. If she stayed at home, she'd go crazy with worry. He gave her hand a squeeze and she gripped hard in reply.

The private wing of the hospital was a far cry from the lime green walls and frantic activity of the floors below, and there was silence around them as they approached the nurse seated behind the curving wooden counter that also served as her desk. She smiled professionally from behind a vase overflowing with scented lilies, no disinfectant invasion here, and Rob's heart twisted. He'd paid for Jason to be here, but as usual, it felt like he'd done too little too late.

His voice echoed around him. "We're here to see Jason Milburn."

"Of course." She picked up a file and came around to their side of the smoothly varnished wood, her uniform white and perfectly pressed.

"How is he?"

"I'm afraid there hasn't been any change as yet. The doctor was with him about an hour ago. We're just going to have to be patient." She seemed unaware of her pun, and checked her watch as her soft shoes ushered them toward a door on the left of the corridor.

"He already has a visitor. She arrived about half an hour ago, but it should be all right for you all to be in there. Sometimes, in these kinds of cases, familiar voices can help bring the patient out of his coma." She smiled again as she reached for the handle. "Can I get either of you a cup of tea or coffee?"

Rob shook his head as did Kelly, and he wondered who would be up here visiting Jason this early in the morning. Maybe it was his girlfriend from the pub the other night. Nodding a thank-you at the nurse—Barbara, her name tag informed him—he stepped inside, still holding Kelly's hand.

The first thing Rob noticed was the perfectly French-manicured fingernails of the hand holding Jason's, and he knew he'd gotten his original guess wrong. This woman's slim build had none of the ageing tiredness of the woman he'd seen in The Plough, and although dressed in jeans and a blouse, these were not the kind of casual items you'd pick up anywhere near Streatford. This woman was designer labeled from head to foot, and as he studied the glorious dark hair that was pulled into a loose ponytail, his heart missed a beat, forgetting itself in the shock of recognition.

The face that turned toward him was as beautiful as it had ever been; its lines and curves of bone more defined now that the fullness of youth had dissipated. It was the eyes that finally confirmed it for him though, that wonderful blue so bright that if he hadn't known better he'd have thought she was wearing contact lenses. So blue and full of pain, just like they'd been the last time he saw them.

"It wasn't me, Rob. I had nothing to do with this. What's happening?"

Her terrified words echoed through the past, and Rob stood frozen in the doorway. Gina. Gina was back. For a moment the world spun, and then a quiet shuffle beside him prompted him back to the present, to the strange formality of adulthood.

"Kelly, this is Gina Grace. Gina, Kelly Hollingsworth. You may remember her from school."

Gina's eyes barely glanced at Kelly, and Rob too, found himself forgetting she was there. "How did you know? How did you know to come here?" His hand slipped away from Kelly's as he stepped forward.

Gina's voice was like tremulous velvet. "I got your message and came back. I didn't want to, but I knew I couldn't stay away. I knew it had to be something serious for you to call." Her eyes slipped to Jason for a second. "But not this. I didn't expect this."

Rob watched as her brow furrowed and she swallowed hard, allowing her to gather herself before she continued. Maybe she had cared about the three of them, after all. Maybe she had cared about *him*. She came when he called. Something in the thought sent a shiver down his spine.

When she turned back to face him, he noticed that her eyes glistened, but no tears fell. She always had been such a contained little girl, so wary of showing emotion. Apart from that last day. That last awful day.

"I got here early this morning and met my solicitor to pick up the keys. He told me about poor Carrie and then that Jason had been found at the house where the police were searching for a little girl that had gone missing. What's going on, Rob? What's happening? I don't understand it. Any of it."

"It's my little girl that's gone. Tabitha." Kelly had stepped up beside Rob and taken his arm. Gina said nothing in response, and Rob suddenly felt awkward standing between the two women. There were things he needed to say that only Gina would understand, but he didn't want to hurt Kelly. It seemed that she felt the change in atmosphere, because suddenly his arm was alone and she took a step away from him.

"Look, you two obviously have some catching up to do. I know Sharnice is in this hospital somewhere, so I think I'll go find her. I'll come back in about half an hour." Looking into her hurt face, Rob felt a pang inside him. *Don't be a bastard again, Black,* he told himself. She doesn't deserve it. Leaning forward, he kissed her on the cheek, but her response was cool, and he let her leave without saying a word.

Waiting for her to close the door, he knew the ache he was feeling. He'd felt it so many times before. Guilt. Guilt at wanting her to leave so he could spend some time with Gina. Beautiful, elusive Gina. Guilt at wanting her out of the way just for a little while.

Kelly found Sharnice two floors down in the women's ward. There was no private room for her, but the weary nurses had made sure she had a bed by the window, so that when she had the curtain pulled round her tiny space in this enormous hospital, she could look out at the sky and have natural light.

The ward nurse told Kelly that since coming out of intensive care Sharnice had kept the thick blue drapes closed as much as possible. She was pleased the girl had a new visitor but told Kelly not to expect too much. The physical scars may be healing, but the emotional ones were going to take a lot longer. What those boys had done to her was terrible. Kelly nodded impatiently, and then pulled back the curtain and stepped inside.

"Hi."

Looking at the girl sitting up in the bed looking so young and fragile, no makeup masking the child, Kelly was almost glad that Rob had been such an arsehole upstairs. If he hadn't frozen her out, then she'd have never come down here. She sat on the edge of the bed. "I thought I'd come and see how you were doing. You're looking good." She kept her voice as soft as possible, and eventually Sharnice brought her hollow eyes round to meet Kelly's.

"I'm okay. It's nice to see you, Miss Hollingsworth." There was no hardness in the girl's voice, none of the cheeky arrogance Kelly was used to seeing in the classroom where Sharnice had a reputation to live up to. But then, Sharnice's world had changed all too dramatically over the last few weeks. Despite the way she looked younger here than Kelly had ever seen her, Sharnice's childhood days were gone forever.

"I think you can probably call me Kelly now, if you'd like."

Sharnice didn't say anything for a moment, but just studied her teacher's face. "You look tired, Kelly." Her voice kept the same low tone, and Kelly wondered if maybe part of this calm exterior was due to painkillers. The girl seemed a little bit spaced out. *Not too spaced out to see how tired you look. Not too spaced to notice that.*

"I am tired. You know my little girl, Tabitha? She went missing the night before last."

She hadn't come down here to talk about this, she'd just wanted to get away from Gina Grace and the way Rob was looking at her, but now that she'd found Sharnice, it seemed to make sense to tell her about Tabby. To talk about the house.

Sharnice nodded, her face betraying no surprise, but Kelly was sure that she saw those pale eyelids open wider for a moment.

"Where did she go missing?"

Kelly's heart started pumping up into her throat, and

ridiculous as it sounded, she felt suddenly as if she were in the presence of an old wise woman.

"The police have been searching up at Syracousse," she whispered. "I found her slipper there, and a man with a broken back. He's here in the hospital in a coma."

Sharnice nodded, gazing somewhere past Kelly.

"It's a bad place. I could feel it, but Lee and Darren couldn't. We should never have gone there. Never."

Kelly reached for Sharnice's hand, bringing her attention back. "What do you mean, 'it's a bad place'? Tell me, Sharnice. I need to know."

A lank strand of hair fell into the girl's face, and she left it there as a disguise for the tear that fell from her eye. She couldn't keep her gaze on Kelly, but instead looked blankly out of the window as she spoke.

"You know, when I got out of intensive care, a policeman came and told me that the boys had tried to kill themselves after they'd given themselves up. I think he thought it would make me feel better, you know, to know that they felt that bad about what they'd done." She paused, chewing her bottom lip, worrying at the skin there. "But it didn't. It didn't make me feel better at all." She looked back at Kelly. " 'Cos I knew something that policeman didn't. That it wasn't their fault. None of this was their fault. They were my best friends."

Kelly gently pushed the hair out of Sharnice's face. "What happened at the house? What made them do that to you?"

"I'll tell you, but only if you promise to do one thing for me."

"What?"

Sharnice pulled herself up on her pillows a little further, wincing slightly.

"When you've got your little girl back, I want you to try to see Lee and Darren. Tell them that it's okay. I know it wasn't their fault. I've had lots of time to think about it, and I know they didn't mean it. I'd write and tell them

252

myself, but no one will let me. They don't think it's healthy." She smiled a small, cynical, adult smile. "Will you do that for me?"

Kelly nodded. "Of course I will."

Sharnice nodded, as if happy with the agreement.

"I've told some of this to the police. Probably all of it at the beginning, but I think they thought what happened had made me fucking crazy. Anyway, they didn't believe me. The house made the boys do what they did. I didn't want to go in there in the first place, but I'd made them leave the Rec, so I figured I'd better go along with it.

"It's weird that we'd never thought of going there before, but I'd forgotten the place was there, and I reckon if it wasn't for Lee's dad working at that solicitor's office, then he'd have forgotten it, too. Anyway, when we got there the door was open, and the electric was suddenly working. It was warm, too, like someone had had a fire in there, not like a house that had been empty for ages. The boys loved it, but I didn't. There was something weird about it, something not right, and then Lee told us what had happened there, with that murder and everything, and how the daughter wanted it left empty forever."

She looked up to check that Kelly was following, and Kelly nodded at her to continue, eager to hear what she had to say. Eager to hear anything that might help her find Tabby.

"I was a bit pissed by then, and I started saying how we should burn it down on bonfire night, you know, do the owner a favor? The boys thought I was joking, but I wasn't. If I could've, I'd have done it right there and then. I didn't like it in there. There was something about it that made me feel trapped. The kind of place that I wouldn't spend the night on my own if someone offered me a million quid. Worse than that, though. It felt like somewhere that had gone bad. I can't describe it properly.

"Anyway, I got them going on the idea and we started to plan it, you know, how to get the petrol and everything, and it was then that things started to go funny. The room went cold to start with. Really cold. Like one minute it was all warm, and the next I wanted to put my coat on. But the boys wouldn't give it to me. They were looking at me funny. And then the light went out."

Kelly stroked her hand. "It's all right, Sharnice. You don't have to say any more."

The girl continued, as if she hadn't heard. "Afterwards . . . afterwards I can remember them crying. Really crying. I hurt so much I thought I was dying, and every time they tried to move me, I just screamed for them to let me go, to leave me on the floor to die. But they wouldn't." Her forehead furrowed with the memory, and her voice fell to just more than a whisper. "They wouldn't leave me there. They were scared to leave me in that house alone. They knew. They knew it had made them do it. They carried me so gently, you know? Carried me out into the lane. Into safety."

Kelly's own tears were falling now, listening to the girl's broken voice. Sharnice sniffed hard.

"That's why I say it's a bad place. Because it is. Something's wrong up there. I hope you find your daughter all right, Miss Hollingsworth. I hope it hasn't done anything bad to her."

Behind them, the curtain rustled and the ward nurse appeared carrying a small tray, a vision of normality.

"That's enough for one day, I think. You've still got a lot of recovering to do. I've brought you a cup of tea and your medication." She looked at Kelly. "You can always come back another time."

Kelly nodded, still unsure of what to make of Sharnice's story, and stood up to leave. "I will. Thank you." She looked at Sharnice. "Thank you, too. You're very brave, you know. Very brave and very special. Is it okay if I visit again?"

The girl in the bed nodded, but her face was serious. "You won't forget what you promised me?"

Kelly shook her head. "I won't forget. You can trust me."

* * *

She went back to meet Rob and Gina, and the three of them walked out of the hospital together, Rob immediately taking her arm. Somewhere inside, she felt better for that. The fresh air raised her spirits, and she leaned her body toward his, forgiving him for his coolness earlier. He responded by squeezing hard against her elbow.

"How was Sharnice?"

She shrugged. "It's difficult to say. She's not the same girl anymore. Nobody would be after that." She paused. "It's strange how people find ways of healing. She says she doesn't blame the boys. She seems to have gotten it into her head that the house made them do it. She called it 'a bad place.' Weird, huh?"

Rob's body stiffened, and she looked up to see him exchange a look with Gina. A secretive, worried look. What was going on with these two? Something Gina had said when they first met her in Jason's room flashed into her mind, and she felt the urge to question her on it.

"Gina, what did you mean when you said, 'it was nothing to do with me'? How could what happened to Jason be anything to do with you?"

Gina's beautiful, pale face flinched, again her eyes darting to Rob, and Kelly felt her frustration rising. "Look, will someone just tell me what's going on? What is it that you don't want to tell me?"

She may as well not have been there as Gina and Rob stood silently looking at each other as if they could hear each other's thoughts without speaking. It was Rob who broke the moment.

"I think we need to go back up to the house, Gina."

She nodded, as if having expected his words. "I've got a set of keys. If the police aren't there anymore we should be able to get in without too much of a problem."

Kelly tugged at Rob's arm. "Are you going to let me in on this? Why do we need to go back up to the house? The police have searched it and they can't find Tabby any-

255

where. Why are you so concerned about that fucking house?" The pain and anger of the week was welling up inside her, and she could feel it all about to explode inside her. All she wanted was her baby back. Screw Rob and Gina. Screw all of this. All she wanted was Tabby.

Rob pulled her close, and gazed intently at her. "Just bear with me on this, Kelly. Let's go back up to the house and find out if there's anything to be worried about. If there is, I'll tell you the whole fucking story, okay? I promise."

Gina stepped up almost between them. "No Rob, you can't . . ."

He cut her off. "I'll do what I fucking want, Gina. I'm tired of carrying it all around inside me. I'm tired of secrets. Anyway, Tabby's missing. I think she has a right to know, don't you? She's part of all this now."

Part of all what? Kelly felt Gina's blue eyes reappraising her, reassessing her importance to Rob, before the elegant woman shrugged. "Okay. She'll think we're crazy, but okay."

CHAPTER THIRTY-FOUR

Stepping onto the gravel outside the main gates to Syra-cousse, Kelly felt relieved to get away from the icy atmosphere within the car. The tension had radiated from Rob all the way through their silent journey, and from her position in the backseat she'd noticed again and again the looks that flitted between Rob and Gina. Her twinges of jealousy were getting stronger, and she couldn't help thinking that her pale blond looks were dull and ordinary next to Gina's striking beauty. It was also obvious that these two seemed to have some kind of history. What was it he'd called himself? The king of the meaningless fling. Maybe she was about to find out the truth about that first-hand. She tried to squash this new pain inside her. Well, at least he'd warned her. But why the hell had she let herself get so involved?

Waiting for Gina to finish struggling with the padlock on the main gates, Kelly took in the view of the house from this new angle. At first, she'd thought that coming back up here was going to be a waste of time, but now that they'd arrived, now that she was looking up at the building, all she could think about was how sure she'd been that she'd heard Tabby calling for her in there. It had been her baby's voice, somewhere just out of reach.

Finally, Gina got the padlock off and pushed the reluctant gates open. The hinges groaned, and the metal seemed to resist Kelly as she helped wedge the left one back against the hedges. Not that there was much chance of it swinging shut. Obviously, not many people came in this way anymore, if at all, but she thought that with all the activity yesterday, the hinges would have loosened up a little. Apparently not.

Following the other two up the drive, their footsteps seemed too loud in the silence. There wasn't even a breeze to make the trees rustle, and Kelly found herself holding her breath. Letting the air out, she glanced around, half expecting to see shadows moving between the bushes, watching them. It was too quiet out here, and it felt eerie. *It's a bad place.* Sharnice's words didn't seem too strange now that she was here.

Don't be stupid, she told herself, bringing her attention back to Gina whose hands seemed to be shaking as she fiddled with a key in the lock. *It's just your imagination. Nothing's wrong.* But still, a shiver ran down her spine, and she stopped where she was, a few paces away from the front door.

"That's weird. It seems to be stuck." Gina was bent over the door, now trying to pull the key out. Rob moved closer.

"Is it the right key?"

She paused and looked up at him. "I think I know the keys to my own house. Of course it's the right one."

Her voice was irritated and snappy, but Kelly could understand why coming back here would make Gina anxious. Her mother murdered her father here, and that memory must be awful to relive. What she couldn't understand was why Rob was so uptight about it.

Feeling completely left out, Kelly took another step backwards and almost tripped over a stiff weed growing up through the driveway. Looking behind her, she saw several more running all the way back to the gates, the green shoots distinctive against the gray. How odd. She couldn't remember seeing them on the way in. Could she have walked through them without noticing? Puzzled, she turned back to Rob and Gina, who were concentrating on trying to get the door open. She was about to speak when movement above distracted her. She gazed upwards and her eyes widened. The weeds didn't seem so important anymore.

She could hear Gina cursing under her breath, muttering quietly, and she knew she should say something, warn them, but her vocal cords seemed frozen as her brain tried to work out what it was seeing, because she knew it had to be impossible. Had to be.

It must have started at the back of the house, because the ivy that was growing so rapidly, reaching round and sucking at the walls, must have come from the neglected vine near the back door of the house that she'd seen yesterday. She almost giggled as she saw the thick green fingers sliding across the roof. *This stuff doesn't need any plant food, it's doing just fine by itself.*

Her breath was coming in shallow waves, and she gasped as the edges of the front of the house turned green, the plant life covering it whole, no bricks visible, as one by one they succumbed to the hungry onslaught of the snake-like vines. What was going on? Just what the fuck was going on? This couldn't be real. It couldn't.

Her eyes following one thick strand as it slid unnoticed across the bottom of the house, Kelly finally found her voice. "Rob. Gina. I think we should go now. Something's happening. Look at the house." Neither of them moved, and her serene calm of disbelief broke as the ivy sped its way to the front door.

259

"LOOK AT THE FUCKING HOUSE!"

Rob started, and looked at Kelly before following her eyes upwards. "Jesus Christ."

Gina screamed and kicked out with one foot. The tendril Kelly had been watching had reached its destination and was now trying to slip its flexible form around Gina's ankle. Watching as the woman turned this way and that trying to avoid its clutches, still screaming for help, Kelly had the horrible feeling that if the plant gripped her, it would never let go. Never. More ivy was slithering in to join the first shoot, and as if finding confidence in the approach of its allies, the green rope finally made contact with Gina's jeans.

Standing on the sidelines, unable to move, Kelly watched as Rob grabbed Gina's arm, pulling her roughly back, freeing her from the plant that hadn't quite secured its hold. The house was almost totally green now, as if it were being devoured, absorbed by the ivy, and Kelly was certain she heard a wail of disappointment emanating from the abnormal growth. She probably would have stayed there forever, if Rob hadn't pulled at her arm.

"Come on, Kelly. Run!"

Turning round, she faltered for a second at the sight ahead of them. Weeds like the one she'd tripped over were springing up everywhere around them and they were growing and growing, some almost knee high. Rob shoved her forward and she began to sprint, trying not to notice the insanely twisted bushes and trees that seemed to reach for her, and the sharp tickling of the weeds nearly strong enough to pull her down.

Gina was next to her, matching her pace for pace, with Rob urging them on from behind. Twice Kelly thought she would fall as her feet caught on sharp stalks and slippery roots, but her fear kept her upright. They were going to make it. They were going to make it. The gates couldn't be too far now.

"Run faster! They're shutting!"

Bringing her eyes up from the dangerous terrain, Kelly's stomach went to water. Oh shit. Oh bloody, bloody shit. The weeds and plants had wound their shoots through the railings of the gates and were pulling them shut, and close as they were Kelly thought they should be able to hear that awful rusty creak of the hinges, but this time there was nothing. This time they seemed to be moving all too easily, all too willingly.

With a grunt of exertion, her legs feeling like lead on fire, she threw herself forward, running at an almost impossible angle. She couldn't see Gina beside her anymore so she fell through the gap in the gates, turning as she did so to reach for the other woman's arm, dragging her over the threshold to safety. Her legs kept moving until she hit the hedges lining the other side of the lane. The leaves rustled as Gina and then Rob slammed into it next to her, sending the vibration through her shaking body.

Shutting her eyes, feeling her internal heat burning her face, she leaned backwards into the bush, unable to think about anything other than the exhaustion that was flooding through her.

"I think I need to start going to the gym." The words came in panting gasps, and she heard Gina attempt a light laugh beside her.

"You're not the only one."

When her breath returned to somewhere near normal, Kelly opened her eyes and sought out Rob. He was standing a little in front of her, staring back through the gates. *The gates empty of plant life. The gates with the padlock securely relocked between them.* Rob forgotten, she stepped forward, ignoring the ache in her cooling limbs, and stared at the house on the other side of the lane. The drive was free of weeds and the pale yellow of the bricks showed no trace of the ivy that had crawled all over it, suffocating it, only moments ago. This was crazy. Totally crazy. How could the house look as if none of the madness she'd just been through had ever happened? She spoke without looking at either of the people beside her.

"I think someone should tell me what's going on here. This isn't right. This isn't *normal*." For a moment she thought she would cry, the mixture of overwhelming emotions rising inside her, but she swallowed it down, forcing the feelings away against her own will. She had to be strong for Tabby. Tabby was all that mattered. As she stared at Syracousse in front of her, a chill settled in her stomach. She'd heard Tabby calling for her in that house. She was sure she had. What if Tabby was in there somewhere, lost and alone? After what she'd just seen anything was possible. Anything.

Rob turned his back almost defiantly on the house. He looked tired and sad, as he took Kelly's hand.

"Let's get out of here. We can go to my house. I think I need a drink before I share this story. At least after what you've just seen it's going to be easier to believe."

Kelly made sure she took the front seat on the drive back to town. This time it was her turn, and there were some things worth fighting for.

CHAPTER THIRTY-FIVE

It had been dark for such a long time that when the bright sunshine hit his eyes, Jason squinted and flinched, as if someone had shone a flashlight in his eyes in the middle of the night. He felt a wave of nausea as he adjusted to the light, and it took him a couple of minutes before he realized where he was. He was back at school, standing in front of the class in Miss Jones's room, listening to a voice whose words he couldn't yet make out. The wooden, ink-stained desks in front of him looked small and different, as did the classroom, and he looked down at himself, mild surprise working its way through his system as he saw himself all grown up. All grown up but back in school. How peculiar.

Examining his tatty leather jacket with the crumpled pack of cigarettes hanging out of the pocket, he had a vague memory of being outside in the cold, his fingers numb. He'd been outside in the dark and he'd been afraid. He frowned a little. That couldn't be right, because he wasn't afraid of the dark, and anyway it was summer outside.

His mind still dulled with the feeling of having just woken up, he glanced over the kids before him, spotting Carrie's pretty face looking all pinched and tight, and then settling on Rob, old Rob, *Robster*, his face pale under the summer tan. For a moment Jason almost smiled, but the way the boy was looking stopped him. Robster was staring at him in horror, his mouth moving slightly, involuntarily.

He'd seen that look before, once, a very long time ago, and suddenly Jason realized *exactly* where he was. He wasn't just back in school. He was back in school on *that* day. That last day of term in that last happy summer. The voice he could hear was his own, and it continued, almost independently of him, as he glanced at the teacher leaning against the far wall to confirm his thought. It was Mr. Fricker, the P.E. teacher, his eyes shut in the warmth, not really listening to the boy at the front. Miss Jones was off school that day, gone on holiday early. She would have been listening. She would never have let Jason tell his tale. But Miss Jones wasn't there the first time round, and she wasn't here now, and Jason stood and spoke uninterrupted, betraying his friend all over again.

He could hear the words clearly now, like needles stabbing at him, but he seemed unable to stop them. He was supposed to be giving a talk on the most interesting thing that had ever happened to him, a holiday or the birth of a sibling, and that would have been easy. He could have made something up. But that's not what he did, that's not what he was doing. He was telling the story of the day in the attic, about The Ministry of Defense, about how he'd found all those crazy pyramids, and about how his friend—no names mentioned, but the sniggering faces around the room showed that they knew exactly whom Jason was talking about—had cried and cried.

He could hear the venom in his voice and wished he could just shut it up, shut it up once and for all. He didn't want to relive this day all over again, he'd done that enough times in his dreams, and anyway, what was the point? What was done couldn't be undone, and he had a niggling feeling that he had bigger problems to be dealing with before it was too late. The strength of the thought made him pause, and he wished he could think straight. What did he mean, 'too late'? Too late for what? Concentrating hard, he heard another sound beneath that of his treacherous voice. It was like the sound of bellows pumping, regularly sucking in and pushing out air, its beat too even to be anything but mechanical.

That's when it'll be too late. When that sound stops.

His brain was feeling clearer, and with relief, he managed to stop himself talking long enough to hear the noise outside the classroom. It was a dog barking. He stared at the classroom door for a few seconds, and then everything began to make sense.

"I'll be back in a minute." He spoke without facing the children, his voice suddenly grown up like the rest of him, and he wondered why he'd said it at all, because he knew he wouldn't be back. He'd never come back here. This was just a clever distraction. You couldn't mend the past from the past.

He pulled open the door, already knowing what he'd see, and a warm smile spread all over him, tingling down into his toes. Teacher was sitting there in the corridor in front of him, whole and healthy, that glorious golden coat glossy and full, his brown eyes shining. Whining eagerly as Jason approached, moving his weight from one front paw to the other, Teacher's tail thumped at the floor. Crouching down beside him, pulling the dog close, Jason was unable to speak, almost unable to feel, the sensations flooding through him, completely overwhelming him. He buried his face in the fur, relishing the musty smell. It was exactly the same. Exactly the same. Teacher was back. And he was perfect.

"It's good to see you, boy. I've missed you." The dog licked his face in reply, and Jason laughed, wiping the wetness away. His hand froze halfway back to stroking the dog, and he stared at it, numbness tickling at him.

His scars were gone. How could that be? How could his scars be gone? Holding both hands in front of him, he turned them this way and that, examining the perfect skin. His eyes shifted from his hands, to Teacher, who sat panting patiently, and then back again.

Of course the scars are gone. Teacher's here and he's just fine. And if he's fine, then you never saved him from the fire, did you? Ergo, no scars.

He shook his head as he played with the dog's silky ears, ears that had burned to nothing last time he saw them. He looked into the brown eyes that stared solemnly back, and the strangeness of it all washed away from him. They were here for a reason. There was something they had to do, and he had a feeling they were the only ones that could do it.

"So, we have to go back then?"

Teacher barked once, loud and confident, and Jason stood.

"Well, come on then. Let's get it done."

The house wasn't happy to know they were back, and it raged to itself, not knowing how they got in. No one could get this far in. They were beyond the rooms, the bricks and mortar, the surface interior. They were far inside, as if in the guts or heart of it.

Jason kept his hand locked in Teacher's warm fur. Despite the madness that he could see around him, he knew where they were. They were in Syracousse. He could feel it.

"It doesn't like us being here."

Teacher whined as if whispering in agreement, and Jason had never felt happier for having the dog close. Taking a step forward in the gloom, a pain shot through his neck and back like a bolt of lightning, and for a moment he stumbled, his head filling with the image of a white room and the machine that made the sound inside him, but he pushed it away. Those things were far away and unimportant, not real to him now. Steadying himself, he felt Teacher's tongue on his fingers and the cold nose against the palm of his hand. "It's okay, boy. I'm not going anywhere." *I hope*, he added silently.

The air around them was dark and cold, with corridors spreading out far into the distance on all sides. Jason peered to his left and right, unsure of which way to go. Strange, unrecognizable sounds echoed out from the distant blackness, some like inhuman wailing and shrieks; others more subtle, occasional scuttling, scurrying sounds made by creatures with too many legs as they whispered by. None of them were pleasant.

Jason shivered as he stood and thought, the damp breeze that teased him easily working its way through his clothes. He looked down at the dog that was sniffing the ground intently, working around each of the corridor entrances.

"I think we need to find Rob. Can you take me to Robster, Teach?" His own voice echoed loudly back at him from a dozen directions, making him jump. Shit, this place was freaky. Freakier than he'd ever imagined.

The dog sat down and let out a short, adamant bark. Jason knew that bark. It was the same one Teacher used to give whenever a bath was mentioned when he was a puppy. It was a definite 'no.'

He sighed, puzzled. He'd been sure they'd been here to help Rob. Looking around again, he felt lost. Lost and confused. Well, maybe they were here to help Robster, but just not directly.

"Is there something we need to do here? Something important?"

This time the dog stood up, his tail wagging.

Jason shook his head and smiled. It seemed that Teacher knew more than he did about whatever the hell was going on, so he may as well just go with the flow.

"Okay, I'll take your word for it, but you're going to have to lead the way. Whatever the hell it is you're looking for, I don't think this house wants us to find it."

Teacher carried on sniffing the ground for several minutes before his ears pricked up at the mouth of one corridor. Turning to Jason, he whined.

"So, it's down that way?"

The dog barked impatiently, and trotted forward, leaving Jason to follow.

As the darkness swallowed them up, Jason kept his feet in time with the gentle padding of the paws beside him, trying to ignore the sounds reaching his ears from the depths of the house. "Well, I hope to shit you're right, Teach," he muttered under his breath, "because the sooner we can get out of here, the better I think I'll feel."

Despite the haziness of time inside his head, it seemed to Jason that they'd been walking for hours, Teacher relentlessly seeking out a scent and then following it, only pausing when unsure of which way to turn. The air had grown colder as they ventured farther and farther inside the house, and Jason's fingers stung inside his jacket pockets, his eyes aching from trying to make out shapes in the total blackness around them. He was no longer really afraid of the sounds around them, no monsters having yet attacked them, and Teacher seemed completely unaware of them, which reassured him. But then Teacher seemed different, too. He seemed as if he'd grown up while he'd been away, just like Jason had, and he sniffed and searched with a serious intentness that he'd never had as a bumbling puppy.

Taking one of his frozen hands back out into the cold he patted the dog's head. "Good boy, Teach. Good dog." Briefly, the dog brought his nose up to lick Jason's fingers, and then got back to his task. Jason's skin burned where the cold saliva had touched, but he didn't care. For the first time in a long time he felt whole again, and he even managed an uneasy smile, as the constant rattling of the machine far away inside told him he was probably physically a fucking long way further away from being whole than he'd ever been in his so-far sorry life.

Realizing Teacher had stopped, Jason halted alongside his four-legged friend. "What's the matter, Teach? Are we lost?"

Stroking the dog, he realized that Teacher's head was tilted, all his muscles stiff and taut with concentration. What was he listening to? Straining hard, trying to shut out the noises both inside and out, Jason sought for the sound that had grabbed the dog's attention, but to no avail.

"What can you hear, boy?" His whisper was more to himself than the dog, but the words broke Teacher's freeze, and the dog started trotting forward, making Jason jog alongside him in the dark to keep up.

The wind picked up, whistling around them, an invisible, bitter assailant trying to push them backwards, forcing Jason to lower his head to protect his stinging eyes, but as the two of them kept moving, the air feeling as if it was shredding his skin, Jason felt his adrenaline rising. *He could hear it.* Only just, but he could hear the sound that had attracted Teach. It was the sound of quiet crying, but unlike all the other noises that surrounded them, this one seemed real. He pushed on faster, putting blind faith in his feet not to stumble in the blackness, and Teacher easily matched him.

Behind them, a deep rumble started, probably way back where all the corridors met, where Teacher had brought them in, and as the mass of resonance grew, the ground beneath them started to vibrate, gently at first, but growing rapidly more violent, shaking Jason's whole body, making him weave unsteadily as he ran. *What the fuck was going on?* It felt as if they were in the middle of an earthquake.

Stumbling sideways, he fell into the wall, his hand slipping into a wide crack. A wide crack that was getting wider. *Earthquake*. He paused momentarily, letting the information sink in, before a belch of dust hit him from the bowels behind them.

The corridor is collapsing. That's what is happening. The corridor is collapsing and it's rapidly catching them up.

"Go, Teach, go!" he yelled as he burst into a sprint, his panic overcoming the unsteadiness beneath him, ducking instinctively as the bricks began to crash down a few paces behind them. Feeling his muscles stretch as he ran, and knowing that this wasn't funny, this wasn't funny at all, he couldn't help the wild laughter that rose from his throat. What was the house trying to do? Didn't it understand? It couldn't hurt them, no matter how much it might want to. *Because we aren't really here. Not real flesh and blood here.* He was strapped up to some godawful machine in a hospital somewhere, and Teach? Well, Teacher was dead. *We're here but not here. Figure that one out, Robster, you're the brains.* But Rob wasn't here with any answers, and Jason's legs pumped quickly toward the small glimmer of light that appeared as the corridor veered round to the right. This was no time to take chances, because here or not, all this shit was feeling pretty real to him.

Following Teacher into the golden glow, he brought himself to a halt as the ground spread out into a place he vaguely recognized. The awful noise of destruction that had been chasing them stopped abruptly, and glancing behind him, Jason saw the space they had come through knitting itself into a solid wall, within seconds no longer any evidence remaining that a corridor had ever existed. He didn't feel any surprise. He didn't think there was anything this house could do that would surprise him.

But he did feel a vague sense of disquiet. Something was niggling him. How would they get out if they couldn't get back to the core of the house? That was the way they came in. Somehow, he didn't think that the front door was going to work for him and Teach. They were operating on a different level.

The dog whined, and he turned away from the wall, leaving the thought with it. They could worry about getting out later. Anyway, he smiled to himself, maybe Teacher had a plan. He'd had most things sussed so far. Pulling a cigarette from the battered packet in his top pocket, Jason found his lighter and lit it, inhaling hard before looking around at their surroundings.

They were on the wide landing at the top of the beautiful, curved staircase that Gina's grandfather had built with such care for his family. It was just as Jason remembered it, except that its beauty was now destroyed by the spider webs and dust that hung languidly from the ceiling and covered the banisters. There were patches of damp on the walls, and an unpleasant smell rose from the rotting carpet. He looked around with disgust. Had time done this? He didn't think so. Gina had people to look in on it. They wouldn't let it get into this state. The house had done this to itself. But why? Why? Or maybe Gina had done it from wherever she was.

A glow of light touched the landing from downstairs, and through the gloom he picked out the figure of a tiny girl, hugging her knees tight to her chest and peering through the banisters. Something about her was familiar, and a vague memory tickled at the back of his mind, but when he pushed to recall it, all he could think of was pain. Shooting, agonizing pain eating at his back and neck.

The little girl, her long hair hanging down in untidy curls, whimpered, a small mewling sound she seemed unaware of, and Teacher whined in response, nudging Jason's leg gently with his damp nose.

"Okay, okay."

He walked over to her and she looked up at them silently, her face impassive apart from a slight flickering in her eyes as she glanced at Teacher who sat beside her, panting his hot breath into her face. Cautiously, she raised a small hand and stroked him, as if to confirm that he was really there.

Jason crouched down leaving Teacher between him and the child, so as not to frighten her.

"This is Teacher. I think he likes you. I'm Jason. What's your name?"

She kept her eyes on Teacher. "Tabitha. But my mummy calls me Tabby." Her voice sounded dry from crying and Jason had to strain to hear it as she continued. "Are you the reason the voice is so angry?"

Jason lowered himself down so that he was sitting cross-legged.

"What voice, Tabby?"

She shrugged, her face tilting up to meet his. "It lives here. It made me come here and now it won't let me go. I thought it was nice, but now it frightens me. It won't let me go." She leaned forward slightly. "It says it doesn't want to be alone anymore. It says it wants *her* to come back." Her voice trembled. "I think the loneliness has driven it mad. That's what I think."

Tabby's talking about Syracousse. The voice is Syracousse.

Jason's head swum as he listened, the memories closing in around him. Carrie had been right. They had gotten it wrong. So wrong. It had never been Gina at all, not Teacher, not Philip Grace, not even the broken glass on the kitchen floor. None of it. None of this. Wherever Gina was, she was innocent. Lost in the awful realization of it all, of the hate he had wasted, he felt bile rising, burning his chest.

It was only when Tabby tugged at his sleeve that he realized she'd asked him a question.

"What did you say, honey?"

"Can you take me home. Can you?"

Jason glanced at Teacher who slid downwards until he was lying with his nose between his front paws. The dog didn't look up. He looked back at the pleading little girl and smiled gently, pushing a curl out of her face.

"No. No, we can't."

Her face crumpled, small tears glinting in the half light, and Jason realized suddenly why he and Teacher were there.

"No, we can't take you home, but someone's coming soon who can. We'll keep you company until they get here, and then we'll make sure you get home." He patted the head of the toy she clutched under one arm. "You and your teddy bear."

"You won't leave me?"

He shook his head. "No. We won't leave you."

Tabitha looked back between the banisters. "It keeps showing me the same thing over and over like a film that's gone funny. It shows me again and again, but I don't understand it." Her head tilted slightly, confused little furrows forming at the top of her nose. "I think the man's my granddad. He sounds like my granddad, but he looks different."

Jason peered between the carved wooden poles to see, and the full canvas opened up below him.

The glow that was filtering its way up the stairs was sunlight, and Jason could see the Graces' mahogany sideboard with the old-fashioned rotary phone sitting on its neatly polished surface, as it had done all those years ago. His eyes rested there for only a second before being drawn in wonder to the delicate figure sitting on the second to bottom stair.

Camilla Grace's blond hair was piled up in a loose bun at the back of her head, and she looked as beautiful as she ever had to Jason, despite the red that was smeared across her face, and the deep crimson that stained the bottom of her shoestring cotton summer dress. Her hands clung to the ornate, thick banister below and she rested her elegant head against it, like a child seeking comfort.

Lost in shock, she didn't flinch when the air was filled

with Gina's voice shouting, 'NO, NO, NO' over and over again, and watching the past being played out before him, Jason knew that somewhere off-stage, a younger version of himself, and Carrie and Rob were running as fast as they could as far as they could, away from Gina, away from the leaking body on the kitchen floor, away from each other.

After a few moments, Gina's screams turned to wails, long soulless sounds that were a thousand times worse than her shouts of denial, ripping at Jason's insides. He reached for Teacher and found a tiny hand clinging to the shaggy fur. Covering it with his larger palm, he heard the large brass knocker on the front door calling out three times. This, and not the sound of her daughter's agonized voice tearing through the house, roused Camilla from her seat, and she stared at the door for a few moments, with what looked to Jason like hope in her eyes, before hurriedly rushing to open it.

CHAPTER THIRTY-SIX

Jack Hollingsworth pressed the Play button on the answering machine for the second time, listening as Kelly's tired voice repeated itself.

"Dad, I'm at Rob's. Gina Grace is here, too." She paused, and Jack could almost see her fiddling nervously with her hair at the other end. "Something really strange happened up at Syracousse and Gina seems to think she's got something to do with it, that it's got something to do with Tabby going missing." Another pause. "I don't know. I think I'm going crazy. Anyway, I'll be back a bit later, but I'm here if you hear anything. Anything at all."

The long beep started and Jack turned off the machine. Staring into space, he couldn't bring himself to move, his insides hollowing out with so many mixed emotions. Gina was back. Gina and Kelly were together at Rob's. It was so hard to believe, but deep down he knew he'd always expected this day to come. He'd only hoped it would be later. Always later.

His heart ached in ways it hadn't for years, the old memories coming back as if they'd never been away. It seemed that the truth was determined to come out; it had always been determined to come out. Anger at the stranger he was all those years ago bubbled up inside him. He should have let the truth come out when it was meant to, on that awful afternoon. He should have faced up to it then. He should have done what Camilla wanted. He should have listened to his heart. Leaning back against the wall, ignoring the pain in his hip, he shut his eyes and let the memory loose, let his guilt play with him one more time.

Camilla had said there'd been an accident, and the alarm bells should have started ringing then, but his heart was too busy thumping in his chest, reminding him that some things were never over, no matter how much you pretended they were.

He glanced backwards, a force of habit from times gone by, before rapping the knocker three times. It was a few moments before she pulled the door open, and then the bells kicked in hard. He stood frozen, staring at the blood that laid trails across her cheek, at the way her whole body trembled, and then into her eyes that seemed open far too wide.

"Oh sweet Jesus, Camilla."

She tried to smile, her mouth twitching terribly. "You'd better come inside."

Moving past her, and shutting the door behind them, he paced into the hall, his guts churning. He tried to keep his voice calm. "Tell me what's happened. Whose blood is that on you? Whose?" Coming from the kitchen behind him, he could hear someone sobbing, a girl crying, and relief flooded through him. It wasn't Gina's. Thank the Lord for that. It wasn't Gina's.

Camilla tugged at her hands as she sat on the stairs, and Jack noticed the streaks of blood that were drying on the banister. Oh Christ, what the hell had happened now?

Her voice was as soft as a child's. "It wasn't me. I swear it wasn't me. He was shouting at me again, calling me selfish for not wanting to sell the house, and I was just wishing that he'd shut up, thinking how much easier life would be if he'd just *die*, and then . . . and then it was like the knife was tugged out of my hand and all I could see was it stabbing him. Stabbing him over and over." She gazed up at him, pleading with those beautiful eyes that were almost purple.

"You know it wasn't me, don't you, Jack? You believe me, don't you? It was just one of those things. Those things that happen. You remember them, don't you, Jack?"

He sighed and rubbed his face, fighting the urge to throw up, fighting the pain of hearing Gina sobbing over the body of the man she thought was her father. Yes, he remembered those things. Those strange events. He looked at Camilla and shook his head slightly. "I heard about the dog, Camilla." The flinch in her face told him everything he needed to know. "I think these things are getting out of hand, don't you?"

She said nothing, and Jack felt his duty like lead inside him. "Is he in the kitchen? I'd better go take a look. We've got to get Gina out of there."

Leaping from the stairs as he tried to pass her, Camilla grabbed his arm. "Not yet, Jack. I need your help."

Stroking her hair, trying to calm her down, Jack felt his heart breaking inside. "I can't help you, Camilla. No one's going to believe any of your strange stories, true or not. No one's going to believe you didn't do it."

She shook her head impatiently. "No, no. I don't want your help for me. Not for me. I want it for Gina. Take her home with you. Tell the truth about her. I don't want her to go to Philip's family. If she goes there, she'll hate me for the rest of her life. Please, Jack. Please."

Jack felt numb, listening to her words but not really hearing them. There'd been a time when he could have done what she wanted, but not now. Not now.

"I can't. You know I can't. I've got my own wife and daughter to think of. I can't do it. It's better this way."

Tears shimmered angrily in Camilla's eyes. "Gina's your daughter, too."

"I would have left my wife for you." He took her by the shoulders so that they were face to face. "When you were pregnant, I gave you the opportunity. We were both going to leave and have our own family. Do you remember? Do you remember how happy I was? But you couldn't do it, Camilla. You were too afraid. And now things are different. I've got Kelly." He pulled her gently to him and kissed her on the forehead. "I would have done anything for you, Camilla, and I still would. But I won't hurt Kelly. The moment for the truth has passed, you know it as well as I. I have to think of my family now. Gina doesn't even know who I am. I'm a stranger to her. To tell her the truth now wouldn't be fair to her."

He stepped backwards, letting Camilla go. She didn't resist, but stared blankly at him. "And now I'm going to get your daughter out of the kitchen, and then I'm going to call the police. Okay?" Hearing his own confident, even footsteps ringing out beneath him, Jack was amazed at his exterior calm. Inside he was numb and twisting in the throes of dawning comprehension. Philip Grace was dead, and Camilla was going to go to prison. There was no get-out clause, no happily ever after.

"I love you," Camilla whispered as he walked away, and Jack paused for a second, unable to turn back, feeling in that instant as if it were he who had been stabbed in the heart.

"I love you, too." He wondered whether she noticed how his voice cracked with the words.

When he came back out of the kitchen, leaving the awful scene behind him—although never to be left behind in his mind, it would live there forever—Camilla was sitting back down on the stairs, humming to herself, and nothing he said could rouse her. Gina was still crying, and getting no response from her mother. Jack pulled her close and rocked her gently as they hugged. It was the first and last time he'd cuddled his eldest daughter.

The memory tasting bitter in his mouth, Jack opened his eyes and felt the time that had passed from then till now settling in his joints. Robert Black's words from the night before echoed in his head. *Strange things at Syracousse.* What had he called them? *Gina things.* He stood thinking for a few moments more, before turning the answering machine back on and picking up his car keys and coat. He knew where he needed to go. Somewhere he should have been before, but he'd been too busy running away. Well, he was too old for running now, and if the truth was on its way, then it was time to stand and face it.

CHAPTER THIRTY-SEVEN

The three of them had drunk their steaming coffee laced with brandy while Rob slowly retold the story of Teacher to Kelly—the real version this time—and then found the rest all coming out in the same dull monotone: Carrie, the judge, the computer, the last day of that summer, the Gina things. He wasn't quite sure how long he'd spoken, but the sip of coffee he took when he finished was cold and greasy.

Kelly kept her head down as she listened, her tense, pale face obscured by wisps of that baby blond hair. Afraid of what he'd see in Kelly's eyes, Rob found it easier just to look at Gina. Gina, who knew all of this all too well already. Gina, who was already contaminated by their history. Gina, who beautiful as she was, Rob suddenly realized was no way as special or important to him as the fragile blonde sitting beside him. Gina was a childhood fantasy; Kelly was an adult reality. The fear of losing her so soon after finding her punched him in the guts, and he reached for her hand. She squeezed his fingers, and looked up. But not at him, at Gina.

"Okay, let's say that all this stuff is true, that it really happened, and after what we saw this morning I'm not really in any position to argue, but there's one thing I want to know. Have you been able to do any of this stuff since you were a child?"

Watching her, Rob was once again amazed at Kelly's strength. Her child was missing, she'd witnessed something this morning that was like a bad acid trip, he'd just told her a story that would make most people think he was a loon, and she absorbed it all and came out with a question he hadn't even thought of asking. A question that was central to everything.

Gina shook her head. "No." Her voice was soft, but still so much in control. "No, nothing like that ever happened again. Every day I dreaded it would. I couldn't relax. Not for one second. I used to have what I called my thought police, a small part of my brain, monitoring my thoughts for anything dangerous. After a while, I found it easier just to keep myself apart from other people. Friends were too much of a worry. What if someone made me angry? Or hurt me by accident? What would happen then?" She smiled slightly. "Of course, as time passed and nothing strange happened it became easier to let people in, but even then, I tended to choose people I would never really truly care about to share my life. Just in case. I've been doing it so long now, I guess it's hard to break the habit."

Her words made Rob's heart ache and those blue eyes looked into his with such honesty that he couldn't help wondering where they would be if the past had been different. They would have been together, of that he was certain. Would they have been happy? Had kids? He watched her, a little sad for what could have been, and was struck by the intensity with which she returned his gaze.

Was that hope in her eyes? Did she think that if they could sort out this mess, then the past would be erased and Kelly would disappear? He broke her stare, not wanting to think about how time played tricks on people, not offering what was wanted until it was too late. Lighting a cigarette, he brought himself back to the problem at hand. Everything else was inconsequential.

"Carrie's message said that we'd got it wrong. Wrong about Teacher. What if you weren't doing any of it? What if it was the house itself? My computer said, 'make her come home.' Maybe the house wants you back."

Kelly was nodding. "That would tie in with what Sharnice said. They were talking about how Gina was never coming back and then the lights went out."

Gina sighed and took one of Rob's cigarettes. "Well, if that's the case, then why wouldn't it let me inside today? Why scare me half to death? It doesn't make sense."

Rob said nothing. Gina had a point, but still his gut was telling him that he was on the right track. God, it was frustrating, all this craziness, and somewhere a little girl was lost. The smoke rose like a haze in front of him.

"I don't have the answers, Gina. All I know, all I *think* I know, is that Tabby is in that house somewhere, and it doesn't want to let her go."

Kelly's eyes glistened with fresh tears, although none broke over the brimming edge. "But why Tabby? Why her? I've got nothing to do with all this. This is your shit, not mine!" Her face twisted with anger and fear, and Rob knew the aggression wasn't meant personally. God knows, she was dealing better with all this than anyone else he could imagine. His own voice stayed gentle.

"Your dad went to Syracousse on the day Philip Grace died. He answered Camilla's call. Maybe that's the connection."

Behind her cigarette, Gina's body stiffened. "Of course! I remember him now! My mother was sitting on the stairs oblivious to me, and he hugged me and hugged me for ages, telling me everything was going to be okay. He was a very kind man. He hugged me until I'd stopped screaming, and then he rang the police."

Rob was aware of Kelly speaking as ideas pulled reluctantly together in his head.

"I don't get this, any of it, but I do agree with Rob. I think Tabby's in that house. I can feel it. I could hear her calling for me. It was horrible. She sounded so close and so afraid, but I couldn't find her."

The room was silent and Rob couldn't bring himself to fill the void. Staring at his watch he saw that it was only just coming up to two in the afternoon. It was hard to believe, with everything that had already happened today, but Rob was starting to realize that there was more to come before the day was over. Far more.

He got suddenly to his feet, and the women looked up at him, startled.

"I'm going out for a couple of hours. There's something I need to find out, and I think I need to do it on my own. There's wine in the cupboard. Help yourselves, but don't have too much. We need clear heads." Leaning forward, he kissed Kelly on her forehead, which was furrowed with confusion.

"I love you."

The words were whispered out, and Rob knew that if they had any power at all, then it would be needed when he got home. Glancing at Gina, the other lady in his life, he left the room and was gone before either woman had time to speak.

CHAPTER THIRTY-EIGHT

The Hurstone Hospital in Ashburtle had once been hidden away, lost in the countryside surrounding it. Now, although still set in its own vast acreage behind the high electric gates, it was only a mile or so from the nearest new housing development. Rob idly wondered how long it would be before the old manor house was sold off and turned into luxury apartments; the residents pushed on to strange and new places or becoming victims of that wonderful invention, 'Care in the Community.' Still, that was a worry for another person on another day.

The middle-aged nurse at the reception desk smiled as she finished processing the information card she'd handed him on arrival and pressed the buzzer to the side of her neatly organized desk.

"Someone will be along to take you to Mrs. Grace shortly."

Rob nodded in acknowledgment. "Thank you for letting me see her at such short notice. How is she?"

"The same as she's been since she arrived as far as I know. I've been here ten years, and there hasn't been any change in that time. She's very fragile. Most of her time is spent in a world of her own. She has responsive spells, but they don't last long. I think she's happier shut off from the rest of us. Still," she smiled thinly with a hint of reproach, "maybe having visitors will do her some good."

Rob said nothing, and within seconds a young male nurse was walking toward him, smiling.

"It's good to meet you, Mr. Black. I'm a great fan of your work." He shook Rob's hand eagerly as he spoke. "Especially *The Pyramid Man*. Wonderful insight into an unhinged mind. So sympathetically dealt with. You really are a very talented writer."

Always uncomfortable with praise, Rob shrugged. "Thanks. It's nice of you to say so." Leaving the older woman behind, he followed the young man down a silent corridor toward the back of the building. The nurse pushed open two large glass doors.

"Mrs. Grace is in the garden. I think she likes it out here. Anyway, it's more relaxing for visitors." He smiled. "Isn't it strange. She doesn't have any visitors for years, and now two in one afternoon."

Rob was barely listening as he scoured the vast green area in front of him. Finally, his eyes found the figure he was looking for.

"It's okay. You can leave me here if you want. I can see her." He pointed in the direction of the wheelchair-bound patient and the figure sitting on the bench beside it.

Leaving the nurse at the doors, he walked slowly across the forty yards or so of grass until he was standing beside the bench. The woman in the wheelchair still had the ghost of beauty in her delicate features, but her eyes were dead as she stared into nothing, and her lips sagged as they hung slack in her face. Rob searched for the Camilla Grace of his childhood, willowy and elegant, but this tragic old woman had swallowed her up for good, the blond hair now gray and untidy, the ageing face free of powder and paint.

Jack Hollingsworth held one of her limp hands in his, and he looked up at Rob, no surprise in his eyes. After a few seconds, he turned his attention back to Camilla. Rob sat beside him on the bench.

Rob spoke softly. "You were having an affair with Camilla, weren't you?"

Jack didn't look at him, but shook his head slowly. "Not when Philip died. It had been over for a few years by then." He sighed and stretched one leg out in front of him, grimacing slightly. "But I still loved her. I still do, I guess." He paused for a second before looking at Rob. "How did you know?"

"It was something Gina said when talking about that day. She said you hugged her and then called the police. It made me wonder why you'd gone up there on your own. It was just a hunch. I wasn't sure until I saw you sitting here."

Jack smiled, his face wrinkling into a thousand folds of life. "You could have been a policeman with thinking like that. You've got the ear for it."

Rob shrugged. "I think of it as a writer's ear. Same kind of thing, I guess."

Jack nodded. "How's Gina?"

"As elusive as ever. I've left her at my place with Kelly. We've had a strange morning."

Looking at the older man's eyes, at the way they seemed to be looking at the past and the present at the same time, Rob knew they had prevaricated long enough. "Are you ready to tell me about it, Jack?"

The ex-policeman nodded, turning his gaze back to the woman in the wheelchair. "I think I am. I think I've been ready for a long time, waiting for this day. I always knew it would come out, you see. Secrets in small towns are like corpses in water. They stay hidden for a while, rotting and bloating beneath the surface until you almost believe they were never there at all. But just when you start to relax, all that awful gas makes them float to the surface, as if they want to be part of the world for one last time. One last grand, grotesque entrance." He let out a short, humorless laugh. "But I guess this one's been rotting and bloating inside me for long enough. It's time to let it float." His tone was conversational and Rob listened, absorbed, drifting into the story.

"Camilla and Philip's marriage went sour after he put her parents in the old folks' home. She never wanted that, and I don't think she ever forgave him for it. For my part, even though I'd married Jane, I'd always had feelings for Camilla. When I was a young man, I'd thought she was out of my league. She was so beautiful she could break your heart with a glance." He paused and smiled at the memory. "And she knew it, too. Anyway, that's no excuse for what we did, but one day it just started. I couldn't have stopped it if I wanted to, and the truth of it is, I didn't. I wanted it to go on forever. Philip was always in London until late, so I spent as much time as I could up at that house with her. I'd tell Jane I was working late and she, God rest her soul, always believed me.

"I should have felt bad, I know I should, but I didn't. Not when I was up at Syracousse anyway. Afterwards, when I was home, the guilt would eat away at me, but never when I was there. When I was there, everything seemed perfect."

He looked over at Rob, his eyes back in the present. "Do you remember what you said the other evening about weird things happening? 'Gina things,' you called them."

Rob nodded, not wanting to say a word and interrupt Jack's flow.

"Well, those weren't Gina things, no matter what you think. Those things were happening long before Gina came along. They happened all the time around Camilla. She could move things on the other side of the room. No, I'm telling it wrong. She couldn't move them; she was adamant about that. But things moved if she wanted them to. Or if she was likely to hurt herself. The first time I saw it I thought I was going crazy, but she just laughed. She said it had been happening since she was a child. She decided that her father had put so much love into building the house for her that some of it had lingered behind to look after her when he was gone. I don't know how true it was, but it was a nice story. I'd have loved her without all that stuff, but with it, I just couldn't fight it off. Jane seemed so *ordinary* next to her.

"The relationship lasted about two years, until she got pregnant with Gina. The baby was mine and we both knew it. She and Philip had been going through one of their bad spells, and he was sleeping in one of the other bedrooms. I guess as soon as she suspected she was carrying she rectified that situation, because as far as I'm aware he never questioned that he was Gina's father. Up until then we'd been planning to come clean and start a new life together. I was going to tell Jane, she was going to tell Philip, and then we were going to live happily ever after at Syracousse. I wanted us to have a clean break, to move away, but she'd never leave that house." He glanced sorrowfully at the old woman in the wheelchair. "Not of her own free will at any rate.

"Somehow the pregnancy brought the reality of the situation home to her, and she changed her mind about divorcing Philip. She was frightened of what people would say. How we would be ostracized. It wasn't really done in those days. Not around here. Streatford's always been about twenty years behind the rest of the world. In some ways I was relieved when she told me. Underneath everything, I was as afraid as she was. Probably more." He looked up and smiled. "Men have never been too brave in matters of the heart, have they? Still," he nodded to himself, as he stared back into the distance, as if the past were playing itself out on the horizon, "I would have done it, even though it would have broken Jane's heart and been the end of my career. I would have given it all up for Camilla if she'd wanted me to. But she didn't, and there was no way I could carry on with things the way they had been. Not now that I knew that it would remain an affair forever. It was as if it suddenly had become sordid. Something to be ashamed of.

"The first year after the baby came was the worst. Every time I saw Camilla out with that pram, and then the pushchair, I felt as if someone were pulling my guts out with a hook. My little baby girl who didn't even know I existed. My life was on autopilot. Everywhere I went I seemed to see their faces. I thought it would be the death of me, I really did. All that pain was eating me up from the inside and I couldn't see an end to it.

And then something happened to end all that. Jane got pregnant, and Kelly came along. After that, the pain just seemed to die away. Not all at once, and not completely, but I had my own family to think about then. Kelly changed the world for me. Everything she did fascinated and amazed me. It still does. I still thought about Camilla and Gina, but I could never imagine hurting Kelly. Not even Camilla was worth that to me." He squeezed the small, withered hand of the woman beside him as if in apology.

"There was still something between us and always would be, so when Philip. . ." He stumbled, trying to find the right words. "When Philip *happened* it was me she called. My direct line, not the switchboard. She wanted me to take Gina. To tell the truth, she didn't want Philip's family to have her." His voice dropped to a painful whisper. "But I couldn't. I wouldn't."

Listening to Jack's story, Rob found himself dragged back into his own memories. Standing in the kitchen at Syracousse looking at that awful, bleeding body, the knife planted in its chest.

"What did she say happened that day?"

"That the knife just flew out of her hand. They'd been having an argument, and she was thinking how much easier life would be if he was dead, and then bang. The knife

289

was gone." His breath hitched for a second. "And so was Philip."

In Rob's mind, the memory was reliving itself in split-screen. Gina outside. *He never shuts up. Never. I wish he'd just die.* Camilla Grace inside, wishing her husband dead as vehemently as her daughter, probably more so, that sharp knife chopping up and down in her hand. Why had they never thought of her? Why? *Because we were kids, that's why. Because when you're kids, adults don't really exist, do they? Not for stuff like this, not for magic.*

Rob leaned forward, his elbows resting on his knees; his fingers interlocked to stop their shaking from seeming so visible. "Did you believe her?"

Jack sighed and frowned slightly. "Yes, I guess I did in the main. I believed that she hadn't wanted to kill Philip, and I believed that the knife did just shoot through the air like she said it did. But I didn't believe it was nothing to do with her. I figured she had subconscious telekinetic powers or something, and her hate for him was that strong at that moment that her subconscious just took over." He took a sideways glance at Rob, as if to see whether the younger man was laughing, before he continued.

"If anyone had asked me even a few months before if she was capable of it, I would have said no without hesitation, but until then, I'd only seen good things come out of that strange power. You know, protective things." He let out a long sigh.

"I guess that somewhere in the back of my mind, I'd been worrying about something like this happening ever since I heard about that dog falling into the fire. A dog falling into a fire and not able to get itself out? I'd have a hard time believing that story from anyone, let alone someone as high-strung as Camilla. No, it didn't make any sense. And my daughter lived in that house. Yes, after hearing about the puppy I think I was always worried that this strange stuff was getting out of control, and I was right. All I can be grateful for, sick as it sounds, is that it was Philip Grace and not Gina who ended up on that kitchen floor."

Rob felt like the world had tilted all over again, and his stomach flipped. *Teacher. He was talking about Teacher.*

"Are you saying that you think what happened to the dog was Camilla's fault, not Gina's?"

Jack shook his head impatiently. "Why should it have had anything to do with Gina? I told you, this stuff was going on before Gina was born, and anyway, Camilla never liked dogs. She thought they were dirty and clumsy. They made her nervous. I can imagine how angry she was when Philip brought that puppy back to the house. She would have been livid." He paused for a moment, and looked at Rob.

"Are you saying you kids all thought it was Gina? You thought she did it? You thought she made that dog go into the fire?"

Rob nodded slowly. "Yeah, we thought she did it. We thought she killed Philip Grace, too." He flinched, thinking back to that day in the kitchen, the three of them running and running, leaving Gina standing and staring in horror. His voice fell to a whisper. "Worse than that, she believed she'd done it, too. She's believed it all these years."

The two men sat in silence for a moment, awed by the awfulness of it all, before Rob spoke. "But you know what's worse? I think we were all wrong. In fact, I'd bet every penny I've got in the bank that we were all wrong, all of us except Carrie-Anne. I think she was closer to the truth than anyone." He looked at Jack. "I'll tell you on the way home. I'll tell you about that day, and then I'll tell you about all the shit that's been happening since I got back, finishing with what happened up at the house this morning. And then we'll go and explain to the girls how we're going to get Tabby back and end this."

Jack pulled himself to his feet and picked up the walking cane that was resting on the back of the bench. He leaned heavily on it as Rob carefully turned Camilla's wheelchair around to push her indoors.

"Rob." The older man's hand was on his arm. "Am I going to have to tell them?"

Rob didn't have to ask who. Gina and Kelly. He nodded, wondering how his heart could get any heavier.

"Yeah, I think you are. I think the time for secrets is over, don't you?"

Jack nodded, the answer expected. "Well, let's go and get it done then."

CHAPTER-THIRTY-NINE

Rob noticed the two women had opened a bottle of wine, and were both nursing half-full glasses, as he opened the door to the sitting room. Even so, he could feel the cool air of tension between Gina and Kelly.

"Dad, what are you doing here?"

Jack had come in behind Rob, leaning heavily on his cane, probably more from the weight he was carrying inside him than any pressure on his hip. When she saw him, Kelly leapt to her feet.

"Is there any news? Have the police found something?"

Jack touched her on the arm and shook his head, keeping his gaze low. Rob wondered how the old man could bear the strain as he watched Jack's eyes flick between his two daughters, one blonde, one brunette, as different as yin and yang.

Nodding Jack toward the armchair under the bay window, Rob sat on the sofa.

"I think we've figured out where we've been going wrong. Carrie was halfway there. She realized that Gina didn't have anything to do with Teacher's death or

Philip's. She figured out that Gina had never had any kind of power at all. It was the house that had the power. Syracousse did those terrible things, and I think Carrie thought it had done them *for* Gina. Because that was what she wanted. To protect her."

He looked up at Gina, whose perfectly made-up blue eyes were wide and watery. Her hand trembled around the forgotten wine glass she held.

"You mean I didn't do any of it? Not the broken glass, not anything?" She paused for a second, almost unable to get her breath to speak. "I didn't do it. I didn't do any of it." She moaned slightly. "But it's still my fault. The house did those terrible things because of me, because I *thought* them."

"No, no, no." Rob shook his head. "This is where Carrie's theory, if it was what she was thinking and trying to get us to realize, is only partway right. After all the things Sharnice said, and the message on my computer, we automatically thought it was Gina the house wanted back, but we've been thinking of the wrong girl." He leaned forward in his chair, his voice soft.

"It's not you the house wants, Gina. It's your mother. Camilla. The little girl it was built for. The little girl who lived there all her life. It wasn't your thoughts Syracousse was tuned into all those years ago. You just happened to have some of the same angry thoughts at the same time."

Gina was shaking her head, gazing at some spot on the carpet. "But that can't be right, it can't be right. What about all the things that happened when there was only me there? What about the things that happened around you? She wasn't even there for most of them."

Rob shrugged. "You were the most important thing in her life. Syracousse would have known that. If Camilla wanted you safe and happy, then I should imagine the house would do its best to make that happen." His voice rose slightly, forcing Gina to meet his gaze. "Don't you see what this means? You can let it all go now. It was nothing to do with you. You're as much a victim of all this as Teacher and Philip."

Tears were streaming down Gina's cheeks, her lifetime of composure ebbing away with them. "But you all thought it was me. I thought it was me. How could a house do anything? How? And even if it could, why start again now? It's crazy. The whole thing is crazy."

"I agree. It's crazy, but I think it's true. I think after Camilla and you left, it just waited for her to come back, like a dog waiting for its owner. Just waited for all those years. It probably would have waited forever if those school kids hadn't broken in and talked about you wanting the house to crumble, and how your mother was locked up and never coming out." Gina flinched at the mention of her mother, and Rob wished they had time to let her take all this in slowly, especially as the worst was yet to come. Jack still had to tell his part in everything, and the clock was ticking around to that.

"It's taking its revenge on us. Maybe it loved us a little as well, and what did we do? We all abandoned it and separated it from the one person it loved the best. The one person it had done everything to make happy."

Gina's head was shaking. "But what can we do? Is it going to try to kill us all?"

Rob's voice was firm, and this time he looked at Kelly as well. "No. No, it's not, because we're going to give it what it wants. We're going to take your mother up there. Jack spoke to Keery on our way back here, and said that he wants to take her out for the day tomorrow with you, under the guise of seeking out any little hidey-holes at Syracousse you might know about that the police might have missed. Maybe if we take Camilla there, the house will give us Tabby back. Maybe it'll finish all this."

Her face full of fear, Gina met his eyes. "Yes, but how? How will all this end?"

Rob didn't have an answer.

"But why the hell did it take Tabby in the first place?

And where have you been with my father? What does he have to do with all this?" Kelly's voice was sharp, and Rob could hear the panic and confusion rising in it. He looked up at Jack, who let out a long, heavy sigh.

"Why don't you go and put a pot of coffee on or something, Rob?"

"Are you sure?" He studied the wrinkled, worn face and saw that the older man's eyes, although tired and bloodshot, held an expression of steel.

"Yes, I'm sure. This is something I need to do on my own."

Nodding, Rob got to his feet and headed out to the corridor, giving the other man's shoulder a squeeze as he passed, then shutting the door and heading into the kitchen where he stood leaning against the breakfast bar, his arms folded, waiting for the fallout. He didn't bother filling the kettle. Coffee wasn't going to cure this. He didn't really think anything could cure this.

CHAPTER FORTY

The scorpion scuttled by, six legs tapping loudly against the dusty wooden floor, its enormous stinger waving in their direction as it paused before running toward them, stopping angrily when it reached the barrier of Jason's coat and sneakers, which made a semi-circle from the wall, he, Tabby and Teacher were sitting against. Somehow it seemed these creatures of the house's imagination couldn't cross the barrier of his clothing. Two unreals don't make a real, Jason had supposed. Maybe his lack of substance and theirs just couldn't connect, like something in an old Star Trek episode. Or maybe the creatures couldn't get near them because Tabby, the only flesh-and-blood entity present, *believed* they were safe behind their wall of fabric. The old trick of mind over matter.

Whatever the reason, the huge, shining bug with the judge's old and wizened face grotesquely stretched across it, sneered from the other side of the black leather jacket but approached no closer. The bloodred eyes burned madly as its pincers clicked and clacked like the clenching and unclenching of a fist.

"Look where you've brought us," it hissed, the open mouth revealing nothing but darkness. "Look what you did to me! LOOK WHAT YOU DID TO ME!"

It paced up and down in front of them, making quick, precise turns from right to left, the hellish version of a mythical centaur, cursing and swearing under whatever repulsive breath it had.

Tabby trembled, and snuggled in tighter between the man and the dog, tucking her face away. "I don't like it," she whispered. "Make it go away, please, make it go away."

Jason squeezed her tight. Disturbing as the sight of the creature was, Jason felt no fear of it, aware that it was a trick, a game, and that the judge wherever he was, was not part of this beast in front of him. Tabby, however, brave as she was, was only four, and there was only so much she could take.

"Oh, you don't want to be scared of a silly thing like that. Look at it. It looks ridiculous." He kept his voice light and cheerful. "It's like those boys at school who think saying rude words is really big and clever. Do you know boys like that?"

He felt the small head, hidden by curls nodding against his chest.

"And what do you do when those boys bore you by being silly?"

This time there was a pause and then a shrug.

"Oh come on, you must do something. What do you do?"

"I stick my tongue out at them." Her voice was quiet, but he could feel the small body relaxing slightly, and he laughed softly.

"Oh you do, do you? Right. Then that's what we'll do."

Leaning forward slightly, he stuck his tongue right out at the abomination that was calling his mother a whore in that unnatural sibilant voice. "Na, na, na, naaa, na, you can't get to us!"

Tabby's head tentatively turned to see what he was doing, so he repeated the action. She glanced at Teacher, who let out a playful bark.

"Come on! I feel silly doing this all on my own." Grinning at Tabby, he nudged her in the ribs, egging her on. *Make it a game, Jase. Make it fun.*

This time he put two fingers in his mouth and stretched it out sideways, wiggling his tongue. There was a giggle beside him, and then Tabby did the same.

Within five minutes, they were laughing so hard that the scorpion hissed and spat before wandering off.

Jason kissed her on the forehead, still laughing. "See. It's only scary if you make it that way."

Tabby nodded, and he could see that, for the moment at least, she was convinced.

The unexpected pain threw him back against the wall, his head hitting it hard as he felt himself sucked away, nausea flooding his system as a weight landed on his chest, bright light filling his vision—there was something on his face, something covering his mouth and why couldn't he move, why couldn't he move?—and then a face loomed over him, a face he didn't recognize, its mouth shouting instructions to someone, one of the people whose shadows flitted across the whiteness, and beyond it all he could hear an awful long tone, like the tuneless note you hear when someone's hung up the phone and left you unwanted on the other end, and then the white was turning to gray. . . .

Something tugged hard at his sleeve, pulling him, dragging him back to consciousness, and he tried to shake it off, but it wouldn't let go, whining and yanking, and it sounded just like a dog, just like a dog. . . .

"Teacher?" His voice sounded raw, and he opened his eyes to see the bleak darkness of Syracousse spread out before him. His head hurt where he'd banged it. Figure that out. His heart pounded rapidly, and as he glanced around, he listened for that rhythmic bellows sound deep inside him. It was still there. Still definitely there.

Tabby stared at him, trembling with more fear than he'd seen since his part in this madness had begun.

"Are you okay, sweetheart?"

She gazed at him, almost distrusting. "Why did you go thin like that? I almost couldn't see you. Where were you going? Were you leaving me here?" The panic was rising, her voice thinning out as it rose in pitch. "Don't leave me here, please don't leave me here."

"Hey, hey. . ." Trying to stop the tears that brimmed in her eyes, he tilted her chin so that she was looking up into his face. "I promised you I wouldn't leave until you were safely out of here, and I'm not going anywhere until then. Me and Teacher are staying right here. Isn't that right, Teach?" He looked over to the dog, who barked in agreement and then laid his head in the little girl's lap, covering it completely.

"You promise?"

"I promise. Now you curl up with Teacher and Mr. Pickles and try to get some sleep. Okay?"

"You won't go anywhere?"

Jason shook his head firmly. "I won't move an inch."

When she had finally settled and was dozing, mumbling quietly in her peaceless sleep, Jason let out a long sigh and shut his own eyes. *Come on, Robster, come on. I don't think we've got much more time.* He paused in the thought, a wave of sadness flowing over him. *I don't think I've got much more time.*

CHAPTER FORTY-ONE

The sound of sobbing escaped the sitting room as the door was flung open and Kelly ran down the corridor into the kitchen. She faced Rob, her chest heaving with emotion, her pale skin deathly. He stepped toward her.

"Kelly. . ."

"Don't." Her voice was like ice, and she held up one hand to stop him from coming closer. "Don't. Whatever you've got to say, I don't want to hear it." The hate in her eyes stabbed at the very core of him.

"Kelly, I'm so sorry, but this isn't my fault."

"Isn't your fault?" she sneered as her voice rose, her mouth quivering. "If you hadn't come back, then none of this would have happened. None of it."

"But it already has happened. It happened a long time ago." He reached for her, wanting to comfort her, but she pushed him away.

"But I wouldn't have known about it! It wouldn't have happened for me! And what about Tabby? Would she still be here if you hadn't come back? Can you answer me honestly that all this would still have gone on?" She ran a hand through her hair, pacing sideways and up and down, as if the strength of what she was feeling inside made it impossible for her to stand still. "None of this has anything to do with me and Tabby." She paused for a moment to point an accusing finger at Rob. "We don't have any sordid little secrets that need digging up. We've just been sucked into your mess." She spat the words at him, tears now rolling down her cheeks as Rob stood helpless, no words coming to him.

"I wish I'd never laid eyes on you. I hate you for what you've done to me." Jack had followed Kelly out of the lounge and now stood behind her. She ignored him, her eyes burning into Rob's.

"I hate you, Robert Black. And I never want to see you again." She paused, sucking in a deep breath, trying to control herself. "I just wanted you to know that."

Turning on her heel, she shoved Jack into the wall and stormed down the corridor and out the front door, slamming it hard behind her. Rob felt his heart break with the sound. Standing in the doorway, Jack seemed to have shrunk, his body hollowed out somehow, his shoulders slumped. His eyes met Rob's and for a few seconds they said nothing, but stared at each other in the company of Gina's distant crying. Eventually, Jack broke the gaze.

"I'd better go after her. Will you look after Gina?"

Rob nodded. "You know we still have to do this thing tomorrow, Jack. If we want to get Tabby back."

Jack paused and looked back over his shoulder. Rob didn't like what he saw in the man's eyes. The way he was looking at him with a mixture of dislike and disgust. *He thinks this is all my fault, too. He wishes I'd stayed away. He thinks I have no heart.*

"Yes, Rob, I know we do, and I'll be there. Just let me get through tonight first, all right? I've just wrecked my little girl's memories, and God knows what that other woman in your lounge is feeling. I think we should worry about them tonight. The rest can wait till tomorrow."

He turned away without saying another word and limped slowly to the door. It shut more quietly this time, and then it was just Gina and him. Last two of the four. Pushing himself away from the breakfast bar, Rob walked on heavy legs back to the sitting room where he stood for a moment in the doorway watching Gina crying into her hands, her hair loose from her ponytail covering her face.

"Can I come in?"

She looked up and nodded, her face destroyed with emotion but still achingly beautiful through the red blotches and the makeup that had abandoned the carefully applied areas of the morning.

Rob refilled her glass from the red wine bottle on the table, and took Kelly's glass for himself before sitting on the floor in front of Gina. "I think you should drink some of that. You need it. It'll calm you down."

They sat in silence for a while, sipping their drinks, Rob watching Gina as she stared out through the bay window at nothing and everything. Eventually, she brought her liquid eyes to his, a half smile wistful on her lips.

"I knew today wasn't going to be a normal day, but this. . . God, I wasn't expecting this." She shrugged helplessly, biting back a sob. "How am I supposed to deal with this?" She slid off the armchair, and sat on the floor by Rob, her knees drawn up under her chin. "I don't know what to feel. I don't know what I'm supposed to feel. What a mess. What an awful, awful mess."

The weight of it all seemed to be making Rob's muscles ache as he struggled, as ever, to find the right words.

"There are positive things that have come out of all this, too. Try to think about those."

"Like what?"

Rob put his arm around her, letting her head fall against his shoulder and feeling like a coward. He didn't want to look into her eyes. He'd had enough of studying other people's suffering close up. It seemed that some things hadn't changed in all this. He was still a selfish bastard.

The memory of the hate in Kelly's eyes made him flinch. Yeah, there weren't many people left who had a high opinion of him, and he couldn't blame them. He didn't have too high an opinion of Rob Black himself. He let out a long breath before speaking.

"Well, at least you know now that none of the strangeness was due to you. You don't have any uncontrollable powers to be afraid of. No more guilt. You didn't kill poor Teacher, and you didn't kill your father."

She stiffened against him, her words bitter.

"No. No, I didn't kill him, but even if I had, I wouldn't have killed *my father,* would I? Philip Grace was never my father. My father's that stranger who just walked out the door."

Rob mentally cursed himself. How could he be so good at words on paper, and so shit when it came to the words that counted? He rested his head gently on her hair, feeling the heat coming through her skin.

"Don't think like that. Philip *was* your father. In all the ways that count, anyway. He brought you up. He loved you. And you loved him. Those are the things you have to remember."

"I don't want to remember. I don't want to remember anything. I feel like the person I always thought I was has just been wiped away as if I never existed. Worse than that, all the people I thought I knew, it turns out I didn't. I don't know who to be. I don't know who *I* am." She sniffed loudly, the sound making Rob smile. It was an un-Gina sound, and yet was so natural.

"You can be whoever you want to be now. No guilt. No fear. Just beautiful Gina. You can be the person you were meant to be."

"You make it sound so easy."

"It's as easy as you want it to be."

She looked up at him and smiled, strands of hair tugging across her face where they had become trapped in his shoulder. "I feel like you're the only person in the world I know, Robert Black. I think I know you better than I know myself. I *recognize* you. Inside and out." Her finger reached up and traced his mouth. "That same smile you had all those years ago. I always had faith in that smile."

As she stared into him with those gorgeous eyes that used to keep him awake as a boy, he felt his stomach flipping slightly. *Oh Christ no, don't even think about it. Not now. Not ever. It's Kelly you love, however mad and hurt she is now. Don't even think about doing this. It's not fair. It's not fair on anyone.*

His mouth felt dry, and he didn't trust himself to speak, suddenly aware with every inch of his body of how close Gina was to him. Her voice was soft and sweet.

"I've often thought about you, you know. I guess it was hard to forget you, seeing your picture in the papers and in all those bookshop windows over the years. I'd buy your books just so I could hear your voice in my head. Stupid, huh?"

Rob shifted slightly, feeling awkward. God, it seemed like her body was giving out so much heat. Was it her or was it him? Who the hell knew; the only thing he was sure of was that he shouldn't be feeling like this. He shouldn't be *wanting* like this.

"Look, Gina . . ."

Her finger came up and pressed itself to his lips, sending shockwaves exploding through him.

"Let me speak, okay?" She pulled herself upright, keeping her face close to his. Rob groaned internally. Oh shit, this was hard. This was very hard. Worse than that, *he* was hard. Was she doing this to him deliberately? Was she still a manipulative little girl underneath all this emotion, toying with him like she did when they were kids? Her words dripped like liquid into his ears, tempting him, teasing him.

"Have you ever wondered how things would have been between us if that summer had never happened?"

Her face held all the vulnerability that it had hidden

during her childhood, and Rob glanced away in an effort to keep his resolve. *Yeah, you're tempted, Black. You're more than tempted. But don't blame her for it; you've always been a grade-A shit to the ladies.* His voice shook slightly.

"But that summer did happen. You can't just wipe it away."

Leaning forward, Gina's breath whispered past his face. "You're not answering my question, Rob. Did you ever wonder? Or was it only me?"

A vein started to throb in his head. "Yeah. Yeah, I wondered. Sometimes."

She watched him for a few seconds, before she spoke, tears reforming in the corners of her eyes. "It's been a long and terrible day, Rob. I lost my identity today, and now I want to stop thinking for a few hours. I want to stop thinking with you." Her lips brushed his, and the moan escaped Rob before he could bite it back, just as it had all those summers ago.

"Help me, Rob. Help me be whole again. You're the only one who can." Her tongue slipped into his mouth, and hating himself, his resolve, his thoughts of Kelly melted away.

"It was meant to be," she whispered, before their mouths were unable to speak any more.

CHAPTER FORTY-TWO

It was half past three in the morning, but the moon was high beneath the clear sky, and as Rob looked out the window over the garden from the darkness of the bedroom, he could see all the way down the length of the lawn to the shadows of the garage a hundred yards away. He had just come back from a quick trip downstairs. He'd put on jeans and without a t-shirt on, goose pimples covered his arms and chest, but he didn't mind. In some ways the cold felt good. He sucked hard on his cigarette, cancer the least of his worries, as Gina stirred in the bed behind him.

"Where did you go?"

Her voice sounded drowsy, as if she'd been on the verge of sleep. He envied her that. Sleep wasn't something he could imagine for himself tonight.

"I phoned the hospital to check on Jason." He didn't turn around, but heard the rustle of sheets as she pulled herself upright.

"Has there been any change?"

"No. He's still in a coma and needing the ventilator." *And they almost lost him a couple of hours ago.* He didn't need to tell her that. That was something he wanted to carry on his own. His own private guilt.

"Why don't you come back to bed?"

Glancing over his shoulder, Rob looked at Gina, who was naked from the waist up, leaning on one arm, hair tumbling free over her shoulder, and he felt nothing except the urge for her to be gone. Out of his bed, out of his house and out of his life. Oh yes, he'd really fucked up this time.

"I don't think so. I'm going to get dressed and make some coffee. You stay here."

Even through the gloom, he could see her face clouding over.

"Are you feeling guilty about Kelly? I know she'll be upset, but she'll get over it. It's not as if you've known her that long. Once this is all over then we can go anywhere we want. Get away from this town for good, and just be you and me. Imagine that, Rob. Just you and me."

Rob sighed and paused on his way to the door. There was no easy way to do this. His voice sounded cold in his head, devoid of emotion, detached from the situation.

"Look, Gina, there is no you and me. Maybe once there could have been, but not anymore. All we've done tonight is find that out. It was a mistake, and if I could undo it, I would. I love Kelly, and I can't change that, not even for you." He paused before adding, "I'm sorry. I really am, but there's nothing I can do about it."

She looked like she'd been slapped in the face, an expression he'd seen on so many women's faces over the years when he'd destroyed their illusions of love. He'd never expected to see it on Gina's, though. Strange how life worked out.

As he picked his t-shirt up from the floor where he'd abandoned it after ripping it off so eagerly only hours before—*Oh yes, you're a shit all right*—he could hear Gina's breath coming rapidly from the bed.

"I don't believe you."

"Believe me, Gina. Please." There was a hint of the spoiled child he'd known all those years ago in her voice, and Rob wondered whether a man had ever done anything other than proclaim undying love for Gina in all her adult life. Probably not. And a month or so ago, he'd have been one of them.

"Well, maybe I'll tell your precious Kelly all about tonight. Tell her how you needed no encouragement. She won't ever want you back then, will she? Not perfect Kelly who everyone cares so much about."

She sounded bitter and harsh, and Rob couldn't blame her for that, but he didn't have the energy for rows and recriminations. He tugged his t-shirt over his head and as he walked to the door, he said, "Do whatever you have to, Gina. This is my fault, not yours. I'll always care about you, but I can't make myself be in love with you." His weariness echoed in his voice. "If you want to tell Kelly, then go ahead. I can't stop you."

He pulled the door closed behind him and padded down the stairs. It wasn't until he was in the kitchen that he turned a light on, as if he could somehow find solace in the gloom. Gina didn't follow him down, and for that he was grateful.

CHAPTER FORTY-THREE

"He's here."

Rob had been watching for Jack's blue Escort from the front room window, and it pulled up outside the house at exactly nine o'clock. What kind of night had Jack and Kelly had? As sleepless as his own? He pushed the memory of his own night's activities aside as he felt his stomach twist with his old friend guilt. What was done couldn't be undone, they'd all learned that, and he'd done enough dwelling on the past to last a lifetime. What would be would be.

He grabbed his keys, eager to get out of the house, and was pleased to see Gina waiting by the door. She'd eventually gotten up at five-thirty, and there'd been no more mention of Kelly and love. Instead, she cooked them both a breakfast neither of them really wanted to eat, and drank endless cups of coffee with him, talking in that soft, sweet voice of times gone by, of Jason and Carrie, reminding him of the good times so easily hidden by the bad.

Her pleasantness at first had surprised Rob, and then

made him uneasy. She was being a little too nice, like someone who knew she was going to get her own way in the end. He didn't trust her, and that wasn't her fault, but common sense told him you couldn't trust someone who'd lost everything. They had nothing left to lose.

"Come on. Let's go."

He pulled the door shut behind him and trotted down the path to the car, taking the front passenger seat. Glancing over his shoulder, seeing only Gina getting in, Jack pre-empted his question.

"Kelly's going to meet us up at Syracousse in an hour."

Swallowing his disappointment, Rob nodded. So she hadn't wanted to come. God, all he wanted to do was see her, make sure she was all right. He had to make sure they put everything right. For all their sakes.

They drove out to Hurstone in silence, the bright eyes in Jack's craggy, time-weary face occasionally darting to the rear-view mirror, not to check on traffic, but to peek at his other daughter, who sat so still and quiet in the backseat. Rob stared out at the passing visions of normality, people emerging from their houses to go about their daily business, and wondered if they were the only ones whose lives had been tinged with madness, or whether each street had its dark and unnatural secrets, the inhabitants of which were too scared to share.

Jack pulled up on the gravel in front of the imposing building instead of using the visitors' parking lot to the rear and turned off the engine, before glancing over to Rob.

"Are you going to wait here?"

Rob nodded. "Yeah. I think just you and Gina should go in." He looked behind him at the woman whose face had grown pale. "Are you okay? It's been a long time."

She nodded, regaining her composure. "I'll be fine."

Sliding out of her seat, she slammed the door and waited for Jack. He took a deep breath before joining her in the fresh air, leaving Rob alone with his thoughts.

* * *

Gina was going up the stairs ahead of him, and Jack took two painful steps at a time to catch up. He needed to talk to her before the day's events swallowed them up. Touching her gently, he stopped her before she buzzed for reception to let them in.

"Gina, I just wanted to say. . . I'm sorry about running off like that after Kelly last night. I knew you'd be safe with Rob, and she's very fragile at the moment, with Tabby missing. I didn't want to leave her on her own. It doesn't mean I don't care about you. I care about you very much. I always have, and I regret not being braver and bringing you back into our house, our family, all those years ago."

Gina stared at him, her face noncommittal. If only he knew her better, then maybe he'd be able to read that expression, to guess what she was thinking, to find the best way to help her. So many ifs, and only himself to blame for not knowing the answers. Well, maybe it wasn't too late to try to build some of those bridges. He glanced down at his knotted hand that touched her arm. He didn't have enough time left to waste with wishful thinking and regrets. It was time to start taking action and trying to put things right.

"You know, I was thinking that maybe after all this is over we could get to know each other a bit better. I'd like the opportunity if you'd let me."

Her eyes flitted away toward the heavy door, and Jack sighed. "Well, think about it anyway."

The nurses had Camilla dressed in a cream linen trouser suit and ready for them in the reception hall. Jack noticed they'd even tried to put a little makeup on her and done her hair. He watched as, trembling, Gina stepped forward and kneeled by her mother's chair. It felt surreal to be reunited with his first family like this. At times in his life, he'd wondered if the three of them would ever meet with the truth out in the open, but he'd never imagined it would be like this, in these terrible circumstances.

The nurse pulled him gently to one side.

"I just thought I'd let you know that Mrs. Grace is capable of walking with some assistance. We normally walk her around for half an hour or so each day to stop her from getting sores and to keep her muscles active. There's no physical reason for her not to walk on her own, but she just doesn't ever do it."

Jack nodded. "We'll have her back by this evening." *I hope.* "Thank you for everything you've done to make her look special. It's nice for her daughter to see her looking so pretty."

Smiling gently, the nurse shook her head. "That's no problem. Maybe seeing her daughter again and getting out of here for a few hours will do her some good. She's no threat to anyone, just a poor, lost old lady. All I ask is that you take good care of her."

"We will. Thank you."

Looking into the kindly face to say good-bye, Jack felt like a Judas all over again. First, he'd betrayed Camilla by not taking responsibility for their daughter, and now he was promising to look after her when who knew what the day would bring. What was going to happen when they got up to the house? None of them could answer that, not even the poor, crazed woman he was pushing down the wheelchair slope next to the stairs, and she knew Syracousse better than anyone.

The wheels bounced loudly on the gravel as they headed to the car, and Rob got out to help him ease Camilla into the backseat and do up her belt. God, she was as light as a feather, and holding her in his arms again, Jack couldn't help remembering with pain how he had carried her so many times before, up those beautiful stairs to the bedroom, her head thrown back and laughing. Yes, he'd been her lover and her betrayer. Maybe if he'd done what she asked of him her sanity would have survived that awful afternoon.

After stowing away the chair in the trunk he got in the front seat and shut the door, Gina having already scrambled into the back to take her absent mother's hand again. Jack could hear her low, painful whisper, begging for recognition.

"It's me. It's Gina. Can you hear me, Mum? Don't you recognize me? It's your little girl. I'm so sorry for leaving you, I'm so sorry. I won't do it again, I promise. I won't ever leave you again. Cross my heart, Mum, cross my heart and hope to die."

Jack looked over at Rob, whose jaw clenched and unclenched, almost in time with Gina's tired, quiet, shameful sobs.

"Are you ready?"

Rob nodded, starting the engine.

"Let's go then."

CHAPTER FORTY-FOUR

Hearing the sound of tires crunching along the stones of the lane, Kelly smiled a little with relief. Not that she would be pleased to see them, not Rob, not her father. It was way too early for that yet, and she had a suspicion that she would never be ready to forgive them. But standing up here alone, even keeping her distance from the house, filled her with an unsettling fear, like that of something you just can't quite see but are sure is out there somewhere waiting for you. The kind of fear she hadn't felt since she was a child not much older than Tabby. The kind of fear that sent your imagination running wild, and was now filling her head with images of Jason lying cold on the track. Jason who'd come up here on his own and now lay broken and ruined in that hospital just one breath away from death.

She shivered slightly although the breeze was mild, and walked forward to greet the car. Yes, sometimes any kind of company was preferable to only your own. Even that of those whose deception had stolen your daughter and broken your heart. She'd never really understood that expression before, *a broken heart,* but she did now, and the shards of her splintered emotions stabbed her somewhere deep inside as Rob stepped out of the car and walked toward her, his eyes a reflection of her own sad weariness. For a moment, Kelly's heart squeezed a little with remorse. But not enough. Seeing he was about to speak, she cut him off.

"I'm here to get my daughter back. Everything else can wait."

Kelly watched him flinch as though her words were acid before she pushed Rob aside to see the others getting out of the car. Her eyes fell to the frail woman her father was easing into the wheelchair, and she could almost taste the bitterness in her mouth.

"So this is what you were screwing while my mother sat at home waiting for you."

Jack's face spun around, so much guilt there that it seemed he was a stranger.

"Kelly, please. Not now."

"No accounting for taste, is there?" Her pale face was flushed with anger, and she sneered at Gina, who held the old woman's hand, tears still wet on her cheeks. Gina's expression hardened.

"Well, that's men for you." She smiled. "You never can rely on them to keep their dicks in their pants."

The knowledge in that controlled voice shook Kelly, and she glanced over at Rob, who had walked to the gates farther up the lane and was staring at the house. What did Gina mean by that? He couldn't have. He wouldn't have. *The king of the meaningless fling, remember? Of course he fucked her. You saw the way he was looking at her yesterday even when he was telling you he loved you. Just words. Just words. You're nothing. You're an outsider in all this.* Oh, but it hurt to think of them together, one more hurt to add to her new and painful collection. She followed the others to join him at the gate, fighting back the tears.

Rob didn't look at them, but carried on gazing at Syracousse, his voice calm.

"I think Kelly and Gina should wait out here. Jack, you and I can take Camilla in. I think the fewer people going inside the better."

"My mother's not going in there without me." Gina's voice was sharp. "We don't know what's going to happen. Anything could happen to her."

Jack sighed. "The house loves Camilla. She's safe enough, but I think Rob's right. We need you girls to be out here in case . . . in case someone has to go get help. I'd be happier if neither of you were inside."

Kelly couldn't even bring herself to look at him. *Oh, Dad, suddenly showing so much fatherly concern for* both *your daughters. You're the only one who's benefited from all this shit, aren't you? You've got yourself a whole new pride and joy. Lucky, lucky you.*

Gina refused to let go of the wheelchair, unaware of her mother's quiet, happy humming beneath her.

"You are not going in there without me. Not with my mother. I go, or no one goes. As the owner I can refuse to let you in and call the police if you try. It's our house. If anyone belongs in there, we do."

Kelly held up her hands in frustration, eager for the stalemate to be over. Just wanting Tabby back. Tabby's pure love, unencumbered by secrets.

"I'll stay out here. Just leave me the car keys. I don't want to go in there anyway. All of this is your mess, not mine. You lot sort it out."

She held out her hand and Jack gave her the leather fob with the key on it. Taking the key, she grabbed his wrist with her other hand, gripping it tight, feeling the bones through his skin. Her voice was low and cold as she met his gaze.

"Just get my daughter back. I don't care how you do it. Just get Tabby back to me. You owe me *and her* that." Behind her, she could hear Gina pushing the wheelchair over the gravel toward the gates where Rob was waiting. She released Jack's wrist, but he stayed where he was, staring at her for a second.

"I love you, Kelly. More than anyone in the world. Try to remember that. There were never any lies about that."

"Not now, Dad. This isn't the time." She turned away from him, and didn't look around until she heard him moving forward, one footstep heavier than the other as he limped to the gates.

Tears threatened her again as she watched them leaving her behind, Rob and her father pushing open the gates, little resistance this time, Gina resolutely pushing Camilla into the drive. Her father didn't look back, but Rob hung behind the others and just before stepping across the threshold of Syracousse, he looked over his shoulder, a half smile, almost wistful, on his face, his eyes seeking hers, and in that moment she knew that no matter what did or didn't happen with Gina last night, he loved her, wholly and completely.

But was it enough? Would it ever be enough to make up for all this? Kelly couldn't give him the response he wanted, no nod, or smile, or wave of good luck. She wasn't ready to let go of her anger yet. If she gave that up, she was terrified there would be nothing left but despair and she would crumble. No, the anger had to stay until she had Tabby back. Until she knew her little girl was safe. After that . . . well . . . after that she'd take it one day at a time.

From behind her frozen mask of indifference, she watched the disappointment on Rob's face before, like the others, he turned his back on her and stepped onto the drive. Her heart froze for a moment as the four of them moved farther away from her—farther away from safety—not sure what she expected to happen, maybe more weeds clutching at them crazily from the ground, but there was nothing except the sound of the footsteps getting fainter and fainter as they walked toward the house.

By the time they reached the front door, all she could hear were the birds that fluttered and flew in the trees around her, and like characters in a silent film, she watched the others disappear inside the house, the door left open behind them, a grinning mouth taunting her for not venturing in.

Her heart pounded in her chest as she checked her watch. Twenty minutes she'd give them, and if they weren't out by then, she'd call Keery, and damn the explanation. Getting in the car, glad to be in a familiar environment of her own, she kept her eyes firmly on the house. Twenty minutes was going to seem like an eternity when there was nothing to do but wait. Wait and pray.

CHAPTER FORTY-FIVE

The silence hung like dust in the air around the four of them as they waited in the desolate hallway. What exactly they were waiting for, Rob wasn't sure. Tabby to come running down the stairs? No, he couldn't see it being quite that easy. And they hadn't considered how they were going to get Camilla out of the house again once they'd gotten Tabby back. What if Syracousse didn't want to let her go? What then?

"What now?" Jack was so close to Rob that the feel of breath in his ear as the policeman spoke almost made the younger man jump.

The sound of humming made them both turn around, the question forgotten. Camilla was squirming slightly in her chair, her eyes still glazed but with more life, more excitement, in them than they'd held for probably years, her lips pressed together pushing out the notes of the uncomposed music.

"Mum?" Gina crouched down beside her, but the old woman ignored her, if she was aware that Gina was there at all. Camilla's head rocked from side to side and her withered hands clenched and unclenched the padded arms of the wheelchair.

Rob looked warily around them. "Something's happening." Invisible pressure was building up, he could feel it almost weighing his body down, and a buzz, like a distant swarm of bees filled his ears. Was it coming from inside him or out? He glanced at Jack.

"Can you hear that?"

The old man nodded slowly, and Jack reached out and touched the wall at the bottom of the curved staircase. His fingers pulled back instantly with surprise, and he pushed them back to the smooth surface.

"The walls are vibrating."

Camilla laughed behind them, a thin sound from a voice rusty from lack of use. "Oh yes!" Her voice was full of joy. "Oh yes!" She continued her humming, but louder this time.

Rob took hold of Jack's arm, his ears aching with the pressure. "It's starting." As they stared at each other, Rob could see his own thoughts reflected in the other man's eyes, hidden behind the determination and strength on the glassy, gray surface. *What the hell are we doing? What the hell have we got ourselves into? How the hell is this going to end?*

Rob stumbled backwards as two things happened at once. Camilla pushed herself out of her chair and the building pressure exploded into music around them, unbearably loud, its strength pulsing up through his body from his feet, a symphony of sound, the instruments unrecognizable, accompanying and overwhelming the old woman's solo humming. Jack clutched at his ears, and Gina cringed as she grasped for her mother.

Rob watched them as if behind an invisible partition. Camilla's arms stretched out wide, her head thrown back as she laughed and spun around and around, pushing Gina away. Bright sunlight flashed in his eyes like a glitterball gone mad, sunlight that couldn't *be* that bright, that couldn't *be* in the house, so bright that he flinched each time it hit his eyes, squeezing them shut.

The real and the unreal were merging around him, and although he could hear Gina calling for her mother, screaming for her above the awful off-key music, when he opened his eyes, he caught glimpses of things that couldn't be there, vases of flowers on sideboards that hadn't been in place for a quarter of a century, pictures on walls, there one minute gone the next, the images changing so quickly that he leaned back against the vibrating wall in an effort to steady himself.

For a moment, the present came back into view, and Rob watched as Camilla danced past him, twirling into the lounge out of sight, her steps as light as a woman thirty years younger. Gina followed her, screaming for her, leaving Jack and Rob alone in the hall.

"We brought her back!" Rob screamed at the walls and the ceiling. "We brought her back for you. To show you she's okay. She's being looked after! Now give us Tabby! Give the little girl back. She doesn't belong here!"

The anger in the increased volume threw Rob back against the wall, and Jack fell into the banisters, holding on to them, his face tight with pain. Rob's own anger rose inside, protecting him from his fear.

"Give her back! We've done what you wanted!"

The music screeched high, no tune there now, and Rob screamed in pain, stuffing his hands into his ears, trying in vain to block it out as sunlight blinded him once again. Forcing his eyes open, for a moment he forgot the whistling agony in his eardrums, as he gazed at the wall opposite to him. The Graces' hallway mirror was back and in it he could see his reflection, but not his reflection from now, the reflection of the little boy he had been all those years ago. But that wasn't what made his breath catch. Not the image of him, he barely glanced at that. It was the figures standing behind his reflection that made him stare. The little boy with the dark hair hanging over his eyes, one hand, one unscarred hand holding the fur of the golden retriever that sat, panting, next to him. Jason? Was that Jason and Teacher?

Jason's reflection smiled at him, a cheeky grin Rob had never fogotten, and pointed one finger sideways. *"Upstairs, Rob."* Rob tilted his head. The voice that came from the mirror was Jason's, but not his childhood voice. This one was deeper. This was the one he had listened to only days ago. *"We're upstairs, Robster. We can't get down."* Teacher barked, and the sound of that more than anything else, brought tears to Rob's eyes. The young Jason's smile fell. *"But hurry. We haven't got much time."*

With a blast of music, the mirror exploded, sending glass everywhere, the shards cutting the back of Rob's hands and arms as he lifted them to protect himself. *How can glass that doesn't exist cut me? How can that be?* He pushed the questions aside and stumbled toward where Jack was curled around the banisters. Jason was helping him, God only knew how, but he was sure of it. The message in the mirror came *despite* the house, not because of it. Jason and Teacher were helping him, and crazy as that sounded, even amongst all this madness, he held on to the thought, it refilling his muscles and tired spirit with energy.

He tugged at Jack's sleeve, making the old man look up at him. Blood was trickling down one side of his face and into the rivulets of his sagging neck, and Rob knew without the help of any doctors that one of Jack's eardrums had burst. He would have liked to spend a few minutes checking that Jack was going to be okay, but that was going to have to wait.

"I think Tabby's upstairs!" Rob shouted over the music whose volume seemed to have lessened a little, knowing that Jack would only have roaring deafness on one side. "You go out to Kelly! I'll get Tabby and then bring the others out. Go!"

He turned to take the stairs and felt a hand clutching at

his leg. Using Rob's body as a post, Jack dragged himself to his feet, one hand gripping Rob's shoulder.

"She's my granddaughter!" he yelled back into Rob's face. "I'm coming with you!"

Looking at Jack's exhausted determination, Rob nodded. They didn't have time to argue, and he guessed Jack had his own guilt to work off in here. "Come on then!"

Trying to keep a firm hold of the banister, Rob made his way up the stairs that were moving under him, sliding this way and that, teasing and taunting his feet, which were desperate to find some kind of secure purchase. Glancing backwards, he could see Jack several steps behind, both hands on the rail, feet tentatively moving forward. Rob felt the urgency eating away inside him. What was it Jason had said? *We don't have much time.* He gazed up at the stairway that twisted and turned like a snake before him.

"Oh bollocks," he muttered under his breath before closing his eyes and launching himself upwards, taking the stairs two at a time. His feet hit their targets, slipping at the last two, but only enough to make him stumble, not lose his balance completely.

When he opened his eyes, relieved to have what felt like stable ground beneath him, the first thing he noticed was the darkness. He could still see the sunlight from below, but there was no light at all on this upper level of the house, and it took him a few moments to adjust to the gloom. Peering over the banister, he saw Jack, still climbing, halfway down. The old man looked up, and waved Rob on with one arm. "I'll catch up! Find Tabby!"

Turning his back on the brightness, Rob stared at the dark ahead of him. This wasn't the house as he remembered it. This had a feel of vastness that Syracousse never had. Looking into the blackness, Rob had a feeling that if he walked into that corridor, he'd be walking forever. Fear chewed at his stomach again, and he could almost feel the house mocking him. *Come and play, Robster. Step inside.* Knowing that the words came from his own head, his own imagination, didn't stop the shiver running down his spine. He had a feeling that if this mad place could speak, then that's exactly what it would be saying.

After the wildness downstairs, this sudden quiet stillness unsettled Rob and he felt as if he were walking into the dragon's lair, only in this case, unlike all the fairy stories, the dragon wasn't sleeping; it was very much awake. Awake and angry. Knowing there was nowhere else to go, he edged tentatively forward, his feet shuffling along the floorboards, fear gnawing at his stomach at the thought of chasms that dropped forever and ever opening up beneath him, hidden by the blackness. Ignoring the pain that burst into life from his bleeding cuts, he held his arms out in front of him, feeling the warm liquid running into his sleeves cooling against his skin, and stretched out his fingers, desperate to find a wall to guide himself along, not wanting to play this insane game of blind man's bluff where the rules could change at any minute.

"Where is she, Jase? Where the fuck is she?" he muttered under his breath, immediately regretting it, the words deadened and lifeless in the heart of the house, eaten up by the dark. With every step, the dim glow from the stairs behind him faded, and he fought the urge to turn and run. There was a little girl in here somewhere, and if she was having to cope with her fear, then he was going to have to do the same. The thought didn't give him any more courage, but his feet continued their hesitant moves forward despite himself.

Feeling something soft make contact with his left shoe, Rob let out a gasp of air that in his head was a skull-splitting scream too terrifying to be released without making him flee as far from this place as he could get. *Oh Jesus Oh Jesus Oh Jesus* . . . Freezing on the spot, he waited to feel it, whatever *it* was, slither and slide against his leg, or like the ivy, squeeze around him. His heart hammered so hard in his chest he couldn't distinguish between the beats. Where the hell was Jack? How far behind could he be?

Rob waited, counting to sixty in his head, but the thing beside his foot didn't move, and holding his breath, he crouched down, one invisible, shaking hand reaching for it, ready to recoil in an instant. He senses recognized the feel immediately. Soft, worn leather. Picking the item up, Rob held it to his face, the smell confirming what touch had already told him. Running his hands over it, feeling the cigarettes and lighter in the top pocket, his fear was for a moment overrun by his confusion. This was Jason's jacket. He was sure of it. When they'd found him in the lane, he'd seen the pack of Marlboros resting in it. But how could that be? How could Jason's jacket be here? *And while you're on the subject, how could Jason talk to you in mirrors? Answer me that one, hotshot.*

A glint of light caught the corner of Rob's eye and he looked up, the jacket dangling from one hand. A small patch of darkness beside him was filled with crackling sparks of electricity, and it was getting bigger. Taking a step sideways into what he hoped was safety, Rob found the wall he'd been looking for and leaned against it, his eyes absorbed in the glitter of light in front of him, spreading outwards into an oval shape, the surface bubbling as if something was pressing outward from the other side. The flickering whiteness made him flinch and turn into the wall, pressing his face into his hand, his slashed forearm squashed against the cool plaster. Sounds were coming from the light now, voices, indistinct but recognizable, a man and a child chattering to each other excitedly. *Jason and Tabby. Jason and Tabby were coming through the light.*

Turning his face back to see, hope rising in his stomach, Rob tried to pull his arm away from the wall, and yelped as it was tugged back. In front of his eyes, the figures were taking shape, bright and light and beautiful; Tabby whole and undamaged, Jason glowing and sparkling with Teacher beside him, their bodies fuzzy at the edges, as if they weren't really there at all, but—Oh God what was happening to his arm, and why couldn't he get it off the fucking wall, and why did it feel as if there were mouths sucking at him, what were they sucking, oh jesus not my blood, not my BLOOD. . . . .

"Rob! Tabby!"

Jack's voice stabbed through Rob's panic, and he looked up to see the outline of Jack stumbling toward them.

"Over here!" he screamed, giving his panic some free rein in his voice. "Over here!"

"Granddad!"

Looking beside him, Rob saw Tabby, clutching her teddy bear, smiling in delight as Jack fell to his knees in front of her, pulling her into a hug, her arms tight around his neck. "Oh thank God, Oh thank God you're okay." Picking the little girl up, he reached for Rob. "Come on. We'll get the others and get out of here while we still can."

Jack ignored the glowing figures of Jason and Teacher as he spoke, and Rob realized that he couldn't see them. As far as the policeman was concerned they just weren't there. Tabby could see them, though. Rob could see her smiling and waving over her grandfather's shoulder.

His arm felt numb and tingly with the pressure of that awful sucking, but still he tried to tug himself free, knowing deep down that it was useless. He shook his head at Jack.

"My arm's stuck in the wall! You're going to have to go without me. Get Tabby and the others out and then send help back!"

Jack stared at him silently, and in that moment Rob was glad for the gloom. He didn't want to see the hopelessness in the other man's eyes.

"Go! Get out of here!" His anger shone from his voice. "Get Tabby back to Kelly! We owe her that!" He paused, and with his free hand squeezed the old man's arm. His voice was quieter this time. "I'll be okay. Whatever happens, I'm okay."

Jack didn't move for a few seconds and then took a step away. "Hang on. I'll send help. Just hang on."

Rob raised a smile that he hoped wasn't wasted in the dark. "I'm not going anywhere."

He waited until Jack and Tabby had disappeared down the distant staircase before turning to speak to Jason. Tiredness was washing over him, and he wondered just how much of his blood the house had consumed by now.

"Help's not going to get here in time, is it?"

Jason shook his head.

Rob let out a sigh. "I didn't think so." Sadness filled him as he thought of Kelly outside hating him, unfinished books never written, all those years that would never be lived. He bit it back, trying to crush it, almost succeeding, but not quite. Christ, he'd known life was shit, but he'd never thought he'd end his days back here. Although, on reflection, maybe there was some kind of mad logic to it after all. Syracousse had been a shadow over his life; it made sense that it would have some part to play in his death. Death. It was hard to associate that word with himself, even now when it was imminent. He wanted to lash out with frustration, but tiredness was eating at him, winning the battle against anger.

"So what now?" The world seemed to be getting black at the edges, and the numbness had spread all down his left side.

Jason grinned at him, that old cheeky grin he'd had when they were kids. "I'm going to wait for you, and then whatever's out there, we'll go together."

"You're going to wait for me?" Rob's heart squeezed. *I won't die alone. Not alone at all.*

"I don't think it'll be long. I can hang on a few minutes longer."

Tears stung the back of Rob's eyes, his voice slurring as unconsciousness started to claim him.

"Where are we going, Jase?"

He was sure that he felt his friend take his hand as he drifted off.

"I don't know, Robster. But Teach'll lead the way. He'll look after us."

Rob murmured a contented sound, the world slipping away from him. *Maybe everything is going to be okay, after all. Maybe we'll hook up with Carrie . . . an adventure, just like the old days . . . maybe.* And then he was gone.

CHAPTER FORTY-SIX

Jack ran down the stairs, which were stable this time, ignoring the agony in his hip and busted ear, the pain and anger in his heart far outweighing them. It wasn't fair, it wasn't right. Rob shouldn't be trapped and waiting to die upstairs in the dark. It should be him. The guilt was his. He didn't deserve to be lucky. Oh God, what mess had he made all those years ago? How many people were going to have to pay for it?

The only thing keeping him going was knowing he had to get the others out of here to safety. He had a feeling the house wasn't finished with them yet. As if in agreement with him, Syracousse let out a rumble, flakes of dust falling from the high ceilings as the foundations shook.

Reaching the hallway, he headed for the lounge door, banging his head on the frame as he passed through it. Reeling with the agony that ran down one side of his head, white pain making him deaf, he stood confused for a moment. He'd never had to duck to come through. Never. Staring at the doorway, realization dawned on him. *The door was shrinking. And it was shrinking fast.*

Moving awkwardly, his balance gone with his eardrum, Jack ran toward Gina, who was frantically trying to grab her mother as she danced by, her hands deflected inches away from Camilla's body by something unseen.

Tears were pouring down Gina's face, her beautiful pale cheeks now red and blotchy. "I can't catch her! It won't let me touch her! It won't let me touch her!"

Still holding Tabby on one hip, Jack grabbed Gina's arm, spinning her around to face him. "Take Tabby and go. I'll try and bring your mother out."

Gina shook her head wildly. "No! It won't let her leave! I won't leave without her. I won't!"

Jack pulled Gina toward the door, the door that was now only up to his waist, and shoved Tabby into her arms, before taking her shoulders. "There isn't time! I may not have been a father to you before, but I'm damn well going to be now." Beyond the lounge, somewhere farther into the house, upstairs maybe, the house roared as ceilings collapsed. Gina's eyes widened with fear as Tabby buried her head into her shoulder. Instinctively, she covered the little girl's head with one hand and glanced toward her mother.

"I can't leave her." Gina wasn't screaming this time, and Jack had to read her lips to understand.

He nodded. "Yes, you can. She'd want you to." From the corner of his eye, it seemed as if the exit had gotten smaller still. Gina was going to have to crawl. "I'll try to get your mother and me out the window. You've got a niece and little sister to look after. Think about them. They need you. Now get out!" Briefly kissing them both on the forehead, not having time for everything he wanted to do and say to try and make things better—why was there never enough time?—he pushed Gina to her knees, forcing her through the small space, their hands touching briefly for the last time as she reached back to pull Tabby through.

"Run!" Jack shouted as the hole closed up in front of him. "Run!"

His energy spent, he rolled himself sideways and leaned against the wall, tired eyes watching Camilla spinning and turning, dancing and singing along with her precious house. He wished he could hear her voice. It might make all this seem a little better. But even the sight of her made his fear lessen a little. This was how it should be, and now that it was so close, death didn't really seem like much of a price to pay, after all.

If he'd been able to hear, maybe he would have had some warning and been able to move out of the way as the large chunk of plaster fell. The first he knew about it was when it landed on him, crushing his hips and legs in front of him. He screamed and screeched, the sound loud and real in his head, just like the pain, *Oh God the pain*, as Camilla danced and danced in front of him, oblivious. Jack's upper torso writhed, desperate to be free of the crushing weight, to be free of consciousness, his mind cleared of everything but the exquisite agony that filled him. But he didn't pass out, his every nerve alive with tortures beyond his imagination as he screamed and screamed until the small capillaries at the back of his throat burst with the strain. *Oh God, just let me die, just let me die, please, just let me die.* The thought pleaded in vain inside his skull, but oblivion stubbornly refused to come. *Maybe there was a price to pay after all.* Camilla danced past him, her delicate feet brushing past his useless ones, sending tidal waves of throbbing, unbelievable pain through his soul, making him scream all over again.

CHAPTER FORTY-SEVEN

Kelly ran one hand through her hair while the other tapped absently on the steering wheel, her eyes fixed on the silent building that rose up a hundred yards away on the other side of the gate. They'd been gone more than twenty minutes now, each of those minutes seeming like an eternity, and she would have called Keery, but her damned mobile couldn't get a signal. Ten more minutes, that's what she'd give them. Ten minutes, and then she'd drive and get help.

Unable to sit still any longer, she got out of the car, needing the cool air to help calm her rising panic, and walked toward the gate. The lane seemed unnaturally quiet, as if even the birds had deserted her. Just where the hell were they? She stared at the house and it glowered silently back at her. Once the others had disappeared inside, her anger had vanished, and now all she wanted was for them to come back safely. Tabby, Rob, her dad, and even Gina and Camilla. Nervousness eating at her stomach, she pushed away a wave of nausea and rubbed her damp palms on her jeans. Oh God, just let them be okay.

Please just let them be okay. She'd never ask for anything for the rest of her life, but please just grant this one prayer. Please.

Her heart leapt into her mouth, as in the distance she saw a figure emerge running from the house. Fear forgotten, she grabbed the gate and started yanking one side open fighting the resistance she felt, ignoring the squeals of the hinges. Leaning back, using all her weight, Kelly pulled it open far enough for someone to get through and still straining and tugging, looked up to see who had come out of Syracousse. It was Gina who staggered towards her. It was Gina, and she was carrying someone in her arms. *Tabby. She was carrying Tabby.*

Oh thank God, Tabby was safe. Tabby was safe. But what were they running from, and where were Rob and her father? Where was Camilla? Gina was halfway up the drive now, and Kelly called out to her.

"It's okay, Gina! You're nearly there! Come on!"

Hearing her voice, Tabby looked around, and Kelly's heart leapt. Her baby. Her baby was back. Everything was going to be fine. Rob and Jack must be following with Camilla, that's where they were. They'd be out in a minute. Any minute now.

Gina stumbled through the gap in the gate, and Kelly grabbed Tabby out of her arms, needing to hold her and hug her forever, burying her face in that soft, warm tangle of curls, desperate to feel those chubby hands wrapped around her neck.

"Oh baby, you're safe now. You're safe. Oh, I love you, Tabby. I missed you so much."

The little girl pressed her face into Kelly's neck. "I missed you too, Mummy. I'm sorry."

Kelly stood and held her daughter for a few moments, unable to speak or move, just reveling in the relief, until a sob from beside her made her look up at Gina, and then the house. Nobody else had come out; there were no figures running up the drive as she'd expected.

Her stomach felt cold as she looked with dread into Gina's anguished face.

"Where are they, Gina? Where's Rob and my father? Where's your mother?"

Gina said nothing, but stood weeping and shaking her head.

Beneath them the ground trembled unnaturally, but Kelly ignored it, pushing Tabby back into Gina's arms. They couldn't leave them in there. They couldn't. *Oh no, not her dad, not Rob. They had to get out somehow. They just had to.*

"I'm going back in to get them! We've got to get them out of there!"

Gina grabbed her and pulled her backwards. "You don't understand, Kelly!"

Kelly looked at the older woman, this stranger who was her sister, not wanting to know what was obvious from the pain in her face.

"What don't I understand?"

Gina's voice was soft, her breath hitching with tears. "It's too late. It's too late for them. We can't help them. They're gone."

Kelly looked from Gina to the house and back again, her whole body numb. Gone. They couldn't be. Not her dad. Not Rob. They were here twenty minutes ago. They couldn't be gone. Just couldn't be.

"No. I don't believe you."

The grumbling beneath them became louder and the trembling more violent, as a deep moan seemed to come from the house like the dying wails of a ship going down in the ocean.

Gina dragged Kelly back behind the car and pulled her in close, so the three of them were hugging tight, the two women forming a protective circle around the little girl.

"What's happening?" Kelly whispered.

Gina stared sadly at the house. "I think it's ending."

The noise was getting louder, and Kelly's ears filled with

mounting pressure as the image of the house ahead of them seemed to shake in a haze. Tabby was crying, softy and fearfully, the wind whipping up into a sudden frenzy around them. Gina didn't seem to notice the pressure or the breeze that lashed her hair around her face.

"Yes. I think it's ending now," she whispered.

A few seconds later, the house imploded.

EPILOGUE

The two women and the little girl were already there and waiting when Kieran pulled up at the site, even though he was right on time. Waving hello, he pulled the lorry into the drive. Why two beautiful young women were setting up home together, he didn't want to know, although the boys who had done the work pulling down the old farmhouse had come up with some pretty lurid ideas. Still, if you were that way inclined, then moving out of Streatford to the tiny hamlet of Nash might give you the privacy you wanted. Not that either of the women had said that's where they came from, but Buckinghamshire wasn't that big a place, and he'd recognized the faces from those newspaper stories a few months back when that writer died, even if they had changed their names.

Stepping down from the cab, he walked over to them, smiling.

The dark-haired one, who called herself Georgina, shook his hand.

"So are you all ready to start building?"

337

Kieran nodded. "Yep. The foundations are all laid, so today we start on the bits you can see."

The women shared a smile and squeezed the hands they were holding of the little girl between them. The blonde, Karen, let out a small squeal.

"I'm so excited! A new beginning starts today!"

The builder gave them a moment to calm down before speaking.

"The boys are right behind me, so you three better go and get yourselves somewhere safe, away from the dirt and noise. You can come and see how we're getting on tomorrow."

He waited until they'd gotten in their car and driven away before he pulled back the tarpaulin from the back of the truck. It was silly really. Not as if they were going to recognize the bricks or anything. And it wasn't as if he were ripping them off. He'd bought them as a job lot months ago; they had been too cheap to pass by, and this was the first job big enough to use them on. There was no way the women could ever know the bricks came from that house that collapsed, and what did it matter anyway? Bricks were just bricks. What harm could it do?

FIEND

JEMIAH JEFFERSON

In nineteenth-century Italy, young Orfeo Ricari teeters on the brink of adulthood. His new tutor instructs him in literature and poetry during the day and guides him in the world of sensual pleasure at night. But a journey to Paris will teach young Orfeo much more. For in Paris he will become a vampire.

Told in his own words, this is the story of the life, death, rebirth and education of a vampire. No one else can properly describe the endless hunger or the amazing power of the undead. No one else can recount the slow realization of what it means to grasp immortality, to live on innocent blood, to be a fiend.

- -

JAMES A. MOORE
RABID GROWTH

People change all the time. But Chris Corin is noticing some pretty extreme changes in the people around him. His best friend is suffering from a strange fever and acting in ways that just don't make sense. And some oddly familiar people in town have started stalking Chris, blaming him for bizarre changes they've noticed in themselves.

Things get worse when the changes become physical. Hideous mutations appear around town. Can these changes somehow be responsible for the violent murders that have occurred—murders that point directly at Chris? Something definitely wants Chris dead, something very powerful.

TIM LEBBON

DESOLATION

Cain is eager for a new beginning. After years of virtual imprisonment by his insane father, and intense therapy following his father's death, Cain is finally ready to see the outside world. He rents an apartment and moves in with only a few meager belongings, including a very special trunk that contains his most guarded secret—something unimaginable. Something unnatural.

The outside world isn't what Cain expected. He soon discovers that many of the other tenants are *very* strange and downright terrifying. His nightmares are becoming more hideous and more frequent. The pressure is building. If it continues to build, Cain might be forced to open his trunk....

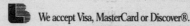